TEN YEARS GONE

AN ADAM LAPID MYSTERY

JONATHAN DUNSKY

Ten Years Gone
Jonathan Dunsky

BOOKS BY JONATHAN DUNSKY

ADAM LAPID SERIES

Ten Years Gone

The Dead Sister

The Auschwitz Violinist

A Debt of Death

A Deadly Act

The Auschwitz Detective

A Death in Jerusalem

The Unlucky Woman (short story)

STANDALONE NOVELS

The Payback Girl

To my mother and father

1

The nightmare tore me out of sleep before dawn.

I opened my eyes, but all I could see were fragments of the dream. Barbed-wire fences and watchtowers. Thick smoke shooting out of tall chimneys, blackening the Polish sky. Uniformed men with evil faces and cruel laughs. Guard dogs straining at their leashes, foaming at the mouth. A huddled mass of frightened, disoriented humanity on the train platform.

With me among them.

What brought me out of the nightmare and into the present was the heat.

July in Tel Aviv was murder, with blazing temperatures and stifling humidity. Nighttime brought only minor relief. It was a favorite topic to grumble about among Tel Avivians.

As hot as it was outside, my room was even hotter. And stuffier. Which was to be expected, I supposed, since I slept with all my windows closed.

I was probably the only person in Tel Aviv to do so.

Or maybe I wasn't. After all, I wasn't the only person with

nightmares. Maybe other people were also worried their screams would wake up the neighbors.

Faint echoes of my scream still reverberated in the dark room. My jaw hurt, a sure indication I'd been clenching my teeth during my sleep. I blinked twice, consciously slowing my breathing, until all I could hear was the deep silence of the enclosed room, and all I could see was the darkness around me.

Groaning, I rolled to a sitting position, lowering my feet to the cool floor tiles. Working my jaw from side to side, I stood, stepped over to the window, and pulled it open.

Night air flowed inside, chilling the sweat on my skin. I looked three stories down to Hamaccabi Street below. No people were about. No cars were moving. Somewhere a night bird hooted. Across the street, a baby howled for its mother. The number tattooed on my left forearm itched, and I absently scratched it. I tapped a cigarette out of the half-empty pack on my nightstand, struck a match against the sill, and lit up.

By the time I crushed out the stub of my cigarette, dawn was beginning to paint the sky gray. The nightmare was gone, but it had left its mark. The memories were there, just below consciousness, trying to dig through like burrowing beasts and infest my mind. I had to work hard to keep them away, where they couldn't hurt me.

And I was tired. Dead tired.

Too many fractured nights. Too many nightmares.

I glanced at my bed, at the sheet I had dampened with the sweat of my night terror, at the thin blanket I had twisted around me. I needed sleep badly, but I feared the nightmare would return. There was only one way to keep it at bay, but it wasn't possible tonight.

And I needed my sleep.

With a sigh, I closed the window, got into bed, and pulled the thin blanket over me.

I shut my eyes and waited for the nightmare to reappear.

————

"Adam Lapid?"

I looked up from my chessboard at the woman who had said my name.

She was a small woman. Five foot two and thinner than she had any business being. Lackluster blond hair pulled back from a high forehead. A faded yellow dress that had been made with a fuller woman in mind. She held her bag in front of her pelvis, worrying the handle with both hands. I recalled that my mother used to hold her bag like that sometimes.

It was half past four and I was seated at my regular table in Greta's Café. Greta's was a homey café located near the center of Allenby Street, on the block between Brenner and Balfour Streets. Bar and kitchen on the left. A dozen small round tables scattered about the rest of the square space. Above, a lazy ceiling fan rattled with each slow revolution, but did little to dispel the heat. Some of Greta's other customers groused about the rattling, but I hardly noticed it anymore. I frequented Greta's nearly every day. It was more than a place to eat and drink. It was a second home to me.

"Yes," I said and gestured to the chair on the other side of my table. The thin woman lowered herself onto it, setting her bag in her lap. "And you are?"

"My name is Henrietta Ackerland," she said in the tentative Hebrew common to those speaking a new language. She had a pronounced German accent, and for a moment I was about to suggest we conduct our conversation in that misbegotten language. The impulse died fast. Her accent was grating enough as it was.

"Want some coffee?" I asked. "Greta makes the best coffee in Tel Aviv."

3

Henrietta began shaking her head, but changed her mind when I told her I was buying. Greta had been watching us from her post behind the bar. I raised two fingers in her direction.

While we waited for the coffee, I examined Henrietta Ackerland more closely. She had been beautiful once, but time and circumstances had changed that. Dark bags bulged beneath her washed-out blue eyes. Her lips were thin and colorless. Deep lines ran across her forehead and shallow ones webbed at the corners of her eyes. The lines of someone who did more frowning than smiling.

She was frowning now, two parallel lines etched between her eyebrows. Desperation was weighing heavily on her, crushing her soul. She fixed her tired gaze on me.

"I understand you're a private investigator," she said.

Among other things, I thought. "That's right."

"And you used to be a policeman. A police detective."

"You're well informed."

She said nothing, but the question was clear in her eyes. *Why aren't you a policeman any longer?*

I hated this part. I did not relish sharing my history. Or explaining my present. But clients needed to be reassured that you could do the job.

"I was a detective with the Hungarian police before the war in Europe. After the war, I came here."

And in between? Well, I couldn't see how that was any of Henrietta Ackerland's business. Nor was it relevant to my abilities as an investigator. Neither was my decision not to become a policeman in Israel.

Thankfully, Greta chose that moment to come over with the coffee, sparing me more of my potential client's questions regarding my past or present. Leaving, she gave me a look that said, *Be careful with this one, she's fragile.* Greta had a good eye for people. And a good heart for them, too.

Henrietta took a careful sip from her cup, closed her eyes, and nodded appreciatively.

"See?" I said. "I told you it was good."

She gave me a smile that died within one breath of being born. Those smile lines would not be getting deeper any time soon.

I drank from my own cup. "Where did you get my name?"

"From a policeman. Reuben Tzanani. He told me I should see you."

Good old Reuben.

"And you want to hire me?" I said.

"Yes. My son. I want you to find my son."

"He's missing? How long?"

"Ten years."

I raised both eyebrows. "How's that?"

"The last time I saw my son, Willie, was on February 27, 1939. Ten years ago."

Ten years and four months, actually. It was now July 6, 1949.

"And the police couldn't help you?"

"The first officer I spoke with told me it was pointless, that too much time has passed. The second one told me that since the last time I saw Willie was outside the borders of Israel, he couldn't help me. I could see in his eyes that he thought I was a bad mother." There was a sharp edge to her tone, as if this were the greatest insult she had ever suffered. "The third policeman I saw was Reuben Tzanani. He told me you might be able to help."

She was running ahead of me. It was a common phenomenon with clients. They spoke as if you already knew what troubled them, that the formality of hiring you was all that was needed for you to get started on their case.

"Why don't you tell me the whole story from the beginning?"

Instead of speaking, she unclasped her handbag and brought out a small brown book. From its middle, she withdrew a small photograph and handed it to me. The photograph was three

5

inches wide and four inches long. A small piece near the top-left corner had been torn off. The photo was yellowing with age, but the image it showed was clear enough.

A sunny day. A lake in the background. Trees looming on the far bank. Patches of white where sailboats cut across the placid lake surface. A much younger, better-fed Henrietta Ackerland at the front. I could tell it had been a cold day, because she was coated and gloved. A small hat perched on her head. She was cradling a baby. Her son, Willie?

Henrietta was staring directly at the camera, a broad smile across her face. I was right. She had been beautiful once. And happy. The woman who sat across the table from me did not seem capable of such happiness.

"Where was this taken?" I asked, lowering the picture.

"Krumme Lanke. In Berlin. Do you know the city?"

"No."

"It's very beautiful. Or it was, before the war."

"You lived there?"

"Yes. I was born there, went to school there, and got married there. My husband, Jacob, took that picture."

"And this is your son?"

"Yes. Willie is his name. But I said that already, didn't I? He was six weeks old that day."

"Big boy," I said. I would have guessed his age at ten weeks. Neither of my two daughters had looked as big as the baby in the picture at six weeks. "This was how long ago?"

"November 2, 1938," Henrietta said without hesitation.

I turned the picture over. No date on the back.

"You know the date by heart."

She nodded. "It was the last time I was happy, the last time all three of us were happy together. Jacob, Willie and me. Things were turning dark for Jews in Germany, but I had my little bubble of sunshine around me."

6

Her tone was one of resigned sadness, a sadness that had had time to settle like silt in every vein and artery, never to be dislodged by the passage of blood or time. Her eyes remained dry. I got the sense she had cried so many tears over the past ten years that she had very few left.

It struck me that whatever her story was, I did not want to hear it. I had enough such misery of my own. *Goddamn it, Reuben, why did you have to send this woman my way?*

Henrietta said, "One week later, November 9, was Kristall-nacht. Jacob was working at the shop. When he did not come back, I thought of going to look for him, but I was too frightened. The noise, the smoke from the fires, the screams. And there was no one to watch over Willie if I went out. The next day, I learned that men had broken into the shop where Jacob worked, dragged him out into the street, and beat him. Then he was arrested. I was sure they would release him soon, but..."

"But they never let Jacob go," I finished her sentence for her when it became apparent she was unable to.

She shook her head. "I tried to find where they took him and kept hoping they'd let him go. After two weeks, I was starting to lose hope. Earlier that year, a cousin of mine decided to leave Germany. She told me I should take my family and leave too, that Germany was no longer safe for Jews. I told her she was exaggerating, that the Germans would soon come to their senses, that the hate couldn't last much longer. By the time I realized she was right, it was too late. Jacob was arrested. I did not want to leave Germany without him. But I could get my son away."

"You gave away your son?" I asked, in a tone of shocked incredulity.

Henrietta flinched as if I had raised a hand to her. "I could think of nothing else to do. I was scared. So scared. I felt that I had to get him out of Germany."

She paused, as if waiting for my approval that she had done the right thing.

"Go on," I said, ashamed of myself. Who was I to judge other people for the decisions they had made in trying to protect their children, considering my failure to protect my own.

"A schoolmate of mine, Esther Grunewald, had decided to immigrate to Palestine. I asked her to take Willie along with her, told her I would follow in a few weeks, three months at most. At first she refused, but I begged and pleaded, offering her nearly all the money I had. Finally, she relented. She and Willie took the train from Berlin to Zagreb on February 27, 1939, and that was the last time I saw my son."

"Why didn't you follow them?"

"I spent the next six weeks making inquiries after Jacob. Then I got a warning that I was to be arrested. Apparently, all my poking about had made someone angry. I used the little money I had left to buy false papers, but couldn't get a passport. I left Berlin, settled in Frankfurt with my new identity, and stayed there throughout the war, hiding in plain sight. With my blond hair and blue eyes, no one suspected me of being Jewish. I looked like the perfect Aryan woman from Nazi posters."

"When did you get here?"

"Two months ago. After the war, I spent some time looking for Jacob, but found no trace of him. I no longer have hope that he's alive. Then I boarded a ship to Israel, but the British stopped the ship and sent us to a prison camp in Cyprus. It was there that I learned Hebrew."

"And once you got here?"

"I started looking for Willie and Esther. I asked the immigration official which newspaper had the biggest circulation in Israel. *Davar*, he said. I posted an ad there six weeks ago. No one has contacted me. I went to the police, like I told you. Only Reuben

Tzanani did anything to try to find Willie. Yesterday he told me he had done all he could and suggested I see you."

"What actions did he take, do you know?"

She nodded. "He told me he checked the civil register, but found no Esther Grunewald or Willie Ackerland listed there. He checked criminal records. Also nothing. Then he searched death certificates from 1939 to today. Nothing." She paused, lowering her eyes for a moment before raising them back to mine. "He told me there was nothing more he could do. I told him I wasn't ready to give up, so he said I might talk to you."

Rubbing the back of my neck, I made a mental note to thank Reuben for leaving me with the unpleasant task of telling Henrietta Ackerland the truth. Which was that her son was dead. It could have happened a number of different ways, but Willie Ackerland was dead, of that I had no doubt. Maybe he and Esther Grunewald had died en route to Palestine. Or maybe Esther Grunewald simply took the money Henrietta Ackerland had given her and dumped the baby somewhere. Maybe she never intended to take him along with her. 1939 was a bad year for kindness. It was a desperate time. In such times even good people do evil things. Maybe Esther Grunewald was such a person.

But whatever had happened, it was clear that no one by the name of Esther Grunewald or Willie Ackerland was living in Israel now or had died here in the past ten years.

I knew I had to tell it to her straight, but that didn't mean I relished the prospect. I delayed by slowly draining my coffee cup. Her eyes didn't leave my face the whole time.

"I wish I could help," I said when I felt I could delay no longer. "But Reuben is right. He checked everything there was to check and found nothing. Finding someone after ten years is almost impossible in the best of circumstances. In this case, there is no hope. With the work Reuben did and the newspaper ad you placed going unanswered, there is only one conclusion to be drawn: Your son is dead."

I didn't tell her I was sorry for her loss. From experience, I knew such a sentiment would provide her with zero comfort. I simply told it to her like it was. The unvarnished, awful, gut-wrenching truth. She would have to deal with it in her own way.

And what she chose was denial. "My son is not dead," she said forcefully, and there was suddenly some color in her cheeks.

"Listen, I—"

She cut me off. "I said he's not dead. If he was dead, I would have known it, I would have felt it. Here." She pointed to her heart. "Do you understand? Do you?" Her face had taken on a resolute cast, her skin stretching taut across her facial bones. It made her look even thinner, as if she might suddenly tear apart from within and whatever was inside of her would come spilling out. "My son is not dead. He is out there, somewhere, and I need to find him. He needs me to find him. I have no one else to turn to. Will you help me?"

I didn't answer. I couldn't. My throat had constricted and my tongue felt too heavy to move. With my heart racing and the blood pounding in my ears, all I could do was stare at her, at this woman who had harbored an irrational hope for ten years, that at some point she'd be reunited with her son. It was this hope, I was sure, that had kept her going during the long years of the war, even as Germany was reduced to rubble around her. It was this hope that drove her to get up each morning, to put food and water in her mouth, to live.

It took me a long moment to realize I was not breathing. I made myself draw a breath and let it out. Once I was breathing normally again, I knew two things. The first was that she would never give up on finding her son. If I refused to take her case, she would find someone who would. Some in my profession were not the most scrupulous of men. She might stumble upon someone who would not think twice about squeezing her for every penny she had, feeding her tidbits of false hope to keep the money flowing. I would not do that.

The second thing I knew was that I had to take her case. For my sake, not hers. When she told me how she would have felt it had her son died, it was like the butt of a rifle had slammed into the pit of my stomach. I could still feel my insides churning.

I swallowed hard, but the taste of ashes lingered in my mouth.

"All right," I said, my voice nearly cracking. "I'll give it a try."

2

After ordering each of us another cup of coffee, I asked, "You said Esther Grunewald and your son boarded a train from Berlin to Zagreb. How were they supposed to get from there to Israel?"

"Esther said they would take another train to Greece," Henrietta said. "A ship was to take them the rest of the way."

"What's the name of the ship? What was the departure date?"

Henrietta didn't know. Nor did she know which port the ship sailed from. Only that it was somewhere in Greece.

"Esther didn't know herself," she told me. "All she knew was that she and other Jews from all over Europe were to gather in Athens on March 1."

She did not have the names of any of the other passengers, nor those of the people who had arranged for the ship.

"If all had gone according to plan and you had followed Esther and Willie here, how were you supposed to contact them?"

"Esther was supposed to send me a letter as soon as they arrived and got settled. No letter ever came."

I did not voice my thought that this was another indication

that Esther Grunewald and Willie Ackerland had never made it to Israel. Instead, I asked Henrietta to tell me about Esther.

"She was the most beautiful girl in our school. I remember being quite jealous of her. Her hair was black and shiny, her face exquisite, her skin like marble. Boys would follow her with their eyes wherever she went."

"She never married?"

"No. I'm sure there were suitors, but no."

"How tall was she? What was her build like?"

"She was tall. Five foot ten or so. And she was slim, but not like —" Henrietta paused to look down at herself, and a shadow crossed her face "—she was slim in a feminine way."

"And what was she like?"

With an abashed look, Henrietta admitted that she and Esther Grunewald had never been close friends. More acquaintances than anything else. I realized that she was embarrassed to admit she had given her son to a woman whose heart and character were unknown to her.

She did tell me that Esther Grunewald had no siblings and that both her parents had died in a car accident in 1937. Esther Grunewald left no one behind when she emigrated from Germany.

By the time I ran out of questions, I had filled little more than three-quarters of one page in my notebook. I flipped it closed so I wouldn't have to look at the dearth of information I had to go on. What did it matter? This was a hopeless case anyhow.

Henrietta told me she shared an apartment in the south of Tel Aviv with two other women and that she worked as a cleaning lady. She did not have a telephone in her apartment, but one of her clients did. I wrote down the number and the day of the week she cleaned there and told her I'd call her with a report in two weeks, or sooner if I found anything. Then I told her what I normally charged as a retainer.

"I can't pay twenty liras right now," she said. "I can give you ten now and the rest next month."

I said that would be fine. I had no doubt she would come up with the money. To do otherwise would be to disgrace her son, not just herself.

After she left, I took the empty coffee cups to the bar. Greta was there, looking at the doorway through which Henrietta Ackerland had just exited.

"I feel guilty for not bringing that girl something to eat. She's skin and bones," she said.

"That *girl* is thirty years old."

"When you get to be my age, Adam, you'll understand that thirty is still very much a girl."

"You going to finally tell me your age, Greta?" There was a running bet among the regulars as to Greta's age. I estimated it to be fifty-eight, but it could have been anywhere between fifty and sixty-five.

Greta smiled. "Not today." She had on a flower-pattern dress and was leaning against the bar, her heavy breasts resting on the bar top between her meaty forearms. Everything about Greta was big—her calves, arms, hips, bust. Even her head was big and crowned with a nest of salt-and-pepper curls. "She's a new client?"

"Uh-huh."

"You don't sound too happy about it. Can't you use the money?"

"Of course I can use the money. How else could I afford to come here every day?"

"Yes. I have no idea how you get by. It was nice of you to order coffee for her. Very generous."

We both smiled. Four months earlier, soon after I had returned to prime condition following my time at the hospital, I helped Greta handle a problem. A brawny man was pushing her for protection money. I took the man aside and explained to him with my fists that Greta was off-limits. After he hobbled off never to be seen again, Greta offered to pay me for my help, but I said I didn't want her money. She didn't like the notion of not paying, and she found that having me around made her feel safe, so she said I could eat and drink her debt to me.

Since then, I'd probably eaten and drunk three times what she would have owed me, if not more. But neither of us mentioned it. I kept eating on the house, never abusing the privilege too much, and she kept liking having me around.

"I just don't think I can do what she hired me to," I said.

"Then why take the case?"

"Because it's better for her to feel hopeful."

"Is she in trouble?"

"No. But she is troubled."

"Poor girl," Greta said.

"At least she has a photograph," I answered.

Back at my table, I discovered I was wrong. On the tabletop lay Henrietta's picture. I picked it up, rushed outside into the heat of Allenby Street, and looked in all directions. Henrietta was nowhere to be seen. Back inside, I sat at my table and examined the picture once again. It told me nothing I didn't already know. Why would it?

I carefully placed the picture between the pages of my notebook and slipped it into my pocket. Then I surveyed the chessboard I'd been playing with when Henrietta arrived.

I played chess almost every day. Greta kept the board and pieces behind the bar for me. I always played both sides and always a lightning game, with no time to think over moves. A lightning game is the only way to keep things interesting when you play with yourself as an opponent. I found that it also took my mind off things, which was usually a blessing.

This particular game, white was in a hopeless position, behind by one rook and a bishop. But in a lightning game anything can happen. I kept on playing, making rapid moves, hoping that white would somehow rally to a victory. Maybe I was looking for a sign that a hopeless situation, like the new case I had taken on, could still end well.

White lost in four moves.

3

A little after seven I folded the chessboard and went over to the bar so Greta could stow it away for me.

"When are you seeing Rachel Weiss?" she asked me as she took the board from my hand.

"Seeing her? That's not exactly how I would put it. You trying to avoid thinking unpleasant thoughts?"

"Wipe that smirk off your face and answer my question."

"Tonight," I said. "I'm going over to her place tonight."

Greta gave a thoughtful nod and eyed me long and hard, as if trying to memorize every inch of my face, or perhaps say a prayer over me.

"You watch yourself, you hear?"

"It'll be all right," I said, discomforted by her concern. "Don't worry."

"I'll worry all I want. And you should worry, too. If you're not worried, you're being arrogant, and arrogance can get you in trouble."

"I have done this sort of thing before, you recall."

"I know, but tonight may be different. So watch yourself. I'll see you tomorrow."

"Tomorrow," I said in a somber voice, as if making her a promise. But in truth, I was not worried and couldn't see why she should be.

Outside, it was still hot, but not as oppressive as earlier. The broad, tree-lined sidewalks of Allenby Street were teeming with pedestrians, and on the road a bus laden with passengers was maneuvering around a truck that had parked with its tail end blocking part of the way. A handful of cars waited patiently for the road to clear. There was a sense of optimism in the air. And why shouldn't there be? Israel's War of Independence was, to all intents and purposes, over. We Jews had won. It was a costly victory, with six thousand dead and many thousands injured, but we had our state. A two-thousand-year-old dream had come true. Armistice agreements had been signed with Egypt, Lebanon, and the Kingdom of Transjordan. Rumor was that an agreement would soon be signed with Syria, Israel's sole remaining belligerent neighbor. Maybe now we would have peace. Maybe.

Not that everything was rosy. Far from it. The economy was in tatters. Thousands of impoverished Jews were pouring into the country on a monthly basis. There was nowhere to house them all, so tent towns had sprouted in various places across the land. Conditions there were miserable. There were also widespread shortages of basic products, including food. A few months ago the government had announced a rationing policy, which included meat, cheese, butter, eggs, and a variety of other items. A number of substitutes such as powdered eggs and chicory coffee were introduced, none of which tasted very good. The rationing gave birth to a thriving black market, with nearly every citizen participating in it, as either seller or buyer. I was one of the latter.

The government made great efforts to crack down on black marketeers, but it was a futile battle. Jewish mothers were not about to let laws and regulations deprive their children of proper nourishment. Good for them.

Hamaccabi Street, where I lived, was an unassuming residential road tucked between the much larger King George and Tchernichovsky Streets. I lived on the third floor of a ten-year-old building that no architect was likely to point to as the pinnacle of his achievements. My apartment comprised a closet-sized bathroom; a walk-in-closet-sized kitchen; a balcony big enough for two people, as long as both held their breath; and one room that served as dining room, living room, and bedroom all rolled into one.

The furniture consisted of a bed, a nightstand bearing a shadeless reading lamp, a closet, one chest of drawers, a scratched-top dining table, and two mismatched chairs. There were no paintings or pictures. Bare walls were good enough.

The rent was cheap, the neighbors unobtrusive, and Greta's was a short walking distance away. It suited me just fine. Compared to some of the places I'd been, it was a palace.

Upon entering, I removed my shirt and draped it over one of the chairs. Then I went into the kitchen, filled one of the three glasses I owned with water and drained it in one long gulp. From the icebox I withdrew the little butter I had left from that month's rations. From a cupboard over the sink I got a box of sardines I had bought on the black market.

I sliced two pieces of bread, put them on a plate, smeared them with butter and stacked some sardines on top. I set the plate on the dining table and sat down to eat. Before the World War, this would have seemed like a poor meal. These days I knew it for what it truly was—a feast.

I rinsed the plate when I was done, made some tea, and took the steaming cup with me to the bedroom. I checked my watch. 20:11. There was time to burn before I was to go see Rachel Weiss, as Greta had put it. I leaned my pillow against the wall and sat on

19

the bed with my back to it. On the nightstand lay a dog-eared paperback western by Max Brand and next to it was an English-Hebrew dictionary, in case I encountered any unfamiliar words. I flicked on the reading lamp, picked up the novel, and began to read.

A few minutes later I realized that I had read the same page over and over and could not recall a word of it. My mind kept returning to Henrietta Ackerland and the hopeless case I had agreed to take on. I flipped open my notebook, read through my notes—it took but a minute—and gazed once more at the picture Henrietta had left behind.

Are you still alive, little one? Or is your mother living on a fool's hope? And will she be able to survive when that hope flickers out?

Maybe she would. She looked frail, but looks could be deceiving. In Auschwitz I had seen men continue to live for months even as their muscles dwindled, their cheeks hollowed out, and their limbs thinned to sticks. And had I not survived when everything had been taken from me?

Stop it! Just stop it! You have other business tonight.

It was no use. The memory flooded my mind without warning. I shut my eyes against its assault, but it had already commandeered my consciousness. It was the first day, that miserable cold day, after we had spilled out of the stinking, cramped cattle cars into that hell on earth called Auschwitz, after the men had been separated from the women and children, after the initial selection that determined who would live to see that day's end and who would be gassed and turned to ashes before sundown.

With the other men who were to live, I had staggered along toward the barracks, the guards shouting obscenities at us, the whimpering of once proud men like the cries of birds with broken wings around me, the air smoky with an unknown and unimaginable stench. Suddenly a pain, sharp and rending, deep in my stomach and chest, unlike any pain I had ever suffered before or since. My chest constricted and my vision darkened. I stumbled forward and would have landed on my face had the back of the man marching in front of me not been in the way. A pair of strong hands straightened me up, and a voice whispered in Hungarian, "Keep walking. Don't give the bastards an excuse to beat you."

Putting one heavy foot ahead of the other, I shambled forward, pushed ahead by the men behind me. Tears were streaming down my cheeks, and my ears were pierced by an unrelenting internal shriek. For in that moment I knew, with a certainty that snuffed out all hope of denial, that my two daughters had just died.

So when Henrietta had told me her son was alive, that she would have felt it had he died, I could not dismiss her words out of hand. Against my better judgment, against all logic, I allowed a tiny part of myself to be convinced that this case had merit, that I had to pursue it.

Damn her! Damn her and that dead son of hers for making me remember what I wanted most of all to forget.

I opened my eyes. They were dry. Like Henrietta Ackerland, I was all cried out. With a sour taste in my mouth, I rose from my bed, went into the kitchen, and guzzled water from the tap. My heart, which had been beating erratically, calmed to a steady rhythm. Returning to the bedroom, I gave the paperback another longing look. But it was pointless. It would not take my mind off the bad memories.

But something else could. At least for a short while.

I went about the room, drawing all the shutters closed. The only light came from the bare bulb that hung at the center of the ceiling. Shadows pooled at the corners, but they did not disturb me. The closet was lighted fine. I knelt before it.

The closet had two sections. On the right were shelves, where I stored my few shirts, pants, socks, and underwear. On the left was a bar with three hangers dangling from it, two of which were taken by jackets, the third by nothing at all. At the bottom of the left section I had stacked a few sheets, pillowcases, and a winter blanket. These I removed, setting them on the floor. Then I lifted the false bottom I had installed at the foot of the closet and set it aside. Beneath it I had hidden a wooden box, a foot long and half that across, with a tarnished metal clasp. I took out this box and placed it beside me on the bed. I undid the clasp, lifted the lid, and gazed at what lay within.

Immediately, I felt myself grow calmer. A feeling not unlike satisfaction filled my chest. A grim satisfaction it was, but I could not recall the last time I had experienced any other kind.

For in the box, neatly arranged, were my souvenirs from Germany, mementos of the months I had spent in that wretched country in 1946 and 1947 after I had recovered from my time at Auschwitz and Buchenwald and until I arrived in Israel in September 1947. A good time it was, a healing time. A time I wished could have lasted longer than it did.

The first item I took out of the box was a Luger pistol. It was wrapped in a black cloth. I unwrapped the gun and hefted it in my hand. Black and deadly, smelling of gun oil. I had cleaned and oiled it two days before. I possessed two full magazines for the pistol, as well as a pouch holding several dozen loose shells. One of the magazines was lodged in the butt of the gun, ready for firing. The intoxicating sense of power holding the Luger gave me could only be appreciated by those who had experienced true powerlessness.

The gun had belonged to an SS officer whom I had met in a bar in Hamburg in late 1946. A few beers had loosened his tongue, and he had bragged about what he had done to Jews in Ukraine as the German army swept eastward toward Russia. Later that night, I broke into his home, finding him alone in his bed. A smile curled my lips as I recalled his look of astonishment when, a moment before I killed him, I'd revealed that I was a Jew.

I set the gun on the bed, reached into the box, and took out a switchblade hunting knife with a swastika stenciled on its pearl handle. I had taken the knife from another Nazi officer, this one in Munich, after I had shot him in the back of the head.

I pressed the release button. The blade sprang into view with a dull twang. Not long, but made from sturdy metal, the kind that could lodge itself in bone without breaking. The blade glinted as it caught the light. Reflected in the shiny steel, my left eye stared back at me. I could read nothing in my gaze, or maybe I did not wish to. I quickly shifted the angle of the weapon so it reflected something other than myself.

I had often wondered why I held on to these two weapons. I could easily have found replacements for them. But both the Luger and the knife were special to me. They were reminders that I was no longer the weak, pathetic creature that I had been reduced to in Auschwitz. They were symbols of the time I had set forth on my journey of vengeance, when I had brought some of my—and my people's—oppressors to justice. They helped me alleviate some of the guilt I felt for surviving while the rest of my family, and so many others, did not.

I swept the knife through the air, describing glittering arcs of deadliness. It felt like a natural extension of my arm. Then I placed it on the bed by the Luger. My eyes shifted from one weapon to the other as I considered which I should take with me tonight.

The Luger was tempting. It would certainly send a forceful message. But it was also risky. Having a gun brought you one step closer to using it, and this might spell trouble, not just for me, but also for Rachel Weiss. A gunshot is deadlier than a knife wound. Rachel Weiss had not hired me to kill anyone. Not to mention the idea of having to dispose of a body did not fill me with enthusiasm.

And besides, I was certain I could make do without it.

The knife, then.

I wrapped the Luger in its cloth and placed it back in the box. I folded the knife and slid it into my pocket. Then my eyes fell on another item I had acquired in Germany. A leather billfold, brown and creased, with a small metal J stamped into its top-right corner. I brought the billfold to my nose and inhaled its scent. Smoke, faint but unmistakable. What fire had impressed its scent on the billfold? Was it the fire of battle? Or the firebombing of some German city? Or was this the smell of Jewish bodies being put to the torch?

I did not know and would never find out. The previous owner of the billfold was dead. I had done the killing. He'd lived alone in a picturesque hamlet outside Frankfurt. When I told him who I was and why I had come to see him, he spat at me. The spittle missed. I did not.

As he lay dying in his blood, I ransacked his house. I found the billfold in the inner pocket of a jacket hanging in his bedroom closet.

I opened it and drew out its contents. First was the money. A sheaf of bills, mostly German and French and Dutch notes in various denominations, but also some Swiss francs. There used to be more, but I had used some to pay rent on the apartment for a year in advance and to procure various black-market goods. In fact, it was through a black-market money changer that I exchanged this money for Israeli liras.

Second, and most important among all my German souvenirs, was the picture. It showed an elegant woman in a conservative gray dress, a gold necklace at her throat, and two children, a boy of eight and a girl of five. The girl had dimples. The boy a gap-toothed grin. All were fair-haired. All were smiling at the camera. A perfect German family.

Why had I taken the picture?

Perhaps I'd wanted to take something from that Nazi officer that was even more personal and valuable than his life.

And why did I hang onto it for as long as I did?

I think I simply liked having a family photo to look at from time to time, since I no longer had any of my own.

Picking up the photo of Henrietta Ackerland and her baby boy, I gazed from one picture to the other. The German matron and her two children were dead. Of that I had no doubt. There had been no trace of them in the house of the man I had killed. I did not know how they died. In an air raid, probably. I hoped their deaths were swift and painless.

And Henrietta's boy, Willie?

He was dead, too, I was certain. I did not know how or where or when, but he was dead all the same. I was chasing a ghost.

I cursed under my breath at the thought of this case. Where should I begin? What would be my first step? I simply did not know.

I glanced at my watch. 21:21. I returned the billfold to the box and the box to its hiding place in the closet. I laid Henrietta's picture on the nightstand. There would be time for it later.

It was time to head over to Rachel Weiss. It was time to shed some blood.

4

Rachel Weiss owned and operated a small restaurant on Hayarkon Street. The street ran parallel to the shoreline, close enough so I could hear waves breaking on the beach and smell the salty scent of the sea.

It was a little after ten when I arrived, finding the door to the restaurant locked. I pressed my face to the glass and peered inside. The main room was deserted and dark, apart from a wedge of light that spilled from somewhere near the rear wall. By the scant illumination I could make out outlines of tables topped with overturned chairs, looking like deformed trees. I rapped on the glass and saw a woman's shadow emerge from the lighted area and pause where the light inked away into darkness.

With hurried steps, the shadow moved toward me, and as she neared, I could make out Rachel Weiss's face. She unlocked the door and pulled it open.

"Thank God," she said as I stepped inside. She hastily relocked the door. "I was scared you wouldn't come."

I had told her I'd be there at ten. I apologized for being late, but offered no excuse. What could I have told her, that I'd lost track of time thinking about the Nazis I'd killed, and half-fantasized about returning to Germany to kill some more?

"It's all right," she said. "Now that you're here, I can stop worrying."

Her face belied her words. Even bathed in shadows, I could see anxiety written all over it, from her pinched mouth to her restless eyes. They kept shifting from the door to me and back again.

"Yes, you can. I'll take care of everything. After tonight you'll have no more problems." To my surprise, an echo of Greta's voice rang in my head, warning me against being arrogant. Irritated at the vagaries of my mind, I added, "Let's step away from the door."

We walked side by side toward the source of light. It came from the kitchen, which opened to the left near the back wall off the dining room. From its entrance I could see the street door, which meant that anyone standing there would also be able to see me. But that was easy to fix.

"Turn on the lights in the restaurant," I told her, and when she did, I flicked off the lights in the kitchen. This way, I would be shrouded by darkness, in prime position to surprise the man when he arrived.

"This is where I'll stand," I told Rachel Weiss. "When he comes, you open the door for him and lead him back toward me. Here." I pointed to a place toward the end of the serving counter, close to the kitchen. "All right?"

Rachel nodded shakily. She was on the short side, curvy and soft-looking, with straight brown hair that fell to her shoulders. The sort of hair that would easily part if you ran your fingers through it. Her eyes were a deep and warm brown, and her mouth, though on the small side, boasted finely shaped lips. Though not beautiful, she was pleasant to look at, even when, as now, her face was tight with tension and fear. She wore a brown dress that covered her from neck to ankle and was too warm for the season. But maybe she felt it afforded her some protection. I could understand why she would want to believe that.

I had first met her a week earlier at Greta's Café. We sat over coffee and she told me of her problem. Three weeks before, a man had appeared one evening at her restaurant. It was near closing time, and he had been the last customer. When he'd finished his beer, he took the empty glass with him and came toward where she stood behind the serving counter, tidying up. The man—he told her his name was Yuri—informed Rachel that instead of him paying for the beer, she would be giving money to him.

"Or bad things will happen," he had warned her, "to your place and to you. Understand?"

"But I didn't understand," Rachel Weiss had told me at Greta's. "I don't know why, but his words didn't register with me. It was like he had just told a very bad joke, and I didn't know how to react to it."

Partly it was his appearance. He was of unimpressive height and build, with a face so bland that, though he kept his eyes constantly narrowed and spoke with a sneer, he simply did not look tough or threatening. There was also the fact that his voice was high-pitched, verging on whiny. Said with that voice, his words inspired not fear but ridicule.

Yuri must have read something in Rachel's face that enraged him, because his expression turned ugly and, without warning, he hurled the empty beer glass at her.

"He didn't hit me," Rachel Weiss said. "The glass flew just past my left ear—" she raised a hand to within two inches of her face, showing me how close it had been "—and shattered on the wall behind me. After that, I no longer found him ridiculous. Now I was terrified of him."

She paid him what he wanted, without hesitation or argument. She could hardly think straight with the fear that had gripped her.

"He told me he'd be back the following week and to have the money ready for him. He warned me not to go to the police. 'The police won't be able to help you, and I'll know about it if you blab to them,' he said. 'I have friends there. If you open your mouth, I will hurt you. Understand?' This time I understood all right. So I kept quiet. Maybe I did not fully believe it had really happened. Maybe I convinced myself that he would not come back again."

"But he did," I said.

"Yes. He did. Exactly when he said he would. And I paid him again. He laughed when I handed him the money. I felt humiliated. That was worse than having to pay him."

I took a sip of coffee and chose not to articulate what was running through my mind. Yuri had laughed, I believed, because he knew he had just vaulted over his steepest hurdle. He himself had not been certain what sort of welcome would be waiting for him that day. But once Rachel Weiss had meekly handed him her money the second time, he knew that he had broken her resistance. This was now an established routine. He could count on her paying him every week. He might even be able to raise her weekly payment without the need for much arm twisting.

And that was what happened for the next two weeks. Twice Yuri came and twice Rachel paid him. This might have gone on for some time had he been satisfied with only money.

Three days before Rachel and I met, Yuri had come to collect once more. Rachel had handed him the money without argument. He pocketed it and then grinned at her. "You're sort of pretty, you know." His voice had taken on a different texture, like something slimy. It made her shiver. He reached for her and caressed her cheek with his full palm. The shiver evolved to a shudder. "Yes. Pretty." He lowered his hand and ran his eyes over her. "Soon we'll get to know each other a bit better. You'd like that, wouldn't you?"

"And then he left," Rachel told me, her eyes lowered, her

29

cheeks flushed a bright red of shame. A tear cut a line across each inflamed cheek, and she began sobbing silently.

I did not try to comfort her. It was hard enough for her to tell me all this, a stranger. I did not wish to augment her embarrassment by intruding on it. But at that moment I swore that Yuri would pay a heavy price for his deeds. I hated all bullies, but those who preyed on women I hated more than most.

When she had ceased crying, Rachel said, "Him doing that— him touching me and threatening to do more—was like a spell had been broken. Doing nothing was no longer an option. I had to do something to stop him."

So she had come to me.

Greta had made the connection. The two women were friendly, and Greta was the sort of woman people confided in. As I had once helped Greta get rid of a similar problem, she suggested Rachel speak to me about it.

"Do you think it's true what he said," Rachel asked, "that he has friends in the police?"

"Maybe not," I told her. "It seems like a lie he would tell."

"So should I go to them?"

"Not if you want a solution to your problem. Because the most the police would do is take him in for questioning. Apart from your word, there is no proof that he did anything wrong, and he'll be able to produce witnesses who will swear up and down that he was with them on the nights in question." I paused, turned my coffee cup ninety degrees clockwise, and continued. "Even if the police arrest him, they won't hold him for long. So far, he has hurt no one and did no real damage to anyone's property. Once free, he can get back at you. He doesn't need to get close. He can throw a brick through your front window or torch your restaurant. The police won't be able to prove it was him."

Rachel turned pale. Her eyes were starting to well up again.

She looked hopeless and helpless. So far, speaking with me did not make her feel any better.

"What you can do is pay a police officer to get a little physical with him."

"Get physical?"

"To rough him up a bit. To hurt him."

Rachel grimaced. "I don't know if I want to do that."

"You don't have much of a choice. It's either that or continue paying him. Of course, using the police for something like that presents a whole different problem."

"Such as?"

"You'd be committing a crime. A serious one. If the policeman you approach decides to reject your offer, you might get locked up."

"And if I hire you?"

"Then I'll deal with this man on your behalf. But you need to accept that it will get violent. There is no other way to send a message across to such a man."

"You're not suggesting...I don't want to...you know."

I gave her a smile, though I wasn't sure what she might see in it. "I'm not a hired killer."

Rachel did not appear to notice that I did not deny having killed people.

She thought it over for a long while, alternately staring into her coffee cup and drinking from it. I let her think things through without interruption. Her hesitation was understandable. Initiating serious violence for the first time is never an easy decision for any law-abiding person. Finally, she nodded.

I told her I'd come to the restaurant the next time she was supposed to pay the man. And here I was.

I could tell Rachel was not enamored of my plan. I well understood why. Asking her to open the door to her tormentor meant that she would need to get close to him. This was not how she had envisioned this night. The way she'd pictured it, I was here so she would never have to be close to Yuri again.

"You can do this," I told her. "Just open the door and lead him to me. Don't let him see that anything is different tonight."

"How do I do that?"

Her voice was shaky and fear was written all over her face. Which was what Yuri would expect.

"Don't think about it. Just be as you are and you'll do fine. All right?"

She nodded. I glanced at my watch. We had less than ten minutes. I told Rachel to get behind the serving counter and make herself busy. Like any other normal day after closing. She did as I said and began folding napkins. I stationed myself in the dark entryway to the kitchen, alternating my gaze between the street door and her. With my right hand fondling the folded knife in my pocket, I found myself looking at her more and more. She seemed intent on her work, and there was something nice about it, something...pleasantly ordinary, something—

The rattling of the front door broke off my train of thought. My eyes veered toward it. A shadow behind the glass, but I could not make out its shape or size. I turned to Rachel. She stood frozen, unable to move.

"Go," I whispered at her, or maybe it came off as more of a hiss, because she gave a start, dropped the napkin she'd been holding, and walked with mincing steps toward the door.

I drew out the knife and pressed the release button. I could feel my pulse throbbing in my neck. My skin tingled. My fingers tightened around the knife handle. I hadn't always been this man, one who is excited by the prospect of battle and bloodshed. But I was such a man now. There was shame in that, I knew. My father, whom I had revered above all other men, would not have approved. But shame should not inspire false denial. I was who I was. And who I was relished the coming violence.

Rachel reached the door. I let out a slow, almost endless breath. I was ready.

I knew there was a problem the moment she opened the door. Rachel let out a noise that was somewhere between a gasp and a yelp. I quickly saw why. There were two men standing on the threshold, not one.

5

I cursed silently.

That's what you get for being arrogant, Adam. That's what you get for not listening to your elders.

Now I wished I had brought the Luger along. Because taking one man by surprise is one thing. Doing the same with two is quite another.

Rachel took a few faltering steps back. The men strode in, one of them shutting the door. I heard the click of the lock being turned.

"Hello, Rachel," the first man said. His voice was high-pitched, and it fairly quavered when he spoke. From excitement, it seemed. "Miss me?"

He had to be Yuri. He fit Rachel's description perfectly—average height and unimposing build, pale complexion, forgettable features, short black hair receding at the temples. The only thing threatening about him was his grin. Wide, almost manic with excitement. That grin made me even angrier than I had been since Rachel Weiss first told me about him. He wore blue jeans and a white shirt with its three top buttons undone. His chest was pale and hairless. His armpits were stained with sweat.

If Yuri had come alone, I would have had no problem. At six foot three, I was taller than he was by about six inches. I also outweighed him by a good margin. And I had arranged things so I would have the element of surprise on my side. Yuri's companion was a different matter.

Stocky and powerfully built, he walked bowlegged with a swaying gait. His arms and hands were short and hairy and powerful. His gray shirt stretched tautly across his torso. I couldn't tell whether his belly was more muscle or fat, but I had no doubt he packed a punch. His crude features, jutting brow, and small dark eyes gave him the appearance of a stupid man. But intellect was not what was going to win the day here. Brute strength, applied correctly, would.

"I decided to bring a friend along tonight," Yuri said, still grinning. "Rachel, meet Max. Say hello to each other."

Max grunted something. It might have been a *hello*, but I couldn't be sure. Rachel said nothing. She kept stepping backward, and I could read the naked fear in her rigid back.

Good girl, Rachel. Keep coming. Bring them to me.

My mind began racing. I had ten seconds at most. Then I would have to act. Two men. I would have to incapacitate one of them in the first second or two to be able to deal with the other on equal terms. I did not wish to kill, but I needed to take one of them out of the fight. But who? The answer came fast on the heels of the question. The stronger of the two. Max.

Rachel was six steps from the edge of the bar, where I had told her to draw Yuri to. Five, four, three.

"I don't think she likes you much, Max." Yuri laughed. "I think you're scaring her. Are you scared, Rachel?"

Two, one. Yuri quickened his step, stretching a hungry hand for Rachel. She retreated, nearly tripped, cried out, and her head turned to where I stood. Her eyes were huge. I sprang forward to attack, but it was already too late.

Yuri, following Rachel's turned gaze, spotted me and shouted a warning to Max. My kick, which had been headed straight for Max's kneecap—and which I would have followed with a slash to his right arm—failed to hit home. Max shifted, and my foot smacked into the fleshy part of his thigh.

He let out a soft grunt. Cursing loudly, I swung the knife in a sideways chop. Max was quicker than his build suggested. He twisted his torso, brought an arm up, and handed me a hard blow close to my elbow. My arm went numb, my fingers unclenched, and my knife clattered to the floor. Now it was Max's turn to attack. He swung a hard right at my head. What saved me was the shortness of his arm. I managed to tilt my head backward just in time, out of his limited reach. His fist blurred past my eyes.

He had invested too much in that one blow. He was too close to me, and his right side was exposed. I brought a knee up, right into his flank. I must have caught part of his kidney, because he moaned with true pain and lowered his guard. My right hand was unresponsive, so I jabbed with my left. I got him right on the nose and heard a low crunch. Blood spilled out of his nostrils, painting his thick lips red.

His nose must have hurt like mad, but he didn't seem to feel it. He swung at me again. I raised my left arm to block him, and his fist smacked into the radial bone. Pain jarred all the way up to my shoulder. My arm dropped like a piece of string at my side. He swung again, this time at my belly. I managed to turn my body at the last instant so his fist caught me on my useless left arm. It was more luck than skill, and I knew it would not last. Next time he would score a hit that would matter.

I shuffled back. Max came at me again, sensing my vulnerability. I surprised him by changing direction, moving forward straight into him instead of retreating. I lowered my head into his face, butting him right on his damaged nose. This time the crunch was louder. It was followed by a couple of cracks and thuds as he crashed backward onto the floor, toppling one of the overturned chairs on his way down. He lay motionless, arms and legs sprawled.

My head hurt where I had butted him, but it did not feel like my skin had broken. Tingling sensation was returning to my right arm. A dull ache had settled in my left. I was breathing rapidly, and my heart was pumping like a frantic sailor in a ship that was taking in water. The bitter scent of fear-induced sweat reached my nostrils. It might have come from Max, but I suspected I was the source.

I studied the fallen man. His face was a mess of blood. The chair, one of its legs busted, lay by his head. For a second, I thought I had killed him. Then I saw his large belly rising and falling. Max was out, but alive.

Where was my knife?

The answer came a second later when I heard Yuri yell, "Max! Max!" and turned toward him.

His right hand was gripping my knife. His left was curled around Rachel, holding her tight to him. The knife's tip was at her throat.

He must have picked up the knife after it had dropped from my hand. Why had he not used it on me? He could have sliced me half a dozen times while I was fighting Max. The pallid face that peered over Rachel's shoulder and his frantic calls to his unconscious accomplice were all the answer I needed. At his core, Yuri was a coward. He might steel himself enough to attack a lonely woman, but he had an inherent fear of fighting other men. Not even when he had a knife and the man standing in his way was unarmed and had all his attention set on another adversary.

"He can't hear you, Yuri," I said, taking a step closer to him and Rachel.

His panicked eyes shifted to me, and he tightened his grip on Rachel. She was utterly colorless, her eyes pleading. Her lower lip trembled. Not that Yuri looked much better. In fact, I would have been hard put to determine who was more terrified—Yuri or Rachel.

"Stay away from me, or she gets it. Right in the neck."

"You all right, Rachel?"

She gave the tiniest of nods. I took another step forward.

"Stay away, I tell you." Yuri's eyes went from my face to Max. He was praying for a rescue. I very much doubted God was listening.

"Max can't help you, Yuri. If he stirs, I'll kick him in the head and knock him out again."

"You son of a bitch. Back off."

There were four feet between us now. I moved right so my body blocked Yuri's view of Max. I wanted his undivided attention. I wanted him to feel he had no way out but what I was willing to offer him. "You got two options," I said, feigning a calmness I did not feel. What I had in mind depended on my having read him correctly. If I hadn't, things might end badly. "Neither of them is good, but one is much worse than the other. Listen closely. Option one is you hurt Rachel in any way. If you do that, I'll kill you. Option two is you let her go unharmed. Then you'll be alive come dawn. Which do you choose?"

He opened his mouth, closed it, opened it again. It stayed open for a while, but not a sound emerged from it. All his plans for the evening had come crashing down around him. Even this moment was not going as it should. He was holding the knife. He had the hostage. He should be the one setting terms. But I wasn't following his script. I was the one who was directing how this little scene would play out. He didn't know what his next line should be. I took another step. Then another. I was close enough to reach out and touch Rachel. If I had the inclination, I could have counted the sweat drops on Yuri's forehead.

"What will it be, Yuri? Life or death. Choose now, or I'll make your choice for you."

We stared at each other for half a minute or so. His hand was shaking, and I worried he might accidentally nick Rachel. "Max," he said, his voice quaking. When no answer came, he cursed in Russian. I could see the wheels turning in his pathetic excuse for a brain, searching for a way out. By the expression on his face, those wheels were stuck in a rut, spinning in place.

Then, with a cry of anger or anguish, directed at me or at himself, he let go of Rachel and pushed her hard to me. I grabbed her and steadied her on her feet.

"Now the knife," I said, steering Rachel to the side. "Put it on that table there."

A final hesitation, and I could imagine what was going through his mind. He had a knife. I was weaponless. Was this the day he would overcome his cowardice? Could he emerge from this day a new man?

I let him work through it, and he did not surprise me. His nature won out. He tossed the knife on a nearby table. Then he straightened his back, tried a sneer on for size, found that it didn't sit right, and let it melt off his face.

"You can have the bitch if you're so keen on her," he said, moving to go past me.

I buried my right fist in his belly. He was soft, hardly any muscle. The fist went deep. He folded with a whoosh of air and fell to his knees, retching.

"Adam," Rachel said with evident surprise, but I paid her no mind. I put my foot in Yuri's side and pushed him over. He landed on his back, still gasping for air.

I knelt by him, stuck my hand in his pants pocket, and took out his wallet. I stood and emptied the wallet of money, placing the cash on the table by the knife. Then I read his full name out loud from his ID.

"Now I know who you are, and I'll be able to find you. If you ever come back here, if you ever bother Rachel again, I'll find you and kill you. Get it?"

He didn't answer. He just lay there, looking pitiful. But I felt no pity for him. He had terrorized and robbed a helpless woman, and was planning on doing much worse. I knew what I had to do.

I stood over him. "I told you I'd let you live, but you still need to pay for what you did here. Extend your hand. Put it right here." I tapped on the floor with my shoe.

Yuri blinked at me uncomprehendingly. I had to tell him again before he did as instructed.

He didn't see it coming, but Rachel did. As I raised my foot and brought it down on his outstretched hand, she screamed, "No! Don't!"

Her words were drowned out by the sound of fingers snapping and Yuri screaming.

Curled on his side, clutching his ruined hand to his chest, he sobbed. The tears dripped from his eyes to the floor.

I went to him, grabbed him by one arm and his belt and pulled him to his feet. I shoved his wallet into his pocket. Max was stirring. I prodded him with my foot. He cracked his eyes open. I yanked him up. He swayed on his feet, but did not fall.

"Don't ever come back here. Yuri will explain what will happen if you do."

His mouth was all bloodied and his breaths wheezed through his caved-in, blood-clogged nostrils. He looked half-dazed, but he got the message. One glance at Yuri was enough to tell him what the situation was. He gave me a quick nod and staggered out, not waiting for his friend. I shoved Yuri out and locked the door and returned to where Rachel was standing.

She had her arms folded across her chest. She gazed at the bloodstains Max had left on her floor. I picked up the money I took from Yuri and held it out to her.

"It probably won't cover what you paid him, but—"

She kept her arms folded. It was warm in the restaurant, but Rachel was trembling as if a cold wind had touched her skin. I suddenly felt cold as well. Maybe it was the battle sweat evaporating from my skin. Maybe it was something else.

"I don't want it," Rachel said, raising her eyes to me. The gratitude I had expected to see in them was nowhere in evidence. It had been replaced by...I wasn't sure what. I felt a stab of disappointment. I realized that I liked Rachel and wanted her to like me back. This filled me with surprise. For five years, ever since my wife, Deborah, died in the gas chambers, I had felt nothing for any woman. Not emotionally and not physically. It was as if this particular passion that had once burned brightly within me had guttered out and not even embers remained of it. Only now I felt glimmerings of that dormant emotion, mixed with a touch of shame, as if I had already betrayed the memory of my wife.

"How could you?" Rachel asked.

I didn't understand. "How could I what?"

"Do that. To him. You broke his hand."

I was beginning to get it. "I had to do it."

"No, you didn't. He'd already put down the knife. He was about to leave. And you just...you just attacked him."

Now I recognized what her eyes held. It was horror, disgust, perhaps even hatred for me.

"If he had gone out of here unharmed," I said, "by tomorrow his mind would have begun painting a different picture of this night. He would have started thinking that he had been too quick to leave, that he could have gotten his way if he'd stuck around. He would have blamed Max or found some other excuse. He would have come back. Maybe not this week or the next. Maybe it would have taken him a month. But he would have been back here. Now he won't, and you know why?"

I waited, but she didn't respond. She just glared at me with those scornful eyes, as if I were something that needed to be kept at arm's length, something dangerous.

"He won't be able to forget the pain, that's why. His hand will heal, his fingers will mend, but the pain will live on in his mind. He won't risk revisiting it. He'll stay away."

"You don't know that," she said, tears springing from her eyes and running down her cheeks. "You're guessing. You're making excuses for what you did."

"I told you that this is what it would take to solve your problem. I told you I would need to hurt him. You agreed."

"I never agreed to this," she said, shaking her head. "Never to this. Know what I think? I think you enjoyed this. You enjoyed stomping on his hand."

I said nothing. What was there to say? Nothing that would change her mind. Nothing that would change the truth.

"I want you to go," she said, fairly spitting out the words. "Get out. I don't want the money. Take it with you and go."

I was still holding the money out to her. I made to lay it on the table. "I'll just leave it here—"

"No." Her voice was strident, almost hysterical. "I said I don't want it. I don't want it near me. You take it. Take it and get out of here."

For a moment I considered disobeying her and leaving the money behind. Then I thought, *Goddamn her. Who is she to suddenly grow a conscience? I risked myself on her behalf and now she behaves as if I have some sickness.*

I took the money. Rachel might have thought it was dirty, but I certainly didn't. I had earned it. The knife I refolded and slid into my pants pocket.

I thought of saying something—maybe to make one final stab at changing her mind, or maybe just to tell her off—but all of a sudden I wanted to leave as badly as she wanted me to go.

I crossed the street and made my way down to the deserted

beach. With each step, my shoes sank deeper into the soft sand until I got to the firmer, wetter soil at the water's edge. Waves frothed white as they broke by my feet. The undulating water reflected the moon a million times over. I gazed upward. A billion sparkling stars speckled the clear night sky. I recalled nights at Auschwitz, where the only way I could see freedom was to look up into the heavens. In every other direction lay barracks, guard towers, barbed-wire fences, mud and frost and misery. And death.

Would the Adam Lapid that had lived before Auschwitz have broken Yuri's fingers? Maybe not. But that Adam would have been wrong. Just as Rachel was wrong. Because what I had done was necessary.

I wasn't cruel. I had my boundaries. Another man would not have thought twice before killing Yuri and Max. I'd taken a risk and nearly paid dearly for refusing to do so. Because I did not kill those who did not deserve it. I reserved death for the truly evil.

I lowered my eyes and stared seaward, at the shimmering expanse of shifting water, all the way to the black horizon. Beyond that horizon was Hungary, where I was born, where I had been a policeman, where I'd married and had children, where my father was buried. God, how I missed him. How I missed Deborah. How I missed them all.

But Hungary was not my home. Looking back at all that had happened, I knew it never had been.

A faraway sparkle caught my eye. A light was glinting in the far distance. Not a reflection of starlight on the water, but a man-made light. A boat.

Or a ship.

In an instant, my mind cleared of Rachel Weiss and her accusations, of Hungary and my dead family. Suddenly I knew with utter certainty the first step I would take in the Henrietta Acker-land case.

I smiled, feeling strangely buoyed. My eyes followed the

glinting light till it vanished in the darkness. Then I turned and headed home.

Back at my apartment, I found the cup of tea I had made for myself earlier that evening. I hadn't touched it before I left. I took a sip. Cold, but sweet. Like revenge.

I got into bed and pulled the thin blanket over me. The room was warm but pleasant. I left all the windows open. Tonight there would be no nightmares, no screams. Tonight I would sleep like an innocent child.

Violent days were like that. They always ended with peaceful nights. I did not know why. And in those twilight moments between wakefulness and blissful sleep, I did not care either.

6

Shmuel Birnbaum did not look happy to see me.

I found him the next morning in Café Tamar on Sheinkin Street, a few blocks from the offices of *Davar*, the newspaper where he worked, the same newspaper where Henrietta Ackerland had posted an ad in the hopes that Esther Grunewald would see it. *Davar* was the party newspaper of Mapai, the left-wing ruling party of Israel, and the most widely read paper in the country. Shmuel Birnbaum was one of its most prominent reporters.

Seeing me approach, Birnbaum set down the paper he'd been reading and began rubbing his jaw. I made an effort to hide my smile. He made none to hide his scowl.

"Good morning, Shmuel. Can I sit with you?"

"If I say no, will you leave?"

I shook my head.

Birnbaum sighed. "Then pull up a chair, by all means. Make yourself at home."

I sat. Birnbaum folded his paper and put it on a vacant chair. He leaned back and ran a hand over his bald scalp, scratching the fringe of light brown hair at the back of his head. He gave me a long probing look.

"Something tells me you're not here to apologize."

"Apologize? For what?"

"For this," he said, pointing at his jaw. "You nearly broke it, you *meshuganah*. And loosened a couple of my teeth while you were at it. I was this close to losing them." He held up a thumb and forefinger close together. "And for what? For singing your praises in the newspaper."

"Without asking me for permission," I reminded him.

"I could have asked you a hundred times, but what good would it have done? You weren't in a position to answer."

"I was in the hospital. Unconscious."

Birnbaum waved a hand dismissively. "Unavailable for comment. When has that ever stopped an enterprising reporter from publishing a story? Especially one as good as yours. You stormed an Egyptian gun position single-handedly and so allowed the rest of your platoon to score a major victory. And you nearly lost your life in the process. How could I resist printing a story like that? It would have been unprofessional. I don't know what you're complaining about. I made you out to be a hero, didn't I? Not that it was hard. Reporting the truth never is. You should have thanked me, you stupid bastard, but what do you do instead? Punch me in the jaw, that's what."

"You deserved it. You crept into my room without permission and took a picture of me in my hospital bed. The nurse later told me she had to chase you out."

Birnbaum's face broke into a wide smile. He had a doughy face spattered with freckles across his cheeks and nose. His eyes were light brown and made larger by horn-rimmed glasses. Seeing him smile, I noticed he had nice teeth. I almost felt bad for nearly knocking some of them out.

But I did not regret hitting him, because he did have it coming.

He had no right to take that picture, and I did not enjoy the publicity his article had garnered me. I liked my privacy and solitude. I felt uncomfortable being called a hero. There were so many others, alive and dead, who deserved the honor more than I did, but never got it.

"She chased me with a broom," he reminisced. "I know you saw some hard fighting against the Egyptians and Jordanians, Adam, but that nurse could have taken on an entire battalion with that broom. What a woman! Ah, here it is."

The morose-faced proprietor of Café Tamar came to the table and set a bowl of soup before Shmuel. Steam whispered up from the bowl in delicate gray curls. The earthy smell of cooked beans wafted about the table.

"Want some bean soup?" the proprietor asked me, in a tone that suggested he couldn't care less what my answer would be.

I told him I didn't. He left without a word or change of facial expression.

"You sure about the soup?" Birnbaum asked. "It's really quite good."

"I'm sure."

"Suit yourself." He spooned some soup into his mouth, swallowed, and sighed contentedly. "Six days a week, about this hour, I come here and have this soup. Even when it's hot enough outside to fry eggs on the hood of a car. It's not much, I grant you, but in these times it's a luxury. Better than going hungry."

"I'm sure it is."

Birnbaum turned somber. "You would know, wouldn't you? You were there, in Auschwitz, and you survived. If you ever feel like telling your story, Adam, I'll be happy to write it."

"Don't hold your breath, Shmuel."

"Why not? I know it was hard, but that's all the more reason to talk about it. It can bring relief, unburden the soul."

"Let it go, Shmuel," I said, and something in my tone made him draw back in his chair. He raised a hand, palm out.

"All right. All right. So tell me, why have you come to see me?"

"I need you to find some information for me."

"What sort of information?"

I told him I was looking for a ship that had set sail from Greece in early March 1939, carrying Jewish immigrants. I did not know the port of departure, how many passengers were on board, and whether it had ever reached the shores of Israel.

"I want to talk to one of the people who were in charge of that voyage. If there's a passenger list, I want it, too."

Birnbaum listened intently, making no noise apart from a low slurping sound each time his lips met the spoon. Then he asked, "And why do you need this information?"

"For a case."

"Thank you, Adam, but I sort of figured that out for myself. Despite your best efforts, I did not suffer brain damage when you clobbered me. What sort of case? What are you hunting for?"

He had taken on a cunning, predatory look. Like a hound, he had caught the scent of a story in the air.

"I can't go into that."

"Oh, come on."

"Sorry, but that's how it is."

Birnbaum set down his spoon. "So why should I help you? I'm paid to write stories, remember? Not to dig up information for private detectives. And you're giving me *bupkes*."

"You owe me."

His eyebrows shot up. "Owe you? What for?"

"For printing that story about me, that's what for."

"Sorry, Adam, but that debt has long been settled. By my jaw. With interest."

"You'd be doing a good deed."

He snorted. Apparently, that was all the response my appeal to his charity was worthy of.

"I could always hit you again, you know," I told him, irritated.

He chuckled and wagged his finger at me. "Not you, Adam. Not you. That sort of thing would go against your nature, wouldn't it? Come on, you gotta give me something if you want my help."

I mulled it over. I could try someone else, but no one I knew had the contacts Birnbaum had. His position in *Davar* afforded him direct contact with government officials and politicians. Everyone wanted to be on his good side and would be keen on doing him a favor in the hope that he might one day reciprocate. He could get this information for me faster than anyone else.

"I tell you what, Shmuel, I'll make you a deal. You do this for me, and when I finish with her case, I'll ask my client to talk to you. If she agrees, you'll have an exclusive."

His eyes gleamed. "So it's a *she*, is it? That makes the mystery even more intriguing. How do I know she'll speak to me? Or that the story is worth my time?"

"You won't. Not until the case is done. But if everything works out, it might be a big story, Shmuel." I didn't let my face show what I thought of the chances of this case ever working out. "Very big."

Those two final words seemed to hang in the air between us like bait. Birnbaum grimaced at my obvious ploy. He did not appreciate being played.

Birnbaum pursed his lips and scratched his cheek. Then he blew out a breath and nodded. "Fine. It feels like a big waste of time, but I'll do it. Maybe that fist to the jaw did rattle my brain after all. Call me at my office in three days. I hope to have something by then."

I thanked him, stood up to leave, then decided to add something.

"One more thing, Shmuel. I don't want you sniffing around while I'm working this case, understand?"

"Would I ever do something like that?" he said, his face a mask of childlike innocence.

"Yes," I said flatly. "You would. I'm telling you right now, Shmuel, that I won't appreciate it. Are we clear on that?"

I had leaned forward, putting my hands on the table, so that I loomed over him. I locked my eyes on his. He gulped and gave another dismissive wave, trying unsuccessfully to mask his nervousness.

"All right. All right. You made your point. Now go on. Get out of here. Let me finish my soup in peace."

Half an hour later, I was at Greta's Café. I was setting up my chessboard for a game when Greta came to my table with a cup of coffee and some toast. She put the food on the table and took a chair. Apart from me, there was just one other customer in the place. The only noise was the rattling of the ceiling fan and the hoot of a car horn outside.

"What happened to your arm?" Greta asked.

I had noticed it this morning when I awoke. Blood had pooled under the skin of my left forearm where Max had punched me the previous night. An ugly purplish lump had formed. At its center, raised like an offering to a vengeful god, was my number tattoo.

"I ran into a little trouble last night at Rachel Weiss's place."

"What sort of trouble?"

"Let's just say that it was a lesson in the importance of not being arrogant," I told her with a wry smile.

Greta did not smile back. "Are you injured?"

"Apart from this ugly thing, no. It doesn't hurt, just looks bad."

"So it all worked out with Rachel?"

"Yes. I solved her problem."

I took a bite of toast and helped it on its way down with some coffee.

"Was that all?" Greta began saying, uncommonly tentative. "I mean, what did you think of Rachel?"

I smiled faintly. Greta was always on the lookout for a woman to dispel part of my loneliness.

"It's not in the cards, Greta. No suitability, I'm afraid."

"I see," she said softly, clearly disappointed.

I shrugged. "The important thing is I did a good job and got paid for it. I'm not looking for romance."

Greta seemed about to say something, but thought better of it. The other customer called for more beer. She went to tend to him. I returned to beating myself at chess.

7

An uneventful weekend passed. I finished one western and started another, tore through a stack of newspapers, and watched Burt Lancaster woo Yvonne De Carlo in *Criss Cross* at Allenby Cinema. In between, I used the money I had liberated from Yuri's wallet to replenish my supply of black-market sardines, eggs and sausages; sat on a bench in Dizengoff Square, watching pigeons peck nonchalantly at hunks of white bread that prisoners at Auschwitz would have killed for; smoked an inordinate number of cigarettes; and cleaned and oiled my Luger. I slept fitfully and woke with the shadowy dream remnants of lost family, blank-eyed *muselmänner,* and dead-eyed guards, wafting in the stifling air of my enclosed apartment like smoke from a crematorium.

On Sunday, July 10, three days after my talk with Shmuel Birnbaum, I strode to the corner of Hamaccabi and King George and entered Levinson Drugstore. The store was run by Zelig and Rivka Levinson, who kept it as clean as an operating room. By the spotless front window, on a small waist-high table, stood a bulky telephone attached to a meter. The meter kept track of how much you owed for each call, taking into account duration and distance. Since nearly none of my neighbors, nor I, had a private telephone in our apartments—hardly anyone in Israel did—the drugstore telephone got plenty of use. I had to wait for five minutes while a neighbor of mine lectured her daughter in Haifa on the proper way of raising her grandchildren.

When she'd finished, I rang the offices of *Davar* and asked to speak with Shmuel Birnbaum.

"Good morning, Adam," he said when he came on the line, sounding chipper. "How was your weekend? Beat anyone up?"

The snapping of Yuri's fingers under my heel sounded in my ears, followed closely by an image of Max's bloodied face as he lay unconscious on Rachel Weiss's floor.

"Not on the weekend, no. Last time I knocked someone out was Wednesday night."

Birnbaum said nothing. I had shocked him into silence. Scratching sounds came over the line. Birnbaum rubbing his jaw? I rummaged in my pocket for a cigarette and stuck it between my lips. A woman cleared her throat. I turned and saw the stern face of Mrs. Levinson frowning at me from behind the counter. She gave a single shake of her head. I returned the cigarette to the pack.

"Got anything for me, Shmuel?"

"Yes," he said, regaining his voice. "And I have to say my curiosity is piqued. I'm looking forward to you telling me what this is all about. Got a pencil handy?"

I took out my notebook and pencil and told him to go on.

"The only ship that fits the timeframe you gave me is the *Salonika*. It set sail from the port of Piraeus, Greece, on March 2, 1939. Forty *maapilim* were said to be on board."

Maapilim was the term used for illegal Jewish immigrants to Mandatory Palestine. Illegal in the eyes of the British authorities who had administered the Mandate of Palestine from 1920 until 1948, when Israel was reborn. Since the 1930s, when Great Britain reneged on its promise of establishing a Jewish national home in Palestine and began severely restricting the number of Jews it allowed to immigrate there, Zionist organizations started smuggling Jews in, mostly by sea. Thousands of Jews currently living in Israel were *maapilim*.

"You're not certain about the number?"

"No," Birnbaum said. "There is no official number nor a passenger list. But that was the number given at the time. What the papers reported at the time, anyway. But what is more interesting is what happened to the *Salonika* and to the people it was carrying."

He paused, as if savoring his possession of information he knew I craved. It was like a scoop, and he lived for scoops.

"Come on, Shmuel. Spit it out."

"On the morning of March 5, while it was in the process of disembarking passengers somewhere north of Netanya, the *Salonika* was spotted by a British patrol ship. The British opened fire. A short battle ensued. Fourteen of the passengers died, as did two crew members. Ten *maapilim* were captured and taken into custody."

"And the rest?"

"Taken to safe houses around the country, I imagine. Lived here ever since."

"Who was in charge of the ship?"

"The Irgun. Which explains what happened next. Those *meshuganahs* were always gung ho."

The Irgun had been a right-wing Jewish militant group that fought to expel the British from Palestine and so bring about the establishment of a Jewish state there. Their methods included bombings, kidnappings, and assassinations of British personnel and soldiers. In addition, they had also striven to bring in as many

Jews as they could to Palestine, regardless of British immigration quotas.

"What happened?"

"The Irgun stormed the prison where the British kept the ten captured *maapilim*. It was a fiasco. Six more died, though they did manage to get the other four out. They also killed five British guards."

Six dead for four liberated. Not a good trade.

"It was no great honor to be part of that raid, you can imagine," Birnbaum continued. "So it's no surprise I only managed to uncover the name of one of the Irgun members involved."

"What's his name?" I asked.

"It's a she. Mira Roth."

I wrote down the name as well as the phone number and address where she worked.

"Thank you, Shmuel," I said.

"Just remember our deal. I'm counting on a very big story from you."

I told him I would do my best and rang off. Luckily, no one was waiting to use the phone. I dialed the number Birnbaum had given me.

Female chatter and laughter in the background. A woman's voice said hello. I asked to speak with Mira Roth. She was called to the phone.

"Mira speaking. Who is this?" Her voice was strong and deep and laced with smoke. A confident voice.

"Ms. Roth, my name is Adam Lapid. I'm calling for information regarding a ship, the *Salonika*. I—"

"Who gave you my number? How did you get my name?" She was agitated. Her voice rose somewhat in pitch.

"From Shmuel Birnbaum. You may know the name. He writes for *Davar*—"

"*Davar!*" Acid dripped over the line along with that single word. "You think I'm going to talk to anyone working for that rag? Don't ever call here again, you hear?"

She slammed the phone down so hard it hurt my ear. I was about to ring her again, but decided to obey her instructions. Besides, she never said anything about not coming to see her in person, did she?

8

The hair salon stood three doors west of the corner of Frishman and Dizengoff, flanked by a stationery store and a photography studio. Through the open door came a similar sound of female festivity to the one I'd heard when I called there earlier. Inside were five women. Two were seated in high chairs in front of mirrors, having their hair done, each attended by a hairdresser. The fifth woman occupied a chair at the opposite wall. She was either waiting her turn or simply enjoying the company of her friends.

My appearance in the doorway had an immediate effect on the merry quintet. Conversation abruptly ceased, and five pairs of eyes flicked my way. I got the distinct impression male visitors were rare in this bastion of womanhood.

"Can we help you with something?" said the older of the two hairdressers, a plump late-fortyish woman.

"I'm here to see Mira Roth," I said.

Four of the five pairs of eyes turned from me to the other hairdresser, a tall, slim woman in her late twenties with wavy russet hair. She blinked at me, not sure what to make of my visit.

"You been keeping secrets from us, Mira?" said one of the customers, a wide-faced brunette woman with a mischievous twinkle in her eyes. "And what a handsome secret he is."

"Careful, Paula," said the first hairdresser. "Don't let your husband hear you talking like that."

Paula made a show of peering under her chair and checking each corner of the salon, calling, "Ephraim, Ephraim, are you here, dear?" She winked at me. "What do you know? It appears my husband is out of earshot."

The other women laughed. All except Mira Roth, who narrowly eyed me.

"So, Mira," Paula said, "you gonna introduce us to your handsome friend?"

"I have no idea who this man is," Mira said, her cheeks reddening.

"Oh?" Paula turned to me. "What's your name, dear?"

"Adam Lapid. I called earlier."

"Nice to meet you, Adam," Paula said, obviously the leader of this little group. "How nice of you to come calling on our darling Mira. I assure you you won't find a better girl, would he, ladies?"

"That's quite enough, Paula," Mira Roth said. The others chuckled. "And the same goes for the rest of you." Recovered from her momentary embarrassment, her voice had reacquired the same strength and authority I had detected in it over the phone. She crossed the salon in three forceful strides and, upon reaching me, planted a firm hand in the middle of my chest and pushed me out onto the sidewalk. She followed me out and shut the door to the salon. "I thought I made it clear I did not wish to speak to you or anyone from your lousy newspaper."

Her mouth was set in a hard line. Her amber eyes were narrowed to menacing slits. Her left hand was planted on her hip. I noticed she was clutching a pair of scissors in her right hand and that muscles bunched and twitched in her forearm, as if she were getting ready to plunge the scissors into my chest.

This was an Irgun member, I recalled. It was quite likely she had killed before. I hastened to defuse the situation.

"You misunderstood me, Ms. Roth. I am not a reporter and I don't work for *Davar*. I'm a private investigator and all I want is to ask you a few questions about the *Salonika*."

"I don't want to talk about that. Not now, not ever. Go bother someone else."

"Please, it's very important."

"It's been ten years. What could be so important?"

"I'm working on a case. My client is a woman named Henrietta Ackerland. Ten years ago, she gave her baby boy for safekeeping to a passenger on your ship and—"

"Esther."

The name had emerged from her mouth in a gasp. We stared at each other in silence. Mira shifted her feet. She seemed surprised at having blurted out the name, but she was nowhere near as surprised as I was.

"You remember her. Do you know where she is?" I asked, feeling my heartbeat accelerate.

Just then came a squeak from behind her back. Mira turned to see that Paula had inched open the door to eavesdrop on our conversation. The faces of the other three women were pressed to the front window, peering at us without a trace of embarrassment.

Mira huffed, went to the door, and wordlessly closed it in Paula's face. Paula stuck her tongue out at Mira through the glass door, then flashed a mischievous smile. Mira did not smile back.

She turned back to me, frowning. "Adam Lapid. Where do I know that name from?"

The old uncomfortable feeling resurfaced, just as it did each time my wartime exploits were brought up. But maybe this time something good would come out of it. What better way to impress an Irgun member than with tales of wartime bravery?

"I was injured during the war. Operation Yoav. The story got some press."

"Ah. Now I remember. I heard about you on the radio. What you did was truly heroic."

I said nothing. She gazed at me and there was something in her eyes that had not been there before. Respect. Appreciation. Perhaps even admiration.

"You're a private investigator, is that what you said?"

"Yes."

She chewed her lower lip, mulling something over. Then she said, "I have to finish doing Carmella's hair. It should take me ten minutes. I don't want to talk about it here—not in front of them. I live close by, on the corner of Frishman and Sirkin. See you there in fifteen minutes."

With that, she turned on her heel and reentered the hair salon.

9

When I was a child, I believed in miracles. I suppose all children do. Just like they believe in magic and monsters. Then, as I grew older and got acquainted with the reality of life, my belief waned. But it never disappeared entirely.

Until Auschwitz.

Now I no longer believed in miracles. But as I walked the few hundred meters from the hair salon to Mira Roth's home, and during the ten minutes I waited outside her building for her to arrive, I considered the possibility that my faith in miracles was about to be rekindled.

Because Mira knew Esther Grunewald and Willie Ackerland. They had been on that ship. In a few minutes I would know whether, by some fluke or miracle, they were still alive today.

"So," I said, "where are Esther Grunewald and Willie Ackerland?"

I was seated on a sofa in Mira's living room. It was a nicer room than mine. Yellow curtains hung at the windows. Small potted cacti stood on a windowsill. Photographs of the Dead Sea, the ruined mountain fortress of Masada, and the Old City of

Jerusalem adorned the walls. In the middle of a colorful rug squatted a low wooden table. Mira had taken a chair on the opposite side of it. She had not offered me anything to drink, and I would have declined had she done so. I desired nothing but answers, and I think she desired nothing but supplying them. I found myself literally at the edge of my seat, and my skin felt as if it were vibrating in anticipation.

"In Nahalat Yitzhak Cemetery," Mira said. Her tightly controlled expression and flat tone made it clear that this was a woman who had had much experience with death.

"Dead?" I asked, feeling foolish the instant the word left my lips. The vibration had faded, leaving a bleak void in its place.

A curt nod.

No miracle. In fact, it was worse than that. A mother parts with her only child to save him from the horrors of Nazi Germany. Against all odds that child and the woman who agreed to care for him make it to the shores of the Promised Land, only to be killed on the cusp of safety. Fury welled up inside me, followed by immense sadness. What sort of God allows for something as sacrilegious as that?

"They were murdered," Mira said, and this time there was a current of anger in her tone.

"By the British, you mean."

She shook her head. "Esther and Willie weren't killed by the British. They were murdered on August 26, 1939, in their apartment in Tel Aviv."

I asked her to repeat what she'd just said. She did. Then she told me the rest of the story. She spoke haltingly at first, as if she had to talk herself into uttering each new word in her narration. Once she got into it, though, her speech smoothed and normalized.

"I met her on the *Salonika*. The ship wasn't much. It was old and patched up, and the engine rattled the whole way from

Greece. But it was the best we were able to find. We arrived a little after dawn and began ferrying passengers ashore. We only had two boats, so we had to make several trips back and forth. We had people on the beach with cars ready to drive the new *maapilim* away. Then the British came."

Her face darkened with the memory. She had strong features —high forehead, pronounced cheekbones, ruler-straight nose, full eyebrows, wide mouth with thin, almost severe lips, and a well-defined jawline. Her hair seemed to be the only part of her appearance that she actively cultivated; it fell in vibrant tresses to her trim shoulders. She wore no jewelry or makeup. The lack of added color just placed more emphasis on her eyes. They bounced back whatever light hit them. Her face was too linear to be beautiful, but there was something about it that arrested the eye.

She was five foot eight and athletic. Long limbs, narrow waist and shoulders. Small high breasts. A body made for running and jumping. A tomboyish figure, but attractive none-theless, and it seemed to fit her character like a glove. She had on a pair of black shoes with a negligible heel and a pearl-colored shirt, which was tucked into the waistline of a blue skirt that showed her knees and calves. I found myself staring at her exposed legs.

"Unlike what the papers said at the time," Mira continued, "there was no battle. Neither I, nor any other Irgun member, was on board at the time. We were all on the beach, getting the *maapilim* already ashore into waiting cars and trucks. The British simply began firing as soon as they had the *Salonika* in range. Some of the passengers who were still on the ship died then and there; the rest—ten of them—were taken into custody. Esther and Willie were among them."

She began pacing the room. It was clear by the set of her jaw how upset reliving that day made her. No wonder the Irgun proved to be such a thorn in the side of the British. They had ample stores of motivation to draw from.

"The British took the prisoners to a makeshift prison camp near Haifa. It was nothing much. A few shacks, some fences, a guard post. A decision was made in the Irgun: we were going to storm the place and get the prisoners out."

"Shmuel Birnbaum told me the raid was a fiasco," I said.

She snorted without humor. "That's mild compared to how it was portrayed by the Hebrew press at the time. We were called terrorists, insane, a danger to Zionism. We were to be shunned. That's why I didn't want to talk about all this at the hair salon. My boss and clients, none of them know I had anything to do with that raid. I wonder how Shmuel Birnbaum knows about it."

"He has good contacts. What went wrong?"

Instead of answering, Mira stepped over to a dresser and picked up a picture that was reclining on top of it. It showed two men and two women. All four were young, fit and tanned, and dressed in khaki short pants and shirts. And all had machine guns slung over their shoulders, hanging in front of their bodies. All four flashed the confident and arrogant smiles common to young warriors.

One of the women was a younger Mira Roth. How old was she when it was taken? Nineteen, eighteen, maybe even seventeen. Her hair had been shorter then, her face slightly leaner. She looked fierce, eager for battle. Fearless.

Mira pointed to the man at the left of the quartet of young warriors. "Yohanan died that night, and Talia..." Her finger lingered on the figure of the other woman in the picture, a willowy brunette. She raised her eyes to me. They glistened with withheld tears. Apparently, Mira had not cried out her share of tears. At least not yet.

"All told, we lost four members. What went wrong? In short, everything. The raid went badly from the get-go. Nothing went according to plan. Of the ten prisoners, six died. We only got four out. We also killed some British soldiers, but that was small comfort. Two of the prisoners we freed were Esther and Willie."

"What happened next?"

"We took them to a safe house, where they stayed until we arranged false papers and an apartment for them. When Esther told me the story of the baby, I suggested giving him to another family for safekeeping. She refused and said she would care for him until his mother arrived. I think she had grown attached to him. I think she loved him."

Mira sat down again and smoothed her dress. She crossed her legs, lacing her fingers on top of her knee.

"The papers we gave them said they were mother and son. We let Esther keep her first name; it eliminated the risk of her making an involuntary mistake if someone called out her name on the street. She chose the surname Kantor—German for cantor—because her father had been one in their synagogue in Germany. She gave the baby his first name—Erich. So that's who they became: Esther and Erich Kantor, mother and son."

Now I understood why Reuben Tzanani had failed to find a death certificate for Esther Grunewald and Willie Ackerland. Both had died under assumed identities. And the people who had been close to them—neighbors and colleagues and friends—knew them by their false names. Which explained why none of them had answered Henrietta's newspaper ad.

But that raised another question. "My client posted an ad in the newspaper, asking Esther to contact her. Didn't you see it?"

Mira asked me which paper the ad had run in and gave a rueful shake of her head when I told her it was *Davar*.

"*Davar*? No Irgun member would ever read that rag. Not with the way it vilified us over the years and still does today. It's the party paper of Mapai. It's pure leftist propaganda."

Of course. I could have smacked myself for not figuring this out for myself. Like all Israelis, I was well aware of the intense enmity between Mapai, the left-wing ruling party of Israel headed by David Ben-Gurion, and the right-wing Herut party led by former Irgun leader Menachem Begin. This enmity had its roots in the 1930s and '40s, when Zionists strove to establish a Jewish state in the Land of Israel. Despite sharing the same overall goal, the divergent politics and tactics of the two factions had led to tragic consequences, including internecine fighting and bloodshed. Even now, with the Irgun disbanded, its fighters absorbed into the Israeli Defense Forces, and its commanders turned to politicians, the hatred between Mapai and Herut burned blinding hot.

This blindness had led Mira, and perhaps other members of the Irgun who knew Esther Grunewald by her true name, to not see a particular newspaper ad. If they had, I would not have become involved in the case, and the terrible duty of informing Henrietta Ackerland that her son was dead would not have fallen to me.

"And the murderer?" I asked. "What happened to him?"

"He was never caught," Mira said.

10

I asked Mira a few more questions about the murders, but she had little information.

"Newspaper reports at the time were vague on the details, but I know both Esther and Willie were killed with a knife. Rumor was the scene was pretty gruesome." She had no idea what the police investigation had uncovered, nor whether there had been any suspects.

Mira offered to make me some tea and started asking me about Operation Yoav and the day I was injured. I told her I had to get going. I needed to inform my client her son was dead.

At the door, Mira asked, "Is that all, then?"

Her question puzzled me. "What else is there?"

She licked her lips. "I thought...well, I just hoped—never mind, I suppose."

I thanked her for her time and left.

It was Sunday, the day of the week on which Henrietta was cleaning the house with a phone in it. I entered a café on Dizengoff Street that had a phone and dialed the number. She answered on the fifth ring.

"Hello," came her voice, tentative and brittle.

"Henrietta, it's Adam Lapid calling in with a report."

"Yes. Yes. Any news?" Her voice had undergone a metamorphosis. Now it was fuller, bolstered by hope.

My mouth opened to deliver the bad news, and in my mind I had already rehearsed what I would say, but no words came out. I could hear her breathing on the other end of the line, and I pictured her pressing the receiver to her ear, eager for the news that would make her life worthwhile again.

"Nothing yet, I'm afraid," I heard myself say. The words sounded strange, as if spoken with another man's voice. "But I'm still working on it."

"Oh. I see." Her disappointment was palpable, and I could scarcely imagine what her reaction would have been had I had the guts to tell her the truth. She also sounded confused, and I could well understand why. I'd told her I would call in two weeks, sooner if I found out anything. Then I *had* called sooner, but said I had nothing to report. I wished I'd never picked up the phone and wanted to get off the line as fast as possible.

"Anyway. That's what I called to say. I'll call again next week. I hope to have something by then."

I said goodbye and ended the call. Laying down the receiver, I felt like the world's biggest coward. *Some hero you are*, I thought.

I must have been staring into space, because the bartender snapped his fingers before my eyes. "You okay? Hey, mister, can you hear me?"

I blinked. "Yes. Just daydreaming."

"Yeah. That happens," he said, giving a friendly chuckle. "Hope you were someplace nice. And not so hot."

I forced a smile on my face and told him to get me a beer.

I took the beer to a vacant table and nursed it for the next ten minutes. What had I gained by lying to Henrietta? What good had it done? Her son was still dead, and I would still need to inform her of that fact. Only a quarter of the beer remained when the answer came to me. On some level, I must have known it from the moment I found myself unable to tell her the truth.

I went back to the phone and dialed a number from memory.

"Hello, Reuben," I said when the familiar, warm voice came over the line.

"Adam, how are you?"

I told him I was fine and inquired after himself, his wife, Gila, and his four children.

"Everyone's doing well. Both the goddess and the angels." He laughed at his own description of his wife and children. "You should drop by, the children would love to see you. It's been some time since you last saw them."

A couple of months, I thought, recalling the visit with excruciating clarity. I did not wish to tell Reuben how his children—his lovely, beautiful children—had reminded me of my own.

"Maybe soon," I said, knowing it was likely a lie. "The reason I called is I need a favor."

"If I can help, Adam, you know I will."

"It's about a case. A murder that happened ten years ago."

"Ten years ago? Does this have anything to do with that woman I referred to you?"

"Yes. I found her son."

"I see. I'm sorry to hear that, Adam. Dreadfully sorry. Did I do right when I gave her your name? I wasn't sure, but she seemed hell-bent on keeping on looking."

"Don't worry about it, Reuben. What's done is done. I want to have a look at the investigation report. Can you get it for me?"

"A case that old would have been archived. I'll ask for it and should have it by tomorrow. Unless it got misplaced over the years. I hope it wasn't."

Me too. Because if I don't get that file, I lied to Henrietta Ackerland for nothing.

"The victims' names are Esther and Erich Kantor," I said. "They died on August 26, 1939. The murders took place in Tel Aviv." I explained that the victims were living under false names because they had immigrated to Palestine illegally.

I heard scribbling on his end as he copied the details.

"I'll call the archive right now. If they find it, I'll have it by tomorrow afternoon."

"Thank you, Reuben. I'll come by tomorrow. Give my regards to Gila and the children."

I paid for the call and went back to what was left of my beer. It had gone stale. Like the murder case, most likely. A crime investigation was like that. It started out with plenty of fizz and bubbles, but they quickly evaporated. What was left was a whole lot of stale information that was largely worthless. When a beer got that way, it got poured down a drain. A case was simply put away, to be forgotten or misplaced. Dear God, I hoped it hadn't been misplaced. Because it was no longer forgotten. Because I knew why I had lied to Henrietta Ackerland, why I had refrained from telling her that her son was dead.

I wanted to find out who had killed him and Esther. I wanted it badly. Maybe, just maybe, if I brought the killer to justice, it would make Henrietta's pain bearable. Maybe she wouldn't crumble to dust when she learned the truth.

I didn't know whether I truly believed that. Maybe it was something I told myself to excuse my lying to her. Maybe I wanted to catch this killer for personal reasons. Because if there was one thing I hated more than anything, it was child killers.

I would never be able to bring the men who had killed my daughters to justice. I did not know their names, and no matter how many Nazis I killed, there would always be more who were involved in the wholesale murder machine that had claimed my daughters, along with so many others. Full vengeance was impossible.

But I might be able to avenge the death of Henrietta's son. And that was what I planned on doing.

11

The following morning, I descended from my apartment and walked west toward Tchernichovsky Street. In my hand was a brown paper bag containing the two western paperbacks I'd finished over the past week.

I turned north on Tchernichovsky and, shortly before the corner of Bograshov, encountered what was now a common sight in Tel Aviv. A long line of basket-wielding women snaked out of a grocery store and halfway down the block. In the store window hung a handwritten sign proclaiming the arrival of fresh eggs that very morning. The number of eggs was not specified. I wondered how many of these women would go home empty-handed. More than a few, I bet.

I turned west on Bograshov, marching toward the sea. The morning sun was at my back and cast my shadow in front of me. A couple of blocks past the turn to the Trumpeldor Cemetery, between a women's clothing store and an insurance agency, was Zion Books. A bell tinkled as I pushed open the door and stepped inside.

The interior smelled of old paper and dry leather. Books were haphazardly stacked on shelves lining two walls, on narrow tables along the front window, and on the counter. Behind said counter sat a narrow-shouldered scholarly man in his fifties, reading a hardback through a pair of very thick glasses. He lifted his eyes at the sound of the bell and, seeing me, set his book aside. He smiled a delicate little smile, but one that spoke of true delight.

"Adam, nice to see you. I was just thinking of you."

"What brought me to mind?" I asked, crossing over to the counter and extending my hand.

The man shook it. His palm was dry and his handshake limp. His strength lay not in his body, but in his mind. His name was Erwin Goldberg, and books were his passion and business. He owned Zion Books and, he once told me in a tone utterly devoid of bragging, he had read over ten thousand books over the course of his lifetime. I would have doubted any other man who made such a claim, but I did not doubt Erwin Goldberg.

The books he sold did not run to type. In his store you could find impenetrable scholarly books on the most esoteric scientific fields; heavy religious tomes analyzing the finer points of not just Judaism, but also Islam, Christianity, and various other faiths; travel books to every corner of the earth; gazetteers, almanacs, and atlases; and fiction novels in a variety of genres.

Goldberg's taste in books matched that of his stock. He read everything and anything. My taste was more focused. I read adventure novels, almost exclusively westerns. Over the months we had known each other, he had tried to steer me to what he called "more serious work," books that would "levitate my soul" and "expand my mind," as he put it, but so far I had resisted.

I slid the two paperbacks out of the bag and laid them on the counter. He glanced down at them. He had a thin face that sloped from his temples to a weak and hairless chin. His mouth was small and seemed perpetually pursed. Lines plowed across his forehead over sparse black eyebrows and earth-colored eyes. His hair was the color and thinness of silver threads. He wore a navy blue suit jacket over a white shirt with a subdued red stripe and a blue necktie. He did not seem to be bothered by the heat.

"You finished them both. Good, good." Goldberg not only found satisfaction in reading himself, but also in books being read by others. "As to your question, some books have come in that I thought you'd enjoy, though I do wish you'd let me slip you something different this time. Some Victorian literature, perhaps?"

I hated to tell him no, but I did just that. The corners of his mouth drooped, but then he shrugged.

"Well, maybe next time."

"Maybe."

He set the two books I had finished aside and bent to look behind the counter. Scratching his head, he muttered, "Now where did I—here they are."

He straightened and laid three slim paperbacks on the counter. All three had creased covers and spines. One had pages that were the color of desert sand. That was another thing about Goldberg. He would buy and sell books in almost any condition so long as no pages were missing. In his store, one could find leather-bound first editions occupying the same shelves as well-thumbed paperbacks.

The three covers had some elements in common. All were colorful, dramatic, and featured a weathered-face cowboy armed with a gun and a steely gaze. One of the books showed an armed woman as well, and I immediately thought of Mira Roth. Two of the books were in English; the third—by Karl May—was in German. I pushed the latter back to Goldberg.

"You don't want it? It's an exciting story. You can read German, can't you?"

I could. Like many Hungarians, I had learned a number of languages in my childhood. Hungarian, naturally, but also Romanian and German. After the war, tens of thousands of ethnic

Germans were expelled from Hungary. Germans were also expelled from Poland and Czechoslovakia. In an ironic, or perhaps tragic, twist of fate and history, many European countries emptied of Germans shortly after the Germans had emptied them of Jews.

"I don't want to read anything in German," I said.

Goldberg stole a peek at my arm. His frown might have been for my number, or the purple stain beneath it, or both. "The language is not at fault for the deeds of those who speak it," he said. "And German is a beautiful language."

Not anymore it wasn't. Now it was the language of ashes and fire and death. A language of cruelty and wickedness. I shook my head. "Not for me, Erwin."

He shrugged and slid the book off the counter, but his expression was sad. Goldberg was a man of words, and he lamented the rejection of any language.

I paid for the other two novels and put them in the paper bag. I thanked him for putting them aside for me and was about to leave, when it occurred to me he might be able to clarify something for me.

"Erwin, you've lived here all these years, what can you tell me about the Irgun?"

"The Irgun? I was never a member myself. I don't like their politics much. Menachem Begin is too extreme for my taste, though I must admit he and his boys fought the British like lions."

"His girls, too," I muttered, thinking of Mira again.

"Excuse me?"

I waved a hand. "Never mind. What I was wondering is how secretive they were."

"Very much so. They had to be. If the British caught them, they would lock them up or hang them. The British were ruthless in that regard, and there were plenty of snitches—Jews too—who would sell them out to the British for money. Shameful. Quite shameful." Goldberg emphasized this last sentiment with a mournful shake of his head.

"What about today?"

"Today? What do you mean, today?"

"Are Irgun members still secretive?"

"Not like they were when the British ruled here, of course. But our government is not a fan of the Irgun or the Herut party that succeeded it. I'd say Irgun members trust each other more than they do other people. But as I said, I've never been a member." He gazed at me thoughtfully. "Adam, why are you asking all these questions about the Irgun?"

"It's nothing important. Just some minor thing I'm working on."

But it wasn't. It was something that had begun niggling at the back of my mind the evening before. A question for which I had no answer. What Goldberg told me did not provide the answer, simply confirmed the validity of the question. It might prove to be unimportant, but what I had learned as a police detective is that seemingly unimportant questions can have very important answers. They often led you to see things in a new light.

I thanked Goldberg and left, heading south. At the corner of Allenby and Ben Yehuda, I walked past Moghrabi Theater and recalled the crowds of jubilant Jews who had danced in the street in front of the theater when, in November 1947, the United Nations voted in favor of partitioning Palestine between the Jews and the Arabs. Continuing south, I soon got to Greta's Café.

Greta served me lunch—soup, rice and cooked vegetables—but the lunch crowd kept her too busy for chatting. Someone had left a copy of *Ma'ariv* and I read through it while I ate. The top headline claimed that Israel and Syria were expected to sign the first draft of an armistice agreement later that day.

After lunch I read a number of chapters from one of the novels I had bought earlier and played a few games of chess. At half past two, I left Greta's and went to pay Reuben Tzanani a visit.

12

His office was on the second floor of the police station at Yehuda Halevi 6. From the outside, the building was an architectural gem, with arched windows, a heavy metal gate, balconies supported on columns, and a wide courtyard. On the inside were frescoes and decorative floor tiles, but it still felt like any other police station I'd been in. Grimy, cramped, loud, and smelling of cigarettes, bad coffee, and body odor. The only differences between it and police stations in Budapest were that there were no mud tracks on the floor and that the air was dry and hot instead of damp and cold.

The policeman at the desk gave me the once-over when I told him my business. Apparently, I still possessed the look of a policeman, because the officer simply nodded and told me to go ahead upstairs. I took the stairs two at a time, turned right, and walked down the hall to Reuben's office.

It was a small office made even smaller by three filing cabinets that took up one wall and the simple metal desk behind which Reuben sat. The desk was piled high with papers, and Reuben was busy scribbling with a pencil on one of them. I stood in the doorway, waiting until he had ceased writing, then said, "Hello, Ant."

He raised his head and gave me a smile. Reuben's smiles were as wide as his heart was big. They radiated light as bright as a flashbulb. I sometimes wondered how a man who had seen the horrors of war could conjure such smiles. I certainly couldn't.

He had received the nickname "Ant" for saving my life. It had happened in October 1948, during Operation Yoav, when we fought the Egyptian Army in the Negev desert in the south of Israel. We were both infantrymen, and on that day our unit found itself pinned down by fire from an Egyptian machine-gun position. Four of our men had already died, and our unit was unable to advance. To this day, I'm not sure what came over me, but suddenly I found myself sprinting forward, zigging and zagging while a hail of bullets chewed into the desert sand at my feet. After what seemed like an hour but was actually less than thirty seconds, I made it to the foot of the small dune on which the gun position perched and lobbed two grenades into it.

The explosions silenced the Egyptian fire. I clambered up the dune, peered into the firing position, and saw two mangled bodies beside the blood-drenched Browning M1919 machine gun. I was about to signal the rest of my unit to advance when I heard a loud pop and felt a searing pain in my belly. A third Egyptian soldier had survived the grenades unscathed by cowering behind some crates at the far end of the gun position. He had shot me and was about to do so again. I raised my rifle and we fired simultaneously. I saw a spurt of red where his left eye had been and felt a massive punch to my chest. The force of the blow knocked me backwards, and I rolled down the side of the dune to the soft desert sand below. There I lay, unconscious, bleeding from two bullet wounds.

I would have died that day were it not for Reuben Tzanani. He had lifted me on his back and carried me over a kilometer to the rear of our lines, where I received the emergency treatment that saved my life. I heard all this much later, after I'd regained consciousness in the hospital in Tel Aviv. At first, the doctors thought I would not survive; then they feared I would be permanently handicapped. But I recovered fully, and, in five weeks minus two days, was discharged.

Reuben's actions that day were made all the more remarkable by the discrepancy in our physiques. I was six foot three, while he was five foot four with army boots on. I also outweighed him by forty pounds at least. For being able to carry more than his body weight, and for saving my life, he received the nickname "Ant." For my actions that day, I received a medal, the rank of sergeant, and was celebrated as a hero in the newspapers and on the radio. I'd always felt that, of the two of us, Reuben was the true hero.

Reuben was a slight, gentle man, who seldom raised his voice. But his tender appearance hid a rock-solid interior. He was one of the bravest soldiers I'd fought alongside of and one of the finest, most honest men I'd ever met. The latter, I suspected, was why he had not made it far on the police force and why he was given an office job instead of a street assignment. The ugly truth was that to get ahead in the police, you couldn't be as pure as a lily. You had to have some dirt on you.

"Adam," he said, "come in. Come in. Clear that chair and sit down. Want me to get you some coffee?"

The second chair—the one not currently occupied by Reuben —was laden with a tall stack of papers. Reuben motioned me to set the papers on the floor, which I did. Sitting down, I said, "No coffee for me, Reuben. I know what police station coffee is like."

He laughed. Then his face turned serious as he picked up a slim brown folder from his desk. He looked from the folder to me.

"I peeked at it. It's pretty brutal."

"I understand they were killed with a knife," I said.

"They were. But that wasn't the extent of it." He grimaced. "To do such things to anyone is unimaginable, but to a baby..." He shook his head and seemed to gaze into a place deep inside himself.

He had the smooth dark skin common among Yemenite Jews and soulful eyes of such a deep brown that it verged on black. His hair was the color of coal and cut in short, thick curls. His features were soft, rounded, almost cherubic. He was thirty years old, four years my junior, but appeared no older than twenty-five. He was dressed in his police uniform, which was, as always, pressed to perfection.

"I think I can handle it, Reuben," I said gently.

He blinked and nodded and handed over the folder. "I don't doubt it, Adam. But what good would it do your client to know the grisly details of her son's death?"

"I don't plan on telling her," I told him, running my hand over the smooth cover of the file folder. "Not yet."

He lifted an eyebrow. "Don't tell me you're going to investigate this case."

"I am going to do exactly that."

"After ten years? What can you hope to find?"

"I don't know. But it's the only way I can think of to help my client. And I know something the cops who worked this case ten years ago did not. I know the victims' true identities. It may lead to nothing, but it does give me reason to hope I can find out something the original investigators didn't."

"Still, after ten years..." He paused, tapping a forefinger on his desk. "You know, Adam, if you're keen on catching criminals, the place for you is in the police force."

"Why? You think if I were a cop, I'd be allowed to work on this case?"

"A case this old? No chance. We're overworked and understaffed as it is. All right, I see your point. But there are other cases, more recent cases. A man like you, who was a police detective—you belong here."

We'd had this conversation before. Reuben couldn't understand why I didn't join him in the police. I never explained to him that I had spent too long in uniform, following other people's orders. I did it in Auschwitz because to do otherwise would have led to my being killed. I did in the army because I wanted to live a free man in an independent country. But I never wanted to do it again.

"It's not for me, Reuben."

He shrugged. "Well, can't blame me for trying, can you? About the report, it doesn't leave the station. There's a vacant room at the end of the hall. Read it there, then bring it back when you're done, okay?"

"Okay. Thank you."

I rose and was almost at the door when he said, "Adam." I rotated to face him. I had never seen him look so grave. "I hope you catch this guy. Whoever did this, he needs to pay."

13

I found the vacant office, closed the door, and sat at the empty desk. I opened the folder and found two copies of the investigation report, one in Hebrew and the other in English. The latter was addressed to the Criminal Investigation Department (CID) of the Palestine Police Force. The CID had been the British unit that oversaw all investigations of major crimes during the Mandate of Palestine. It ceased operations in 1948 when the Mandate ended and Britain evacuated all its forces from Palestine.

I set the English version aside and began reading the Hebrew report.

The bodies of Esther Grunewald and Willie Ackerland (they were identified in the report by their false names: Esther and Erich Kantor) were discovered at nine in the morning on August 27, 1939, by their landlord, Abraham Sassoon. Mr. Sassoon was replacing a burnt-out light bulb on the third-floor landing when he caught the familiar coppery scent of blood. He followed his nose to the door of the apartment occupied by the victims and saw that the wood around the lock was scarred and gouged, as if someone had tried forcing it open. Sassoon tried the handle, but the door was locked. He knocked several times with no answer.

Increasingly worried, Sassoon went to his ground-floor apartment, got the spare key, climbed once more to the third floor, unlocked the door, and stepped inside. He found the two bodies in the bedroom. "I didn't need to check," he told the police later. "I could tell they were dead."

Sassoon did not have a phone, so he told his teenage son to run as fast as he could to the nearest police station and inform them that a murder had been committed in their building. Half an hour later, a police car arrived. The two officers ascertained that indeed there were two murder victims inside and called for a detective and a photographer.

I inspected the photographs one at a time. The first few centered on Esther. She lay on her back, one arm stretched over her head, the other at her side. Her left leg was bent at an awkward angle; her right was straight. She was wearing a nightshirt that covered her to her knees and was barefoot. The nightshirt was white, but its top half was drenched with blood. More blood stained the floor around her head. Some of her long black hair was matted to the floor with it. The source of the blood was a gaping wound that ran across her throat. But that wasn't the extent of her injuries.

Her face had been slashed and cut numerous times. Not an inch of it appeared to have been spared. Her cheeks were scored, her nose gouged, her forehead crisscrossed with lacerations. But that wasn't the worst of the damage. That had been inflicted on her eyes. Both had been stabbed, leaving eye sockets that were saucers of blood and gore.

Reuben had been right. This was gruesome.

The second batch of photographs showed Willie Ackerland lying on his back in a crib. The crib stood by the bed in which Esther must have slept in. One of Willie's stubby hands protruded from between the wooden bars of the crib, his fingers clenched in a tiny fist. He was wearing a white shirt and dark pants. His hair was golden. The blanket that had covered him in his sleep had been twisted and cast aside to the end of the crib. He had been stabbed through the chest several times and his face had received a similar treatment to that of Esther's. His eyes had also been stabbed out. I doubted Henrietta herself would have recognized him. There was much less blood in the crib than around Esther's body. Probably the result of the initial stab wound finding Willie's heart.

I set the photographs down and leaned back in the chair. Intense anger gripped me and I noticed my fingers were clenching and unclenching of their own volition. A low growl escaped my throat. I couldn't remain seated. I stood and looked out the window. A crow was perched on the windowsill. It one-eyed me, tilting its head, as if considering my worth. Then it squawked twice, flapped its wings, and flew away.

I stuck my hands in my pants pockets and paced the small office. Four strides was all it took to reach from one wall to the other. I felt like hurling something at the wall, but figured the racket would draw curious policemen to the office, and I might be made to leave before I finished with the report.

This was no regular murder, and the man I was pursuing was no ordinary killer. This was brutal, depraved, and immensely evil. Whoever did this had a purpose beyond killing. A dark purpose.

When I felt I was calm, I returned to my chair and went on reading.

The apartment had been ransacked. Dresser drawers had been rummaged through and closet doors left hanging open with clothes thrown to the floor. In the living room, sofa cushions had been slashed, while in the kitchen, the killer had gone through drawers and cupboards.

A handbag had been emptied on the dining table. A compact,

a handkerchief, a tube of lipstick, some tissue paper, and a pencil lay scattered. No money. No keys. The killer had taken them with him, which explained the locked door.

The bodies were removed to the morgue, where they underwent a more thorough examination. Various statistics were noted —height, build, hair color—and the many injuries were listed. It was a long list. For both woman and child.

Esther had died of her neck wound. All of her facial injuries occurred postmortem. She had not been sexually assaulted.

Willie had suffered multiple chest wounds and, as I suspected, one of the stabs had gone through his heart. Like Esther's, his disfigurement occurred after death. At least he didn't suffer much. That was some comfort, I supposed.

There were no defensive wounds on Esther's hands, which likely meant that her attacker had managed to catch her off guard and struck quickly. Perhaps the killer was a person Esther knew, which allowed him to surprise her. Or perhaps she had been sleeping when he broke through her door, rose to see what was happening, but was still sluggish from sleep when he came upon her in her bedroom. In short, the lack of defensive wounds did not help me narrow the pool of suspects.

They had both died during the night, between 23:00 and 04:00. Which meant that they might have died on August 27, but their date of death was officially set to the 26th.

Included in the file were two identity cards for residents of Mandatory Palestine. The first bore the name Esther Kantor. Various details were noted on the card. Birth date: April 8, 1919; Place of Residence: Tel Aviv; Occupation: Secretary; Race: Jewess; Height: 5 feet 9 inches; Color of eyes: Blue; Color of hair: Black; Build: slender.

A picture of Esther's face was pasted on the left side of the card. Henrietta Ackerland was right. Esther had been very beautiful. It was as if her face had been carved from marble by an artist's hand. Her eyes were large and deep, her forehead tall, her mouth luscious, her cheekbones high, her nose pert, her features symmetrical. Her hair was pulled back, and not a strand of it was out of place. To have been reduced from such exquisite beauty to a bloodied mangled mess seemed sacrilegious, not merely criminal.

The second identity card bore the name Erich Kantor. I took out the picture Henrietta had given me and compared it to the picture on the card. The boy in the second picture was older, of course. He had been six months old when it was taken. But the resemblance was evident. These two pictures were of the same boy.

"You came so close, little one," I found myself muttering to the dead boy in the photos. "So close."

There was another picture in the file. This one showed both victims together. Esther was sitting on a park bench with Willie on her lap. He was a big boy now, nine months old perhaps, chubby-cheeked and healthy looking, and was leaning back into Esther, like young children sometimes do with their parents. Esther wore her hair loose and had on a summer dress and a necklace of pearls tight around her long neck. Willie had on black shorts and a white shirt that looked a little too big for him. He was smiling a crooked little smile and his eyes twinkled. She had her arms around him and was smiling broadly. The smile elevated her beauty from exquisite to dazzling. She exuded such joy and warmth that my mind rebelled against the notion that she was dead. Mira had been right when she told me Esther had grown to love the boy with whom she had been entrusted. They looked utterly happy and carefree in each other's company. No one would have doubted for a moment that the two were mother and child.

I reread the list of items the police cataloged in Esther's apartment. A pearl necklace was not among them. Nor was any other kind of jewelry—a friend of Esther's had reported her owning some earrings and rings, nothing very expensive. A handwritten note in the margin of the item list read "Killer swiped all jewelry."

Returning my attention to the picture, I recognized the location: Gan Meir Park in Tel Aviv. A date had been scrawled on the back. August 22, 1939. Just four days before the murders.

Would Henrietta Ackerland like to have this picture? Would it ease her hurt to see that her son had been happy when he died? Or would it augment her pain to see him so happy with another woman? I couldn't really say. With a pang of guilt, I slipped the photograph into my pocket. Reuben would not have approved of me taking anything from a police report, but I figured it would do no harm. If I hadn't asked to read this report, no one would have ever laid eyes on it again.

I kept on reading.

Sergeant Shabtai Rivlin was the detective in charge of the case. His notes were written in a black pen, and his handwriting was cramped and slightly crooked. But it was legible, and his notes seemed thorough enough.

His first interview was with Abraham Sassoon. The landlord identified both woman and child as his tenants. Sergeant Rivlin went on to interview the rest of the neighbors, workers in various nearby stores where Esther had shopped and at a dance club she often frequented, and her colleagues at the law firm where she'd worked as a secretary. All expressed shock at the murders. All had nothing but good things to say about the victims. None could point the finger at anyone who might wish to see either Esther or the boy they knew as her child dead. At no point did Rivlin interview any Irgun member or any of the other passengers who were on board the *Salonika*. He never discovered nor suspected that the two victims were living under assumed names.

Rivlin had reached out to police informers to see if they'd heard any chatter regarding the murders. He had also pursued the jewelry angle by visiting pawnshops and bringing known fences in for questioning. Neither effort yielded any results.

Rivlin worked the case hard for two weeks and made increasingly infrequent entries over the next four. But it was soon clear that he had hit a dead end. No leads emerged. No suspects appeared. The case quickly grew stale, then cold. Finally, it was abandoned and set aside.

14

I read the file through twice, scribbling names and dates and places in my notebook, adding my impressions as I went along. Nothing jumped to grab my attention. There was no eureka moment.

I had a look at the English version of the file, but it appeared to be nothing more than a translated copy of the Hebrew report, most of it typed. One thing the English report contained that the Hebrew one did not was a document, dated four weeks after the murders, in which Rivlin detailed his actions during the investigation and explained his lack of progress.

"Where can I find Sergeant Shabtai Rivlin?" I asked Reuben in his office, handing him the investigation file.

Reuben set the folder aside on his desk. He picked up the phone, dialed an internal extension, and asked if Rivlin was around. A moment later he hung up. "There's a café near the corner of Lillenblum and Rishonim. You should be able to find him there. You can't miss him. He's bald and got a big mustache."

"All right. I'll find him."

I thanked Reuben and made my way to Lillenblum Street. I

found the café easily enough and spotted Shabtai Rivlin within two seconds of stepping inside. Reuben's description was dead-on. Rivlin had a brush mustache the color of mud and a bald scalp that glistened like the belly of a fish. He wore a blue shirt with rolled-up sleeves, pants that were also blue, but a shade darker, and black loafers that had not been shined since the reign of King David. He was the only person at the bar, the other three patrons split between two tables. He sat stooped over a quarter-full glass of red wine, almost like he was praying to it.

I walked up to him. "Sergeant Rivlin?"

His weary face turned to me, and it took less than the blink of an eye for me to peg him as a drunk. It didn't make me a master of observation or deduction. The burst of red capillaries on his bulbous nose and the alcoholic flush in his cheeks were a dead giveaway. Add to that the fact that his bleary eyes were equal parts brown, white, and red, and that the stink of alcohol hung around him like a shroud, and the dismal, depressing picture was clear. Sergeant Shabtai Rivlin was a drunk and had been one for quite some time. It was affecting his health. There were purple bags under his eyes, and the skin on his face had a grayish tint. He was paunchy and jowly. His bent posture made it difficult to determine his height. He looked like he had poison running through his veins, which, I supposed, was more true than not.

"Who are you?" he asked me in a gruff voice, though I noticed his speech was not slurred. He was drunk, but not out of it. What remained to be seen was what sort of drunk he was.

"My name is Adam Lapid. I'd like to ask you some questions if you have a moment."

"I don't. I'm busy." He gave a chuckle that sounded like a raven's squawk. "Can't you tell?"

So not a gregarious drunk. A nasty one.

A lanky, balding bartender was watching the two of us with

obvious interest from across the bar. I said to him, "One more glass of wine for him. And bring me one as well."

I eased myself onto the stool beside Rivlin's. He said nothing. The only way I could tell he had heard me make the order was that he emptied his glass and pushed it aside.

The bartender placed two glasses before us. I left mine untouched. Rivlin lifted his. He didn't bother with a toast or a thank you, just took a long slurp. Only after he had swallowed and dried his mouth with the back of his hand did he deign to look at me.

"Who did you say you were?"

"Don't give me that," I said. "You heard my name just fine."

Rivlin nodded, possibly in grudging respect, though I couldn't say for sure. "Well, what do you want?"

"To talk to you about a case you worked on."

"A case? Why do you want to talk about a case?"

"I'm a private investigator."

"Oh, one of those." He chuckled again, favoring me with a derisive grin. His breath was awful. "You think I have time for jokers? I'm a police detective, not some amateur. Go bother someone else." With that he turned back to his glass and took another swallow.

I thought of telling him I'd learned his whereabouts from a fellow policeman, but decided not to. I doubted it would make him more receptive to my questions, and it might get Reuben into trouble. Besides, I had another way to win him over.

"Put the bottle on the bar," I told the bartender, "and step away so we can talk in private."

The bartender didn't appear to be thrilled about the second part, but the look I gave him convinced him it was a good idea. He brought the bottle over and moved away to the far end of the bar. I refilled Rivlin's glass. He considered it for a long moment, his hairy forearms forming a triangle on the bar top, fingers laced. "All right," he finally said. "You bought yourself a minute. What case are you interested in?"

"A murder you worked ten years ago."

He stiffened. By no more than an inch, but I still caught it.

"You expect me to remember a case from ten years ago. Are you crazy?"

"It's not the sort of murder you're likely to forget."

When Rivlin faced me this time, his eyes were no longer bleary. He was looking at me—really looking—for the first time since I approached him. I wondered what he was searching for. I wondered what he ended up seeing.

"Maybe I'm a forgetful guy."

I shook my head. "You know the case I'm talking about. August 1939. Lunz Street. Two victims. A woman and a baby. Do I need to remind you what he did to their faces? Their eyes?"

He sat perfectly still for a few heartbeats, did not even blink. Then he drew a loud breath through his nose, held it in for a long moment, and blew it out of his mouth with a whoosh. He picked up his glass and gulped down half of it with one big mouthful. I didn't need to remind him. He remembered all right.

"Your minute is up," he said, not looking at me.

"I don't think so."

"Well, I do. Beat it."

"Fine. I'll go," I said. I reached for the bottle. He grabbed my wrist, fingers digging into my flesh.

"Leave it here."

I yanked my hand out of his grip. "Only if you talk." Rivlin worked his mouth around for a second or two, and I added, "I'll spring for a second bottle. And here's something extra for your time." I fished a lira note from my pocket and dropped it on the bar. His hand moved fast to cover the bill. He didn't even look around to check if anyone saw anything. He had experience in taking money.

He slid his palm with the banknote beneath it to the edge of the bar, where he cupped the note in his fist and stuck it in his pocket. He brought his hand out—minus the banknote—downed the rest of his glass, poured himself another, and surprised me by taking a sip that was the epitome of daintiness. Then, still not looking at me, he said, "How come you're working this case?"

"My client is a relative of the victims," I said, choosing to refrain from explaining the whole bit about their names being false. I was there to gain information, not dish it out. Besides, he'd had his chance with this case and blew it. It was my turn now.

"No next of kin came forward at the time," Rivlin said.

"She just arrived in Israel and learned about the murders. She wants me to take another look at what happened."

"She wants to catch whoever did it?"

"That's right."

Rivlin shook his head. "Impossible. Not going to happen." He pointed a finger at me. "And if you had any decency, you would have told her so."

I tried to hide the prickle of discomfort that spread across my back. What I'd done was much worse. I had lied to my client. I had betrayed her trust.

"She knows it's a long shot," I lied. "She still wants to have a go at it."

He shrugged. "You read the report?" He had figured out that was where I likely got his name from. Like I thought, he was drunk but not out.

"Yes."

"You certainly have money to spend, don't you?" He had set his gaze on me, and there was a greedy calculation in his eyes.

I didn't correct him. Let him think I paid for the information. He was unlikely to believe me if I told him I got it as a favor. His kind never did any.

"If your information is good, you may get some more of it."

Rivlin responded with a grunt, but didn't press the issue. "If you read the report, you know as much as I do."

"Only the dry facts. What I'm interested in is your impressions, your thoughts."

"My thoughts? Want to hear what I think? I think you're wasting your time and your client's money. You're not going to find out who did it. Not a chance in hell."

"Because too much time has passed?"

"No, that's not it at all. This case was hopeless when it was fresh, when I got it, and it's hopeless now."

"Why?"

He drained his glass and refilled it.

"Think," he told me. "Think how it went down. Think how it happened."

"I want to hear what you think," I said.

He made a face that intimated he considered me to be the dumbest person he'd met in a long, long while. "Fine. I'll tell you. It's the middle of the night. He jimmies the door, gets into the apartment. She wakes up from the noise, climbs out of bed, and sees his face. He's screwed. She can finger him to the cops. All he can think is that she's a threat he needs to eliminate. He has a knife, like a lot of lowlifes do. He slashes her throat. A robbery that escalates to murder. Not exactly unheard of."

"That's the obvious conclusion," I admitted, "but why would he choose to rob Esther Kantor? She was a secretary. She didn't have a lot of money to steal."

"Maybe he thought she had more. Maybe he got the wrong apartment. Maybe he chose it at random. Who the hell can say what went through his mind?"

"Why would he break in at night when the apartment was likely occupied?"

"Maybe he thought it was empty. Maybe he's stupid. Or maybe

he figures it's safer at night. It's a residential building. He comes during the day, some bored housewife might spot him."

I nodded. "All right. But why kill the baby? The baby can't point him out to the police."

"Put yourself in the bastard's shoes," Rivlin said. "He's a thief, not a killer. He's never killed anyone in his goddamn miserable life. But he's just murdered a woman. She's on the floor, blood pooling around her. He's facing the gallows if we catch him. He's on edge, panicked, can't figure out how things could have gone so wrong. All of a sudden, the baby starts bawling his little lungs out. To the killer, it sounds like an air-raid siren. Any second now, some neighbor will start wondering what all the racket is about. He needs to shut the baby up fast, and there's just one way to do it. He sticks him a few times in the chest."

"And then instead of fleeing the scene, he hangs around to scour the place for cash? When he's scared out of his mind?" I shook my head. "Doesn't make sense."

His answer came quick, and I got the impression he'd asked himself these questions a number of times over the years.

"Yeah, it does." Rivlin had taken on a lecturing tone, and for the first time he seemed more intent on me than on the wine. "He's just killed two people. He wants nothing more than to run out the door, to get as far away as possible. But he can't be sure the baby didn't wake someone up before he whacked him. Someone, some nosy neighbor, may be coming up the stairs that very moment. Our killer's got two options: take a chance and meet that neighbor on the stairs, where he's got no advantage, or wait in the apartment, and if a neighbor comes in, jump on him and take him by surprise. So he waits by the door, listening for the sound of footsteps on the stairs. A minute passes, two, three. Nothing. His heart rate slows, his breathing subsides, he's feeling more secure. It's a bad night, but he might as well get something out of it. He tosses the apartment, finds whatever he finds, and grabs the money from her purse." He gave me a satisfied closed-mouth smile. "Get it now?"

I did. It could well have happened like Rivlin said. Except for one tiny thing he'd neglected to mention.

"That doesn't explain what he did to their faces," I said. "To their eyes."

"No," he agreed, no longer smiling. "It doesn't. Nothing explains that. Nothing can explain that. It's crazy. That's my point. That's why you're wasting your time."

"What do you mean?"

He fixed me with his stare, and it might have been a trick of the light, but his eyes appeared to have more red in them than before.

"Crazy is the operative word. A crazy act by a crazy guy. Random. Unpremeditated. Irrational and pointless. Which is why I got nowhere in my investigation. Look, there are two possibilities. One, the killer knew Esther Kantor and came to kill her specifically. Only I talked to the neighbors and everyone who knew her, including the workers at the grocery store where she bought her food. She was a nice person, everyone said. Friendly. Always with a smile. No one could think of any reason why someone would want her dead, not to mention the baby, not to mention mutilating their faces like that. Two, whoever killed them was totally insane. He may have started out as a burglar, but once they were dead, something came over him, some compulsion, and he needed to cut them up and stab out their eyes. Why? No reason. There is no reason with madness. No reason we can understand. That's the whole point."

He had counted out the options on his fingers and was holding two of them in front of my face.

"That's why I got nowhere in my investigation. There were no physical clues. No one saw the killer enter or exit the building. No one had any motive to kill her. The murder didn't fit any former killing. It was a first. All I could do was wait until some clue turned up or the killer struck again. But he never did. The guy did it once and that's it. And I don't have a goddamn clue who he might be."

Rivlin stopped and drew in a breath. He suddenly looked even more weary than he had before. He picked up his wineglass and gazed into it. The red of the wine looked a little like blood. Apparently, he didn't see the resemblance, because he drank deeply from the glass. If he enjoyed it, he showed no sign of it.

"What do you think happened to him?" I asked.

"The killer?" He shrugged. "Maybe he had a heart attack the next day. Maybe he stepped on a land mine during the war. Or maybe he's the sort of killer for whom once is enough. I don't know. I'm not even sure I care anymore. I worked this case hard enough, let me tell you. Not that it did me much good. The brass chewed me out for failing to bring in results. I even had to type daily reports in English to the goddamn CID, explaining why I was getting nowhere, not that they ever offered to help any. So if you think you can waltz into this case after ten years and find the killer, go right ahead. Be my guest. Waste your time all you want, just don't take any more of mine. I'm done answering your questions. Pay the man for a second bottle and then get lost and let me drink in peace."

Having said all that, he jerked his head forward, ignoring my presence. I studied his profile and wondered how old he was. He could have been in his late thirties, but he looked an unhealthy forty-five, maybe closer to fifty. Closer to the end. He had nothing more to give. Not to me, probably not to anyone. I didn't want to talk to him anymore. I didn't want to be anywhere near him. But I had one more thing I needed him to tell me.

I got up from my stool and said, "How long have you been a lush?"

That got his attention. He whirled in his seat and gaped at me.

"Not that I care, but it's important I know if you started before

August 1939. Because I need to know whether your investigation was worth a damn, or if I need to do it all over again."

"You son of a bitch," he snarled.

He lurched to his feet and lunged at me, swinging a round-house at my head. I could see it coming from a long way off and ducked it easily. His momentum took him past me, and I thought he was going to fall flat on his face. But he surprised me by keeping his feet and taking another swing, a short one, this time with his left. I was a little late in jerking my head out of the way this time, and his fist glanced off my mouth. It barely hurt—he didn't put much behind his punch—but it was enough to mash the inside of my lip against my teeth. I tasted blood.

Rivlin stood with his hands on his knees, heaving, his two swings having taken a lot out of him. The urge to belt him one was strong. My fingers were balled into tight fists and itching for permission to plant themselves in his face. I managed to curb the craving. Hitting him was a bad idea. I might get a good night's sleep by doing it, but the downsides were considerable. First, punching a cop is one of the fastest ways to land in the deepest of trouble, even when the cop took the first swing. Second, I still wanted him to answer my question, and he wouldn't be able to do that if I knocked him unconscious. And third, our little party was no longer private. The other patrons had risen from their seats and were standing close by, ready to intervene if they were needed, but clearly hoping they would not be. The bartender was pointing at me. "We don't need no trouble here. Get out!"

"I need an answer," I told Rivlin. Which I did; otherwise I would not have pressed him. Truth was, I felt sorry for him. He was broken, and what I was doing was the equivalent of stepping on the pieces, crunching them into smaller fragments.

"Did you hear what I said?" the bartender shouted.

"I'll go in a minute," I told him. To Rivlin I said, "Well?"

Sweat had broken on the sergeant's brow. He wiped at it with a trembling hand. There was hatred in his eyes now, and in his open mouth I could see his clenched teeth.

"You're lucky I don't bust up your face right now," he said. "You think you're better than me, don't you? You think I'm just some drunk who can't work a case. Well, you're wrong. I did everything I should have on that case. Everything."

His voice cracked on that last word, and his gaze dropped. I couldn't be sure he was telling me the truth. I think he might not have been sure of himself, either. He wasn't going to give me a straight answer. He might have been a drunk ten years ago, or he might have had his drinking under control. Maybe it had affected his work, and maybe it hadn't. I would never know.

"All right," I said, "I get it."

I fished a one-lira note from my pocket, rolled it into a ball, and tossed it to the bartender.

"Get him another bottle," I said.

15

It was past six thirty when I left Rivlin to wallow in his wine and misery and wound my way north. Either the heat had broken or something else was chilling me, because I felt cold. I was also ashamed. A part of me—perhaps most of me—had longed to put my fist in Rivlin's face, even though he posed no real threat to me, even though hitting him would have served no purpose other than personal gratification. My father would have not recognized this part of me. If he had known of it, he would have mourned it.

I lit a cigarette, shaking off my dark thoughts along with the match. My stomach began rumbling, and I realized I was hungry.

On Rothschild Boulevard, I found a small café with a radio that played jaunty European music and had a light dinner. I often had a drink with dinner, but on that evening I found the thought of alcohol repellent. I had seen men destroyed. Watching one destroy himself was stomach turning in a whole different way.

As I ate, I ran my conversation with Sergeant Rivlin through my mind. What he'd said about the killer being a madman who had chosen his victims at random could very well be true, but I didn't believe it. This had nothing to do with facts or logic. I simply did not want to believe this was what had happened.

The reason was simple: If Esther Grunewald and Willie Acker-land were the random victims of a deranged killer, one who had never killed in a similar fashion before or since, then Rivlin was correct. I had absolutely zero chance of ever catching him.

And I wanted to catch him.

I wanted it even worse than I did the day Mira Roth had informed me of their deaths. Seeing their pictures and reading the details of the injuries they had sustained had made me realize I was chasing a monster the likes of which I had not pursued since my Nazi-hunting days. Whoever did this was evil—the sort of evil most men and women cannot imagine nor fathom. Bringing him to justice would be immensely satisfying.

But catching him hinged on Rivlin being wrong, that this was not a random burglary that had escalated to murder, but a targeted killing. Someone had come to kill Esther Grunewald—or Kantor, the name she had been using. She had to be the primary target, since Willie, a mere baby, was unlikely to have enraged someone sufficiently to target him.

I had to assume this was the case and act accordingly, because if it wasn't, then I had no way to investigate this case, nowhere to even begin. Sitting in that quaint café on Rothschild Boulevard, with the radio piping merry polkas, I decided that someone had come for Esther Grunewald, had come for her personally, and that I was going to find out who it was.

In my notebook I'd listed all the people Rivlin had interviewed ten years ago. I planned on talking to as many of them as were still around. But there were people missing from this list, and there was just one person who could tell me who they were.

Half an hour later, I knocked on her door. She was home. She wore short brown pants and a light-blue work shirt and plain brown sandals, the sort worn by farmers in the Negev. I stared at her legs again. They were long and slender and tanned just a shade lighter than her arms. Her ankles were slim, her feet arched.

Mira Roth did not seem surprised to see me. A small satisfied smile flickered across her thin lips, and her amber eyes glowed like molten steel in the orange sunset light that slanted in through the second-floor landing window. "Come in, Adam."

We walked the few steps to her living room. Neither of us sat. We stood a foot and a half apart, and I caught her scent. Clean and stringent and familiar. She had showered recently, using the rough utilitarian soap the government allotted to each citizen. I used the same kind. If she'd washed her hair, it had had time to dry. It was pulled back, revealing shapely ears without earrings.

"I came by to tell you you got your wish," I said. "I started working on the case."

Her smile broadened by half an inch. "Was I that obvious? What gave me away?"

"A couple of things. I started wondering why you had talked to me at all, especially about something you don't want your boss to know. Then I recalled you making sure I was a private investigator when we spoke outside the salon. It all became clear—you told me about the *Salonika* and the botched-up raid because you want me to find out who killed Esther and Willie."

"It appears I made the right decision. You're perceptive."

"It wasn't that hard. It's going to take a lot more than that to solve these murders."

"You can do it," she said, her tone completely earnest.

"That's a nice sentiment, but the likelihood of my succeeding is about the same as that of snow falling tomorrow on Allenby Street."

"But you're going to try."

"Yes. But even if by some miracle I manage to discover who killed them, getting proof that will stand up in court is a whole different matter."

"Don't worry about a trial. Just find out who did it and give me his name. I'll take care of the rest."

I stared at her in blank astonishment, trying to see if she really meant what I thought she did. Her tone had been flat, emotionless, and cold. Her face wore an unwavering expression of calm resolve. Her back was as straight and rigid as a sheet of steel. Only her eyes betrayed what she was feeling. A fire raged within them. All doubt was erased. She was deadly serious. I recalled my earlier impression that she was a woman familiar with death. I just hadn't realized she was comfortable with it as well.

"Is that a problem?" she asked.

It took me a second to find my voice, for in that moment she appeared not merely striking but also beautiful. Like a savage warrior woman of some ancient, extinct culture. "No," I said. "It's not a problem."

And it wasn't. For hadn't I taken it upon myself to serve as judge, jury, and executioner during my time in Germany? Was what Mira suggesting so different? If the only way to bring a murderer to justice was to do it yourself, then I was all for it. I just hadn't expected Mira to feel the same way and to express it openly and without reservation.

"I'll need your help," I said.

"How?"

"To catch a killer, you often need to know the victim. In this case, there were two victims, but one of them was a baby and unlikely to be the main target. Esther is a different story. Someone might have targeted her. To have an idea of who that might be, I need to know more about her, who she was, what her life was like, and so on. I need to talk to people who knew her, people from the Irgun."

Mira nodded thoughtfully. "There weren't many. I can connect you to them. But I doubt they would be able to tell you much."

"We'll see. What're their names?"

"There was the couple with whom Esther and Willie stayed for a few weeks until we arranged papers and an apartment for them. Their name is Klinger. Moshe and Yael. They had a baby of about the same age as Willie, so we figured they'd have clothes and diapers for him. The other person you can talk to is Michael Shamir. After the raid, he and I drove Esther and Willie to the Klingers, and he brought them their false papers when they were ready."

"Will they talk to me?"

"I'll write you notes of introduction."

From a cabinet by the south window, Mira took out a pen and paper and proceeded to write me two notes. She handed them to me and sat, crossing her legs. I took the same spot on the couch as during our previous meeting. I read both notes, searching for code words. I found none. The notes simply stated that I was all right to talk to about the *Salonika,* the prison raid, and Esther and Willie, and were signed with Mira's name. One was addressed to Moshe and Yael Klinger, the other to Michael Shamir.

"Adam, these notes will only get them to speak to you about matters pertaining to Esther and Willie. Other Irgun business is off-limits. All right?"

"I'm not interested in anything but the murders," I said.

Mira handed me another piece of paper. On it she'd jotted two addresses, a Tel Aviv address for Michael Shamir, and one in Netanya for the Klingers.

"This is where you took them that night? To Netanya?"

"No. The Klingers lived in Haifa at the time. They moved to Netanya a while back. I haven't spoken to them in ages. They were what you would call distant supporters of Irgun. Neither ever took part in military actions, but they contributed money and sheltered a number of immigrants over the years."

"And Michael Shamir?"

"Michael is a different story. He's a fighter through and

through. One of the best we've ever had. The sort who is totally dedicated. The sort who leads others. The sort who is willing to sacrifice his career, family, even his life for the greater cause. I wish we'd had more like him."

Her voice had taken on a note of adoration when she spoke about Michael Shamir. I was embarrassed to feel a stab of jealousy deep in my gut. Was she infatuated with Michael Shamir? And what did I care if she was?

I pushed the thought away. "Did you have any contact with Esther and Willie after the night of the raid?"

"Yes. I visited them at the Klingers' seven or eight times."

"Quite a lot."

She nodded. "I took it upon myself to help Esther settle into local society. She spoke Hebrew, which was a big advantage, and I taught her some of the local history and geography, told her where she could buy this and that, how to travel, how not to seem out of place. That sort of thing."

"What was she like?"

Mira placed both hands on her knee, drumming with two fingers of her left hand on the back of her right as she pondered how to begin.

"I'm not sure what to say," she said at length. "I can tell you that Esther was intelligent, curious, a quick study, had a sense of humor..." Her voice broke, and she put a hand over her face. When she brought her hand down, her eyes were sparkling with unshed tears. "Above all, she was excited to finally be in the Land of Israel. It had been her dream to live here since she was a child. But I can't see how any of that relates to her death."

"Any plans for the future? Any aspirations?"

Again she took a few seconds to form her answer. "The usual stuff. She wanted to settle in, find work, and begin her new life. I'm not sure she thought much more ahead than the next year or so."

"How about finding a husband? Starting a family?"

"I'm sure Esther would have found someone eventually, with how beautiful and smart she was, but I don't recall her ever talking about it. As for family, she had Willie. I think she thought of him as her family. I remember thinking how hard it would be for Esther when Willie's mother arrived to take him back."

That brought the conversation to a halt. Mira looked down at her hands. She was probably recalling her time with Esther. I was thinking about Henrietta and wondered how many pieces she'd fall into when I told her what had happened to her son.

"She had no other family here? No friends?" I asked, after a minute.

Mira raised her eyes and shook her head. "None. Esther had no one here when she arrived."

"How about people from the *Salonika*? Did she keep in touch with any of them?"

"No. I gave clear instructions for her not to. It was better that way, so if the British caught any of them, they would not be able to give her away."

"How can you be sure she followed your instructions?"

Mira hesitated for a second and answered cautiously, "I can't be absolutely sure of it, of course, but Esther was a serious girl. I think she did as she was told."

I nodded, accepting her answer. But I knew that if I hit a dead end, I would need to talk to the other *maapilim*. "Did she have a suitor or a lover?"

"Not that I know of," Mira said.

"You did not keep in touch after she moved to Tel Aviv?"

"I ran into her once and asked her how she was getting along. She said she was fine, had found work, that Willie was growing up okay. She said she'd never heard from his mother."

"She said nothing else about her life in Tel Aviv?"

"No."

This was not what I wanted to hear. It meant that Mira basically had no knowledge of Esther's final months, which was when her killer had decided to end her life. I needed a clearer picture of those months, and it was apparent I was not going to get it from Mira.

"You say Esther and Willie stayed for a few weeks with the Klinger family. How did she get along with them?"

"Fine. Esther told me they were treating her well. They all seemed friendly."

"Do you happen to know if they kept in touch after she moved?"

"No. Afraid not."

"All right. I'll ask them about it when I see them."

I was disappointed with my visit. I had expected to learn more from Mira, and I ended up learning almost nothing. The paltry number of contacts she'd provided me with was discouraging. But along with disappointment, I was also feeling a blend of discomfort and something I had not felt in a long while. Desire. My fingers were tingling. I wanted to reach over and touch Mira, to cup her cheeks, to run my hand along her calves. A fluttery heat had settled in my stomach and my mouth had turned dry. Those glimmerings of passion had grown to a low fire.

I felt like I should say something more, but could not decide what. I looked at Mira, but in my mind's eye I was seeing Deborah, my wife. I knew that here was a line and that crossing it would mean a break from my past, a rupture between my life as it was and as it had been. I did not want that. Not yet, anyway.

"Are you all right, Adam?"

Mira was peering closely at my face, a frown of concern notching a crease between her eyebrows. She had leaned toward me, and there was a gap between her thin lips. Through that gap I caught a glimpse of her teeth, small and white and straight. I forced some saliva into my mouth, swallowed hard, and cleared my throat. I couldn't let my mind wander. I needed to remain focused. Because there was still something I didn't understand here, something that had bothered me since shortly after my previous visit to Mira's apartment.

"One more question, Mira."

"Yes?"

"How many Jews would you say you had a hand in helping to immigrate to Israel?"

She looked puzzled, wondering what my question had to do with the murders. "Several hundred. Perhaps as many as a thousand."

"And with how many do you keep in touch?"

"None that I can think of. Why do you ask, Adam?"

"I was just wondering why you care so much for two of them."

A muscle in her cheek twitched, and she seemed unsure of how to answer. I let the silence stretch. Just before it transitioned from awkward to outright uncomfortable, she said, "It's just that I don't like the idea of their killer remaining free."

"I get that," I said. "No one likes to see people they know get murdered. And I get that you liked Esther. But why do you care enough about her and Willie Ackerland to spill your guts to me? Word is you Irgun members are a tight-lipped bunch. Yet here you are, giving me names of other members, telling me all sorts of things, and I don't understand why you're doing it."

"I feel responsible."

"Why would you? Did you have anything to do with their deaths?"

"Of course not," she said vehemently. "How can you think such a thing? It's simply the fact that I had a part in bringing them here, to Tel Aviv, where they ended up dying."

"And you're willing to break the law, act the vigilante, perhaps go to jail for many years just to avenge them? It's more than most people would do."

"Maybe I am not like most people."

That I could believe. But I was still not satisfied with her answers. I leaned forward, elbows on knees, my eyes glued to hers. "That's all it is, Mira? Just some vague sense of responsibility? Nothing more?"

She answered without hesitation. "Nothing more."

I searched for a tell, some sign she was not being truthful. There was nothing. She looked completely honest. I held her gaze for a minute more, and when she didn't flinch or avert her eyes, I gave up. "Okay. I need to get going."

Mira nodded and rose to her feet with me. At the door I turned to her. "If you're keeping anything from me, Mira, now's the time to tell me."

"I told you everything I know," she said, and if she was lying, she should have considered a career in theater.

I nodded and reached for the door handle. I had the door half open when I felt her hand on my forearm. Her fingers were cool.

"Adam," Mira said, and for an instant it seemed she was about to say something important, "good luck."

"Yeah," I said.

———

From Frishman I turned south to Dizengoff Street. At Dizengoff Square all the benches were taken. Dogs on leashes barked greetings at each other. Around the central fountain strolled men and women. Some were dressed in light, airy clothes appropriate for the climate, while others were encased in heavier, more formal attire, which they had brought with them from much cooler lands and from which they could as yet not bear to part. There was laughter and chatter and a sense of optimism. For a fleeting moment it seemed that this was not a country that had just emerged from a terrible war and whose very existence was precarious, but a normal, peaceful land inhabited by people who were not intimately acquainted with disaster and forever fearful of it.

I stopped at a kiosk and bought a bottle of soda that purported to taste like oranges. At least it was cold. I drank it as I continued south to Gan Meir Park, where more of Tel Aviv's inhabitants were socializing, and where a group of young boys was kicking around a soccer ball across the expansive lawn. The children ranged from ten to twelve, and I couldn't help thinking that but for a tragic turn of fate, Willie Ackerland might have been one of them.

I thought of calling Henrietta and confessing my sins to her. *I lied to you,* I would tell her. *Your son is dead.*

I dismissed the notion. For one thing, she did not have a phone in her apartment. For another, I was just getting started with this case.

Then my mind drifted to where I did not wish it to go.

Mira Roth.

Despite her severe, angular features, I found her appealing. This was heightened by who she was—a soldier, one who was not above meting out violent punishment. Unlike Rachel Weiss, Mira would not have scorned me for breaking the fingers of a man who was tormenting her. She would have understood my actions. She would have understood me.

The man I was now was not the same man who had lived before Auschwitz, before he'd lost everything and everyone. That man was no more. Most women would not be able to understand the man I had become. They would be frightened of me; they would shy away. But Mira would not. On the contrary, she would appreciate what I had done, both in Israel and in Germany. To her it would seem right and proper and just. Maybe that was part of her appeal, that I believed she would fully and completely accept who I was.

I finished the soda and tossed the empty bottle in a trash can. The bottle banged against the side of the can, and a scrawny ginger cat bounded out, screeching at me for disturbing his scavenging.

"I'm sorry," I sincerely said to the cat, not for a moment feeling ridiculous for doing so. I knew what it was like to live off scraps.

Continuing south, I couldn't shake off the feeling that Mira had lied to me, that she was keeping something from me. I wasn't certain of it, because she'd been so forthright about everything else, including the botched raid in which she took part, and because she'd seemed so honest when I pressed her on the matter. But to my cynical policeman's eye, Mira had looked *too* honest, her face too controlled, her gaze too steady and level, as if she were trying hard to *appear* truthful.

This bothered me on more than one level. There was the possibility that whatever information Mira harbored—if she indeed did harbor any—might have proved useful to my investigation, and there was the personal aspect. I was attracted to her, and I did not want to believe that she would lie to my face. Yet, this was what I did believe, though I could not imagine a reason why she would do so. For without Mira's cooperation, I would have no case. I would not know that Esther Grunewald and Willie Ackerland had been murdered. Mira was eager to avenge these murders. Why would she hamper my investigation by keeping information from me?

At the corner of Tchernichovsky and Hamaccabi, I debated the wisdom of making this an early night. I was tired, and I had two new books to read. But I did not want to be alone with my thoughts in my apartment just yet. I kept on walking, made the turn to Allenby Street, and a few minutes later entered Greta's Café.

The place was nearly full and Greta waved hello to me while carrying a tray of drinks to a table of four. She was too busy to chat, which was a shame because I felt like talking.

I sat at my table, smoking, playing chess, surrounded by the ruckus of laughter and boisterous conversations, and tried to clear my mind. I gave up after an hour, said a quick goodbye to Greta, who seemed sad to see me leave, and walked back up Allenby Street.

I caught a movie at Migdalor Theater and then went home. After showering, I stood before the mirror and pulled down my lower lip. Rivlin's punch had left twin lacerations across the inside of my lip. Both cuts looked red and raw, but neither was bleeding. I ran my tongue over them, but could not taste blood. I turned off the bathroom light and got into bed.

As I lay staring up into darkness, I wondered whether my getting punched by Rivlin would prove sufficient to keep the nightmares away, or if I had to draw blood for this to happen. I couldn't be sure, because it had been a very long time since I had been hit and not struck back, not since I was liberated by the Americans. I had closed all the windows as a precaution in case I screamed in my sleep. Two hours later, when the dark dreams came, I discovered I had acted wisely.

16

It was around nine in the morning when I flipped open my notebook and looked over the list of names I had gotten from the police report and Mira Roth, trying to decide who I should go see first.

Michael Shamir was the closest. He lived on Gadera Street, which was less than a ten-minute walk from my apartment. There was a good chance he'd be at work at this time of day, but I decided to risk it. In truth, I was curious to meet this man who had inspired such admiration in Mira.

I pulled on a white shirt, blue pants, and black shoes—the other pair I owned was brown—and headed out. The heat was back in force and the air was as still as a dead man's heart. The sun was ascending in the east, with not a cloud in the sky to muffle its scorching rays. I ambled so as not to build too much of a sweat. This worked only partially and prolonged the length of my hike to thirteen minutes.

Michael Shamir lived in a run-down three-story building with a facade that used to be a brilliant white but was now smudged black and gray from exhaust fumes and absorbed moisture. The front door was missing its handle and the corners of the lobby sported an accumulation of dirt and brittle leaves. The lobby smelled stale, as if it had not been washed in weeks. A dead cockroach lay on its back in the middle of the floor with its crooked feet sticking up, and a procession of ants were busy dismantling it. I stepped over both carcass and ants and went up the stairs to the top floor, my shoes making scuffing sounds against the dust on the steps.

I knocked on the door to apartment five and waited. No answer. I knocked a second time, a bit harder, with similar results. I had turned away from the door when I heard footfalls approaching on the stairway.

The first thing I saw was the top of his head. His hair was black and cropped very short. He was toting a grocery bag in each hand and climbed with his head bowed. Then, probably alerted by the landing light that I had flicked on earlier, he paused, eight or so treads from where I stood, and raised his head.

His face was familiar, and it took me a second or two to figure out from where. He was the second man in Mira's picture of the four young warriors—the other, Yohanan, had died during the prison raid. In that picture, he had been a youth of around twenty. Now he was thirty or so and showing the ten years that had passed.

His face looked longer and leaner than it had been in that picture, almost ascetic, giving him a monkish cast. His hair was receding at the temples, though the rest of it was dense. Perpetual frown lines furrowed his tall forehead. His eyes were set deep and the color of walnut and seemed captured in a permanent squint, as if he was staring into the sun. They were intense eyes, the eyes of a man who had seen and done things. Between the eyes began the slope of a Roman nose and beneath that was a mouth that seemed incongruously full. The chin was neither big nor small, neither protruding nor sunken. Chin and cheeks were dusted with black stubble. He had not shaved that morning.

He was five nine and had a wiry build. Lean muscle bunched under the skin of his outstretched, bag-wielding arms, and a vein stood out in each of his biceps. He looked fit, but not as formidable as I had expected him to be. All told, he was not a handsome man. Mira's admiration for him did not stem from his looks.

He stared at me for a long moment, not moving. "Looking for someone?" he said finally, in a soft, velvety voice.

"Michael Shamir. That's you, isn't it?"

"That's right."

"My name is Adam Lapid. I got your name and address from Mira Roth."

His eyebrows rose a fraction. "Mira Roth? Is that a fact?"

"Yes. She gave me a note to give to you."

I fished the note Mira had given me out of my pocket and held it out to him. He climbed the rest of the way, set down the two bags, and plucked the note from my hand. He read it with seeming care. I watched his face while he did so. Not much of a reaction, a slight deepening of those frown lines, an upward flick of the eyes to assess my face. On their way back to the note, his eyes paused for a fraction of a second on the number tattooed on my forearm, but did not give away his thoughts. When he was done reading, he folded the note and did not return it.

"Better come in, then," he said.

While he unlocked the door, I reached down and grabbed one of the grocery bags. He muttered a low thank you, hoisted the other bag, pushed open the door, and led the way inside.

I had expected his apartment to match the rest of the building. It didn't. The walls were freshly painted, the floor clean. The kitchen, which opened to the right a couple of feet from the door, was about the size of mine and immaculate. No crumbs on the counters, no dirty dishes in the sink, no grime on the small window. We set the bags on the floor and he proceeded to unpack them. Bread and dry goods went into a cupboard; cheese, milk, and vegetables he put in the icebox. None of the food items were contraband. Either he was one of those rare souls who did not partake of the black market, or I had caught him on a good day. When the last of the food was in its place, he said, "I'm gonna have a beer. Want one?"

"Too early for me."

He shrugged and tugged out a bottle from the icebox. Condensation sparkled along the glass. He popped the cap, took a swig, smiled a small smile, and said, "I just got back from work, so this is like a nightcap. How about some water?" I nodded and he filled me a glass from the tap. "Let's go to the other room."

The other room wore a number of hats, just like mine on Hamaccabi Street. There was a small table for eating and writing; a made bed, with a nightstand next to it; a low sofa, which was slightly sagging in the middle, but otherwise looking in good repair; and a row of overturned wooden milk boxes arrayed against one wall and topped with cramped rows of books. A poor man's room, but one who took care of what he owned. Also a single man's room, as there was no sign of any woman or her touch anywhere.

A number of pictures hung on one wall. The first was a copy of the picture Mira had shown me. The second, of about the same period, showed a younger Michael Shamir grinning, a cigarette in one hand, a Sten machine gun in the other. The third had him shaking hands with Menachem Begin, the leader of the Irgun. The fourth, no older than a year, showed him in an IDF uniform, army hat jammed low on his head, leaning against an earth bank, rifle stock at his shoulder.

"Where did you fight?" I asked.

"A bunch of places. Jaffa, Jerusalem, the Galilee. Mostly against the Lebanese and Syrians. Were you in the war?"

"Yes. A bit in Jerusalem, during Operation Nachshon, and the rest of the time in the Negev."

He nodded appreciatively. "You boys did good work there. Gave the Egyptians a good licking."

"You guys in the north did not do so bad yourselves."

A shrug. "I wish we'd done better." Then he raised his bottle and added, "To old comrades."

The toast might have sounded funny coming from most men, but it didn't from him. We drank and lapsed into our separate thoughts and memories. I caught a faint whiff of cigarette smoke and, looking around, spotted an empty tin ashtray on the table. I set my glass down and got out my pack of cigarettes. I proffered him one, but he declined, saying he didn't like mixing it with beer. He told me to go ahead, so I did.

He sat in the middle of the sofa with his knees wide apart, holding his beer bottle by its neck between them. I took a chair by the table, ashtray at my elbow. For the first time, I noticed his face was drawn and tired, and I remembered him saying he had worked during the night.

"Where do you work?" I asked.

"I'm a guard at the Reading Power Station."

"Always work nights?"

"Usually. The other guys don't like it much, but I do. It's quiet, and no one's around. I can get some reading done."

"I guess working nights is easier when you're single."

"I'm not single," he said in a low voice. "I'm a widower. But I suppose it amounts to the same thing, as far as working nights is concerned."

His eyes went to a point over my shoulder, and I swiveled my head to follow his gaze. There, on the nightstand by the bed, stood a picture. I had to cant my head and squint to see it fully. It showed a man and a woman standing close together, the man dressed in a suit and tie and the woman in a white dress and a veil that was pulled back, exposing her face. A wedding photo. The man was Michael Shamir and the smile on his face was as bright as a chandelier. The woman was an attractive brunette, and for the second time that day I found myself staring at the familiar face of a person whom I had before only seen in a picture. Mira Roth's picture.

What was her name?

I fumbled in my mind for the elusive memory, feeling it slip through my mental fingers a couple of times, till I finally caught it. "Talia," I muttered. "Your wife's name. It's Talia, isn't it?"

He stared at me in apparent shock, but did not answer. He probably wondered where I had learned the name. I explained about the picture Mira had shown me and watched his expression soften. Now I understood what Mira had meant when she said Michael Shamir had given up his family for the cause of the Irgun. For hadn't Mira said that Talia Shamir had also taken part in that raid and died during it?

"I'm sorry. Your wife was very beautiful."

"Yes. She was." His eyes were downcast, staring, I imagined, past the bottle in his hands, past the soles of his feet and the floor beneath them, all the way to years ago, when his wife was still with him. His voice, which was thick with prolonged mourning, left me with no doubt—he was no competition for the affection of Mira or any other woman. His wife had been dead twice as long as mine, but he was still very much in love with her.

Witnessing his grief, I was ashamed to have been jealous of him. I felt a kinship with this man, for weren't we both soldiers, hadn't we both killed, and weren't we both alone in the world?

I inhaled from my cigarette, tapping loose ash into the ashtray.

"Let me tell you why I'm here. Then I'd like to ask you a few questions. I'll keep it brief so you can get some sleep."

"That would be good," he said, raising his head and taking a quick pull from his bottle.

"I'm a private investigator, and a week or so ago I was hired to locate a woman and a boy who had come to Palestine from Germany in 1939. I managed to learn that they traveled on the *Salonika*, were arrested by the British, and later freed when the Irgun raided the prison where the British took them. Mira told me you took part in that raid."

"That's right, I did."

"Their names were Esther Grunewald and Willie Ackerland, but the false papers you furnished them bore the surname Kantor. You remember them?"

"Yes. Who hired you to find them?"

"The mother of the boy. If you recall, she had given the child to Esther Grunewald for safekeeping and planned on coming after them."

"The mother," he said in surprise. "I was certain she was dead. I always wondered what sort of woman would give her son away."

I was surprised to find myself bristle at this criticism of Henrietta, for hadn't I voiced a similar sentiment, and to her face? "I'd say she saw the future more clearly than most German Jews did, wouldn't you agree?" And most Hungarian ones, I added to myself.

"Yes," he said. "I suppose you're right."

I drew a calming breath. "Anyway, she managed to survive the war and only recently made *aliyah*. Naturally, she was anxious to locate her son and hired me to do it. Unfortunately, both Esther and Willie were murdered in their apartment ten years ago. The police never caught the killer, and now I'm giving it a try. You know about the murders?"

"Yes. It's terrible what happened to them."

"How did you learn of their deaths?"

"Mira told me. I've never seen her so upset. Not before nor since, and I've seen Mira in tough spots, believe me."

"Why do you think that was?" I asked, keeping my voice casual, hoping he might let slip why Mira took the murders of Esther and Willie so much to heart.

He disappointed me. "I don't know," he said. "Maybe it was because a child had died. Women are more emotional than men, especially when children are concerned. Or maybe it was because of how they died."

"What do you mean, how they died?"

"Well, I don't know the details, but I remember the papers implying that the murders were brutal. Was that right, do you know?"

"Not exactly," I said. "They died quickly enough, but the maniac disfigured their faces."

He grimaced, shaking his head. "Hard to imagine."

"Be glad you can only imagine it. I've seen the pictures. They're not pretty."

That brought the conversation to a standstill. I crushed out my cigarette. He finished his beer.

"I'm going to have another," he said. "Change your mind and join me?"

I shook first my head and then another cigarette from the pack. I had ignited it and taken a drag by the time he returned from the kitchen, a fresh bottle in his hand.

He dropped onto the sofa and said, "Are you making progress in your investigation? Any suspects?"

"I'm still working on it," I said, taking another drag.

He nodded sagaciously, and I got the impression he understood full well that so far I had next to nothing.

"Well, I'm not sure what help I can be, but I'll gladly answer any questions I can."

"Good. What I'm trying to do is get a clearer picture of who Esther was. I understand you met her on the night of the prison raid."

"That's right. I drove her to the safe house."

"You and Mira," I said.

"Yes."

"You drove them to the Klingers'."

A short pause. "You know about the Klingers?"

"Mira told me."

"I see. Yes, we went to the Klingers' house in Haifa."

"How was Esther that night?"

"How was she? Scared out of her mind. It's perfectly under-standable. After all, she was just in the middle of a firefight. I was pretty shaken myself. That damned raid." He shook his head, and his tone became agitated. "The plan seemed solid, but everything went to hell within the first moments. If we had to execute the same plan a year or two later, the results would have been differ-ent. But back then we were untrained and inexperienced. We paid a heavy price."

His jaw was tight enough I expected to hear teeth grind. His gaze seemed to be turned inward, to where he stored bad memo-ries. I let a few seconds slither by before asking, "Did you see her after that night?"

He took a quick sip of beer. "I came by with a camera and snapped their picture—hers and the boy's—for the false papers. I later returned when the papers were ready. So I went by there twice, maybe one other time."

"What was she like?"

"Like?"

"Yes. For instance, how was she with the baby? Was she close to him?"

A small shrug. "How close could she have been? She wasn't his real mother."

"Mira told me Esther loved Willie."

He pursed his lips. "Well, then I suppose she did. Mira knew her better than I did. I only saw her once with the baby, when I took their picture. The other time I was at the Klingers', he was asleep in another room."

"Anything else you remember of Esther?"

He thought for a moment. "One time I was there, she told me she wanted to join the Irgun, to take action against the British. She seemed very motivated. But eventually she did nothing. A lot of *maapilim* were like that—they were enthusiastic about taking part in the struggle in the first few days after getting off the boat. As weeks went by, their fervor died down. They became engrossed in day-to-day living—their jobs, that sort of thing—and forgot their previous declarations of dedication and willingness to sacrifice whatever was needed for the sake of the Jewish people." He fixed me with his steely gaze. "You know, the British did not get out of our country because they wanted to. They left because *we* drove them out." He punctuated the "we" by thumping his chest with his fist, and I recalled Goldberg expressing his admiration for the Irgun's fighting spirit, if not their politics.

"Were you part of any resistance group? Did you fight the British?" he asked me in a challenging tone.

"No."

"When did you get to Israel?"

"September 1947."

"Well," he said, mollified, and perhaps a touch embarrassed by his emotions, "by that time the work was nearly done. And you did do your part in the war."

He sipped his beer. I took a last drag and mashed out my cigarette in the ashtray.

"Did you have any contact with Esther after she left the Klingers'?"

"No."

"When you saw her there, did she seem to get along with them?"

Another small shrug. "She and the Klinger woman—I forget

her name—seemed friendly enough. The husband I didn't see after the first night. Not that I missed him all that much."

"Why do you say that?"

His face tightened with anger. "A young, able-bodied man, and all he was willing to do was dole out the occasional contribution and host poor immigrants for a few days. And even that they stopped doing after that time. We needed fighters, not innkeepers."

I leaned forward, my skin tingling as it did when I was on a case and had just uncovered something that might prove important. "Esther and Willie were the last immigrants the Klingers ever sheltered?"

"That's right."

"Why?"

"I don't know. I didn't hear about it directly from them. All I know is that we never brought more immigrants to their house."

Scratching my jaw, I leaned back in my seat and pondered this new fact. It could mean nothing. I wouldn't know till I had a chance to see the Klingers.

"Anything else you can tell me that might help with my investigation?"

He considered, taking a long pull from his bottle. He set it on the floor between his feet and shook his head. "I don't think so. Like I said, I only saw her and the baby a couple of times."

I nodded. I could think of nothing more to ask him. Maybe that bit about the Klingers would lead to something and maybe it wouldn't. Other than that, my talk with Michael Shamir was a bust. I got to my feet.

"Thanks for your time. I'll be off now."

He rose. "Say, weren't you in the papers a year or so back? Something about Operation Yoav?"

I was surprised when the discomfort that usually arose when I was asked about the day of my injury did not materialize. Perhaps because this man was also a warrior. Perhaps because of the matter-of-fact manner in which he had presented his question.

"Yes." I didn't elaborate.

He slapped me on the shoulder. "Nice work." That was the extent of his commendation. I liked that. No platitudes or flowery praise, just a crisp acknowledgment of a job well done, which was how I saw my actions in the war.

At the door, I stopped and offered him my hand. His grip was firm and warm. With his other hand he gestured at my forearm.

"You were there, in the Nazi camps?"

"Yes," I said.

"I understand it was terrible. I'm glad you survived."

It was an odd thing to say, but he seemed completely sincere when he said it. Still, I couldn't think of a proper reply. What should I have said? Thank you?

"I met a camp survivor during the war," he went on. "A French Jew. One night before a big battle in the Galilee, he started telling me what he went through during the war in Europe, how the Germans put him and his family on a train to Poland, to a concentration camp. All his family was dead, he was the only one left. Once he started talking, he didn't stop. Not for a second all through that night. Neither of us got any sleep. I think he felt compelled to tell his life's story because he was worried about the upcoming battle, worried that if he got killed, there would be no one who would know his story or that he had ever existed."

"What was his name?"

"Pierre. Pierre Levi."

"What happened to him?"

Michael Shamir pointed to his neck. "The next day he caught a bullet right here. Died on the spot."

17

I got lucky and caught a bus that was only slightly less warm than a furnace. I sat beside an overweight woman who mumbled to herself in singsong Italian while she stared out the window as if at a picture show. Behind me, two men spoke in animated Yiddish, while in the seats in front of me, a mother was busy hectoring her eight-year-old daughter in staccato Polish. That was the sound-track of Tel Aviv, a cocktail of languages and dialects and accents all pouring past and into each other.

The bus ferried me across town and deposited me near the middle of Rothschild Boulevard. I trekked north, past Bilu Elementary School in whose basement the Tel Aviv Chamber Choir was conducting a rehearsal. Harmonious singing accompanied me as I made the turn to Lunz Street and located the building where Esther Grunewald and Willie Ackerland had lived and died.

There were six apartments, two to a floor. Esther and Willie had lived in number six. I examined the labels on the mailboxes in the lobby, hoping to find that the people who had lived in the building ten years ago were still in residence. Another disappointment. Of the six mailboxes, only one name was familiar to me—Sassoon, the landlord's name—and it appeared on two of the boxes, numbers one and six. I frowned. Did a relative of the landlord now occupy the apartment where the double murder had taken place?

I mounted the stairs to the third floor and knocked on the door marked six. No answer. Back on the ground floor, I rapped on the door to apartment one and heard a gravelly voice rasp at me to wait a minute.

A swarthy, pockmarked man of around fifty opened the door, holding a cigarette in one hand and a steaming coffee glass in the other. The cigarette was fat and Turkish, the coffee thick and the color of mud. I could not determine which emitted a stronger smell. The man wore a white undershirt tucked into black slacks. His arms were covered in dense black curls. More curls sprouted from his scalp and to them he'd pinned a small black *kippah*. He was five foot six, with a spare frame and dark, heavy-lidded eyes that were now peering up at me.

"Abraham Sassoon?" I asked.

He nodded. "And you are?"

I gave him my name and told him the reason for my visit. The corners of his mouth drew down to form a mournful arc when I mentioned the murders.

"Come in," he said. "Come in."

He offered me coffee and seemed not offended when I declined. We sat in two chairs that were more comfortable than they looked. Sassoon smoked and drank his coffee. I added to the stinging odors that pervaded the room by lighting a cigarette of my own. Bluish-black smoke swirled in the air between us. He told me about the day he'd discovered the bodies, touching his *kippah* every other sentence with nicotine-stained fingers, as if needing to reinforce his belief in the Almighty.

"You heard nothing during the night?"

His answer echoed the one he'd given Rivlin in 1939. "Not a thing. It has troubled me ever since, that I slept peacefully in my bed while a ruthless, depraved murderer was killing two of my tenants a mere two floors above my head."

"Are you a heavy sleeper?"

"I'm afraid that I am, but that's not the worst of it. I also snore. My dear departed wife used to say I sound like a locomotive undergoing a coughing fit, but it has never disturbed my sleep."

"When did you lose your wife?"

"It will be eight years in December."

I told him I was sorry for his loss. He accepted my condolences with a heavy nod.

"She didn't hear anything either," Sassoon said. "For the same reason, I suppose." He shook his head again and sucked on his cigarette.

"What can you tell me about Esther?"

He touched his *kippah*. "Not much, I'm afraid. I can tell you she was a good tenant. Never late with the rent, didn't make noise, seemed to get along well with the other residents. But I can't say I knew her all that much. Esther was very friendly with another tenant of mine, Natalie Davidson. Maybe you should talk to her. She and her husband and son lived in apartment three."

I nodded. I had read Rivlin's interview with Natalie Davidson, in which she had presented herself as a friend of Esther, and I was planning on talking to her.

"Do you happen to know where the Davidsons are living these days?"

Sassoon started shaking his head, but paused midway. "I got a letter from them at Rosh Hashanah two years ago. I should have it somewhere...now where did I put it...ah, here it is."

He had been rummaging in a desk drawer and now presented me with a white envelope. Inside was a generic greeting for the

Jewish New Year. Printed on the envelope was a return address on Ben Yehuda Street, in Tel Aviv. I copied it in my notebook.

"Do you know where I can find the other neighbors who lived here at the time?"

The corners of his mouth curled down again, almost to his jawline. "Zelig Joselewicz in apartment two was about eighty when the murders took place. He died in hospital from the flu three...no, four years ago. Yisrael Metzner, who lived in apartment four, was killed in 1940 when the Italians bombed Tel Aviv. Lastly, there's the couple who lived in apartment five, Mr. and Mrs. Rutte. They returned to the Netherlands. They were Dutch Jews. The murders put the scare into Mrs. Rutte. She told me she didn't feel safe here any longer, that she wanted to go back to Amsterdam. You can imagine what happened to them after the Nazis invaded the Netherlands."

I could. I had met Dutch Jews in Auschwitz, though I could not recall anyone named Rutte.

"So," he continued, "the killer is really responsible for the deaths of four people, not just two."

He finished his coffee and set it aside. A dark, muddy sediment clogged the bottom third of the glass. He crushed out his cigarette in an ashtray and brushed tobacco crumbs from his fingers.

"Did Esther have any visitors? Any men who came calling?"

"I never saw any, and it's not that I forbade it, like other landlords do. As long as you pay the rent and don't make trouble, you can do what you please in your apartment. That's the way I run things."

I scratched my cheek. "I've seen pictures of Esther. I find it hard to believe that a woman as beautiful as her did not have any suitors."

"Some men don't want a woman burdened with a child. But maybe she did have someone and I never knew about it. Natalie Davidson might know."

I asked him if I could see the apartment where the murders had occurred. He raised both eyebrows.

"What good would that do you? It's been ten years. Not a stick of furniture is the same."

"Still. I'd like to see it. Who lives there now?"

"My son, with his wife and baby boy."

"The same son you sent to call the police when you discovered the bodies?"

"Yes. Haim. He's twenty-two now." Sassoon must have read the question on my face, because he added, "You think it's strange that I'd let my family live in that apartment. For two years after the murders, I didn't even rent it out. I could have done so in a heart-beat—it's a good apartment. I just couldn't bring myself to do it. Gradually, my aversion subsided. I removed all the furniture, repainted every wall, installed a sturdier door—this I did to all the apartments in the building—and rented it out. Two years ago, when my son got married and told me he wanted to move up there, I was aghast. But he persisted, and I gave in." A small shrug. "At first it felt strange, but ever since my grandson was born, it doesn't anymore. It's like the apartment has a fresh start. Come, let's go up."

We climbed the stairs together. Sassoon was showing his age, or maybe his lifetime of smoking Turkish tobacco, as he huffed with each step, pulling himself up with the metal banister. He knocked on the door before opening it, explaining that he was not sure whether his daughter-in-law was home. She wasn't. We entered the apartment and he led me to the bedroom and pointed out where the bodies had lain.

I didn't know what I expected to find. Some undefined vestige, some ember of the two fires of life that had once blazed here and had been abruptly extinguished. I certainly did not expect to find bloodstains, physical evidence, or some other clue left by the killer. In the end, I found nothing. Whatever mark Esther and

Willie had left on their home was gone or beyond my sensory capabilities.

We were crossing the living room toward the apartment door when, out of the corner of my eye, I caught a blinding flash, like light being reflected from glass. I turned my gaze toward the south window, but all I could see was a strip of blue sky and below that the buildings on the opposite side of the street.

Back on the ground floor, I asked Mr. Sassoon where I might find his son.

"Haim? He's with his army unit up north. He's due back tomorrow morning. But why do you want to talk to him? He has no information that can help you."

"Maybe something will come to him that didn't ten years ago."

He appeared doubtful, but said I was welcome to return at any time. We shook hands and he wished me the best of luck.

Lunz Street ran east to west between Yehuda Halevi Street and Rothschild Boulevard and was two hundred meters long from end to end. I started on the eastern side and began knocking on doors. Only half my knocks were answered, and only half of those by people who had lived on Lunz Street at the time of the murders. One woman, clutching a baby to her hip, turned white as a sheet when she learned of the atrocity that had happened on her street. Another informed me that her upstairs neighbor had always struck her as strange. "I'd take a look at him if I were you," she suggested with a whisper. "He's a suspicious one." The neighbor in question turned out to be a portly, gentle-faced man in his late fifties who had emigrated to Israel from Iraq in 1947. Another neighbor, a black-bearded man in his early forties, remembered the murders well, and Esther even better. "What a beauty she was," he said wistfully. "It's always a shame when a beautiful woman like her dies." And what did he think of Esther, besides her looks? He told me he had never exchanged a single word with her. Willie he mentioned not at all.

By the time I'd made it to the building directly opposite the murder scene, I was hungry and thirsty and frustrated. All my stair-climbing and door-knocking and questioning had yielded nothing. Esther remained a mystery to me. I trudged up the stairs to the third floor with a heavy tread, cursing under my breath for my arrogance in believing I could solve this hopeless case, and knocked on another door.

At first there was no answer, but I could hear shuffling noises from within. So, my foul mood getting the better of me, I pounded on the door with my fist, jarring it in its frame.

The man who opened the door partway looked frightened to see me. I smoothed the scowl off my face and told him I was sorry if I'd disturbed him. He muttered something that sounded like "It's all right," but might have been something else. I mechanically gave him what had by now become my standard opening, which was to give my name and ask how long he had lived on Lunz Street.

"Since 1935," he said.

Good. Four years before the murders.

"Did you know Esther Kantor?"

A slight hesitation. A jerky shake of the head. He was under average in height, thirty-two or thirty-three years old, and had a face rich with poor features—pasty skin; beady brown eyes; small mouth with pencil-thin, colorless lips; an almost nonexistent chin; and a hook nose with gaping nostrils.

"She was the woman who was murdered on this street with her baby ten years ago. Ring a bell?"

"No."

It might not have rung any bells for him, but it did for me. Warning bells. He was the first neighbor who'd lived on Lunz Street at the time of the murders who claimed not to remember them. Murders were rare in Tel Aviv, and the double murder of a woman and baby was the rarest among the rare. It would take a singularly insular person not to know of such a murder, especially when it happened in the building across the street from his own.

I studied the man with revived interest. His name, I knew from a small sign on his door, was Manny Orrin. Now I noticed the furtive brown eyes that twitched onto mine and away like a pair of agitated flies, and the way his bony hand gripped the half-open door, hairless knuckles turning white. He was blocking the doorway with his narrow body, not just depriving me of physical entrance, but blocking my line of sight into his apartment. I shifted my body sideways, angling my head slightly to try to peer past him, but he turned his body in relation to mine, effectively depriving me of the view.

"Mr. Orrin," I said, plastering on a sheepish smile. "I've been on my feet for many hours and I, well, I would be grateful if I could make use of your bathroom."

Before he could formulate an excuse why that was not possible, I uttered a relieved thank you, took a decisive step forward, and pushed the door open, brushing past him into the apartment. I cast my eyes quickly about the room. I had three seconds, no more, before he recovered from my brusque entry.

Everything seemed perfectly ordinary. A dining table on the right. A radio on the left. A big leafy potted plant by the door to the balcony. A sofa, rug, and two padded chairs. Heavy gray curtains on the windows. Bookshelves.

Wait. Eyes back. There, just visible on the floor behind the potted plant. A camera, with an elongated lens like a snout. I moved left for a better view. Black with a chrome top, with the name KODAK stenciled across the front. Sleek, elegant, professional.

The thought flashed through my mind: Camera lens. Blinding light reflected off glass. And right across Lunz Street, clearly visible from the nearby window, was the apartment where the murders had taken place, where I had stood ninety minutes before.

Turning to the man, I said, "You like spying on people, Mr. Orrin?"

He just stood there in the open doorway, gawping at me. His mouth hung open and the tip of his tongue lay pink and quivering across his lower lip like a beached salmon.

I noticed other things. Photographs, a great many of them, adorning the walls—of people, trees, and buildings in Tel Aviv, and of the sun setting into the Mediterranean. Quality photographs.

"You're a photographer?"

Orrin swallowed, recovering from his shock. "I don't take kindly to people who barge into my home. I would like you to leave."

"No," I said simply.

"No?" He became flustered, agitated, shifting his weight from one foot to the other. His top lip glistened with fresh sweat.

"Not until you answer my question: Are you a photographer?"

"Ah, yes," he stammered. "I own a photography studio."

"And you're sure you never heard about the two murders that occurred in that building right across the street?"

Orrin rubbed his hands together nervously. "Well, now that I've had time to think about it, I do remember something. Not the details, you understand, just the general fact that it happened."

"So a moment ago you had no recollection of it and now you suddenly do?" I had pitched my voice intentionally lower and narrowed my eyes threateningly.

"Yes," he said, and offered a self-deprecating smile that served only to make him look more insincere, "I'm afraid my memory is weak and—"

Ignoring him, I knelt down and grabbed the camera from the floor.

"Put that down! That's mine!" His voice came in a screech. He rushed at me, arms reaching forward, fingers curled like claws. Rising to my full height, I thrust one hand on his sunken chest and shoved him away. He fell on his ass and back, yelping in pain. I strode to the door and shut it and turned the key in its lock. This might take some time, and I did not want interruptions. I flipped the camera over and rewound and extracted the film. I set the camera on a table and weighed the film in my hand.

Suddenly, I heard a scuffing sound and sensed motion coming from behind. I instinctively jerked my head aside. The candlestick Orrin wielded swished past my ear and smashed into the wall, gouging an ugly trench in the flowery wallpaper.

I whipped around and sank my fist in his gut, just under the belly button. He was soft around the middle, and my punch folded him in half, knocking the air out of him. He crumpled to the floor, clutching his abdomen. The candlestick clattered on the tiles beside him. I set my foot on it, holding it down.

Taking another quick look out the window and across the street, I saw the living room of apartment six in Mr. Sassoon's building, where his son, Haim, lived with his wife and baby boy. The same apartment where Esther and Willie had lived.

I gazed down at Manny Orrin. He was lying on his back, breathing hard, his cheeks flushed with effort and pain. I loomed over him, holding the film so he could see it. "What's on this that's worth bashing my head in?"

Orrin didn't answer, so I prodded his side with the tip of my shoe. He cringed.

Looking at his miserable face, it came to me. "You like taking pictures of women? Is that what's on this film?"

By the way his eyes dilated, I could tell I'd guessed right.

"Get up! On your feet!" I held out a hand to help him up. His palm was cold and clammy. I resisted the urge to rub my hand on my pants. "Where are the rest of the photos? Where do you keep them?" For there were more, of that I was sure.

"You have no right to touch my possessions." His whining tone grated on my ears.

"Where are they?" I growled. "Either show me, or I'll hit you again."

He didn't say anything, but his eyes roved past my shoulder toward a hall that led deeper into the apartment. I pushed him ahead of me past a bathroom and into a gloomy bedroom. Thick curtains were drawn across the windows. I flicked on the overhead triple-bulb light fixture and saw a room that contained a double bed with a headboard, a three-door closet, a wooden cabinet, and a dressing table with a large mirror. On the dressing table stood jars of cream and lotion, tubes of makeup, pins, and a hairbrush, all laid out in an orderly fashion. A woman's bedroom, which, judging by the heavy winter blanket on the bed and the general sense of disuse, had not been slept in for a long while. Pictures hung on the walls, these of a much-younger Manny Orrin, sometimes alone, sometimes at the side of an old severe-faced woman who I assumed was his mother. There were no recent pictures of them together, which led me to believe his mother was dead. When I flung open the closet doors, I saw old-fashioned dresses hanging neatly on hangers and more female clothing folded on shelves. The clothes smelled thickly of mothballs. It was clear that this had been the mother's room. Orrin had kept it as it had been when she died.

I tried the cabinet. It was locked. "Open it!" I said.

He shook his head.

"I'll tear this whole room apart if you don't. I won't leave one shred of clothing whole."

He gulped, his face tightening in suppressed anger, and I wondered what his anger was capable of driving him to do. But he didn't try anything, and his angry expression morphed into a resigned one. He produced a brass key from his pocket, inserted it in the lock, and pulled the cabinet door open.

Inside, arrayed on three shelves, were rows of photo albums. I grabbed Orrin's shoulder and pushed him toward the chair that stood before the dressing table. "Sit down and don't move."

He did as he was told, sitting with his hands between his knees, looking like a chastened child. I started leafing through the albums, beginning with those on the bottom shelf. The first few albums contained photos of the sort that hung in the living room —innocent pictures of buildings and streets, of Orrin and his mother, and of other people dressed in clothes long out of fashion —but as I got to the second row of albums, the nature of the pictures began to shift.

More and more of the photos were of women, all young and attractive. The early pictures were all snapped in public places. Gradually, the range of scenes expanded and there were photos of women inside apartments and houses, pictures taken through windows, some close-ups and some which had been shot from a distance. It was clear the women had no idea they were being photographed, but none were captured in intimate or sexually revealing circumstances.

Initially, the women seemed to have been chosen at random, none appearing in more than a handful of shots. Then there were whole album sections devoted to a single woman, as if Orrin's obsession had narrowed in focus, fixating on a single target for a time before shifting to another.

At the beginning of each section, over the first picture of the new object of Orrin's obsession, was a label with a woman's name written on it in blue or black ink. It was halfway through the second shelf of albums that I came upon the label marked with the name Esther Kantor and, two inches below that, the first photo of Esther. She was in the living room of her apartment, holding a mug to her lips, her right profile turned to the camera, her raven hair tucked behind her ear. More photos followed, more than had been taken of any other woman. Many of them long shots taken from Orrin's apartment, showing Esther in various clothes and in the midst of diverse activities—ironing, washing dishes, eating, brushing her hair. In one picture, she was holding her arms out sideways and appeared to be in the middle of a twirl.

"What's this?" I asked Orrin, showing him the picture.

"She's dancing. She liked to dance."

Other photos showed Esther with Willie in her arms, standing at the window or sitting on the sofa or feeding him. There were also photos of her outdoors—walking in the street, pushing a baby stroller, lugging grocery bags, drinking a beverage. None of the photos was indecent. Esther was always fully clothed. I stared hard at each photo as I removed it from its place in the album, searching for something, though I was not sure what it was, and failing to find it. With each photo that I laid aside on the bed I could feel my rage mounting, bubbling like lava inside me. Some of this rage was directed at Manny Orrin for stalking Esther and robbing her of her privacy. But most of my rage was for the unnamed killer. For these photos made Esther more real to me, painting a fuller picture of the life she'd had and lost.

On the back of each photo, Orrin had inscribed Esther's name and a date. Looking at the photos, I could follow Esther's life from the middle of May 1939, up to the 26th of August, hours before she was killed, which was when Orrin had taken his final photo of her. This one showed her walking down Rothschild Boulevard, wearing a light summer dress, clasping a bag in her left hand. There were people around her. My eyes went to each of their faces, and in my mind I could hear an irrational scream, "Couldn't one of you have saved her?"

"Why did you kill her?" I said when I finally lowered the picture.

"What?" Orrin looked shocked.

"And the baby? Why did you kill the baby?"

He began shaking his head furiously. "I didn't kill them."

"Were the pictures no longer enough? Did you need to up the thrill?"

"I'm telling you I didn't do it. I never even touched her or spoke to her. I..." He paused, reddening. "I never speak to any of them. I just take their pictures."

"Why?"

He gave a helpless, pathetic little jerk of the shoulders. "It...it's just something I do. I can't help it."

"Why did you choose Esther?"

"She was so beautiful," he said, and the adulation in his voice made my skin crawl. "So lively, so radiant. She was special, unlike any of the others. You can see it in the pictures."

I looked again and saw he was right. Esther was dazzlingly beautiful, even when she was dusting the furniture in her apartment or dragging a mop across the floor, but there was something about her beyond her beauty. Something intangible and undefinable, an aura or an energy that leaped from the picture to my searching eyes. Again I was filled with rage, but even more so with sadness and grief.

"I never would have hurt her," Orrin said in a low voice. "She was precious to me."

I gritted my teeth. "You stalked her. You took her pictures without her permission."

He didn't seem to have heard me. He spoke in a dreamy tone. "A few times I thought of going over and talking to her. She would not laugh at me, like other women did. She was kind and understanding. Maybe, just maybe, she would see something in me others never did. I never built up enough courage to do it."

"And you killed her because you knew she wouldn't want you." But even to my ears the accusation sounded hollow, lacking in conviction.

His voice was plaintive, almost childish. "I didn't do it."

I scrutinized him for a long moment. He was certainly a credible suspect. He was mentally unstable, and he'd had a bizarre fixation on Esther. He might have been driven to rage and murder over her rejection of him, real or anticipated. Moreover, from his living room window, he had a clear view of Esther's building. He could see when all the neighbors had turned off their lights, when the time was right for him to cross the street, climb the stairs, and enter apartment six, where Esther and Willie slept.

He might have killed Willie for the reason Rivlin had suggested, because the baby had awoken and begun crying. But why would he disfigure their faces? Perhaps, again as Rivlin had said, it was simply an act of madness by a person who was clearly insane.

And afterward, with his clothes drenched in Esther's and Willie's blood, he could have crossed the street and entered his apartment without anyone seeing him. Easy.

But could this man, who had lunged at me so ineptly with a candlestick, break into an apartment and slash the throat of a woman before she could mount a struggle? And what of the fact that the killer had not struck before or since that night in August 1939—at least not in a sufficiently similar manner as to arouse Rivlin's suspicion? Manny Orrin, as his photo albums attested, had been obsessed with many women. If he had killed one, would he have been able to resist killing another for ten long years?

There was also the fact that I believed him. It was a belief not based on evidence but on instinct. Another investigator would have hauled him from his chair, slammed him against a wall, and third-degreed him for as long as it took to squeeze a confession out of him. It wouldn't have taken long. A little pressure would have broken him. That would have been enough for a police detective with few scruples. He would have downplayed or ignored the discrepancies between Orrin's confession and the crime scene. Just enough to get a conviction. Cops sometimes do that, especially when they're desperate or when their gut tells them they've got the right man, or when they find someone who deserves to be punished for something, even if he did not commit the specific crime they're investigating.

And Orrin did deserve to be punished for photographing women without their consent. But I did not think he had killed Esther and Willie. He was sick, but not that kind of sick.

Or was I reading him wrong? Was I being arrogant in believing my instincts would not mislead me? Was the killer sitting right here before me?

"I cried when I heard what happened," he said, sitting shrunken in his mother's chair. "I mourned."

There was a metallic taste in my mouth and my muscles were tense. A part of me wanted to hit him. Another part pitied him. He was a lost man. But he didn't feel like a killer to me.

I took a deep breath. "All right. I believe you. Let me ask you something: When you followed Esther to take your pictures, did you see her with anyone? A man?"

"No. But I didn't follow her all the time, just a little."

Just a little, I thought, looking at the five dozen pictures spread over the thick blanket.

"Where are the negatives?" I asked.

They were stored in the final two albums on the top shelf, all neatly labeled. I removed the ones holding Esther's image and put them in my pocket.

"I'm taking these too," I said, gathering the pictures on the bed.

"What? No. Please, don't."

I gave him a stare that made him wilt in his seat.

His voice was beseeching. "Can't you leave me with one? Just one?"

"You had no right to take them. They're not yours." And this, I realized, was how I would punish him, by taking away all his favorite photos.

I glanced at the other albums. I couldn't carry them all with me, nor all the pictures in them—even the stack of Esther's photos was too big to stick in my pants pockets, so I had to hold them in my left hand. But I could do something else. I flipped through all the albums, copying down the names of the women Orrin had photographed over the years. There were over twenty names. If any of these women had been murdered, no matter how, Manny Orrin was my man. If not, then I could be fairly certain my instincts had not failed me.

Orrin didn't ask me what I was doing, but sat quietly through all this, shoulders hunched, thin hands in his lap.

I wasn't sure what else I should do with him. I could sic the police on him, but whatever crime they charged him with would be minor. Maybe he would just pay a fine. Maybe he'd spend a few nights in jail. Neither would do anyone much good.

"I'll be keeping my eye on you," I lied. "If I catch you taking pictures of any more women, I'll pay you another visit. I will hurt you badly."

A shudder went through him. He said nothing. I had no idea if he'd heed my warning. He might try to, but his cravings might prove too powerful for him to resist for long.

That wasn't my concern. I was after a killer, not a Peeping Tom. I left him sitting in his mother's chair in her frozen-in-time room. On the way out, I grabbed his camera. I tossed it into a garbage bin on the street. Let him buy another. This one was tainted.

18

I had knocked on just over two-thirds of the doors on Lunz Street, but after visiting Manny Orrin, I couldn't bring myself to knock on a single one more. I had been climbing stairs and knocking on doors and talking to neighbors for over two hours, and I wanted to get off my feet. In addition, I was clutching a stack of photographs in my hand, and it was uncomfortable to walk around with it.

Ten seconds after tossing Manny Orrin's camera in the trash, while I was briskly walking west in the direction of Rothschild Boulevard, where I planned to grab a bite and a cold drink, I heard a lilting female voice that was five levels too cheery for my mood.

"Yoo-hoo, young man. Yoo-hoo."

It took me a second or two to realize it was addressing me. I turned and tilted my head back to see where the voice was coming from.

"Over here. Yoo-hoo."

She was standing on a second-floor balcony in the building I had just walked past, waving a large straw hat to catch my attention. A chubby middle-aged woman, a little on the short side, gray-haired and round-faced, flashing a smile as big as a house.

"Leaving so soon?"

I frowned in bemusement. I didn't know this woman and was sure we'd never met before.

"Don't go just yet. I've got some rugelach and lemonade here for you. Come on up."

I hesitated. A moment ago I couldn't wait to get out of Lunz Street, but the urgency had been replaced by curiosity. It wasn't every day that I got called up by total strangers to partake of rugelach and lemonade. Especially not when I was hungry and thirsty.

"Coming up," I called back to her.

She stuck her straw hat on her head and clapped once in merriment, like a girl fifty years younger.

"Wise decision. Apartment four." Then she vanished from sight, presumably to open the door for me.

I took the stairs, feeling somewhat silly and amused with myself. She was standing at the door, and I saw she was possessed of kind gray eyes, plump cheeks, and extensive smile lines at the corners of her mouth and eyes. She was smiling now, and her smile exuded warmth and welcome. A pair of glasses dangled from a cord around her neck. Her dress was light gray, with a large pocket across its center. Her shoes were brown and sensible. She had pulled her hair back in a bun, and her ears were studded with tiny silver earrings. She held herself with poise and elegance and extended her hand for me to shake much as a man would.

"Elena Warshavski."

"Adam Lapid."

I clasped her hand in mine, and she gave it a single resolute pump before releasing it.

"It's good that you've come," she said, eying me up and down and nodding once, as if in approval. "I've been sitting on my balcony for the past hour, watching you walk in and out of one building after the next, and I asked myself, Elena, what is this serious-faced man up to? And when is he going to come up here and tell me? But where are my manners? Come in, come in. Let's go sit on the balcony."

She led the way through a cozy living room to her sun-bathed balcony and gestured toward one of the two wicker chairs that stood by a round table, which carried a pitcher of lemonade, two glasses, and a plate of rugelach. My nose told me the rugelach were freshly baked. My mouth watered. I swallowed the excess saliva. Elena noticed and laughed.

"Go on. Take one. Or two. A big man like you—one would hardly suffice."

I took two rugelach and ate them with greater speed than good manners would tolerate. The outer shell was crispy, but the soft dough inside fairly melted on my tongue, filling my mouth with the taste of cinnamon and butter. Elena had dotted each rugelach with raisins, and these had puffed up in her oven, popping like hot balloons when I broke their skin with my teeth.

"Good, huh?" said Elena with obvious relish. "Here, try the lemonade."

She poured me a tall glass and I took a big gulp. The lemonade was tasty and cold and very sweet. I raised an eyebrow.

"You've either been saving up your sugar rations or you have a good black-market supplier."

Elena poured herself a glass and sat down. "Don't tell me you're one of those government hounds always sticking their snouts into other people's business."

"Do I look like one?"

"I wouldn't have invited you up here if you did. When I first saw you from my balcony, I thought you might be a salesman. But you weren't *schlepping* around a sample case or any merchandise I could see. Besides, you don't look like a salesman."

"What do I look like?"

"I can't say, and that's difficult to admit because I fancy myself a good judge of people." She raised her glass and took a sip. "What do I look like?"

"A teacher," I said.

Elena stared at me, eyebrows elevated.

I offered a smile. "Those pictures of you and your students were pretty hard to miss."

She turned her eyes in the direction of her living room, where the pictures I'd referenced filled up one wall. Then she burst out laughing. Her laughter was rolling and musical, and my smile stretched wider in response to it.

She set her glass on the table and dabbed her eyes with a napkin. "Nicely done, Adam. You don't mind if I call you Adam, do you?" I shook my head. "And you must call me Elena. You're right, of course. I am a teacher. Have been one for the past thirty-six years. Geography and history and Hebrew. You get top marks for your deduction skills." She folded her napkin and laid it on the table. "But I notice you have some pictures of your own with you."

I had set the stack of pictures I'd taken from Manny Orrin upside down on the table. I peeled off the top one and handed it to her. She lodged her eyeglasses on the bridge of her nose and studied the picture.

"My God, it's her."

"You remember her?"

Instead of answering, she said, "Can I see another one?"

I handed another picture over. This one had been taken two days before Esther's death and, like the former, it was a street shot, not one taken inside her apartment. Fortunately, Elena did not ask me where I got the pictures.

She glanced at the photo and let out a deep sigh. "Yes. It's definitely her. Poor girl. What was her name? It's on the tip of my tongue."

"Esther Kantor," I said, giving Esther's false name.

Elena handed the pictures back and removed her eyeglasses

from her nose. They dangled from their cord, resting against her chest. "Yes. Now I remember. I remember how shocked I was hearing what had happened to her and her baby."

"So you lived here at the time of the murders?"

"Yes. I've been living in this apartment for fourteen years now."

"And you knew Esther?"

"Not really. We exchanged pleasantries once or twice when we passed each other on the street. That's about it. Are you a relative?"

"No. I'm a private investigator. I was hired to look into the murders, to see if by some chance I can find out who committed them."

"A private investigator. I don't believe I ever met one before. So that's what you were doing here today."

"I was hoping to find neighbors who remember Esther, who knew her."

"Did you find any?"

"Almost none. Some people remembered the murders, but that's about it. The only person who had any meaningful contact with Esther is Mr. Sassoon, her landlord."

"I know him. He's a nice man."

"But even he says he didn't know her well. He told me that Esther was friendly with one of his former tenants. Natalie Davidson. You know her?"

Elena pursed her lips. She picked up a rugelach and nibbled on its edge, averting her eyes to look across Lunz Street.

"What is it, Elena?"

She turned back to face me. She set what remained of the nibbled rugelach on the table and brushed the crumbs from her fingers. She clasped her hands under her chin, her lips twisting like she had a bad taste in her mouth. Things you preferred not to say often tasted that way.

"What is it?" I repeated.

"I hate to speak ill of the dead."

"I'm not here to judge the dead, only those who made them so."

That seemed to persuade her. "Like I told you, I didn't know Esther Kantor, but that doesn't mean I didn't form an impression of her. As I said, I fancy myself a good judge of people, and my instinctive impression of her was very positive. Don't ask me why this was; I can't really say. It was just a feeling I had."

"And..."

"And...well, that all changed one day, or should I say one night. It had to do with Natalie Davidson. Mr. Sassoon is absolutely right; the two were friends. I saw them together on many occasions. They seemed very close."

"Seemed?"

She nodded. "One night, a week or so before the murders, I was walking by the docks when I saw Esther Kantor kissing a man in the street. The man, I'm pretty sure, was Alon Davidson, Natalie's husband."

I let that sink in for a moment. There was no mention of this in Rivlin's report. Not even a hint. Alon Davidson, in his interview, hadn't brought up any kiss.

"You say you're pretty sure it was Alon Davidson. You're not certain?"

"The way they were standing, the man had his back to me. I didn't see his face clearly, only hers. My eyes—well, I'm afraid they've never been very good at night. So if you're asking me whether I would swear in court that it was him, I'd have to say I wouldn't."

"Let's say it wasn't in court. Let's say you were talking to your students. Would you say it was Davidson?"

Elena favored me with an approving smile. "I would have enjoyed having you in my classroom, Adam. That's a very good question. The answer is yes, I would have said it was him. Alon Davidson is not a man who's easy to mistake for another. There is

147

also the matter of location—by the docks. Davidson is a fisherman. I suppose he moors his boat there."

"What do you mean it's not easy to mistake him for another man?"

"Are you planning on talking to him?"

"Yes."

"Then you'll understand when you see him."

She poured herself another glass of lemonade and took a tiny sip. She seemed not entirely happy with the fact that she'd told me what she did.

"The thing is that once I saw her kissing him, my opinion of her changed drastically. I don't approve of any woman who goes around with a married man, but with the husband of a close friend? Reprehensible. I quite disliked her after that." She sighed. "And then she was killed. Murdered. Along with her son. I felt guilty for thinking ill of her."

"Did you tell anyone about this? The police?"

"Yes, but it wasn't until three weeks after the murders. A week before the murders occurred, my daughter gave birth. She lived in Nahariya. I stayed with her for a month to help her with the new baby. It's only when I came back that I learned what happened."

"And then you went to the police?"

"Yes. I talked to a detective. Rivlin—that was his name. I remember him wrinkling his nose when I told him I wasn't positive it was Alon Davidson that I saw. He said that Davidson had an ironclad alibi."

"He did," I said. According to the police report, Davidson had been at sea on his fishing boat the night of the murders. Another fisherman, who was with him that night, had sworn to it. But why had Rivlin omitted his conversation with Elena from his report? Even if he had been certain that Alon Davidson could not have been the killer, there was another person who now had a possible motive and no alibi: Natalie Davidson, the betrayed wife and close friend. If Esther and Alon Davidson had indeed had an affair, and Natalie Davidson had known about it, she would have a pretty good reason to hate Esther. People have killed over less. Yet nowhere in his investigation report had Rivlin listed her as a suspect. Why?

Maybe he had simply not thought Elena's information was worth pursuing, considering her less-than-certain identification of Alon Davidson. Or maybe the alcohol had begun affecting his work and judgment.

Or he might have had another reason. During our conversation, Rivlin had always referred to the killer as a "he" or as a "guy." He believed that the killer was a man. He never considered the possibility that Natalie Davidson could have done it, not even when a possible motive fell in his lap. I was embarrassed to admit that I had fallen prey to the same preconception, that up to this point I had also assumed the killer was male. No longer. Natalie Davidson was now a suspect. A person whom the police had overlooked ten years ago. Just the sort of person I was hoping to find.

"I told no one else what I saw," Elena said. "Why risk ruining a marriage for something that might have been a minor indiscretion?"

She was looking at me as if she was desperate for my approval. "You did the right thing keeping quiet about it," I said, "and the right thing when you told me about it now."

19

When I left Elena Warshavski's apartment, I was carrying two small paper bags, both given me by Elena. One contained half a dozen rugelach, the other the pictures I'd taken from Manny Orrin. At the door, Elena shook my hand. "I'm glad you stopped by, Adam."

"I am too."

"Drop by again sometime, and we'll talk of other, nicer things."

"I will. Goodbye, Elena."

I knocked on some more doors, but learned nothing new. When I finally left Lunz Street, now carrying just the one paper bag with the pictures—I had consumed all the rugelach and tossed the other bag in the trash—it was a quarter to two. The heat was so ferocious that I felt caught between the hammer of the sun and the anvil of the baking sidewalk.

I trekked west, every few seconds tugging my shirt free of my sweat-sticky skin. At home, I dropped the bag with Esther's pictures on the table and drank a tall glass of water. I took a long shower and did not bother to towel my hair dry.

After washing my shirt at the sink and hanging it up to dry, I got into fresh clothes and headed out. In my pocket were the two pictures I had shown Elena, alongside the picture of Esther and Willie I had taken from the police report. At the Levinson Drugstore, I placed a call to Reuben Tzanani.

I asked him to check whether Manny Orrin, Alon Davidson, or Natalie Davidson had a police record, and read him the list of women I'd assembled from Orrin's albums. I said that I wanted him to check whether any of these women had died a violent death.

"Why?"

"Because then I'd have my killer."

I heard a shifting sound, as if Reuben had adjusted his posture. "Who?"

I hesitated, knowing that Reuben would feel obligated to pass on this information to his superiors. I didn't want anyone to interfere with my investigation. "Manny Orrin," I said and explained about the pictures. "But I don't want you to share this with anyone else just yet. Okay?"

"If this man's killed multiple women, Adam, I can't just sit on it."

"Agreed. But so far I don't know that he's anything but a harmless peeper. This is why you need to check if any of these women have been murdered. If they haven't, I doubt he's my man."

"What he's doing is still wrong."

"It is, but even if it's illegal, I doubt it's a serious offense."

Reuben sighed. "I suppose you're right, but I feel strange not doing anything about it."

"Let me wrap up this investigation and then you can do what you feel is right."

He agreed to wait a bit and told me to call him tomorrow afternoon. I hung up, paid Mrs. Levinson for the call, and left. Ten minutes later, I was seated at my table at Greta's, with my chessboard before me.

Just as I'd finished setting the pieces, Greta came over to my table, bearing a glass of orange juice in her hand.

"Here. Freshly squeezed, but not cold, I'm afraid. I can stick it in the refrigerator for ten minutes if you like."

"No. It's fine." And it was, pulpy and tangy and luxuriant as it went down my throat.

Greta sat down. "Guess who I saw this morning?"

"Rachel Weiss."

She raised an eyebrow. "How did you know?"

"I didn't. But it was only a matter of time before she talked to you. What did she say?"

"She told me what you did to her attacker's hand. She got quite emotional."

"I can imagine."

"Not the most pleasant conversation of my life. She accused me of connecting her to a violent madman. Did you have to break his fingers?"

"Yes," I said flatly, and was surprised to note that I felt no anger toward Rachel Weiss. A person such as her could never understand me or what I knew had to be done to Yuri. She did not have the necessary life experience. She was not like Mira Roth.

Greta nodded. "That's what I told her. 'If Adam did it, then it had to be done.' I understand she blew off at you. I'm sorry about that. I wish I never gave her your name."

"Don't. I'm glad you did."

"Really?"

I nodded. "Rachel Weiss was in real trouble, and she might have been seriously hurt if I hadn't been there that night. She may not like how I went about it, but I saved her. That's the important thing. That, and the fact that she paid me."

I smiled and Greta smiled back.

"Besides, helping her taught me an important lesson on not being arrogant."

"What do you mean?"

I told Greta about that night. I kept nothing back, apart from the glimmerings of passion I had felt. Apparently, Rachel Weiss had not told her I'd faced two men that night, because Greta's eyes grew wide when I said this. She shook her head a few times while I spoke, and gasped when I related how close I'd come to being bested by Max. She flinched when I got to the part about breaking Yuri's fingers, but told me I did the right thing. That meant something.

We sat for a while, chatting about the way the rationing regimen was turning thousands of law-abiding citizens into criminals; the thousands of Jews pouring into Israel and the many still stranded in European ports or camps, waiting to make *aliyah*; the heat and humidity of Tel Aviv; and how business at the café was slowly picking up now that the war was over.

After Greta went to serve another customer, I played a few quick games and smoked a series of cigarettes until my throat felt raw. I half-wished I could take the rest of the day off and go home and read. But more than I wanted a break from the case, I wanted to solve it. Or at least see it come to a dead end, at which point I could say to myself that I had given it a proper try and could let it go.

I placed the chessboard and pieces in their box, which I returned to its spot behind the bar. I said goodbye to Greta, hiked up Allenby, and swung a right to Ben Yehuda Street, following it north until, three doors before the corner of Ben Yehuda and Bograshov, I arrived at the address I'd copied from Natalie Davidson's letter to Mr. Sassoon.

I was in luck: the Davidsons still resided there. My luck held when my knock on their door was answered by a fair-haired boy of eleven who, after I asked if his mother was home, hollered, "Mom," over his shoulder.

A woman in late pregnancy appeared at the other end of the hall. Early thirties. Five foot four. Straight dark brown hair framing an open, good-natured plain face. Soft brown eyes that were slightly too close together, a low forehead, a nose that drew too much attention to itself. Her best feature was her skin—it shone with that radiance common to pregnant women. She wore a green-white striped dress with large pockets that ballooned over her distended belly, a thin gold necklace, and no shoes. Even from a distance of a few meters, I could tell her feet were swollen. Both her hands were pressed to her lower abdomen, as if fearful that without their support her belly would burst open under the weight of the child within.

I was struck by a sudden urge to laugh. At myself. This woman, with her bloated feet and swollen belly, did not seem capable of harming a kitten, let alone brutally killing a woman and a baby. The very idea was preposterous. But, I reminded myself, killers came in all shapes and forms, and Natalie Davidson had not been pregnant at the time of the murders.

"What did I tell you about shouting, Danny?" she said, not unkindly, to the boy, placing a hand on his shoulder.

"Not to do it," he intoned, rolling his eyes.

"That's right." The hint of a smile on her lips told me she was well aware of her son's expression, even though his back was turned. My mother had had the same uncanny ability to read my sisters and me. The similarity made me uneasy. If Natalie Davidson turned out to be a killer, I wanted her to be nothing like my mother. If she were innocent, I was liable to cause her some pain today, because I had hard questions to ask and unpleasant truths to share with her.

She shifted her eyes to me. "Can I help you?"

I gave her my name and told her I was a private investigator and that I got her address from Abraham Sassoon. "I want to talk to you about Esther and Erich Kantor," I said, using the names she would have known Esther Grunewald and Willie Ackerland by.

Her hand spasmed on her son's shoulder, squeezing it so tightly that he yelped in pain. She let go without a word, heaved a deep breath, and told me to come in.

I followed her to the living room, with the boy—Danny—close on my heels. His mother noticed his presence.

"Go to your room, Danny."

"But I want to hear," the boy protested.

Her lips bunched up, but then her face softened. From her purse she withdrew a banknote. She held it in front of the boy like a carrot before a donkey. "Take this and go buy yourself some ice cream." Danny reached for the money with eager fingers, a smile plastered on his face. "And take your brothers with you."

The smile vanished from the boy's face, replaced by a pout. "But, Mom, they're too little."

"Either take them with you or go to your room." She made as if to put the money back in her purse, but Danny plucked it from between her fingers and went yelling for his brothers. Two boys, ages six and eight, emerged from an interior room and followed their elder brother out of the apartment, chattering loudly.

After they had gone, Natalie sighed. "May God bless me with a daughter this time." She smiled self-consciously. "That sounded awful, I know, but three boys are a handful. Do you have children, Mr. Lapid?"

"No," I said, a familiar ache squeezing my heart. Whenever I was asked this question, I considered telling about my daughters, but I never did.

She asked me if I wanted anything to drink. I said I didn't. She dropped heavily onto a padded armchair, resting both feet on a low stool, and gestured for me to park myself on the sofa. Judging by the furniture, the new radio, the thick rug on the floor, and the size of the living room, the Davidsons were well-to-do. There was a tall vase filled with flowers on a table to my left and their pleasant scent filled the room.

"I was thinking about Esther earlier today," she said. She had a mellow voice, the sort that is hard to imagine ever being raised. I was again reminded of my mother, who had always exerted a quiet authority, and I had to swallow hard as a cold lump formed in the base of my throat.

"What brought that on?" I asked.

"Oh, nothing. I think of her often."

"I understand you two were close."

Her eyes were glistening. "We were. She was my best friend. We used to spend a lot of time together—us and the children— and I used to watch over Erich for her. He was a lovely boy, a truly beautiful boy." Her voice cracked on that last word, and so did whatever dam was holding back her tears. They streamed down her cheeks in rivulets. She started to heave herself up from her seat, but her weight was making it a challenge. She gestured toward the dining table. "Get me a napkin, please." There were a number of pink napkins standing upright in a metal holder, folded like fans. I handed her one and she pressed it to her eyes.

During my years as a policeman, I'd met people—men and women both—who could turn on the eye faucets at a moment's notice and *voila!* the tears would start flowing. It's a neat trick, one used by the craftiest of criminals. The best have it down to a fine art, where you can't tell that they're faking. Watching Natalie cry, I concluded there were two options. Either she was truly heartbroken by the murders, or she was one of those rare black souls who can cry on command and affect the expression and mannerisms for it to appear natural.

It took a minute for the tears to stop. Then, still watching her face closely, I asked her directly, "Did you know Esther wasn't Erich's real mother?"

There was surprise on her face, but not as much as I'd expected.

I leaned closer. "You did know."

She twisted the napkin between her fingers. Her nails were short. "No. No, I didn't. I knew that some of the things she told me about herself were not true, just not that. I never suspected that. If she wasn't his mother, what was she doing with him?"

I gave her a two-sentence-long version of the truth. It made her weepy again. Half of the napkin I'd handed her had darkened with her tears by the time her sobbing ceased.

"Have you a cigarette, by any chance?"

I lit one for her and another for myself. She puffed on hers greedily a number of times. Coughing, she waved the smoke away from her eyes, laughing a self-deprecating laugh. "I don't even like smoking all that much, but it does soothe the nerves, don't you agree?"

I shrugged. "I just smoke because I like it."

She took a long pull on her cigarette, then handed me the still-burning remnant. "There's an ashtray on the table there."

I crushed out her cigarette and tapped some ash off mine.

"So Esther's real surname was Grunewald? And Erich was actually Willie?"

"Yes."

"I never knew."

This, I believed, was the truth. I could see no upside for her in lying to me about that. Not if she was innocent. Not if she was guilty. Did the fact that Esther had kept her true identity a secret from Natalie say anything about their friendship? It might be an indication that they weren't as close as Natalie claimed. But, more likely, Esther had simply followed Mira's instruction not to tell a soul her real name.

"What did Esther tell you that wasn't true?" I said.

"She told me her husband was a sailor who'd died at sea. My husband is a fisherman. As a fisherman's wife, I know quite a bit about sailing and seafaring, and it quickly became clear to me that Esther didn't, that the story she told me was false."

"Ever call her out on it?"

"Never. I assumed that Erich's—I mean Willie's—father was alive and well, and that he and Esther had never been married. I understood full well why she would lie. Society frowns on women who have children out of wedlock. I didn't want her to feel as if I were judging her, so I never raised the issue."

"You never suspected that she wasn't Willie's mother?"

Natalie inclined her head an inch to the right, considering. "Well, I remember remarking on the fact that she never breastfed him, but Esther said she had no milk. Some mothers are like that; it's actually quite common. With the way she cared for him, with such love and devotion, I never would have guessed she wasn't his mother."

"What did the two of you do together?"

"Just what young mothers do—spend time with the children or talk about them." She gave a faint smile. "You men don't realize how consuming caring for a baby is. It swallows up practically all your time and energy."

"I'm surprised you agreed to take care of Willie, it being so hard."

"Just because it's hard doesn't mean I don't enjoy it. I love children, especially babies. Besides, I was already at home with my own baby at the time, and the little money Esther paid me came in handy. I liked earning my own money. And Willie was a sweet child. Not fussy or noisy. Easy to care for."

"How often did you watch over him?"

"Every day when Esther was at work, and during some evenings when she went dancing. Esther loved to dance. Sometimes she would put on the radio in her or my apartment and we would dance together." A dreamy smile flickered across her mouth and some color seeped into her cheeks. "It was fun. How we would laugh."

"I understand Esther went dancing quite often."

Natalie nodded. "Twice a week. Sometimes three. At a club called *The Sun*, at the bottom of Hayarkon Street."

I nodded to myself. Rivlin had interviewed the manager of *The Sun* and some of the employees who'd worked there. They had all said Esther invariably arrived at the club alone, never left with anyone, and never danced with any particular man. I planned on paying the club a visit later that day.

"She ever leave the baby with you overnight?"

A resolute shake of the head. "Sometimes she would pick him up pretty late. Ten, or even eleven, but she never left him with me at night."

I killed what remained of my cigarette. "The night of the murders, you were alone in your apartment?"

"Danny was with me, of course, but my husband was on his boat."

No alibi, I thought. *And she lived just one floor below the murder scene.*

"And you heard nothing?"

She shook her head. "Not a thing."

"Can you think of anyone Esther may have angered or hurt? Even something that appears minor may be important."

"No. No one."

"What about Esther herself? How was she in her final days? Was she happy? Was anything bothering her?"

Natalie rubbed her chin. "Now that I think of it, Esther did say something about having problems at work. She didn't tell me what it was precisely, only that it was nothing she couldn't handle."

This was new. There had been no mention of any work-related

problems in Rivlin's report. On the contrary, Esther's boss and colleagues had all been effusive in their praise of her.

"When was this?"

"A few days before she died. Two or three, no more than five. A week at the outside."

"Did she mention anyone specifically? Her boss? A colleague?"

"No." She looked at me with widened eyes. "Do you think that someone she worked with could have...?" Her voice trailed off, and it occurred to me that, if she were the killer, she might be making this up, feeding me false information in the hope that I would waste my time looking for something that wasn't there instead of at her.

"Why didn't you say anything about this to the police ten years ago?"

She lowered her chin, her posture a bit defensive. "I'm not sure that I didn't. I don't remember. Like I said, Esther told me it wasn't important."

Was she making this up on the fly? I couldn't be sure. I made a mental note to ask Esther's boss and colleagues about it.

"Was Esther seeing anyone?" I asked, changing the subject.

"No."

"No men came calling? No one hung around the building?"

She shook her head.

"Esther never mentioned anyone? Someone she'd met in the dance club, perhaps?"

"No one."

"Did you find this strange? I've seen pictures of Esther. She was a gorgeous woman."

"I asked her about it several times," she said. "Did she meet anyone at the club or at work? She said she wasn't looking for a man at the moment, that she was still in mourning for her dead husband. Of course I knew that wasn't true. I thought maybe she was still in love with Willie's father. Now I know that this wasn't the case either. But there were times when I'd catch her smiling to herself, as if at some romantic thought. And there were nights when she would come back from the dance club and there would be a glow to her skin that made me think that she had...well, you know—" She trailed off, and this time the red in her cheeks was prominent.

"That she had been with a man?" I completed, as the silence lengthened.

She nodded, looking grateful that I had spared her from having to finish her sentence.

This was not something I had expected. Either Natalie was playing an elaborate game, or she was completely blind to what her husband and best friend had been up to. I felt a sudden stab of shame in the pit of my stomach at what I was about to do. But there was no alternative. Best to do it quickly.

"Is your husband home at the moment?"

She blinked. "My husband? No. He's on his boat, working."

"When will he be back? I'd like to speak to him."

"He won't be back until tomorrow morning. But I doubt he can tell you much. He barely knew Esther."

I raised an eyebrow. "How can that be, you two were so close?"

"Alon—that's my husband—worked very hard during those days. He was away often. He and Esther never seemed to connect."

"Still, he must have had an impression of her."

"I suppose so." She paused, cocking her head to the right and glancing at me through eyes that had suddenly gone narrower. "Why do you ask?"

Instead of answering, I said, "Was your husband away often during the evening and night?"

"Yes. Just like today, he would be at sea."

"Did any of those times coincide with the evenings Esther went out dancing, leaving you with Willie?"

Natalie froze. For a moment, it seemed that she wasn't even

breathing, and I was worried she might faint. Then her eyes twitched and did a wild sort of dance. I imagined that a similar turbulence was swirling through her mind. Emotions rippled across her face, most fading too quickly to read, but the profound hurt she felt was evident. It was clear that my question had surprised, even stunned her. Looking at her, the dagger of shame in my stomach twisted, cutting deeper. This short, homely, pregnant housewife did not look like a killer. She did not seem capable of slitting the throat of a woman, stabbing a baby through the heart, and then disfiguring the two of them. What she looked like was a mother—warm, kind, gentle and loving. In all likelihood, I had just caused an innocent woman a great deal of pain.

She gave a tiny shake of the head, little more than a tremor. I remained silent, not answering the question in her eyes: *Did you just ask what I think you asked?*

Along with the question, her eyes showed instinctive denial swiftly followed by doubt. Was she casting her mind ten years into the past, thinking back on those evenings on which she had babysat Willie? Was she grasping at any explanation that might help her deny an awful truth? I realized that there was no need to tell her of Elena Warshavski and the kiss she'd witnessed, that the seed of suspicion had already been there in her mind. Perhaps it was planted when she'd caught her husband looking at Esther in a particular way. Perhaps it had been the other way around. Or perhaps it was simply the general fear of the plain wife with the irresistibly beautiful unmarried friend, that it would take but a playful bat of the eyelashes or a suggestive sway of the hips for the friend to steal her husband away.

Natalie shut her eyes tight and took a shuddering breath. Her eyes were dry when she opened them, and her entire body was rigid, as if she was exerting tremendous willpower to maintain control of herself. Her hands were pressed hard to her belly. She strained to keep her voice even, but it quavered just a bit when she spoke.

"No, Mr. Lapid. None of the times Alon was away coincided with the evenings I watched over Willie."

I said nothing. I knew she was lying, and she knew I knew.

"And now I think you should leave."

For a few seconds I remained seated, not moving. Her jaw was clenched, her mouth pinched, her eyes unwavering, as if challenging me to call out her lie. I did not. What would be the point? I would get nothing more from her. At least not now. It didn't matter whether the suspicion I raised was justified or not. I was a stranger and I had attacked the thing she valued most: her family. That made me the enemy.

I stood up. She followed me with her eyes. They were hard and cold as freezing metal. I forced myself to meet them.

"I'm sorry if I hurt you," I said.

Her expression did not change. She did not want my apology. She wanted no more words out of me. "Just leave. Just go."

On the street outside her building, I paused to light a cigarette. I wasn't feeling too proud of myself, even though I had only done my job, what I knew I would do once I stepped over Natalie Davidson's threshold. I told myself I'd not caused her pain for nothing. I'd learned some valuable things. I'd learned that Esther Grunewald had had a romantic relationship and that the idea of Alon Davidson having an affair with her was not unthinkable to his wife. Crossing the street, I glanced back and saw Natalie standing at her window, peering down at me. I couldn't read her expression. Seeing my upturned face, she drew the curtain.

I turned west on Bograshov, walked slowly past London Square, and swung south at the coastline, my shoes thudding on the narrow promenade with the sea to my right. The laughter of beachgoers mingled with the crash of waves on the shore, pierced now and then by the bellows of ice-cream vendors hawking their melting wares. Gulls swooped overhead like airplanes on a bombing raid.

I found a table at a seaside café, grabbed a beer and a grilled cheese toast, and sat watching the sea reflecting the softened afternoon sun and the people bathing in the surf. A radio behind the bar was playing something with plenty of violin and cello. It sounded like German music. Melodramatic and dark and foreboding.

At a nearby table, a bearded man with a missing arm sat reading a slim book. He laid the volume on the table whenever he needed to flip pages, before picking it up in his remaining hand to resume reading. I wondered when and how he'd lost his arm. Was it in Europe? During Israel's War of Independence? Or another calamity? There had been so many of them these past ten years. I had a sudden urge to walk over to him, introduce myself, and ask him what had happened.

I didn't. Instead, I gulped the last of the beer and wolfed down the remains of the toast. Neither tasted very good, but I wasn't in the habit of throwing away food.

I continued south past Ha-Knesset Square, where the Israeli parliament held its sessions, and kept walking till I got to the spot where *The Sun* dance club had once been. Once and no more. Now only a blackened, hollow shell of a building stood, its doorway and ground-floor windows boarded shut, the windows in the second floor gaping empty black squares. Shards of glass and garbage littered the narrow courtyard, where yellow and green weeds abounded. The stench of old decay and rot hung over the place.

"Burned down," a hoarse voice to my right said.

I had been staring at the building. Now I turned toward the voice and saw a shrunken silver-haired woman wearing a shabby blue dress so faded that it must have been washed a hundred times or more. A basket dangled from her right forearm. Her accent was Russian. Deep lines gouged her cheeks. She could have been sixty or seventy-five.

"When did it happen?"

"1945. During the summer. There used to be dancing here."

"I know."

"Yes. Plenty of dancing. Not just husbands and wives, but all sorts of men and women." She shook her head, bemoaning the immorality of unattached couples dancing. "The racket the place made, the loud music. It hurt my ears."

"You live here?"

"Around the corner."

"Do you know what caused the fire?"

"Some say it was arson, that a man whose wife spent time there got angry and torched the place. The police said it was an accident. Someone left a burning cigarette, some alcohol caught on fire, and up went the whole place."

"Do you know where I can find the owner, Mr. Segev?"

"Died in the fire. He and an employee." Her lips curled. "A woman. Not his wife."

"And the rest of the people who worked here?"

A shrug. "Don't know. Haven't seen any of them in a long time."

I returned my eyes to the building. Rivlin's interviews with Mr. Segev and his staff had yielded no leads. Still, I would have liked to talk to them myself, to maybe shake something loose in their memories. Now it appeared I had encountered another dead end.

More in desperation than belief, I showed the old woman the three pictures of Esther, the two from Manny Orrin and the one of her and Willie I'd lifted from the police report. "Remember her, by any chance? She used to dance here."

The woman squinted so hard at the pictures, it looked like she'd fallen asleep on her feet. The lines on her face deepened to canals. Then she shook her head, handing the pictures back to me.

"Don't remember seeing her. Who is she?"

"Her name was Esther," I said, the bitter taste of disappointment on my tongue.

"What's she done?"

"She died."

"Oh." The news didn't seem to faze her. "So many people have been dying lately."

20

Punching Manny Orrin had earned me a night of undisturbed sleep. I awoke at six, feeling almost fresh, and stayed in bed, smoking and reading one of the westerns Goldberg had sold me. The protagonist, a Texas cowboy with a shock of blond hair and a sun-beaten face, seemed to never be without a cigarette in his mouth. He smoked when he rode, when he was gunning down bad guys, even while he was having dinner in a cabin with the pretty rancher's widow he was helping out. It was a good yarn. Not the best I'd read, and certainly not original in terms of plot, but still enjoyable. It was seven thirty when I turned the last page and set the book aside with a sense of satisfaction. Then I got up, washed and shaved, and went to the kitchen. I boiled an egg and sliced it into strips, which, along with a couple of juicy sardines, I slapped between two buttered slices of dark bread. After eating, I slipped on some clothes and went in search of more people who had known Esther.

On Dizengoff Street, sandwiched between an accounting firm and a dentist's clinic, stood the offices of *Becker & Strauss*, the law firm where Esther had worked as a secretary. It occupied a two-story square building, with tall windows and no balconies. A sign on the door proclaimed that the firm had been established in 1907, which meant that it had once had a different location, since the city of Tel Aviv was founded in 1909.

Beyond the door was a reception room, at the far end of which was a large desk topped by a typewriter and stacks of paper. Behind the desk sat a young, pretty secretary, and behind her stood a row of filing cabinets.

I stepped up to the desk, introduced myself, and asked if I could see Mr. Strauss, Esther's boss. The secretary told me he was out and wouldn't be in before noon. "But if it's a legal issue, maybe one of the associates can help you."

Maybe they could, I told her, and asked if either of the two associates who had worked in the firm ten years ago were around —Itamar Levine and Alex Fishman.

The secretary's face turned sad. She was eighteen or nineteen, had been a child when Esther died, younger even than what Willie Ackerland would have been today had he lived. She told me Alex Fishman had died fighting in Jerusalem against the Jordanians, and that Itamar Levine no longer worked for the firm.

"I never met either of them," she added. "I've only been working here for six months. The girl I replaced in this job told me about Fishman. I read about Levine in the files."

"Was her name Leah Benowitz? The girl you replaced, I mean." Leah Benowitz had worked as a secretary for Becker & Strauss, alongside Esther, and had claimed to have been her best friend when interviewed by Rivlin.

"No. Leah Benowitz hasn't worked here for a few years. I never met her either. I think she left when she got married."

"Can you give me her current address? Or the last one you have on file?"

She hesitated. "I'm not sure I'm supposed to."

I explained who I was and that I was investigating the murder of a former employee of the firm. "Ever heard of Esther Kantor?"

She shook her head, now looking not just sad but frightened. She absently fingered a fine silver bracelet that hung on her slender right wrist, still hesitant. She gave me a searching look, apparently decided I was trustworthy, and told me to wait a minute. She rose from her chair, went over to a filing cabinet, and began leafing through a row of folders. She tugged one out, opened it, and read off an address on Ibn Gabirol Street.

I scribbled the address in my notebook. "How about Itamar Levine's address?"

She consulted another folder. "He doesn't live in Tel Aviv anymore. He got a job with a firm in Haifa. Modai, Danzinger & Knobel. I don't have a residential address for him, but I got a phone number for the firm."

I wrote down the number and thanked her and left.

Twenty minutes later, a block north of the city zoo on Ibn Gabirol, I mounted the stairs to the second floor of a nondescript residential building and knocked on the door to apartment four.

A woman in her early twenties answered the door. She wasn't Leah Benowitz and had never met her. "Ask the landlady down-stairs. Maybe she knows where this Benowitz woman is."

The landlady was sixty and rail thin and had a reedy voice. "Why're you looking for Leah?" she said, eying me with suspicion.

I produced a smile and told her I was a private investigator working for a law firm. "I am required to notify Ms. Benowitz that her mother's cousin died and left her a sizable inheritance."

That got the desired reaction. The landlady invited me in and asked me to sit while she rifled through a chest of papers and found a forwarding address on Borochov Street. "Her name is Goldin now."

At the door the landlady asked me how big the inheritance was. I winked and said, "It's confidential. I'm sure you understand."

———

Leah Goldin—née Benowitz—was absolutely charmed to learn of my profession.

"A detective? Like Philip Marlowe?"

My bewilderment must have shown, because she explained, "From the movie *The Big Sleep* with Humphrey Bogart and Lauren Bacall. Don't tell me you haven't seen it."

I confessed that I hadn't.

"Oh," Leah said, laying a hand on my arm, "you definitely should. Lauren Bacall is so beautiful, and the two of them together on the screen—it's pure magic." She looked me up and down. "You don't look like Humphrey Bogart." It was unclear whether she meant this as a compliment or a criticism, so I said nothing. "People have told me I could be in the movies. What do you think?"

She still had not invited me in. I was standing on the third-floor landing; she was still holding the front door to her apartment with her left hand. Now she let go of the door to strike a pose. She planted her left hand on her hip, the right she bunched to a fist, except for an extended index finger, the tip of which she'd placed on the underside of her chin. Tilting her head slightly to the back and left, she cocked her right hip. Finally, she parted and puffed out her lips, as if about to give a kiss, while her eyes narrowed in a feeble attempt at sultriness. All in all, it was a weird combination of gestures and affectations, none of which looked natural or appealing, all of which I assumed she'd copied from movies.

After five seconds of increasingly awkward silence, I realized she was waiting for me to answer. Estimating that a compliment was likelier to get me in the door than the truth, I lied. "You have star quality. No doubt about it."

Leah beamed.

She had a face made for beaming, youthful and smooth and

innocent, framed by a shower of brown curls. The smile dug dimples in her plump rosy cheeks and made her light brown eyes sparkle. She had a pert nose and a small pink mouth set in the middle of a round face. She reminded me of pictures of fairies in one of the children's books I had read for my daughters. She was five two and bosomy in a blue housedress with red dots. She was barefoot. Her feet were tiny. If not for the onset of laugh lines at the corners of her eyes and mouth, she might have been mistaken for a buxom fifteen-year-old. Her age, I knew from the police report, was thirty.

Truth was, she was pretty, but hardly on the level of movie actresses.

She looked so utterly happy with my lie that I hated having to ruin her mood.

I told her what I was there to talk to her about. Her face fell. She pressed one hand to her cheek and shook her head.

"What an awful thing. I must have cried for a week straight when I heard the news. Well, come in, come in. I'd be happy to help."

I followed her down a hall that opened onto a narrow kitchen on the left and a larger living room on the right. Children's toys lay scattered on the rug and coffee table.

"Forgive the mess," she said. "The children...they just throw their things everywhere. No matter how often I tell them to tidy up after themselves, they never listen. You have children, Adam? I can call you Adam, can't I?"

"No and yes. No, I don't have children, and, yes, you can call me Adam. How old are your children?"

"Four and two. Boy and girl. Can you believe that I have two children? Most people think I'm too young." She flashed a coquettish smile. Her breath smelled faintly of sugar. "They're at my mother-in-law's now. Which is the only good thing about having her live nearby. I do love the two monsters so, but they can be draining. If it weren't for them, I wouldn't look so worn out." She let out a theatrical sigh of desperation, then peered at me expectantly. It took me a moment to realize that she was waiting for some response from me.

"You don't look tired," I offered lamely, but it appeared to satisfy her. She took my arm and steered me toward a two-seater. She sat next to me, curling her feet under her. Then she shook her head playfully and let out a chuckle.

"Where are my manners? I haven't offered you anything to drink."

"I'm fine," I said.

"Sure? I can make some coffee, or do you feel like some red wine? I know they say drinking alcohol before dinner is bad for you, but I've read that in America lots of people do. Have you been to America, Adam?"

"No."

"I so desperately want to go," she said, her hand still on my arm. "When I see movies, I picture myself in those huge cities with the buildings so high they pierce the clouds. Or when I listen to big band music on the radio, I imagine those nightclubs with all the glamorous people dancing and drinking champagne. I sometimes can't help but feel angry that when my parents chose to leave Poland, they came here instead of America. What were they thinking? Can you imagine how glorious my life could have been?"

I nodded slowly, though inside I was burning with indignation. Leah Goldin, I realized, was the sort of self-centered person who believed she deserved far more than what life had given her, the sort who invariably blames others for her perceived misfortune.

A part of me wanted to grab her by the shoulders, shake her hard, and yell in her face that she should be thankful that her parents had found the fortitude to uproot themselves and immigrate to a land they knew only from Jewish history and tradition. That by doing so, they had surely saved their daughter's life. That I blamed myself for not having the foresight to do the same. That my family was dead because of my blindness.

I gritted my teeth, biting back the words. Hitting her with the truth would do no good. It would only alienate her, and I needed her cooperation.

"Do you have a cigarette?" Leah said, jerking me out of my furious thoughts.

I yanked the pack out of my pocket and tapped one out for her. I fired up a match. She leaned forward toward the light, cigarette stuck in her small mouth, laying a steadying hand on mine as she brought match and cigarette together. Then she took a pull, making a face before tilting her head back and blowing out a cloud of smoke at the ceiling.

"You must be a strong man to smoke such potent tobacco." She was giving me a half-lidded stare, one that sent a message that was impossible to mistake. On the wall above the sofa hung a large framed wedding picture of Leah Goldin and her husband. She was beaming again, all in white—her dress, her earrings, her necklace, her veil, and the bouquet of daisies in her hands. He was a lanky man wearing a three-piece gray suit and a self-conscious smile. He was looking directly ahead, but also appeared to be gazing down at us. I shifted slightly away from her, my back pressed against the armrest.

"About Esther Kantor," I said, "you two were friends?"

"Oh, yes. The very best of friends. We worked together, side by side, every day."

"You were already at Becker & Strauss when Esther was hired?"

"I started two years before she did."

"She settled in fine?"

Leah nodded. "I helped her of course, showed her where everything went, how things worked. She caught on quickly. Esther was a smart girl."

"She told you things about herself, about her life?"

173

"Of course. We would talk a lot. I remember feeling sorry for her because she had to raise a child all on her own. You know her husband drowned?"

So Esther had not revealed her true identity to Leah, and Leah had not seen through her lie the way Natalie Davidson had. But maybe Esther did share other parts of her life with Leah.

"Did she tell you about her lover?" I asked.

Leah blinked, clearly surprised. "You know about him?"

"Yes. Alon Davidson."

A glass ashtray lay on a side table by the sofa behind Leah. She twisted around, showing me her back while she mashed out the cigarette. She turned back to face me. "Yes. She told me about him."

So, I thought, *Elena's eyes had not deceived her.*

"What did she say about him?"

Leah hesitated. "Not all that much. I don't feel comfortable revealing intimate details."

She hadn't needed to tell me that last bit. I could tell as much by her tense posture and the shift in her manner. Her flirtatious bubbliness had evaporated. The gravity of the subject of our conversation had finally dawned on her.

"Did she tell you how serious they were? Whether they had plans for him to leave his wife?"

"Oh, they were very serious," Leah said. "Esther was in love with him, I think, though she never said so in so many words. I asked her if they were going to be together, but she said it was too soon."

"I see. You ever meet him?"

She shook her head.

"What about Davidson's wife? Did Esther ever express any qualms about sleeping with her husband?"

Leah lowered her gaze. A few curly strands of hair fell across her face. "I'm sure she felt bad about it, but sometimes you can't help yourself when you're in love, can you?"

I supposed that was true, but it still rankled. I hated the thought of Esther betraying Natalie Davidson. It changed the way I saw her. Up to this point I'd had an idealized image of Esther. She was this brave, generous soul who had taken a strange baby with her on a long and arduous journey, who had nurtured him for months and was planning on doing so for months more. Her doing something bad and dishonorable—like having an affair with a close friend's husband—had been unimaginable.

Now I saw her in a different light—not as some paragon of goodness, but as a woman of virtues and vices, of good deeds and sins.

It changed nothing. I was still determined to catch her killer. For one thing, he or she had also murdered an innocent baby, and there was no excuse or justification for that. For another, while she had betrayed Natalie Davidson and might have committed other sins I was unaware of, Esther Grunewald had not deserved to die.

"How long was the affair?" I asked.

"Two months, if I remember right."

"Were they getting along? Think back to the final two weeks of her life—did Esther say they had a fight, an argument?"

She thought for a moment. "No, I don't remember anything like that." Then her eyes grew big, making her look more like a child than ever before. "Why? Do you think this man—Davidson —might be the killer?"

"No," I admitted. "I have no evidence to that effect. I'm just asking questions."

"I understand." Leah heaved a breath. "I don't think I can tell you more about the affair. Like I said, Esther didn't tell me all that much about it, about him."

I nodded. Time to move on.

"Did Esther talk a lot about Erich?" I asked.

"All the time," Leah said, clearly eased by the change of subject. "Erich did this and Erich did that, and how cute he was when he smiled, or even when he cried."

"She loved him a lot."

"Oh, yes. Well, it stands to reason, doesn't it? She was his mother."

I considered telling her the truth, but decided against it. Telling Natalie Davidson had yielded no new details. I doubted enlightening Leah as to Esther's true name and identity would prove different.

I said, "I know Esther went out dancing a lot, to a club on Hayarkon Street. Ever go with her?"

Leah said that she hadn't.

"So you have no idea if she ever met a man in that club? Or if anyone ever approached her too forcefully?"

"No, I don't."

"What about at work?"

"What about work?" Leah asked.

"Did any client ever show any undue interest in Esther?"

"No."

"That seems hard to believe, she was so beautiful."

"Oh, I thought you meant did anyone step over the line. Sure, clients used to flirt with her, with both of us. That's what men do—there was no harm in it. You learn how to let them down easy, without hurting their feelings. I taught Esther how to do that."

"No one tried too hard?"

"No. No one. I would have known if anyone had."

Which left Alon Davidson as the only man in Esther's life. Someone who was in an illicit relationship with her, a relationship he had kept secret from the police.

But he had an alibi, I reminded myself. Unless that alibi was false, he could not have been the killer.

I needed to go talk to Davidson. Just as soon as I heard from Reuben whether he had a history with the police.

Having the affair confirmed was enough to make my visit to Leah Goldin worthwhile, but perhaps she could solve another little mystery for me.

"Was Esther happy working at Becker & Strauss?"

"Yes. It's a great place to work. Mr. Strauss is a wonderful man, a wonderful boss. You talked to him?"

"Not yet. I went by the firm earlier, but he was out. So Esther told you nothing about having trouble at work?"

Leah slowly shook her head.

"It would have been in the last few days of her life. According to her neighbor, she was upset about something related to her job. Any idea what it might have been?"

"No. The neighbor didn't know?"

"Esther was vague about it, she said."

"It was probably not that serious, then."

"Maybe not," I said, remembering Natalie Davidson telling me that Esther had assured her she could handle this problem, whatever it was. Still, I was disappointed that Leah Goldin could not fill in this gap in my knowledge.

I scratched my knee through the fabric of my pants. Leah clasped her hands together over one thigh. Her expression was one of solemn reflection. Probably thinking about Esther.

As the silence lengthened, I gave Leah a long look, reconsidering my early assessment of her. She was flighty and self-centered, but that was not all she was. Esther must have known a different side to Leah to have confided in her about her affair with Alon Davidson. In her way, Leah had been a friend to Esther, had cared for her, and had mourned her loss. I could tell by her face that merely talking about Esther and the murders had a deep effect on her. She appeared withdrawn and worn out. Her eyes were downcast, shoulders slightly hunched.

I reached over and touched her shoulder. She started.

"Sorry," I said, withdrawing my hand. "I didn't mean to scare you."

She chuckled. "It's my fault. I was just...someplace else for a minute."

"I understand," I said. "The past can be a dark place."

"Yes. Yes, it can."

"I should get going. Thank you for talking to me."

She walked me to the door and mumbled a goodbye. I heard the snick of the lock before clearing half a flight of stairs.

21

It was just shy of eleven when I exited Leah Goldin's building. Too early to pay Becker & Strauss another visit. Too early for lunch. But Lunz Street was a five-minute walk away, and Haim Sassoon was due back from his army unit that morning, so that was where I went.

Haim Sassoon was so similar to his father, the two might have been cast from the same mold, only twenty-something years apart. Their height and build were almost identical, as were their facial features and hair. But unlike his father's, the skin on Haim's face was unmarked by age or acne scars, giving him a look of youthful innocence.

His father had accompanied me upstairs to his son's apartment. Haim's wife had gone out and taken their baby boy with her, so there were only the three of us. The elder Sassoon and I sat side by side on the sofa while Haim poured coffee into three glasses before taking a chair. The brew had the same scent as the coffee his father had offered me when I visited him—harsh and bitter. I took a careful sip and found that its taste did not stray far from its scent, but both father and son relished it.

Haim Sassoon was in uniform, sleeves rolled up his thin biceps, dog tags hanging on a chain outside his shirt. He had removed his army boots but still had on the thick woolen socks that went with them. He looked tired, as soldiers often do. I told him I was sorry for keeping him from his bed.

He waved a hand. "Don't be. Dad told me what you're doing. I want to help any way I can."

"Good," I said. "You were twelve when the murders took place. You remember the victims?"

"Sure. I used to see them almost every day."

"Did Esther ever talk to you?"

"Oh, sure. She was very nice. Whenever she saw me, she'd ask how I was doing, how was school, things like that. I remember one time I was playing in the street with some friends and Esther walked by. She called out to me and smiled and waved. My friends were full of questions: Who was she? Where did I know her from? How old was she? I felt so proud knowing this beautiful woman." He gave his father a sheepish smile and added by way of explanation, "I was a boy then."

"Did you ever see her with any men?"

"No," Haim said.

"No one you remember hanging around the building?"

No, again.

"Do you remember Alon Davidson?"

"Sure. One time he taught me how to tie a special knot, like they use on boats. For a time, I wanted to be a fisherman when I grew up. First time I stepped on a boat, I got so seasick I thought I might die. That was the end of my sailing dreams."

"Ever see him with Esther when his wife wasn't around?"

He shook his head. I turned to his father, who I could see was frowning at me from his end of the sofa. "How about you?"

"Don't recall seeing them together," the elder Sassoon said

stiffly. He obviously did not approve of the implication of my question. "Why are you asking this?"

"Just something I'm trying to clear up," I said, quickly turning back to Haim and changing the subject. "Think back to the day of the murders. Did you see anyone lurking around, someone who didn't belong?"

Haim took a sip of coffee. "I don't remember anyone. I'm sorry." He looked disappointed with himself that he was giving me so little.

"No need to apologize. What about that night, did you hear anything?"

"Just the baby crying."

"What time was this?" I asked, sitting up straight. Nowhere in the police report had this been mentioned.

"I don't know. I didn't check my watch. I just remember waking up and hearing a baby crying. It wasn't unusual. I'm not even sure I told the detective about it at the time. There were two babies in the building: the Davidson kid and Erich Kantor. Babies cry."

"But you remember it still, so something must have been different."

Haim gave a cautious nod. "If it hadn't been on that particular night, I'd probably not remember it at all, but I remember the crying sounded very loud, louder than it usually did. Then it gradually grew softer, and then it died down completely." He paused. His eyes became huge brown orbs. "Died down—you think that what I heard was the baby being killed?"

"I don't know," I answered truthfully. But it fit in with the scenario Rivlin had painted. I could picture the scene: Willie Ackerland is wrenched from sleep by the sound of Esther being slaughtered. He senses the wrongness of the situation and is struck by fear. The fear rises to sheer panic by the sight of the stranger in the room, by the smell of blood. He opens his little mouth and begins shrieking. The sound reaches Haim's ears. It's louder than usual because this is no ordinary crying. Then the killer acts. Maybe he tries putting a hand over Willie's mouth, partially muffling his cries; or maybe he stabs down with his knife. The knife finds the heart and Willie's cries quickly subside in volume as his life flickers out.

So yes, Haim Sassoon indeed might have heard Willie's death cries.

I said, "Are you sure you can't say at what time you heard this? Not even a rough estimate?"

Haim shook his head, his expression close to despair.

"It's all right," I said, warding off the pointless apology or excuse that I could see coming. "You couldn't have known what was happening." I smiled a reassuring smile, but I was cursing inside. If Haim could have told me at what time he'd heard a baby crying, I might have known the exact hour the murders took place. All I had now was the frustrating sense of being close to a crucial piece of information, only to see it slip from my grasp.

"You did good," I told him, feeding him the lie that would make him feel better. "You helped."

"Yeah?" He smiled, relieved.

"Yeah."

I started to get up, extending my hand to him, when I caught a contemplative look on his face.

"What?" I said.

"It's funny, but a memory just popped into my head. I'm not sure how useful you'll find it."

I sat back down, elbows on thighs, hands clasped together between my knees. "Let me hear what it is and I'll decide."

"It was a few days before the murders," Haim said. "I can't say for sure how many. Two, maybe four or five, no more than that. I was walking down Rothschild Boulevard and I saw Esther sitting on a bench. She was talking with a woman—more accurately, the woman was doing most of the talking. She was angry. She wasn't shouting, but I could tell by her gestures."

"Angry with Esther?"

"Yes. I think so. I couldn't hear what she was saying."

"Did you tell Sergeant Rivlin about this?"

"No," he said sheepishly.

"Why not?"

Haim shrugged helplessly. "I didn't think it was important. He only asked me about men whom I might have seen with Esther." Then he added by way of an excuse, "I was a boy."

There it was again, I thought, Rivlin's assumption that the killer had to be male. And my assumption as well, I hated to admit.

"It's all right," I said. "Was this woman familiar?"

"No."

"You never saw her before?"

"I don't think so."

"How did she look?"

Haim tried to recall her image, but soon gave up. "I don't remember."

"Think," I said. "Take as long as you need. Close your eyes. Clear your mind. Try to reach the memory. I'll help you."

Haim shut his eyes, and I started walking him through what he remembered of that day: what the weather was like, how he was feeling, what time of day it was, the clothes Esther was wearing. It was a technique I had learned as a policeman, whereby getting a witness to recall some details connected to a scene made it easier for him to recall even more details—including those you most wanted him to remember.

I worked at it for half an hour, trying one angle and then another, often asking the same question a half-dozen different ways, but Haim kept drawing a blank. He remembered the scene —the place, the weather, the mood of the participants—and he remembered Esther, of course, but he did not recall a single thing about the appearance of the woman who had been angry with her. Not her build, not her age, not her complexion, not even her clothes. Finally, in desperation, I described the women I had encountered on my investigation—a tactic I knew held the risk of corrupting his memory. Nothing.

Throughout all this, Haim's face bore an expression of intense concentration. I had to give him credit—he gave it his all. It was I who finally decided to stop.

"Stop?" Haim said. "No. Let's try some more." He looked exhausted. I had worked him hard mentally. He seemed so crestfallen by his failure at recollection that I was prompted to offer a comforting lie.

"Not today. We'll try again another time." When I saw that didn't improve his mood, I added, "You did good. You helped a lot."

He brightened. "Yeah?"

"Yeah," I said.

22

After my talk with Haim Sassoon, I spent another hour on Lunz Street, knocking on doors and talking to neighbors who were not home the previous time I'd canvassed the street. I learned nothing new.

Before leaving Lunz Street, I gazed up at Elena Warshavski's balcony, thinking I could use another drink of lemonade. She wasn't there. I thought about climbing the stairs and seeing if she was home, but decided against it. It is one thing to be invited; it is another to try to invite yourself.

Around the corner on Rothschild Boulevard stood the grocery store where Esther had done her shopping. I showed her picture to the manager. He remembered her, but had no information regarding the murders. A canvass of nearby stores proved equally fruitless.

I grabbed a quick lunch at home, changed my shirt, and went out again into the searing heat of early afternoon. It was one thirty when I stepped into the reception room of Becker & Strauss for the second time.

The secretary smiled when she saw me.

"Mr. Strauss is in," she said, "but he's in the middle of a meeting and it might take a while."

"How long do you think?" I said.

"Half an hour, give or take."

I told her I'd wait, and she asked me if I wanted anything to drink. When I said that I didn't, she pointed to a corner with a gray couch, a couple of chairs, and a hat stand bearing a fedora and a homburg. Then she proceeded to ignore my presence, fixing her attention on her typewriter.

I sat on the couch and smoked while she clacked away on her keys with impressive speed. A number of newspapers lay on a low table, and I riffled through them, catching up on the news. Shmuel Birnbaum had a column on the condition of Jewish refugees still stuck in various ports and camps in Europe, desperate to be allowed to come to Israel. He had a good writing style—factual, direct, without the proclivity to flowery language that some of his colleagues suffered from.

While I waited, four men in button-down shirts and ties wandered singly or in pairs in and out from adjacent offices, handing papers to the secretary or grabbing a cup of coffee from the small kitchen. None spoke to me. Maybe they were used to having people waiting.

After twenty-five minutes, the door to Mr. Strauss's office opened and out stepped two men. One was tall and slim, with a full head of metallic gray hair; the other shorter, fatter, with thinning hair combed desperately over his bald pate. They shook hands and exchanged a few parting pleasantries before the fat man walked to the hat stand, retrieved his homburg, and left.

The tall, slim man—Mr. Strauss, I presumed—was turning to go back into his office when his secretary called to him, informing him that he had a visitor. I crushed out the cigarette I'd been smoking, got up, and strode over to him. He watched me approach with an inscrutable expression on his face.

He wore a navy blue shirt tucked into belted gray slacks and black shoes polished to a high gloss. A masculine Adam's apple bulged above the knot of his red tie. His clothes were new and expensive and had either been ironed recently or he didn't make any sudden moves while he was in them. The watch on his left wrist gleamed money. He had a narrow face with sharp features— a long, straight nose, pointed chin without a trace of stubble, pronounced cheekbones, a slash of a mouth, and piercing blue eyes under widely spaced eyebrows. He was between fifty and fifty-five, fit and preserved, with an erect bearing that hinted at vanity. He was five inches shorter than I was, but still gave the impression of looking down at me. He didn't ask who I was or what he could do for me, but waited for me to speak.

"Mr. Strauss, my name is Adam Lapid. I was wondering if I could have a few minutes of your time."

His eyes went over my hair, face, and clothes. He didn't seem to find much he approved of.

"I'm very busy, Mr. Lapid. If this is a legal matter, Dana can see whether one of my junior associates is free to see you." His tone was that of a man speaking to an inferior, one he had no patience for.

"It's not a legal matter, Mr. Strauss. It's regarding one of your former employees. Esther Kantor."

A slight movement of his mouth was the only reaction. "What about her?"

"I'm a detective, and I'm investigating her murder. I would like to talk to you about it, about Esther."

"I've already spoken to the police about it at the time."

"I know. I read the police report and spoke to the detective who handled the case." I was trying to make it seem as if I had the cooperation of the police and that it would be wise of him to speak to me. If this made any impression on him, he was doing a good job of hiding it.

Those penetrating blue eyes appraised me for a moment; then they shifted to my right. From the corner of my eye, I could see Dana, the secretary, her body tilted forward, clearly engrossed in our conversation. I suppose typing is always duller than murder.

Strauss frowned, and I thought he was going to rebuke her. Instead he turned to me and, in a tone that suggested he would rather have his wisdom teeth pulled, said, "All right. Come in. But I haven't got long, so you better keep it short."

His office was spacious and well-appointed. A gleaming wooden desk; a pair of sturdy ladder-back chairs; a sideboard with bottles and glasses on it; and a wall hung with framed pictures of Strauss beside various dignitaries, including at least one government minister I recognized and a former mayor of Tel Aviv. On another wall were various academic diplomas. He'd studied in Jerusalem and Beirut. These days, of course, the latter city was in an enemy country. On the desk lay tidy stacks of papers, a couple of expensive-looking pens, a humidor, and a glass ashtray housing a number of fat stubs. The rich scent of cigar smoke permeated the office.

Strauss poured himself a tall drink, then walked behind his desk and sat down. Only then did he think of asking if I wanted anything and seemed relieved when I told him I didn't. He instructed me to take one of the two visitors' chairs. He sat with his hands on the blotter, fingers laced, his posture relaxed.

"Your name is Lapid?"

"Yes."

"Never heard of you. Been in the investigation business long?"

"Since I arrived in Israel two years ago."

"A newcomer, eh? Where are you from?"

"Hungary."

"I thought it was something like that. Your accent and all. You should give Dana your name before you leave. We sometimes employ private investigators. Maybe we can find some use for you. We pay well."

"Thank you, but at the moment I'm not looking for more clients." This was a lie. My schedule was far from full, and I could always do with extra cash. I just didn't like him trying to put money into my hand when *I* was there to question *him*.

"Who is your client on this case?" he asked.

"A relative of Esther and her baby."

"You can't say the name?"

"I'm not at liberty to. Confidentiality. As a lawyer, I'm sure you're familiar with the concept."

He smiled tightly. "Isn't it the responsibility of the police to investigate murders?"

"It is, but the police have given up on this case. Now I'm having a go at it."

"What makes you think you'll succeed where they failed? You have experience with murder cases?"

"Some."

"How did you acquire it?"

I didn't owe him an answer, but his haughty tone made me want to give him one just the same. "I was a police detective before the war. In Hungary. That's how."

The way his jaw twitched told me he hadn't expected that, and I enjoyed a flash of triumph. He curled his right hand around his glass and slowly sipped his drink. It wasn't wine he was drinking. The liquid was amber, giving off a faint scent of vanilla and honey.

Setting his drink down, Strauss said, "If you read the police report, I've got nothing to tell you you don't already know."

"Maybe if I ask the right questions, something new will come to light."

He muttered something under his breath, not bothering to hide his skepticism and impatience. It was clear he viewed me and my mission as a waste of time. Mostly his.

He waved a hand. "Well, go ahead. Ask away."

"Thank you. I understand Esther worked here for four months."

"In the neighborhood of."

"Who hired her?"

"I did."

"What qualified her for the job?"

"She could type in Hebrew and English. It was the latter that was important."

"You had dealings with the British authorities?"

"Of course. They were the ones in charge."

He said this without a hint of apology. Most of the Jews who had profited by their dealings with the British during the Mandate of Palestine took great pains to hide those dealings now that the hated British were gone from Israel. Strauss apparently saw no reason to do so. At least not to me.

"What area of the law does your firm practice?"

"Business law. Contracts, real estate, that sort of thing."

"No criminal law?"

"No." He offered a tight-lipped smile. "The money is better in business law, and the clientele is of a noticeably higher quality."

"How long have you been with the firm?"

"Over twenty-five years. It was founded by my father-in-law, Mr. Becker. He died seven years ago. If you're going to ask me what he thought of Esther, save your breath. He'd retired before she began working here."

"Yes. The police report said as much. Apart from her typing skills, was there any other reason you hired Esther?"

He took another sip from his glass. Whatever the liquid was, it seemed to go smoothly down his throat. "She impressed me. A smart girl. Most German girls are smart."

"You're from Germany?"

A curt nod. "I was born in Hamburg. My parents and I came here when I was nine."

He still had an accent, but it was very faint. The influence of his German upbringing was more apparent in his impeccable clothing, his arrow-straight posture, and his overbearing manner. He was one of those Jews who retained an admiration of Germany and German culture and habits, even though their former country had rejected them utterly and attempted to wipe them off the face of the earth. I had run across a number of such Jews in Israel and understood none of them.

"How did Esther come by her English?" I asked.

"I don't recall," Strauss answered.

"Is typing all she did?"

"And filing and dictation and making coffee and fixing drinks for clients. The usual secretarial functions. I fail to see what all of this has to do with her murder."

"Just some background information, Mr. Strauss. I appreciate your patience. Were you satisfied with Esther's work?"

"Yes. She was a fine secretary."

"No complaints from any clients?"

"None."

"Any ever show an interest in her?"

"Meaning?" he asked, though his tone made me suspect he knew exactly what I was asking.

"Meaning that Esther was a beautiful woman. Did any of your clients ever express an interest in more than her typing skills? Any of them ever ask you about her? If she was married, for instance?"

His voice came out as dry as a crust of leftover bread. "I run a law practice here, Mr. Lapid, not a matchmaking service. If any of my clients had his eye on Esther, I am not aware of it." His eyes narrowed. "I hope you're not suggesting any of my firm's clients had anything to do with these murders?"

"Not suggesting anything, Mr. Strauss. Merely exploring the possibility."

"Well, cease your exploration this instant. I can well imagine the sort of people you run across in your line of work, but our clients are of a different class. We have no criminal element among our clients."

"It's been my experience, Mr. Strauss, that murderers come from all classes of society."

He sneered. "Maybe that's true of Hungarians, but it isn't true of any of our clients. Is that clear?"

"Yes. Quite clear," I said, biting back what I'd been about to say, that Germans made far more adept murderers than Hungarians.

"Good. Because I can tell you right now that I will not stand idly by if you foolishly decide to bother any of our clients with this nonsense. This firm has a reputation to maintain."

"Is your reputation more important than finding Esther's murderer?"

The flash of anger in his eyes, like light reflected on ice, told me he didn't like that last line one bit. "If that was the case, I would throw you out this instant. And if you step out of line again, I will."

"I'll be sure to remember that. Tell me, was Esther happy here?"

"Happy? I treat my employees well, but I don't have heart-to-heart chats with them. She seemed perfectly satisfied."

"It's just that a few days before she died, Esther confided in a friend that she was having some difficulties here."

Strauss did not look surprised by this revelation. "I see."

"You have an idea what was troubling her?"

"I do. It's quite straightforward, actually. Esther asked me for a raise in her wages; I refused to give her one."

"When was this?"

"As you said, a few days prior to her death."

"You told the police nothing about it at the time."

"Why would I? It was a routine matter, of no relation to her murder."

"In fact, you're on record saying how good Esther was at her job."

"She was."

"Then why did you refuse her this raise?"

"Because she'd only worked here for a few months. If she had waited until she'd been here a year, I might have made a different decision."

"That was all? That was the only thing?"

"Yes."

I stared across the desk at him. He was as calm and relaxed as before, his hands clasped around his nearly depleted glass. It suddenly struck me that this latest line of questioning was the first that had not engendered impatience or irritation on his part. In fact, he had answered these last few questions almost without inflection.

"Do you regret this?" I asked.

"Regret what?"

"Not acceding to her request for a raise, considering what happened soon after."

A frown carved two crooked lines across his brow. He did not answer for a few seconds. "What possible difference would that have made?" he said finally.

"None. It's just that she might have been happier during her last days if you had."

He glared at me, raising his chin. "No. I have no regrets." It seemed he was about to add some biting remark, but swallowed down the words before they passed his lips. Another first.

"All right," I said, thinking that Strauss was either a very proud man or a very cold one. Or both. "How did Esther get along with her coworkers?"

"Fine. She was very close to the other secretary, Leah Benowitz —she's married now; her last name is Goldin."

"What about the others—Itamar Levine and Alex Fishman?"

Strauss let go of his glass, sliding his hands to the edge of the desk. "They were cordial to each other, professional, but I don't think they knew Esther outside the office. Leah knew her best. Of course, she was also interviewed by the police ten years ago, an interview you must have read. But I suppose you'd want to be able to tell your client that you left no stone unturned in your investigation."

His mocking tone was getting under my skin. I was on the verge of informing him that I had already talked to Leah Goldin, when I was struck by a sudden realization.

I turned to look at the office door, behind which was the reception area and, in it, Dana, the secretary. The only secretary.

Turning back to Strauss, I said, "Ten years ago, you had two associates?"

"Yes."

"How many do you have now?"

"Six." Strauss's thin lips arched in satisfaction. "We have expanded."

"Business must be good."

"Hard work has made it so. That and meticulous, diligent, and quality service."

German efficiency, I thought. *The sort that gets the job done.*

"Why did you require two secretaries ten years ago, when you only employ one now, when your business is much larger?"

Strauss tensed. He had good facial control, so I might have missed it were it not for his eyes. If the look he gave me had a temperature, I would have gotten frostbite.

"I don't think how I run my firm is any concern of yours, is it, Mr. Lapid?"

"I was just curious, Mr. Strauss," I said, intrigued by his apparent discomfort.

"An admirable quality in your, eh, profession. I'm sure it serves you well when you stalk the occasional wayward husband or wife." He glanced at his wristwatch. "But now I'd like you to leave. I'm a busy man and you have taken enough of my—"

I raised a hand. "Just one or two questions more, Mr. Strauss."

He exhaled in resignation. "Go on."

"Where were you the night of the murders?"

His eyes blazed. "Are you suggesting I might have had something to do with this crime? Are you insane?"

"It's a question you were asked ten years ago."

"If you know that, then you must know the answer as well. I was home, with my wife, all night."

He was right. I did know that from the police report, but I wanted to see his face when he said it. He appeared truthful.

"Your wife can vouch for you?"

"She did at the time, but if you'd like to talk to her yourself, I'm afraid you're a bit late."

"What do you mean?"

"My wife is deceased, Mr. Lapid," he said flatly. "She died three months ago. Cancer."

"I see you're still in pieces over it," I said.

Strauss shot to his feet, planting both palms on his desk. His jaw muscles rippled with anger. He spoke through gritted teeth. "How dare you? Just who the hell do you think you are? Consider my earlier offer rescinded—do not leave your name with Dana on your way out. And don't come back here, either. Now get out!"

I stood, feeling an odd satisfaction that I had gotten a rise out of him. It was silly and pointless, but it sure felt good.

I strode to the door. Strauss stood riveted, following me with his eyes. I grasped and lowered the handle, drawing the door open. "Thank you for your time," I said before stepping out and shutting the door.

Turning from the door, I saw Dana staring at me from behind her desk. I offered a smile. She reciprocated. She had a nice smile. I was about to bid her a good day when she spoke.

"I'm glad you found her."

I had no idea what she was talking about. "Who?"

"Leah Benowitz—Goldin, I mean."

I approached her desk. "How do you know I saw her?"

"She called earlier. I told her you were asking about her, and she said you'd been by."

"She called you? I thought you two didn't know each other."

"We don't. It's the first time I've spoken with her. She called for Mr. Strauss."

I swiveled my head to look at the closed door to Mr. Strauss's office while my mind strove to digest, process, and make sense of this new piece of information. I also hoped fervently that Strauss would remain ensconced in his office for just a while longer, because I had a few more questions for Dana, the pretty secretary.

"Did she say anything about me?" I asked.

"Just that you two met."

"Did she say why she wanted to speak to Mr. Strauss?"

"No."

I could tell by her face that she did not listen in on their talk. She might prick her ears if an intriguing conversation was being conducted within earshot, but she wasn't the sort to eavesdrop on a private telephone call.

"Was this the first time she called since you started working here?" I asked.

"Yes. Unless she called on my lunch break."

"I wonder why she called Mr. Strauss today of all days."

"Perhaps to ask him for something. Mr. Strauss is a very generous man."

"Is he now?"

"Yes. He gave me this." She displayed her left wrist, from which dangled the silver bracelet I had noticed last time. "Isn't it beautiful?"

I agreed that it was.

"He said it was a gift for all the good work I've been doing. I was stunned."

She was a slim woman, with a heart-shaped face and soft dark hair. Her eyes were large and brown and guileless. Her mouth was full and lush. She really was lovely. Not exquisitely beautiful as Esther was, but attractive, in an innocent, youthful way. Fresh, inexperienced. Maybe that was why she didn't know men were not in the habit of giving silver bracelets to pretty women thirty years younger than themselves without aiming to get something in return.

"Is this your first job?" I asked.

She said that it was.

"He must like you a lot," I said, noting the slight flush that crept up her neck. Apparently she hadn't considered how odd it was for a law firm to hire an inexperienced secretary, no matter how good at typing she was.

I heard the door at my back swing open, followed by the hard, clipped voice of Mr. Strauss.

"I thought I told you to get out."

Dana tensed, eying me warily. I winked at her before turning to her boss.

"I was just admiring Dana's bracelet," I said, and walked out.

23

I took an inner-city bus downtown to the central depot and there boarded another bus to the coastal town of Netanya, some thirty kilometers north of Tel Aviv. The bus, painted red and nearly full, was twenty minutes late in departing and another forty in arriving at its destination. Along the way I was treated to the sight of rolling sand dunes, dense groves of bananas and oranges, and copses of pine and ficus trees. Looking at these divergent landscapes—arid sand to one side of the road and fertile cropland to the other—it occurred to me that this was a fair representation of Israel as a whole: a small country in which existed diverse climates and religions and ethnicities, all in close proximity to and without clear borders between one another.

The bus dropped me off at Zion Square in the center of Netanya. Along the square and the many streets that branched from it were small shops selling a large assortment of goods. Outside the shops, on stools and chairs, sat shopkeepers drinking coffee from small glasses, chatting with each other in loud voices.

At a kiosk, I bought a bottle of soda and asked for directions. The directions proved accurate ten minutes later when I found myself looking at the home of Yael and Moshe Klinger. It was a medium-sized house, one story with red shingles and a white fence framing a well-tended courtyard. Flower beds bloomed under the windows, and mowed grass flanked the cobbled walkway that led from the street to the front door. There was something distinctly European about this small garden. Someone had put a lot of effort into cultivating it.

Taking in the scent of flowers and watered earth, I knocked on the door and waited. The pear-shaped woman who opened it had fiery red hair knotted at the back of her head and sensible brown eyes set in a square, freckled face. She wore a red apron over a white housedress and was clutching a wooden stirring spoon. Flour feathered her apron and more of it was smudged above her right eyebrow.

"You've got some flour there," I said, "over your eye."

She blinked and wiped her forehead with her palm, an action that served only to add more flour to her skin. She laughed when I told her so.

"I was baking," she explained unnecessarily, as the enticing smell of baking dough wafting from inside the house told the tale well enough. "I don't believe I know you."

I gave her my name and said I was there to see her and her husband, Moshe, and that I'd got their address from Mira Roth. This elicited a slight frown and a shifting of her feet. For a second, she seemed unsure of what she ought to do, but then she made up her mind and invited me in, telling me she was expecting her husband shortly.

She showed me to the living room, where I sat on a padded armchair next to which stood a tall Zenith radio. She excused herself, saying she needed to wash her hands. In the backyard, two girls, eight or nine, were playing with a white ball and a black puppy. The girls, I noticed, were identical twins. For a second, the image of my two daughters wavered before my eyes, and I felt my throat constrict.

Yael Klinger returned, minus the apron, and handed me a tall glass of water. I'd consumed half the water when I heard the front door fling open. A man bearing a crate of fruit appeared at the entrance to the living room. The name of the agricultural cooperative Tnuva was splashed in white paint on one side of the crate. The man had on a khaki shirt and shorts and sandals. His muscular arms and legs were tanned a healthy brown. Between his aquiline nose and generous mouth grew a thick black mustache. He was six feet tall, athletic and handsome, with a full head of jet-black hair—the sort of man whose picture would feature prominently in Zionist posters, extolling the new Jew that was reborn along with our nation. He saw me and sent his wife a questioning look.

"Moshe, this is Adam Lapid," Yael Klinger said. "Mira Roth sent him to us."

"Hold on a minute," he said, his voice an attractive baritone. He went into the kitchen, set the crate of fruit on the counter, and began scrubbing his hands at the sink. His wife joined him there, and I could hear whispering followed by slicing and scraping noises. A minute later, they returned to the living room, each bearing a plate laden with sliced bananas and apples and oranges.

Yael took her plate to the two girls in the backyard, while her husband set his on the coffee table and plopped himself on the sofa, directly opposite where I was seated. He plucked a few pieces of fruit and tossed them in his mouth. "Go ahead," he said, munching. "Help yourself."

I did. The fruit tasted wonderful. Moshe read the pleasure on my face and grinned. "Good, eh? There are some benefits in working for Tnuva."

"So I see. How long have you been working there?"

"Thirteen years."

"In what capacity?"

"This and that. Driving mostly, but I'm also a mechanic. Where do you work?"

"I'm a private investigator. I work for whoever hires me."

"Exciting work, is it?"

"It has its moments. Mostly it's just talking to people."

"You're working for Mira Roth?"

"No. She's just someone I met during my investigation. Here." I dried my hands and handed him the introductory note Mira had given me.

He read it over a few times, his face not showing much. Yael reappeared, closing the door to the backyard behind her, and sat down beside her husband. He handed her the note. She let out a small whimper when she read it, covering her mouth with her hand. Tears sprang to her eyes.

"Come now, sweetheart," Moshe Klinger said, patting her shoulder with a measure of awkwardness. "Let's have no more of that."

Yael shook her head, her tears flowing freely now. She mumbled something unintelligible, rose to her feet, and hurried to the bathroom.

"Yael is a sensitive woman," Moshe explained, looking embarrassed. "She and Esther were close."

"More than you and Esther were?"

"Oh, definitely. I saw very little of Esther. I worked long hours. Yael was at home, so she spent more time with Esther and Willie."

"So you didn't know Esther well?"

A shake of his head. "No, I can't say that I did."

He leaned forward, took some more fruit, and chewed on it. Yael returned, her face damp and her eyes reddened. She resumed her seat, sitting very close to her husband, legs touching. "Excuse me, Mr. Lapid. I didn't intend to get all emotional."

"No need to apologize. I'm sorry I upset you. And please call me Adam."

She gave a curt nod and her husband said I should call them Moshe and Yael. I explained how Henrietta Ackerland had hired me to find her son, how I'd learned of the murders, and that I was hoping to discover who had killed Willie and Esther.

"Imagine that," Moshe said, "after ten years, she suddenly shows up here in Israel. Isn't that something, Yael?"

Instead of answering her husband, Yael said to me, "What is she like?"

"Resilient," I said, realizing that I knew very little of Henrietta and had only the barest of impressions of her. "Smart and resourceful. A good woman."

"I feel for her," Yael said. "Tell her that for me when you see her."

"I will. What I was hoping you'd tell me was your impression of Esther. If I get a clearer picture of her life, of who she was, maybe I'll find out who killed her and Willie. They stayed with you for how long?"

"Three weeks?" Moshe asked his wife.

"Five," she answered, which prompted another grin from her husband. He seemed to have a face made for them: easygoing, confident, a bit cocky even.

"I told you I wasn't here much," he said to me.

"This was in Haifa?"

"Yes."

"Did you know she was coming that night? She and Willie?"

"They didn't tell us anything," Moshe said, a bitter edge to his voice. "Like they didn't trust us."

"The Irgun, you mean?"

"That's exactly what I mean. Had to maintain security, they said. Like they were afraid we wouldn't be able to keep our mouths shut." He shook his head. "We didn't even know a raid was in the works. They just showed up on our doorstep in the dead of night."

"Woke the baby up," Yael said in a faraway voice, like she was reliving that long-past moment.

"That's right," I said, remembering Mira telling me why she chose to bring Esther and Willie to the Klingers. "You have another child."

Right then, the front door flew open and into the living room burst a boy of eleven. His face was flushed, his left knee bloodied, and his shin marred by raw abrasions.

Yael bounded to her feet, her mouth open. "Oh, Dror, what happened?"

Dror Klinger affected nonchalance. "Nothing, Mom, just fell down playing. Hardly hurts at all."

"You come with me. We need to wash your knee and put some iodine on it."

He made a face, but went with his mother into the bathroom without argument. Moshe grinned. "She can't help but fuss over him. To her he's still a baby. I mean, it's not like a bloodied knee is such a big deal. It's part of growing up. Right, Adam?"

"Right," I said absently, thinking that Dror Klinger resembled neither of his parents. He was blond, slim like a beanstalk, with blue eyes and fair skin reddened by sun exposure.

"I tell her to stop worrying over him, that she'll spoil him, but she doesn't listen. Is your wife the worrying type?"

"I'm not married," I told him, eager to change the subject. "How long ago did you move here from Haifa?"

"Here? Oh, years ago. Why do you ask?"

"No particular reason." I noted that he hadn't answered my question, and also that his eyes had narrowed and that he was scrutinizing my face.

Yael and Dror emerged from the bathroom. The boy had a

bandage on his knee and purple smears on his shin where his mother had slathered iodine.

"Maybe you should stay home the rest of the day," Yael said.

"But I want to play. The guys are waiting for me."

"Let him go, Yael," Moshe grumbled. "Go play with your friends, Dror."

The boy grabbed a few pieces of fruit and ran out the door, yelling a goodbye over his shoulder. His mother looked after him, her face a mask of worry. "I hope he doesn't fall again."

"Let the boy be, Yael. He'll be fine. Come now, sit down. Let's answer the rest of Adam's questions."

Yael gave her husband a sharp look, clearly not appreciating his commanding tone, but she wordlessly did as he said. He, in turn, seemed completely oblivious to her displeasure.

Moshe said, "It was two o'clock in the morning when the four of them arrived on our doorstep."

"By the four of them you mean Esther and Willie with Mira Roth and Michael Shamir?"

"You know Shamir?" Moshe asked, and when I confirmed that I did, he added in an admiring tone, "One of the best fighters the Irgun ever had. That the Jewish people ever had. I would have loved to have fought alongside him, but with a wife and baby at home, well..." He trailed off, rubbing his hands, his eyes not meeting mine. He radiated shame, which I felt was justified. His excuse was a weak one. Many of the soldiers in my unit had had families. Many had left widows and orphans behind.

"We did our part," Yael said, laying a comforting hand on his knee. He nodded twice and looked at me.

He said, "Michael and Mira told us about the prison raid, that it did not go well. They said our side suffered casualties, but that they managed to get away without the British following them. They left Esther and Willie with us and drove off."

"Who told you Esther wasn't Willie's real mother?"

"Mira did," Yael said. "At first she thought he might stay with us, at least until his mother came, but Esther insisted on keeping him."

"I understand she loved him very much."

"Yes," Yael said. "She did."

"How did you explain their presence to your neighbors?"

"We told them Esther was my cousin, visiting with her son. No one questioned our story."

"What was their stay with you like?"

"Good," Yael said. "Esther helped with the chores. It was nice having her around. And Willie was a lovely baby."

Moshe grinned. "Yael has a soft spot for babies."

Yael did not smile. "The house felt sort of empty when they left."

"Did you keep in touch after they moved to Tel Aviv?"

"At first, yes. Esther and I would write to each other."

"What did she write about?"

"Oh, just everyday stuff. How Willie was doing—she used the name Erich, of course, in case her letters fell into the wrong hands—her new job, her apartment, how life was like in Tel Aviv."

"Did she ever write about any men she might have met? Anyone whom she was seeing?"

"No," Yael said.

"What about Alon Davidson? She ever mention him?"

She frowned. "I don't think so. I don't remember."

I rubbed my forehead, exasperated. I had hoped that Esther would have felt comfortable sharing some intimate details of her life with Yael Klinger, considering that Yael knew her true identity. But apparently Esther had been a private, perhaps even secretive person in general, not just when told to be one by Mira.

"Do you still have her letters?" I asked, hoping against hope, and felt searing disappointment when Yael said she'd lost them when they moved to their new home. I was getting used to the feeling. A lot of facts and clues and memories get lost in ten years. Like ashes blown in all directions by a capricious wind.

"After two months or so," she said, "the letters began tapering off. Finally they ceased completely."

"You never met again in person?"

She shook her head.

I turned to Moshe. "How about you? Did you ever see Esther after she and Willie left your house?"

He said that he didn't.

"Did Esther have any visitors during her and Willie's stay with you?"

"Only Mira Roth and Michael Shamir," said Yael. "He came over—I think it was twice—and brought Esther their new papers. He never stayed long. Mira came more often and stayed longer."

"She and Esther got along? They were friendly?"

"Yes. They seemed to like each other a lot."

I drummed on my thigh with two fingers, wondering what to say next. I wanted to ask more about Mira and Esther's relationship, but couldn't think of a way of doing so without it seeming odd.

I cast my eyes over my hosts. Moshe reclined with his legs wide apart, one arm draped over the back of the sofa. Yael sat close to the edge of the seat, knees pressed together, hands folded in her lap. There was some tension in her body, I noticed, while her husband appeared completely relaxed. Perhaps it was as he'd said, that his wife was closer to Esther and Willie than he was. By what she told me, that was indeed the case. Maybe she simply cared more than he did whether their killer was brought to justice.

I hated to admit it, but it seemed that my trip to Netanya had been a wasted one. I could think of nothing more to ask either of the Klingers. Wait a minute, that wasn't entirely accurate. I did have one more thing I wanted to know.

"Why did you stop sheltering immigrants after Esther and Willie left?"

I hadn't meant anything by the question, but apparently it had touched a sore spot. Husband and wife blinked in unison. They exchanged weighty glances. Moshe lowered the arm he had draped over the sofa's back. He no longer looked relaxed.

"Who told you that?" he asked.

"Michael Shamir."

Moshe grimaced, and I had a good idea why. Like Mira, he idealized Michael Shamir, and he hated the fact that his idol was aware that not only had he refrained from fighting the British, but that he had also closed his door to needy Jewish immigrants.

"I still gave money to the Irgun," he offered lamely.

"That's not quite the same thing, is it?"

He didn't like that one bit. He sat forward, eyes flaring, and pointed a finger at me.

"I did plenty, all right? Plenty. More than most people. Probably more than you. Were you part of the resistance? What did you do to get the British out?"

"Nothing," I said, "but I did fight in the War of Independence and took two bullets in the process. Where did you fight during the war?"

Moshe's face was red. He almost spat out his words at me. "What are you implying, that I was a coward? That I was not committed? Damn you, is that what you're saying?"

"I was just wondering," I said, already regretting provoking him. I needed information from him and his wife, not to triumph in some contest of who did more for Israel and the Jewish people. From his reaction, I knew that Moshe had never fired a gun at the enemy, let alone was fired at. There were many men like him, fit and healthy men in their prime who'd managed to weasel out of proper military service. The war might have ended sooner if not for men like him. But the war was over, and I gained nothing by shaming Moshe in front of his wife.

Yael placed a hand on her husband's shoulder, trying to calm him, but he shook her off. He rose to his feet, looking like he was about to take a swing at me. "I don't need to hear this. Not in my house, I don't. Get—"

"It was me," Yael said in a voice loud enough to still her husband. Her eyes met mine and didn't let go. "It was my decision not to take in more immigrants, not Moshe's."

"Why?"

She hesitated for a second before saying, "I got scared, all right? I worried that one night British troops would break down our door and arrest us, and then what would become of our son? Can you understand that?"

I stared at her. Her eyes were once again wet and in her temple a vein was pulsing wildly.

"This fear came upon you all of a sudden, just after you had Esther and Willie in your home?"

"Yes."

"It had nothing to do with Esther?"

"No. I swear that it didn't."

I would have liked to have been able to read her expression just then, but she buried her face in her hands and began sobbing. Moshe put a hand on her shoulder. "Get out," he told me. "Before I throw you out."

I did as he said.

Outside, three doors down from the Klinger home, a skinny woman in her late thirties was weeding her yard. When I passed by her house, she said, "Friend of the Klingers?"

"Yes," I replied, not wishing to explain my visit to her.

"Don't remember ever seeing you around here."

Ah, she was one of those. There was someone like her on every street. The nosy type who liked to know everything about everyone.

"First-time visit," I said, and was about to bid her good day and walk off when I thought of something. "You know them long?"

"Ever since they moved here," she said. "Nearly ten years."

"Sure about that? I thought they didn't live here that long."

"Sure I'm sure. My husband and I have been living here since August 1939. Moshe and Yael moved in a month after that, in September."

The month after the murders, I thought, recalling how Moshe had evaded telling me precisely when he and his wife had moved to Netanya from Haifa. Now I got to wondering why they'd chosen to move in the first place.

24

A handwritten schedule posted at the central bus terminal in Netanya informed me that the bus to Tel Aviv would be leaving in half an hour. I went in search of a phone and found one at a grocery store a few doors west of the terminal. The proprietor wanted money in advance. I paid him and rang Reuben's number. He picked up in the middle of the second ring.

"Where are you?" he asked.

"Netanya," I said.

"What are you doing there?"

"Interviewing a couple who knew the victims."

"Come up with anything?"

"Not on the face of it, no. How about you? Did you find anything?"

"Yes." I could hear the rustle of papers being moved on his end. "I checked those names you wanted. I'll start with the list of women. All but one are alive and kicking. The one who's dead passed on during childbirth. The child died too, but I guess that has no bearing on your investigation, does it?"

"No," I said, feeling a pang of sadness at the thought of the dead woman and baby.

"I suppose that means Manny Orrin is off the hook."

"It's not proof positive, but I think so. I didn't like him for it anyhow. Does he have a record?"

"No. Neither does Natalie Davidson. Her husband, Alon Davidson, is another matter."

"What did he do?" I said, liberating a cigarette from the pack in my pocket and sticking it between my lips. I struck a match and lit up.

"He was arrested eight years ago on suspicion of assault. He cut up some guy pretty badly in a bar brawl. According to the report, the guy spent a week in the hospital. Davidson spent two nights in jail before being released. He was never charged."

"Why not?"

"The only person who said he saw the whole altercation from start to finish swore the other guy initiated the fight by swinging a bottle at Davidson. Davidson had a knife on him. He's a fisherman, apparently, and he claimed the knife was a tool he used on his boat. He said he acted in self-defense."

"A week in the hospital, that's some defense."

"I'd say."

"He used a knife—that's interesting."

"I thought so too. Think he might be your killer, Adam?"

"I don't know," I said, tapping ash to the gray tile floor of the grocery store. "I haven't seen him yet, and he had an alibi." I took another drag. "Reuben, if this was a bar fight, how come only one witness?"

He sighed. "You know how it is, Adam, most people don't want to get involved. Some said they saw nothing, that they were facing the wrong way and that it all happened too fast. Others said they couldn't tell who got physical first."

"What caused the fight?"

"The guy who got sliced said Davidson made some remark about his wife. She was in the bathroom when it happened, so she saw nothing. Davidson swore the guy was lying. The witness corroborated his version."

"What's the name of the witness?"

"Let me see...Saul Mercer."

I frowned, reaching into my pocket for my notebook. I began flipping pages. "What was that name again?"

"Mercer. Saul Mercer. Why? You know him?"

I found the right page. What I read there got my mind working. "No," I told Reuben. "Never met the man."

"That's all I have on Alon Davidson. That one arrest. Other than that, he's clean."

I thanked him and once again he invited me to drop by to see his children. I said that I was too busy at the moment, but maybe when I was done with the current case, I'd pay them a visit.

I placed another call, this time to Itamar Levine's law firm in Haifa. The secretary who picked up told me he'd gone home for the day. I asked her whether he had a phone at home and she said he didn't. "He'll be in tomorrow," she said. "Call back then."

There was a falafel stall by the bus stop and the vendor filled a pita for me with falafel balls and salad and a liberal amount of *tehina*. I sat on a metal bench and ate. When I was done, I wiped my mouth with the paper napkin the vendor had provided and balled it up and tossed it in the trash. Then the bus arrived. Forty-five minutes later I was back in Tel Aviv. Forty minutes after that, I was at the Tel Aviv harbor.

Walking down the pier, I came upon a grizzled, weathered-faced man who was rolling up the sail of a fifteen-foot boat and asked him if he knew where I could find Alon Davidson. He said he hadn't seen him that day and pointed to two men who were smoking on the pier fifty feet further south. "They're Davidson's men. Ask them."

The two men were both Bulgarian Jews, recent arrivals in Israel, and their Hebrew was heavily accented and rudimentary. But we managed to communicate, and one of them, the one who spoke better, told me Davidson had gone home a few hours ago. "He be back—I not know, tomorrow in the morning, maybe?"

I told them I'd come by tomorrow and they both nodded as if they didn't care, which they probably didn't. They didn't ask who I was or why I was looking for their boss.

By now it was around seven and my stomach was sending me signals. I walked east and by seven thirty was at my regular table at Greta's, a melted cheese sandwich, a steaming cup of coffee, and my chessboard before me.

I stayed at my table for the next two and a half hours, had two more cups of coffee and a soda, and ate a second sandwich. I played one game after another, striving to clear my mind of all I'd learned over the past two days, of the possibilities that new knowledge aroused, of the case in its entirety. It worked only partly—I enjoyed brief snatches of mental liberty, in which my mind became joyously free of Esther and Willie and Henrietta and all the people I'd met and talked to during this investigation. But my mind never stayed liberated for long. It seemed intent on submerging itself in the swamp of details and facts that I'd learned, and in the questions and suppositions that those facts and details gave birth to.

What I really wanted, I realized, was to talk about the case, to voice my thoughts and see how another person reacted to them. So I remained at my table until I was the sole remaining customer in the café, until Greta had locked the door and flipped over the open/closed sign, until she'd flicked off half the lights and came over to my table.

She dropped onto a chair with a sigh. "Long day. My feet are killing me."

"You should soak them in hot water. Give me a minute; I'll hop to the kitchen and fill up a bowl."

When I returned with a large stirring bowl, she removed her shoes and socks and gingerly slipped her feet into the water. A smile spread slowly on her lips.

"That feels good. Now why didn't I think of it myself?"

"That's why you keep me around, to solve problems for you."

Her smile widened. "And you do a fine job, I must say. Even if you do eat me out of house and home." Her face turned serious. "You look tired. Sleeping okay?"

"As usual. It's not lack of sleep that's the problem; it's this case I'm working on." I told her about Henrietta Ackerland and how a hopeless missing person case morphed into an equally hopeless double murder investigation. I related to her the various steps I'd taken and described the people I'd met and the conversations I'd held with them over the past few days. I listed the things I'd learned and the open questions that had cropped up. I told her about Alon Davidson. Greta listened in silence, her wise eyes focused on my face, full of compassion and sorrow.

"The thing is," I said, "Davidson is the only good lead I have. He was Esther's lover and he hid this fact from the police. It's more than enough to make him a suspect. But until I talk to him, I won't have a sense of whether I like him for the murders, and a part of me doesn't relish the prospect of meeting him at all."

"Why not?" Greta asked.

"Because if he turns out to be innocent, or if I'm unable to reach a certain conclusion as to his guilt, I'll be left with close to nothing. No real leads. No suspects. No way to catch this killer. And I want to catch him pretty badly."

"You in a hurry?"

I nodded. "I can't take forever on this case, because I owe it to my client to tell her the truth about her son. She needs to start mourning if she's ever to rebuild her life. You think I did the right thing by not telling her?"

She pursed her lips. "Your heart was in the right place. But I'm not sure catching the killer will provide her with as much comfort as you may suppose."

It's more than I ever got, I thought bitterly, but I suspected Greta was right.

She said, "But it's not just the sense of time running out that's bothering you, is it?"

"No."

"What, then?"

"A couple of things. One is the feeling that I'm too late, that too much time has passed, that no matter how hard I work this case, how long I stay with it, or how many people I talk to, I will fail to uncover the killer. I fear the information that could have solved this case is gone along with the people who held it, or that it's buried under ten years of more recent memories, or simply distorted the way old memories often are. The second thing that's weighing on me is that for all my efforts, I'm not sure I'm any closer to knowing who Esther Grunewald really was. I'm learning new things about her, some good and some bad, but who she really was still eludes me. It feels as if her true self is just around some nearby corner, but I don't know where that corner is, so I can't turn it." I sighed, running both hands over my tired face. "Am I making any sense?"

"Perfect sense," Greta said. "You feel like you're chasing a ghost."

"Maybe you're right. Maybe that's it."

"And deep down you know that ghosts cannot be caught."

I looked at her and got the impression that the sorrow in her face was not limited to Esther and Willie and Henrietta, that some of it was meant for me. She reached her big hand across the table and laid it on mine. Her palm was warm, her fingers strong as they closed around my hand. Her blue eyes radiated kindness. "You're afraid she'll haunt you, aren't you? Esther Grunewald. That if you don't catch the killer, she will never let you be."

I swallowed hard, knowing Greta was right. I had enough ghosts haunting me already. I did not want another one to invade my dreams. The thing was, the more I learned about Esther Grunewald, the fuller her shape and character became in my mind, and the less I wanted to fail her. If I did not bring her killer to justice, maybe one day soon she'd start to appear in my dreams, like the family I'd once had and failed to protect or avenge.

"Am I that easy to read?" I asked.

"You do have an expressive face, Adam. What about the baby? Are you worried he'll haunt you, too?"

I considered her question for a moment, then shook my head. "I don't think so. Willie Ackerland is just as much a victim as Esther was, but I know almost nothing about him besides what he looked like in his photographs. My mental image of him is far hazier than Esther's. She's the one I'm worried about."

Greta squeezed my hand once and let go. My hand felt cold without her enveloping fingers.

"But you're still not done, so don't despair. Maybe something will pop up. Now let's talk of more pleasant things. Mira Roth. Tell me more about her."

I had kept my description of Mira to a minimum when I told Greta about the case, but it appeared that she had seen something in my face, or perhaps heard it in my voice, when I spoke about her. So I told her a little more about Mira, how she looked, what she'd done for the Irgun, her desire to punish the killer herself. As Greta listened, the corners of her mouth curled upward into a smile.

"What?"

Her smile broadened. "I'm simply enjoying hearing you talk

about her. You like her quite a bit, don't you? She appeals to you. Good. I think that's very good."

Suddenly I felt embarrassed, like a self-conscious boy caught staring at a pretty girl. "Don't get your hopes up, Greta."

"Why not? Up is where hopes are supposed to be. What should we hope for? To be down?"

"You know what I mean."

"I do, Adam. I do." Her smile had gone and the sadness was back in her eyes. "But it's all right to hope. You know that, Adam, don't you?"

I didn't tell her that in my experience hopes usually ended up being dashed.

"Do you still think she's keeping something from you?" she asked.

"Mira?"

"Yes."

I nodded. "That's the way it feels to me. Though what it might be, I cannot imagine."

"It seems odd, given how much she wants you to catch this killer."

"That's the thing I don't understand myself."

We talked some more and gradually the conversation shifted from the case to mundane things. I told her about Erwin Goldberg and the books he'd sold me. She told me about a government inspector who'd come nosing around the café, hoping to catch her using black-market food in the kitchen. "The man must have been blind. There were all these restricted items spread out on the work counter and he didn't see them. Just shook my hand and thanked me for being a good citizen."

After a while, she remarked that the water in the bowl I'd brought her had gotten cold. I fetched her a towel to dry her feet. After she'd put on her socks and shoes, she asked me if I might help her to tidy the place up. I turned the chairs over on the tables and swept and mopped the floor while she washed, dried, and put away the dishes. We worked in companionable silence and had the place clean and ready for tomorrow's business in a little over thirty minutes.

"I still have some accounts I want to go over," Greta said. "Come. I'll see you out."

At the door I turned to her and gazed into her compassionate blue eyes that stared right back at me. I wanted to say something, maybe thank her for taking the time to listen to me ramble, and was forming the words in my mind, when she held up a hand. "It's all right, Adam. You go on home now. Sleep tight."

We said goodnight and I stepped out onto Allenby Street. The street was deserted, all the shops and restaurants and cafés closed for the night. Darkness blanketed doorways and storefronts where light from streetlamps failed to reach. A solitary car cruised by, its engine humming. Then it made the turn onto Sheinkin Street and was gone, leaving an empty road behind.

Hardly anyone owned a car in Israel. Only the very rich could afford one. Even during the day, privately owned cars were a distinct minority of the vehicles in Tel Aviv. Most of the traffic consisted of trucks and buses and government-issued cars, such as police cruisers and army vehicles. Horse-drawn wagons were not an uncommon sight. At this time of night, traffic was almost nonexistent.

I drew a long breath. The heat of the day had broken and a nice breeze was blowing from the south, freshening the air. I began walking north toward my apartment and was in the process of extracting a cigarette from its pack when I caught a fast movement from the corner of my eye. A large shadow had detached itself from the darkness pooling in a recessed doorway and was hurtling across the two meters that separated it from me. It swallowed the distance in one quick bite. In the split second before it was upon me, my mind registered that it was a man, very tall and broad, and that one of his huge hands was bunched into a fist that was flying at my head. I didn't have time to duck or sidestep or bring up my hands to block his blow. All I managed to do was turn my head a little, so that instead of on the mouth, his blow caught me behind the ear.

It was like being hit with a hammer. A supernova of hot white pain burst in my head, and all sense of solidity drained from my body. My knees gave way and I crashed sideways against a lamp-post. Then I melted to the pavement.

And then everything went dark.

25

I must have been out for no more than a couple of seconds, because when I came to, I was still lying on that same strip of sidewalk on Allenby Street, and my assailant was standing over me. He grunted something I couldn't make out and leaned down. One of his hands curled itself into my hair, pulling hard, making my scalp scream. His other hand grabbed a fistful of my shirt. The son of a bitch was as strong as an elephant. He easily dragged me along the sidewalk, into the recessed doorway where he had waited to ambush me.

He hurled me against the door. My head banged painfully against the wood, making me feel like my brain was being rattled inside my skull. The side of my head throbbed where he had hit me, and my ribs hurt where I had banged them against the lamppost. I thought about crying for help, but worried that Greta would hear and come out to investigate. What could she do against this man? He would crush her like a bug.

I could hear him breathing fast and heavy above me. Then, through eyes that were sending me blurry, unfocused images, I caught him shifting his weight and saw his foot rushing toward me. I could do nothing to defend myself. My arms were limp and useless. I couldn't even brace myself for the kick before his foot drilled itself into my stomach. I let out a choked grunt and folded in half, retching violently. Bile rose to the base of my throat, clawing to get out. Breathless and in agony, an incongruous, panicked thought shrieked in my mind. *Don't throw up. Mustn't waste food. Who knows when you'll eat again.* The shock and pain had transported me back to Auschwitz, where starvation was the norm.

"You been filling my wife's head with poison, you little shit. Telling her all sorts of lies about me and Esther Kantor." He had a rough voice, hard and merciless. I could make out his outline. Elena was right, Alon Davidson was not a man you were likely to mistake for another. Massive, both in height and width—though exactly how tall I could not determine from where I lay. He shifted his feet, the soles of his shoes scuffing against the pavement. Then he kicked me again, in the lower stomach, right where one of the bullets I'd taken in the war had left a scar. All the air went out of my body. I couldn't draw breath and my vision turned dark.

He said, "I'm going to make you hurt." Then came a click and the smell of sea salt and fish close to my nostrils, followed by the awareness that he had crouched down beside me. He grabbed my hair again, pulling my head up, and if my eyes were open, they weren't sending my brain any signals, because all I saw was black. I knew that pain was coming, bad pain, like the time a sadistic prison guard in Auschwitz had whipped me a few dozen times and I thought I would die from agony.

I tried bracing myself for the pain, for that was the only thing you could do when you were helpless and about to be hurt. You could suffer through it with as much dignity as you could muster so that later, if there was a later, you could stare at yourself in the mirror and not drown in shame and self-loathing.

So I told myself to be ready, to take it without shaming myself, that there would be a day of reckoning, of revenge. There had to be. I wasn't about to die in the street like a dog, not after all I'd survived. But another voice, a nasty voice I barely recognized as my own, whispered that I knew full well that people die anywhere, anytime. Even good people. That death has no order or reason. It simply takes what it wants when it wants.

I caught a glint of something slicing through the veil of darkness in my eyes—a knife?—then came the sound of running footfalls, and Davidson turned and muttered, "What the—" and he let go of my head so it dropped to the pavement, sending a new stab of pain through my skull.

Now came the sounds of thuds and smacks and grunts. Heavy breathing. Shuffling feet. A metallic clattering sound and then a deep smack closely followed by a groan of pain. Fighting. Someone was getting hurt and it wasn't me. I tried to make my eyes see, to scatter the film of blackness that had descended across my vision like a theater screen. Instead I felt myself drowning in a pool of unawareness as consciousness slipped away.

26

The sensation of something cool and wet on my head coaxed me back from unconsciousness. My eyes cracked open to slits, and I tried to orient myself. I was slumped in a chair and someone was working a wet cloth over the spot where Davidson had first hit me.

It was Greta, her face inches from mine, one of her hands cupping my chin, the other holding a large white cloth. On the table was a bowl filled with water. The water held a reddish tinge. Greta dipped the cloth in the water and used it to clean the wound behind my ear. Then she set the cloth aside and uncapped a small bottle filled with a purplish liquid. A stringent medicinal scent wafted from the bottle. Greta moistened a dry corner of the cloth with the liquid and dabbed my wound with it. It stung quite a bit. Then she dropped the cloth on the table, capped the bottle, and proceeded to put two large plasters across the gash. We were in the café, at my table. The same ceiling light that she'd kept on during our conversation earlier that night shone on her face. She looked more worried than I'd ever seen her.

My mouth was dry and my tongue felt like a woolen sock. I

worked my mouth around, trying to induce some saliva, and managed to croak, "What happened?"

Greta's eyes, which had been focused on her ministrations, flicked to mine, and she let out a sigh of relief. "Thank God. You're awake. How are you feeling? Are you all right?"

I considered her question and answered truthfully. "I ache in more places than I have any desire to count, and my head feels like it's been bounced around some, but I think I'll be fine. How did I make it back here?"

She gestured toward the southern wall. "He brought you."

My eyes turned to where she'd pointed, and there he was, leaning nonchalantly against the southern wall of the café, about three meters away. He wore a thin brown jacket over a dark shirt and pants, and his head was covered by a black flat cap, which he'd pulled low over his forehead. He gazed at me calmly with his brown eyes, his expression blank.

"Michael?" I said, surprised. "What are you doing here?"

"I was passing by on my way to work when I saw him drag you into the shadows," Michael Shamir said. "The son of a bitch was about to cut you up."

He pushed himself off the wall, came forward, and laid a folding knife on the table. It was a crude instrument, not as finely crafted as mine. Crude or not, press it against skin and it would slice through easily. I realized that the click I'd heard when I was on the ground at Davidson's feet was him opening the blade, locking it into place, readying it for use.

I raised my eyes from the table to Michael. His face bore no bruises or cuts. If he had sustained any injuries during his fight with Davidson, they were hidden by his clothes. Before we first met, I had felt a strange jealousy toward him, born out of Mira's obvious admiration of him. During our meeting, that jealousy was supplanted by a sense of affinity. I saw something of myself in this man, this former soldier and widower, this quiet, orderly loner.

But now he had saved me from serious harm, perhaps even death, and, apart from gratitude, I found myself filled with that same emotion Mira and Moshe Klinger felt toward him—admiration.

"Thank you," I told Michael. "I'm lucky you showed up when you did."

He shrugged again. "Don't mention it." Then he gave me a small smile. "I sort of enjoyed it."

"This man said not to call a doctor or get a taxi to take you to the hospital," Greta said, her tone making it clear that she doubted the wisdom of this decision.

I took quick stock of myself. "Michael is right. I'm banged up, but I think I'm okay. If I start to feel worse, I'll get myself looked at."

"He also said this is the brute who assaulted you, but to leave it to you to decide whether to call the police."

Only then did I notice the large figure out cold in a chair to the left.

Alon Davidson.

Even in his slumped position, with his head lolling against his chest, Davidson looked massive. Six foot five or six, very wide across the shoulders and deep across the chest. Tanned, muscular arms like tree trunks that culminated in hands the size of melons. Instinctively, I ran my tongue over my teeth, thinking how many of them I would have lost had I not moved my head just before Davidson's fist had struck.

My gaze shifted from him to Michael. How had Michael, who was much shorter and lighter, managed to overpower this giant? And he seemed to have done so without getting a single scratch in the process.

I said to Michael, "You dragged him in here?"

Michael nodded.

"He was around earlier," said Greta, gesturing toward Davidson. "I saw him peering through the window. He didn't come in."

He wouldn't need to. He could have gotten my description from his wife. Or from someone else who knew me, another customer at the café maybe. So he came around to make sure I was at Greta's, and then he waited outside in the dark. He must've waited for hours, giving his anger time to build to a boil. And when I came out, he pounced.

If it hadn't been for Michael, I would likely have been severely injured. Perhaps even killed. Maybe Davidson would have disfigured my face. Like he'd done to Esther and Willie? I glanced again at the knife on the table.

"Who is he, Adam?" Greta asked.

"Alon Davidson," I said, leaning forward for a better look at him. He had on gray work pants and a yellow shirt with very short sleeves that showed his developed biceps. There were bloodstains on and around the shirt collar. His hair was black and cropped very short. Blood glued the short hairs at his crown. I couldn't see his face with his head drooped forward.

"Can you wake him up?" I asked Michael.

Without a word he stepped forward, reached one hand toward Davidson's face, and made a twisting motion. Davidson jerked in his chair, a sharp cry escaping his mouth. His head came up, eyes popping open. They were set very deep and a very dark brown. Purple bruising circled the left eye, the skin there already starting to swell. Blood caked along his eyebrow. More blood clogged his nostrils, and his large masculine nose was either badly bruised or broken. Two or three days' worth of bristles grassed his cheeks and chin. His brow and jaw and chin matched his physique—all were large and made up of inelegant lines, like a pile of rocks had been sown together atop his barrel of a neck. The result wasn't as ugly as it sounded. If you rinsed off the blood, some might consider it a handsome face, in a brutal sort of way.

Davidson turned his head this way and that until finally his eyes came to rest on my face. A sneer curled his lips, his eyes burned hot, and his body drew tense like a loaded spring. For a second I thought he was going to lunge across the table at me, bloodied as he was. Then Michael laid a hand on his shoulder, surprisingly gentle, and said softly, "I think Adam has some questions for you. You'd better answer them." Then he stepped back to lean against the wall, got out a cigarette, and put it in his mouth.

Davidson didn't answer for a moment. He just stared at Michael with fear on his face. Alongside the fear was wonder, as if he were asking himself, just like I had a minute ago, how this much smaller man had bested him. He turned back to face me.

"You're lucky this guy got me from behind," Davidson said. There was a swagger in his voice, but his body was no longer tense.

"Otherwise?" I prompted, resisting the urge to remind him how he had ambushed me. *Stay focused on getting the information you want*, I told myself.

"Otherwise I'd have given you a well-deserved beating."

"Deserved? For what?"

"For telling my wife lies. I come home after a long night on my boat, my wife sees me walk in the door, and she starts bawling. Accuses me of having an affair with a friend of hers, Esther Kantor. I ask her who put such lies in her head and she gives me your name. Took me all day to find you."

"Find me to do what?"

"To teach you a lesson you weren't about to forget anytime soon."

"But not for lying about you. Because I wasn't lying, was I, Alon?"

"Yeah, you were. I never had an affair with Esther."

"Now you're the one who's lying, Alon. Esther told a friend of hers about you, about the affair."

His eyes bulged. "What? She's lying. Tell me who this bitch is. Why, I'll—" He bit off the rest of his sentence.

"You'll what? Punch her in the face?"

Davidson shook his head. "I don't hit women."

"This friend isn't the only person who saw you and Esther together. A neighbor saw the two of you kissing."

"More lies."

"By the docks. A few days before the murders. Ring any bells?"

By the way his eyes darted this way and that, I could tell that it did. He shifted in his seat, looked from me to Greta to Michael and back to me.

"You want to ask me questions, she and him have to be around to hear me answer them?"

"Yes. You brought this on yourself by attacking me. Now answer the goddamn question."

He let out a theatrical sigh. "Fine. I did kiss Esther by the docks, all right? Happy? I admit it. But I didn't have an affair with her."

"What, then?"

Davidson wiped blood off his nose with his hand. "She was something, Esther was. Like one of those models you see in magazines. I wanted her as soon as I saw her. Her being around my wife and our apartment so much didn't make it easy to approach her. I tried catching her eye a few times, to gauge her interest, but I couldn't read her. Then, one evening, as I was starting to head back home from the docks, I saw her getting out of a truck and walking down the street toward me. She was wearing a white summer dress, showing her legs. Beautiful. We got to talking and then I kissed her. I just pulled her to me and kissed her."

Beside me Greta let out a small sound. I didn't turn to look at her. I kept my eyes on Davidson, feeling my anger toward him mount.

Davidson licked his lips, as if reliving the kiss. Then he grimaced. "The bitch slapped me. She told me I should be ashamed of myself, me a married man with a wife and baby at home. I told her I couldn't get her out of my mind. She told me to forget about it, that it was never going to happen. She said even if she wasn't friends with my wife, I had no chance with her." He gritted his teeth and the anger he must have felt ten years ago was still there, like glowing coals ready to be stoked to flame. "She looked at me like I was dirt."

"It got you mad, didn't it?" I said. "That she rejected you like that?"

He didn't answer, but the hateful expression on his face was answer enough.

"Getting slapped, that must have made you mad. Bet you were itching to return the favor."

"I told you, I don't hit women," Davidson said, not denying he'd had the urge to do just that.

"What about slashing their throat? Ever find yourself doing that?"

He stared at me. "Huh? What the hell are you talking about?"

"Did you kill her because she turned you down? Or was it because you were scared she'd tell your wife?"

"I didn't kill Esther."

"And why did you cut her face? So she'd be ugly in death? Was that a part of your revenge? Why kill the baby?"

"I didn't kill them, I tell you." He was shouting now, face taut and eyes blazing. His words bounced off the walls, hanging in the air like a death cry. Beside me I could hear Greta breathing sharp and fast. Michael, on the other hand, was unmoved by this outburst. He held a cigarette loosely between two fingers, his posture loose and relaxed.

I said nothing. Davidson, his face softening to a triumphant smile, leaned back in his chair. "The police questioned me about Esther ten years ago. I had an alibi. I was on—"

"Your boat," I said. "I know. I read the report."

"Then why are you making these stupid accusations? You know I couldn't have done it."

"You were on your boat with someone, am I right?"

"Yes. A fellow fisherman. We were out all night at sea."

"Saul Mercer?"

He hesitated, but could see no harm in answering. "Yes. Saul Mercer."

"He's a friend of yours."

"Well, yes. Yes, he is."

"He must be a good friend, twice he got you out of trouble with the law."

Davidson sat as still as a boulder. His mouth had dropped open in the shape of an O, like a train tunnel going into his big head.

"I asked a policeman friend of mine to run a check on you. He told me how one time you got in a bar fight and cut a man up pretty badly after an argument about a woman. Did you use this knife here, or one just like it?"

"I was defending myself," Davidson said. "He came at me with—"

"A bottle. Yes, I know. That's the story you told. You and Saul Mercer. The same man who said he was with you on your boat the night someone took a knife to the woman who spurned you and her baby."

Davidson opened his mouth to speak, but I waved a hand, cutting him off.

"The cops who questioned you about that bar fight did not think to check whether Saul Mercer was in the habit of covering up for you. And the detective who investigated the double murder ten years ago had no reason to suspect that Mercer was lying about your alibi. What do you think would happen if I go to the police and enlighten them? They'll pay Mercer a visit. They'll lean on him. Ask him if he was one hundred percent sure you were on that boat with him that night. What do you think he'll do? Maybe he'll stick up for you. Or maybe he'll say he made a mistake, that he got the dates mixed up. It could happen to anyone, nothing sinister about it. Maybe he'll leave you with no alibi. What do you think?"

Davidson's mouth dropped open further. Big as he was, he no longer looked intimidating.

"All that would be left for the cops to see is a man with a reason to get back at Esther Kantor, a man in the habit of cutting people with a knife."

He swallowed so hard it was audible.

"So tell me, Alon. Where were you really that night?"

I'd been putting on an act this past minute or so, ever since I'd mentioned Saul Mercer. Because if Davidson had indeed been on that boat, then nothing I'd said would have any effect on him. He would—smugly, no doubt—inform me that his friend would vouch for him. Which he might well do, even if he were lying. But I could see no other way to shake his alibi, to shake him. I'd rolled the dice and was now waiting to see what numbers came up.

For a long moment Davidson didn't speak. Then he averted his eyes, cleared his throat, and said in a low voice, "I was with a woman."

"What was that? Speak louder."

He raised his eyes. "I was with a woman, you little turd. You happy?"

"That night? The night Esther and Erich were killed?"

"Yes. Saul and I, we cover for each other sometimes. We tell our wives we're on the boat together overnight, but one of us stays ashore and spends the night with another woman."

I noticed he used the present tense, meaning that he cheated on his wife regularly and had done so for at least ten years. My hands were below the table, bunched into fists. Natalie Davidson had defended her husband and tried covering up for him by lying to me. He didn't deserve her love. He didn't deserve her.

"So you were cheating on your wife, just not with Esther?"

"Yes," he said.

"You were with this woman all night?"

"I was at her place until four or five in the morning. Then I went to the docks to wait for Saul to bring the boat in."

"Are you still seeing this woman?"

He shook his head. "I got tired of her. You know how it is." And the lowlife actually grinned a man-to-man grin at me, showing his big teeth. Still grinning, his eyes drifted, passing over Greta as if she weren't there, and came to rest on Michael's face. Michael did not smile back. Instead, he eyed Davidson with such cold menace that the smile melted off Davidson's face like ice cream in an oven.

I could guess what was going through Michael's mind. Probably something similar to what was going through mine. He had lost his wife like I had lost mine, and he'd probably do anything to get her back—just as I would have done anything to be reunited with my Deborah. And here was this lucky moron with a loving wife and three children with a fourth on the way, and it wasn't enough for him. He was willing to risk it all for a thrill. Not only that, but he was actually gloating about how little he cared for his lover. No wonder Michael looked on the verge of beating him up again.

"Michael," I said, and when his eyes turned my way, I could tell he got my message. *Calm down. Don't go crazy now.*

Michael nodded and dropped his cigarette to the floor, crushing it with his foot. Then he jerked his eyes to Greta, sending her an apologetic look for dirtying her floor.

"I need this woman's name," I said.

"What for?" Davidson asked.

"So I can talk to her, see if she corroborates your story."

"It was ten years ago."

"Still. Tell me her name."

He hesitated. "I'd rather not. She's married, you see."

"It's okay for you to sleep with a married woman, but it's not okay for me to talk to her?" I leaned forward, making sure I didn't wince when my stomach twinged where he'd kicked me. "Listen to me now and listen good. Give me that woman's name or I go to the police and tell them you lied about your alibi and that maybe you weren't defending yourself when you cut that man. Your choice. What's it going to be?"

The hatred in his eyes was as hot as a bonfire.

He said, "How do I know you won't go to the police anyway?"

"You don't. I can give you my word and that's it. I won't tell the police Saul Mercer lied for you, and what happened here tonight will stay between us four. Unless you're the killer and unless you try to harm me or anyone I know. But you need to make your choice now."

I could see him trying to find a way out of this and having no luck, so he told me her name was Shulamit Hendleman and gave me the address where she lived when he was seeing her. I wrote it down in my notebook.

I slipped my notebook back into my pocket, even that small movement causing me pain; then I sat back, drumming my fingers on my thigh. I had one more question I wanted to ask Davidson.

"Did the police ever question you about you kissing Esther?"

"Yeah," Davidson said.

"Sergeant Rivlin?"

"I don't remember his name. The same guy who talked to me earlier, the one I gave my alibi to. He said there was a rumor Esther and I had a thing going on. I swore we hadn't. He said he might need to look deeper into it, that he was sorry if it would cause me problems at home. I could see what he was angling for. I said I'd appreciate it if he didn't spread lies about me. I slipped him some cash and he went away."

So that was the real reason why Rivlin had not included Elena's sighting of Esther and Davidson in his report. Since he did not believe Natalie Davidson could have done the killing, and since Alon Davidson had been alibied, Rivlin saw no benefit in recording Elena's testimony. But he could still parlay the testimony into cash. That greedy drunken excuse for a detective. I regretted not punching him when I had the chance.

I looked at Davidson. Michael had hurt him good. By tomorrow that eye would be swollen halfway shut, and his nose and head would probably hurt him for days. But it wasn't enough. Not by a long shot.

"Anything else?" I asked, looking at Michael and Greta. Both shook their heads, Greta looking a little surprised at my question.

Davidson, following this, said, "Good. Then we're done here, right? I'll head on home. Hopefully my wife's had time to cool down."

I turned my eyes once more to Davidson. Despite the bruises and caked blood on his face, he looked self-assured, smug. In some perverted way, his telling us about his mistress had boosted his self-esteem. He'd shown us what a man he was, and he was feeling good about it. No. What Michael had done to him wasn't nearly enough.

"Just a minute. There's one last thing I'd like to get straight: You said you were going to teach me a lesson, is that right?"

Davidson smiled. "That's right."

"By giving me a beating."

"Yes. And I did, didn't I? Before your friend came along to save you."

I pointed at the knife. "A knife isn't used for beating. What were you planning on doing to me?"

Davidson licked his lips. A look of wariness came to his eyes. "To scare you a little, that's all. So you would stay away from me and my wife."

"I think you're lying. You said you were going to hurt me, not scare me."

"That was just talk. Swear to God."

"You weren't going to cut me up?"

He shook his head. He looked worried all of a sudden. Something he saw in my eyes or heard in my voice made him reassess the situation. He sensed trouble.

I got to my feet. It was a process. First I sat forward; then I placed both hands on the table and used them to push myself up. I stood still for a few heartbeats, my head swimming. When I felt relatively steady again, I slipped the damp cloth with which Greta had cleaned my wound off the table and, walking slowly around the table with my hands behind my back, wrapped the cloth tightly around my right fist, padding the knuckles. Davidson watched me approach, a frown on his face. I must have looked like I was about to fall down at any second. With my legs all wobbly and shaky, that was how I felt.

"Hold on now," he started saying. "Just hold—"

I cut him off. "I think you were going to use your knife on me, but I'm willing to give you the benefit of the doubt. That said, I'm certain you were aiming to hurt me pretty badly. Knock some of my teeth out, probably. Maybe do something even worse. Leave your mark on me somehow." Another step and I was in front of his chair. "I can't just let you get away with it without paying you back myself."

"Just a minute." He began pushing himself up, raising his hands to defend himself.

"Sit down!" Michael ordered.

Davidson's eyes jumped from me to Michael, and in that moment I brought my right fist from behind my back and, putting my entire body behind it, landed it right on the side of his mouth.

His head snapped sideways and the rest of him followed, toppling out of his chair and onto the floor like a felled tree. The blow jarred my arm all the way to my shoulder and my knuckles felt as if they'd been stepped on. Tugging the cloth loose from around my knuckles, I was gratified to see my hand wasn't bleeding. Flexing my fingers to alleviate the pain, I watched as Davidson laboriously raised himself to hands and knees. Blood dripped from his mouth. He shook his head, coughed, and spat some more of it out. Something white glistened among the blood on Greta's floor.

"Help me throw him out," I told Michael.

We each grabbed Davidson under one arm and dragged him to the door. Outside, we dragged him a few doors away and leaned him against a wall. His mouth was a mess, but he was conscious and breathing as well as could be expected. I crouched beside him, bringing my face close to his, our eyes at the same level.

"If you ever try to hurt me again, you'll lose more than your teeth. Understand? Be grateful I don't want to leave your wife without a husband and your children without a father. Now get up and go home. Be gone in five minutes, or I might change my mind and let you have some more."

I rose and Michael and I went back into Greta's café.

Inside, Greta was busy with a bucket and mop, cleaning the mess on her floor.

"Here, let me do it," I said, reaching for the mop.

She waved me off. "You're in no condition to do anything but go home and sleep. Sure you don't need a doctor?"

"I'm sure," I said truthfully. My head was clear and my feet no longer felt like jelly. I was still aching, but pain was something I was familiar with. "Sorry you had to see that, Greta."

"Don't be. He had it coming, the beast. And don't you worry about me, either. I'm not the sort of woman who goes weak in the knees at the sight of blood." She paused in her mopping and looked at me. "Are you really not going to report him to the police?"

I nodded.

"It's your call, but I wish you would."

"You think she's right?" I asked Michael.

He had lit up another cigarette and took it out of his mouth to speak. "Nothing good ever came out of getting cops involved. That's been my experience, anyway."

Probably born out of his years in the Irgun, when he was among the hunted.

Greta threw up the hand not holding the mop. "Have it your way. But what if he's your killer?"

"If he is, then there isn't any way to prove it," I said. "Not yet anyway. For all I know, his friend will stick by him and his alibi for the night of the murders will hold. Or this woman, Shulamit Hendleman, will corroborate the version he gave us tonight. I could get him charged for assaulting me, but he'll get off relatively easy. And the police might not look kindly on me for having broken his teeth long after he was subdued."

Not to mention the fact that if I turned him in, it would make it harder for Mira to exact her revenge. If I became convinced Davidson was the killer, of course.

"What if he comes after you again?" she said. "A man like that, he doesn't forget easily."

"He's not going to blindside me twice, I promise you that. If he tries, I'll be ready for him." But to be on the safe side, I decided that I would be armed until this case was done.

She gestured at the knife on the table. "What do you want to do with this?"

"Throw it out with the trash."

"With pleasure. Can you get home all right?"

I assured her that I could. She did not seem convinced. To Michael she said, "Can you walk him?"

He asked me where I lived and glanced at his watch when I

told him. "I'm already late for my shift, but I can walk you to the corner of Allenby and Tchernichovsky."

"That's close enough," I said.

I squeezed Greta's hand and told her again that I was sorry for bloodying her floor. She told me to hush about that and to come by tomorrow so she could see I was all right. To Michael she said, "Thank you for stepping in when you did. Most men wouldn't have."

He seemed embarrassed by her gratitude, assured her it was nothing, and nodded with a smile at her offer of a free meal whenever he wanted.

Outside, he tossed the remnants of his cigarette into the road. I got the crumpled pack out of my pocket, got two cigarettes out, and offered him one. At the corner of Allenby and Brenner I said, "I owe you one, Michael."

He blew out some smoke. "Forget about it, okay?"

"Okay. I will. In about five minutes. But while I still remember it, know that I owe you one."

After a few more steps I said, "What'd you think about Davidson?"

Michael snorted. "Sleazy. Full of himself. Not as tough as he looks, and not half as tough as he thinks he is. But don't make the mistake of assuming he's too banged up to cause you trouble. He likely has friends who are just as vicious."

"Don't worry. I won't be taken by surprise again. But what I meant was, do you think he might be my man?"

He considered it and shrugged. "I'm not a detective."

"A part of me hopes it's him."

"Why?"

Because then he would absolutely merit killing, I thought. What I said was, "Because he's the best lead I've got."

We passed the turn to King George Street, the road angling northwest.

I said, "You miss your wife, Michael?"

He jerked his head to look at me, surprised.

"Sorry," I said, "I didn't mean—"

"It's all right," he said.

"It's just that I'm also a widower. Five years now. I miss her like mad."

He drew in some smoke, held it in for a beat, and let it out. When he spoke, his voice was thick with smoke and sorrow. "I know what you mean."

There was that sense of affinity again, the feeling that this man and I were very similar. I suddenly realized how long it had been since I had a friend I could talk to openly, without reservation, without fearing that I would be misunderstood or judged. Not even Greta or Reuben knew all my secrets. But maybe Michael could.

"She died in Europe," I said. "In Auschwitz. I feel guilty, that I should have protected her more."

"From the Germans?"

"Yes."

"Was there something you could have done? Could you have resisted?"

I didn't want to answer because the truth was unbearable and shameful. "No. Nothing. But I still can't shake the guilt over what happened to her, over what happened to my children."

"Your children are also dead?" he asked, and I could only nod in response, as my throat had closed up. "I'm sorry," he said. "I know what you mean about guilt." But otherwise he remained silent, offering no platitudes or hollow words of encouragement. There was no pity in his eyes, and he made no effort to affect an expression of commiseration. I was grateful for that. Too many Israelis, those who had lived in Israel while the Nazis strove to eradicate the Jews of Europe, did not know how to act around survivors such as I. The discomfort we aroused in them was palpable. They sought to ease their consciences by trying too hard to ease our pain. I liked that Michael did not try to make me feel better. He probably knew all too well that there was no way to do that. The loss of his wife would have taught him that some wounds cannot be salved by mere words or sympathy.

At the corner of Allenby and Tchernichovsky, we said our goodbyes. We shook hands, and for a second I thought of suggesting I'd walk him to the Reading Power Station. But I was dead tired and ached all over. I needed to get in bed.

"Let's meet at Greta's one of these evenings. You can claim your free meal."

"I'd like that," he said. "She seems like a good woman."

"She is, and her food is excellent. Tell you what, I'll give you a number where you can reach me. Just let me know when you plan to stop by." I recited the number at Levinson Drugstore and he repeated it back to me. We shook hands again and he walked off. I watched him for a few seconds, then turned to Hamaccabi Street.

At home, I peeled off my clothes and let them drop to the floor. In the bathroom mirror, I examined my torso. Beside my two bullet wound scars, there were patches of discolored skin where Davidson had kicked me. My lower back was abraded from being dragged across the pavement. I turned on the shower, standing under the hot jet for five minutes, letting the water sluice off the sweat from my skin and the tension from my body, but took care not to let any of it touch the plasters on my head.

After drying myself, I crawled into bed, leaving all the windows open. My mind started to drift, but it didn't get far. In less than ten seconds I was asleep.

27

It took me all morning to find her.

I woke up after nine, groaning as I rolled out of bed, my body aching and sore in multiple places. I stumbled into the shower, and this time let steaming water run over my head. The water loosened the plasters and stung the broken skin behind my ear. Gently, I peeled off the bandages and prodded the side of my head. A tender lump the size of an olive had blossomed behind my ear. I was happy to find that the wound was already scabbing over. A second lump, smaller and less sensitive to the touch, had grown on the back of my head where it had hit the door Davidson had flung me against. My torso looked like a few canisters of fresh paint had been upended over it.

Despite the pain, I was feeling refreshed and alert. I could not recall the last time I had slept so deeply, but it had been years ago.

I closed all the shutters, then retrieved my box of souvenirs from its hiding place and took out the Luger. I doubted Davidson was in any shape to attack me again today, but I was taking no chances. I got dressed, stuck the Luger in my waistband, and put on my light jacket to hide it from sight.

I made some toast and coffee, consumed both quickly, and discovered I was still hungry. I toasted two more pieces of bread and carried them with me as I left my apartment. I munched on the toast as I made my way north toward Ussishkin Street, where Shulamit Hendleman had lived when Alon Davidson was her lover.

She wasn't living there any longer. In fact, she hadn't lived there for about nine years. I learned this from one of her neighbors, who also informed me that the Hendlemans had gotten a divorce at about the same time. "She was involved with another man," the neighbor told me, shaking her head at the tragedy of a broken marriage. "Cheated on her husband. And Ethan is such a nice man. That's Dr. Hendleman. Imagine, she's married to a doctor and she goes behind his back. Foolish woman."

Dr. Hendleman, the neighbor told me, worked at Hayarkon Hospital. I hiked there and asked the reception nurse if I could see him. She told me Hendleman would be done with his rounds in twenty minutes or so. I found a bench and parked myself on it, the sight of patients hobbling along the hall and the heavy scent of disinfectant conjuring unpleasant memories of my own time in the hospital.

Dr. Hendleman was a scrawny man with round eyeglasses and a shrinking hairline. He offered a kind smile when he introduced himself and asked what ailed me. The smile vanished when I told him I was healthy and that I was looking for his wife, Shulamit.

"Ex-wife," he muttered. "She hasn't been my wife for nine years now."

"Know where I can find her?"

He hesitated. I explained who I was and that she might have information pertinent to a case I was working on. I assured him that she was in no trouble.

He sighed. "Why should I care if she were? But I do care, even after all these years. Look, Mr. Lapid, I haven't seen or spoken to

Shulamit since our divorce. But I've heard that she remarried some years ago and moved to Herzliya. Her husband's name is Ayalon. If you see her...well, I'd prefer it if you don't mention you talked to me."

From a phone in a nearby restaurant, I called the Herzliya town hall and asked a sleepy-voiced male clerk for Shulamit Ayalon's address.

"I'm not allowed to give out that information," the clerk droned in my ear.

"Listen, the reason why I need to find Mrs. Ayalon is for a story I'm working on."

"A story?"

"Yes. I do research for Shmuel Birnbaum at *Davar*. What did you say your name was?"

"Greenspan," he said. Then, suddenly more alert: "Wait a minute. Why do you need my name?"

"So we can cite you in our story as a helpful source—if you can spare the time to find that address for me. Give me your first name, too. Spell it out for me, so I'll know I got it right."

Prompted by the promise of negligible fame, it took Yuram Greenspan less than five minutes to find Shulamit Ayalon's address. "When do you think your story will be published?"

"Anytime in the next thirty days," I told him. "Keep your eyes peeled for it."

After hanging up, I caught a bus downtown, and there switched to another bus that conveyed me the twenty kilometers north to the town of Herzliya.

It was a small town made up of tidy streets with modest one-story houses. It took me less than twenty minutes to locate the Ayalon residence. My knock was answered by a five-foot-five gentle-faced woman with tight brown curls and sloping eyes, cradling a two-year-old boy on her hip. She confirmed that she was indeed Shulamit Ayalon.

"My name is Adam Lapid. I'd like to talk to you for a few minutes about Alon Davidson."

Whatever I was expecting, it wasn't what happened next. Her face, pale enough to begin with, went three shades whiter, and she began trembling. For a moment, I worried she might lose her grip on her son. She looked terrified out of her mind.

"You're a friend of Alon?" she asked, her voice quavering. She took a small step back, arm tightening around her son.

"Hardly," I said. "In fact, I don't like him very much. I'm a private investigator, and I'm working on a case Davidson may be connected to. Do you recall a double murder of a woman and child that took place ten years ago in Tel Aviv?"

I told her a little about the murders, and she said she had a vague recollection of them.

"How awful. You think Alon may have had something to do with it?" She seemed surprised, but certainly not as shocked as she would have been if the notion of Davidson being a killer had struck her as outlandish.

"I was hoping you might be able to help me determine that. You see, Davidson told me he was with you the night the murders took place."

Her cheeks turned pink. "So you know."

"Yes," I said. "But I am not here to judge you, Mrs. Ayalon. All I'm interested in is Alon Davidson."

We were still standing on her threshold. With a sigh, she opened the door wider. "You'd better come in, Mr. Lapid. I don't want my neighbors to catch wind of any of this."

It was a three-room house, and she kept it tidy and neat. She set her boy in a playpen, where he began piling blocks on top of each other, then asked me if I wanted a glass of ice tea. I said that sounded good, and she poured each of us a tall glass.

Sitting across a low table from each other, we each took a sip. I was formulating an opening question, but she beat me to it.

"I met Alon shortly after I moved to Tel Aviv. Ethan—that's my first husband, Ethan Hendleman—was just starting out as a doctor. He worked very long hours, including night and weekend shifts. I had come from a kibbutz and knew no one in Tel Aviv. I was lonely, out of sorts. I think he recognized that in me."

"Davidson?"

She nodded and took a quick, nervous sip from her glass.

"I didn't see it then, of course. What I saw was this tall, imposing, handsome man. The sort of man who could wrap me up in his arms, keep me warm, and protect me from anything. I was surprised he took an interest in me. It was flattering." A pause, another sip. "I didn't plan on being unfaithful to Ethan—I loved him very much—but when Alon put his hands on me, I just didn't say no."

"How long did the affair last?"

"Eighteen months, give or take. We would see each other most weeks, once or twice, on nights when Ethan was at the hospital. I betrayed my husband in our own bed." Her eyes filled up and tears hung on her eyelids before tumbling down her cheeks. She wiped her eyes with the heel of her right hand. "I'm an awful person, aren't I?"

I shook my head. "I don't think so. You're just weak like the rest of us."

Her son, alerted by his mother's tears, began whining. Shulamit said a few reassuring words to him, went into the kitchen, and returned with two cookies. The smile she had on her face as she handed the cookies to her child looked forced, but the boy did not seem to notice. He quieted down, happy with his treat. She returned to her seat opposite me.

She said, "I fell in love with Alon. Or at least I thought I did. He told me he loved me, said he would leave his wife for me, but he always had reasons and excuses why now was not a good time for him to divorce her—usually something along the lines that she

245

was not well or in an emotional state, that he felt sorry for her. Things like that. I foolishly believed every word of it."

"So you kept seeing him."

She nodded. "I couldn't be without him. That's how it felt, anyway. Eventually, I got tired of waiting. I told Ethan I had met another man, that I wanted a divorce. When I told Alon about it, I thought he would be happy, that it would prod him to break up with his wife. Instead he got very angry. He shouted, he raved, he called me names. He..." She paused and a haunted look came into her eyes.

"He hit you?" I asked.

A jerky nod. "Slapped me. Twice. When I began crying and accusing him of lying to me. The first slap might have been to quiet me down, but the second one...I think he enjoyed that one." She took another sip then set her glass down on the coffee table. I did the same. "He said he wanted nothing to do with me, that he didn't love me. He said I was stupid, that he would never leave his wife. Then, when I threatened to tell her everything, he gave me the coldest of stares. 'Better not do anything foolish, Shulamit,' he said, 'or you might not live long to regret it.' I remember those words perfectly and how he sounded when he said them. I kept hearing them in my dreams for months after."

"You think he was serious?"

She rubbed her arms as if a chill had settled on her skin. "I think so, yes."

"Is that why you weren't shocked when I raised the possibility of him being a murderer?"

"I suppose so. Although...I can see Alon hurting me or another woman, but you said a baby was also killed."

"Yes."

"I can't see Alon harming a child. Or maybe I just don't want to believe I was intimate with such a man."

"Davidson said you were with him the night of August 26, 1939."

"He might have been, but I can't swear to a specific night. Not after ten years. I'm sorry, Mr. Lapid."

"That's all right. Tell me, on nights he was with you, when would he arrive and when would he leave?"

"He'd be at my door anywhere between ten to midnight and leave around four or five in the morning. Does that help?"

According to the police report, the murders took place between 23:00 and 04:00. Would Davidson have been able to commit the murders and still make it to Shulamit's apartment at the usual time? I did some rapid calculations and decided that he would. Davidson could have killed Esther and Willie at eleven p.m. and arrived at Shulamit's apartment by midnight or slightly later. He wouldn't even need to have run from Lunz Street to Ussishkin Street—a brisk walk would have sufficed. It was unlikely that Shulamit would have remembered it if he'd been fifteen or even thirty minutes late. Not after ten years.

Of course, it was possible that Davidson had not seen Shulamit that night at all. He could have killed Esther and Willie and spent the rest of the night elsewhere. But if Dr. Hendleman was working that night, if Shulamit was home alone, she could have provided Davidson with a backup alibi, in case his first one fell apart under scrutiny. Which was exactly what had happened last night at Greta's.

But Davidson's affair with Shulamit raised another question.

"In the time you had the affair," I said, "could Davidson have been involved with another woman?"

Shulamit mulled it over. "If you had asked me this question then, I would have said no, but now? Yes, I suppose it's possible."

"But you saw no sign of it?"

"No. Nothing. Why do you ask?"

I didn't answer her. My mind was churning, swirling with questions.

Davidson could have denied having an affair with Esther,

because he figured it would cast him as a suspect. But why had he insisted on it even after I told him a colleague of Esther had confirmed the affair? At that point, Davidson believed his initial alibi was strong, that he was beyond suspicion. He should have felt safe enough to come clean about the affair. It was only later that I revealed to him what I knew about Saul Mercer and got him to admit he had not been on his boat the night of the murders.

What Davidson had said about the night he forced a kiss on Esther by the docks could explain what Elena Warshavski had claimed she saw. What it couldn't explain was what Leah Goldin had told me. She'd said that Esther had told her she was having an affair with Alon Davidson. So either Esther had lied to Leah at the time, or Davidson had lied to me yesterday, or...I rubbed my face. Someone was lying, and I desperately needed to find out who.

Regardless of whether Davidson and Esther were having an affair, he could have killed her. He had motive. He had opportunity. He knew the layout of the building and the habits of the neighbors. He knew that he would be able to get in and out of the building without being seen. Davidson was vicious and violent and capable of harming women. He had lied about his alibi. He was the best suspect I had.

But if he had been truthful about not having an affair with Esther, it would cast doubt on his guilt. Just as his giving me Shulamit's name and address, despite knowing she was unlikely to speak of him fondly, did not seem like something a guilty man would do. On the other hand, I'd threatened to go to the police if he didn't cooperate.

Shulamit was looking at me, and I recalled that I hadn't answered her last question.

"It's not important," I said, getting to my feet. "Thank you for seeing me."

At the door I turned to her. "I apologize for making you relive painful memories."

"No apology is necessary," she said. "Actually, I want to thank you."

"Thank me?"

"Yes. I feel better now for having talked about those bad times, like a weight's been lifted off me. Do you know what I mean?"

I said that I did, though in truth I did not. How could talking about your awful experiences make you feel anything but lousy?

28

An hour later, back in Tel Aviv, I found a deserted café with a stooped, hatchet-faced barwoman and a telephone in the rear. It took a while, and a good number of calls, but eventually I managed to find the former manager of Moshe Klinger, back when he'd worked for Tnuva in Haifa.

He had a gruff, well-fed voice, and I could picture him in my mind: tanned skin lined by sun exposure; thick mustache; heavy frame with a bit of a gut, but not soft; thick arms dotted with sunspots; Shorts and sandals and strong legs sporting brown or black curls; and a face that was showing its forty-something years, but might stay that way for the next twenty. His name was Menashe Harel.

"I understand Moshe Klinger worked for you," I said into the mouthpiece.

"Who wants to know?" he demanded. A busy man in the middle of a busy day.

"Sergeant Dov Remez," I said, taking the first name of one government minister and stitching it to the last name of another. "Tel Aviv police."

A long pause. Breathing on the other end. In the background were sounds of men shouting instructions to each other and truck or tractor engines growling. The sounds were muffled, like Harel was in an office in a loading area with the door closed.

"Police? What's this about? Has Moshe done anything?"

"No, Mr. Harel, he's done nothing wrong," I said, aiming for a tone that signaled both assurance and weary impatience. I was committing a crime by impersonating a police officer, but I doubted I would ever be punished for it. Besides, I wanted to get answers quickly, without begging or wheedling, and couldn't think of a better way of getting them. People like Harel have respect for authority. "But his name has come up in connection with an investigation we're running, so I'm doing a little background check on him. Your full cooperation would be appreciated. Now, did Moshe Klinger work for you?"

"Yes, he did," Harel said, eager to help. "But not for, oh, ten years now."

"Yes. That fits in with what we already know," I said. As an interrogator you learn that it's always good to look like you already know a great deal. It makes people less likely to lie or hide things from you. "What exactly were his duties?"

"Driving. He also did some work on vehicles; he was pretty handy with a wrench. But his job was to drive a truck, delivering produce."

"What was his route?"

"He didn't have just one. He'd drive wherever I'd tell him."

"Including Tel Aviv?"

"Sure." A pause. "Listen, Sergeant, Moshe still works for Tnuva. If he's suspected of something, we should—"

"We're interested in Klinger as a potential witness, not a suspect. Tnuva has nothing to worry about. Now tell me, did Klinger's work ever require him to stay the night away from home?"

"On long trips, yes."

"Where would he sleep? Hotels?"

Harel snorted. "Hardly. In the back of his truck, most likely. It's what most drivers do if they don't have family who can put them up for the night. It's not as bad as one might think; I've done it a few times myself over the years."

He sounded right proud of it, as if it proved that he was a down-to-earth sort, one who could do with little and not complain about it. Not that I believed he knew the first thing about how little people could get by on. After all, he had been in Israel since at least 1939, not in Europe.

Not that it mattered. What did matter was that Moshe Klinger was often away from home at night. Could he have been away the night of the murders? Moshe had no motive that I could see, but he had evaded telling me that he and his family had moved from Haifa to Netanya shortly after the murders. And I suspected his wife had not told me the whole truth about the reason they had stopped housing immigrants after Esther and Willie.

"You keep a list of drivers and routes?" I asked.

"Sure. I have to know I got everything covered."

"Do you still have Klinger's work schedule?"

I could almost hear Harel's eyebrows crank up. "After ten years? Are you kidding?"

No, just hopeful. So there was no way of knowing whether Klinger was away from home that night. I was ten years too late. Again.

I kneaded the back of my neck. The wound behind my ear throbbed. "Were you satisfied with his work?"

"Yeah. He did his job fine. Truth is, there's not much to excel at. It's a simple job: you take stuff from one place and drop it off at another. As long as you're on time and nothing turns up missing, I'm happy."

"What kind of man is he?"

"What kind?" Harel sounded bewildered. "I don't know. A regular kind. We weren't close or anything. Like I said, he did his job. That's all I cared about."

"No problems with other employees or customers?"

"What kind of problems?"

"Anything. He ever get angry or physical with anyone?"

"No, nothing like that." He had said this slowly, suspicion creeping into his voice. I had asked a question that seemed out of place—if indeed I was not interested in Moshe Klinger as a suspect of a crime.

"When was the last time you saw him?"

"His last day of work here. He moved to Netanya and now works for our outfit there."

"What made him leave Haifa, do you know?"

"No," Harel said. "Now that you mention it, that was the only time I was angry with him."

"Why?"

"Because he hardly gave me any notice. Look, I run things in an orderly manner here. I plan things in advance. Klinger just came into my office one day and told me he was moving to Netanya in a week's time. Just a week. I had to scramble to find a replacement driver. Lucky for him I didn't make any noise about it, or he would have been out of a job, you can believe that."

"Why the sudden move?"

"I don't know. I asked, and he mumbled something about his wife. That made me even angrier. It's a cowardly thing to hide behind your wife. You're a man, stand by your decisions."

"But you don't remember the exact reason?"

"No. Listen, I gotta ask you, what's this about? Why do you care about what happened ten years ago?"

"It's confidential," I said, knowing that I would get no more from him. "I can't talk about it, and I'm instructing you to keep quiet about it as well. It's police business. Don't mention our talk to anyone. Is that clear?"

"Yeah, yeah. I gotta get back to work, all right?"

I considered asking him for names of colleagues of Moshe's, but decided not to. Harel would likely keep his mouth shut about our talk; anyone close to Moshe wouldn't. For the time being, I saw no upside in Moshe knowing that I was considering him as a suspect.

———

I handed some money to the hatchet-faced barwoman.

"For the call," I said. "Can I get a coffee?"

"Ran out of the real stuff yesterday," she said, tucking the money into a box below the bar. "Chicory coffee okay?"

It wasn't, so I ordered an orange soda. It was lukewarm and flat. Something told me this café wouldn't be in business for long.

"Thanks," I said and toted the bottle with me back to the phone. I swallowed some more soda. It did quench some of my thirst. That was something.

Taking another sip, I called Itamar Levine's law firm. The same secretary as yesterday picked up.

"He just came in," she said once we got through the introductions. "Hold on a minute."

I did and soon heard a soft male voice: "Hello, this is Levine."

"Mr. Levine, my name is Adam Lapid. I'm an investigator from Tel Aviv."

"An investigator? Police?"

"No. Private," I said. Pretending to be a policeman is a risky tactic with lawyers.

"I see. What is this about?"

His voice was soft and cautious. The voice of a man who

doesn't step off the curb before checking at least twice in both directions that the road is clear.

"Esther Kantor," I said.

A sharp intake of breath. "I haven't heard that name in a long while."

But from the way he said it, I would have bet the name had cropped up in his mind not that long ago.

"You worked together at Becker & Strauss."

"Yes. But why are you asking me about Esther?"

I told him.

"What hope is there after ten years?"

"More than there was two weeks ago," I said.

"If you say so. I don't know what I can tell you. I cannot imagine who might have killed her. I certainly didn't, if you're entertaining any such notion."

"I know you didn't," I said. "I read the police report. You were away."

"Yes. In Cairo. A conference. A very boring conference. But I did get to see the pyramids, which I doubt most Israelis would ever have the chance to see. When I returned, I learned Esther and her child were dead."

"How well did you know Esther?"

"As well as one can, professionally. As you said, we worked in the same firm. I was a young associate. She was a secretary."

"Was she a good secretary?"

"Excellent. Very bright and orderly. The best secretary I've ever worked with."

"And how was the other one?"

"The other one?"

"Leah Benowitz."

A short pause. "Not as good as Esther," Levine said, measuring his words.

"Can you tell me why Becker & Strauss would need two secretaries, when today there's only one?"

"Is there just one? I haven't been at the old place or spoken to anyone there in ages."

His tone was casual, but I felt that he was straining to keep it so. There was an undercurrent of tension at the bottom of every word, as if he were walking a tightrope as he spoke. In particular, the term "old place" rang false to me, like giving a term of endearment to someone you're known to dislike.

"Only one," I said. "A very young and pretty one, actually."

Another pause. This one had weight to it. "Why are you telling me this, Mr. Lapid?"

"Because I was wondering if that was unusual, or if all of Mr. Strauss's secretaries are young and pretty."

"I don't really know what you mean," he said, trying very hard to sound sincerely perplexed and utterly failing at it.

I ran a hand over my face. I was tired, and the lump behind my ear was radiating pain all over my scalp. "Mr. Levine, may I be frank? Over the past few days, while I've been investigating these murders, I have been lied to more times than I can count, I've had information withheld from me for no apparent good reason, and I've run across people that one would be fortunate to never meet in his life. All the while, somewhere, the killer of a woman and a child is roaming free. I'm fresh out of patience. Do you understand me? I want answers."

"I've given you answers. I've answered each and every one of your questions."

"Yes. In a lawyerly way. You skirted or weaseled your way around giving me straight answers. Or you pretended not to know what I was talking about."

He put on an indignant tone. "I don't know where you get off speaking to me this way. I'm not sure I wish to continue talking to you at all, Mr. Lapid. Now—"

"You'd better talk to me, because I'm sitting here by the bus terminal in Tel Aviv. The bus to Haifa leaves in twenty minutes. I can be on it and at your firm in three hours. If you're not there, I'll return tomorrow and the next day after that. I promise you I will make some noise."

"Are you threatening me? I'll call the police on you."

"Fine. We'll have a party. Your colleagues will talk about it for months. Especially when I start yammering about the young woman who worked with you and was murdered with her child. I know you didn't do it, but I doubt any of them will take the time to read the police report. They'll always wonder if there's any chance that you had something to do with it. That should do wonders for your career and social life."

Levine was silent for a long moment. His breathing sounded fast and shallow over the line. At length he said, "I don't want trouble."

"Me either."

"It's not my colleagues I'm worried about."

"Who, then? Strauss?"

He didn't answer.

"If he asks, you can tell him I called you and you told me to get lost. I'm not going to tell him different. The man practically threw me out of his office."

"Well, Mr. Lapid, I can see how one might tire of your presence."

He said this in a tone so dry and free of inflection that I burst out laughing. After a second, Levine joined in the laughter. I didn't hear a crack, but just like that the barrier between us had crumbled.

"Call me Adam, all right?" I said.

"And I'm Itamar. I'm sorry for giving you a hard time. At least now I know why Strauss has been looking for me."

"He called you?"

"At the firm. Twice. Once yesterday and once today. Urgent

business, he said. I've been putting off getting back to him for as long as I can."

"He'll tell you not to talk to me."

He sighed loudly. "Which is all the reason I need to do just that. Go ahead; ask me what you want."

I drank some more soda and wiped my mouth with the back of my hand.

I said, "Did Mr. Strauss hire Esther because of her looks?"

"I'm sure that was one of his considerations. Perhaps the primary one. But as I said, she was very good at her job. She had to be. Leah was so lousy at it."

"And Strauss kept Leah on because..."

"Because she was his mistress. Because it was easier to give her money that way without his wife finding out. He paid her much more than any secretary ought to get."

Which was probably why Leah Goldin had said Strauss was a wonderful man, I thought.

"Are they still involved?" I said.

Levine said he didn't know.

"Are you certain Strauss had his sights set on Esther?"

"No doubt about it. I saw how he looked at her."

"Did he act on it?"

"If he didn't, he was about to."

"What makes you say that?"

Levine sighed again and said in a disgusted tone, "Because of the necklace."

"What necklace?"

"Two weeks before I left for Cairo—three weeks or so before Esther was killed—I saw her in the office with a string of pearls around her neck. I knew right away she couldn't have bought them herself, not on her salary, but I thought maybe the pearls were some heirloom or a present from a suitor. I asked her about it and she said Strauss had given it to her. A gift, he said, for all—"

"The good work she's been doing," I completed his sentence, my insides twisting into a cold knot. So that was where the pearl necklace in the picture of Esther and Willie had come from.

"How did you know that?" Levine asked.

I told him about Dana, the pretty secretary, and the silver bracelet she had received from Strauss.

"That lecherous son of a bitch," Levine said, anger and hatred dripping from every word.

I finished my soda and set the empty bottle on the floor.

"Were Leah and Esther as close as Leah says?"

"They looked friendly enough," Levine said. "But were they close friends? That I cannot say. The only person Leah seemed truly close to was Mr. Strauss."

"Wouldn't she be upset or jealous seeing him set his sights on Esther?"

"It's logical. But maybe she was blind to it, like Strauss's wife was blind to all his philandering."

I wedged the receiver between my jaw and shoulder and lit a cigarette. It wiped away the overripe aftertaste the soda had left in my mouth.

I said, "A few days before she died, Esther told a friend she had some trouble at work. Any idea what it was?"

"No," Levine said. "I don't. Whatever it was, it must have happened while I was in Egypt."

"Strauss told me that Esther was upset because when she'd asked him for a raise, he'd refused. But given that he'd bought her an expensive necklace, it doesn't seem logical he would refuse her a raise, does it?"

"No. No, it doesn't."

"Why would he lie about something like that?"

"I don't know, Adam. The man is not above lying, that I can tell you."

"Is he also capable of killing?"

Levine was silent for a long, hollow moment. At last he said, "I don't know. He's ruthless in business, but that's not quite the same thing, is it?"

"No," I admitted, watching cigarette smoke undulate before my eyes.

"And I just can't picture him killing a baby. I hate him. I despise him. I fear him. But I can't see him doing that."

That was the thing, wasn't it? So far, none of the people I'd encountered were the sort who would kill a baby. But then again, would you recognize such a person? Would you see their depraved nature on their face? A madness like that was coiled deep inside the dark recesses of the soul, where no one could see it. It only emerged when opportunity allowed it to, or, as in Auschwitz, when the reins of civilization were loosened and madmen were given license to satisfy their maniacal urges.

"Do you think Strauss did it?" Levine asked.

"He had an alibi. His wife told the police he was with her that night."

"You think she was lying?"

"Wives have been known to do that. But it's too late to find out."

"I know. But what would be his motive?"

"I don't know," I said, staring at the burning tip of my cigarette. Strauss's smug face hovered before my face. I stabbed at it with the cigarette, and it vanished.

Levine and I spoke for a minute more. He asked me again not to say anything to Strauss about our talk. I was about to inquire what Strauss had done to earn his hatred and fear, but dismissed the idea. Why would Levine want to relive painful moments? What good would that do?

After hanging up, I returned the empty bottle to the bar and paid for my call.

"Come again soon," the woman said, her tone as cheerful as a funeral dirge.

29

My hands jammed deep in my pockets, I hiked uptown. The heat was intense and the sun was harsh on my eyes. I kept my gaze aimed at a point three meters ahead on the gray sidewalk, ruminating on this mess of a case.

The first problem was that there were too many lies and withheld truths, and too many people guilty of one or both. I counted them off in my mind.

Alon Davidson had lied about his alibi and had tried to lie about kissing Esther. He might have lied about not having an affair with her. Moshe Klinger had lied—or obfuscated the truth —about the timing of his family's move from Haifa to Netanya, and his wife, Yael, had lied about the reason why they had stopped sheltering immigrants. Leah Goldin had not told me about the affair she'd had with Strauss, and I was beginning to suspect she had also lied to me, but I wasn't sure about what. She had also called Strauss, presumably to inform him of my talk with her. Strauss, in turn, had lied about the reason why Esther had been troubled during her final days.

Each of them could have perfectly innocent reasons for their lies and evasions, or they might be trying to cover their tracks. I needed to find a way to separate the innocent from the guilty.

The second problem was that, as far as I knew, apart from Alon Davidson, none of the men and women on my list had a motive to kill Esther Grunewald. And none of them, including Davidson, had a motive to kill Willie Ackerland, not to mention deface the bodies. Maybe one of them had gone crazy, as Rivlin believed the killer had done. If so, the killer just might be some random stranger, but I had based my entire investigation on the assumption that he or she knew Esther and had a reason to kill her.

My instincts told me that assumption was correct. This was no random murder, but a targeted killing. The killer had gone after Esther specifically. My task was to figure out the *why* to be able to finger the *who*.

Which was easier said than done.

I let out a grunt of exasperation and stopped walking, leaned against the fence of a deserted schoolyard, blew some cool air down the front of my shirt, and fired up a cigarette.

Raising my head to blow out the first plume of smoke, my eyes lighted on the display window of the store directly across the street. It was a bridal shop, and three female mannequins draped in wedding dresses stood erect behind the glass. Shifting my gaze away, I took another drag, then paused as an itch started in the back of my mind. I pushed myself off the fence, waited for a bus to burble by, and crossed the street.

The leftmost mannequin was in a clingy gown, high at the neck, made of some smooth fabric—silk or satin. The middle one wore a conservative number, with long sleeves and lots of lace, a small white bag hanging from the crook of an arm. The third had on a low-cut dress with frills and a cap with a veil on its head. But the dresses weren't what had brought on that itch. It was what encircled the long neck of the third mannequin. A pearl necklace.

White dress and white necklace.

Twenty minutes later, I stood on her threshold. She wore a smile on her face when she cracked the door open partway, but it would not have fooled a blind man. She wasn't happy to see me.

"Mr. Lapid," she began, aiming for and failing to achieve a lighthearted tone, "I was not expecting you."

"I have a few more questions to ask you, Mrs. Goldin."

She had on a green dress that went an inch past her knees and clung advantageously to her heavy breasts. Her mid-heel shoes were black. She'd swept back her curls, clipping them on either side of her head. Like last time, she looked to be in her teens.

"I'd be happy to answer them, but I'm afraid that this is not a good time. Perhaps if you came by tomorrow..."

"Just one question regarding Esther's lover, Amir Davidovitch," I said, making up a name similar to Alon Davidson.

"All right," Leah Goldin said. "What about him?"

Closing my eyes, I inhaled a deep lungful of air and let it out one molecule at a time. My head throbbed. The bruises on my torso tingled. So Davidson had been telling the truth. He had not been Esther's lover. Leah had lied to me. I felt a mixture of disappointment and anger. I'd wanted Davidson to be the killer, but that had just become a little less likely. I had lost my best suspect.

I opened my eyes and stared silently at Leah. Her eyes narrowed under my gaze, her frown adding years to her childlike face.

"What?" she said. "Why are you looking at me like that?"

"His name is not Amir Davidovitch, but Alon Davidson," I said. "You never heard either name until I told it to you, did you? He wasn't Esther's lover. You lied to me."

She froze for just an instant, recovering quickly. "No, of course not. Why would I? I just got the names mixed up, that's all." She let out a self-deprecating chuckle. "I'm very bad with names, and the children kept me up half the night, so my mind is—"

"Is your husband home, Mrs. Goldin?"

She blinked, taken off balance by the abrupt shift. "Eh, no...but I'm expecting him home soon, at any moment." She'd added that last bit in a rush. It was clear she was lying, that she had only said her husband was on his way home in the hope that the imminent presence of a man would persuade me to leave. I could guess what she'd do if I did leave—sprint for a telephone and call Strauss to report my visit and get his instructions. "So you'll need to excuse me. I have to get back to my cooking."

"All right," I said. "Go ahead. I'll wait for your husband out here. I got all the time in the world."

Stepping back, I leaned against the landing railing. I turned my head aside, as if no longer interested in her, but in my peripheral vision I could see her fidgeting.

"Why do you want to talk to my husband?" Leah said.

I turned my eyes back to her. "To ask him if he knows his wife was sleeping with her boss."

Leah's face lost all color. She attempted a laugh that came out like a caw, cleared her throat, and said, "I have no idea what you're talking about."

I pushed myself off the railing, moving forward quickly, crowding her. She took a faltering step back, her eyes widening as she looked up at me.

"I know," I said. "I know you were Strauss's mistress. Or maybe you still are. I know you called him at the office right after I left here yesterday. Which is why he had a lie ready as to what had upset Esther shortly before she died. And I know one thing more: the pearl necklace you have on in your wedding picture came from him."

I shoved my hand into my pocket and brought out the picture of Esther and Willie in Gan Meir Park. I held it before her face. "It's the same necklace, isn't it? The one Strauss gave Esther. You will tell me how you got it. You will tell me everything that happened in that office. If you don't, I will expose you before your husband—I'll tell him what I know, and what I think I know. I'll make stuff up if I need to. When I'm done talking, I doubt he'll want anything to do with you."

She began trembling, looking as if she might fall to pieces, but I didn't care. She had lied to me. She had hidden things from me. And she'd done other things. I just didn't know what they were yet.

Her voice quavered. "Please. Not now. My children are home."

That at least wasn't a lie. Sounds of the children laughing, chattering, and banging something against the floor emanated from within the apartment.

"We can talk in the kitchen," I said. "It has a door."

She hesitated for another second, but then gave a resigned nod, and I followed her into the apartment. I waited behind while she went to the living room and I heard her instruct her children to stay where they were, that she would soon come play with them. Then she re-emerged and we entered the kitchen. She slid the door closed behind her and leaned her back against it, shoulders sagging, looking small and powerless, her eyes on the floor. I stood by the refrigerator, four feet away. The unmistakable scent of overcooked powdered eggs clogged the narrow space.

"Who was Esther's lover?" I said. "And don't you dare lie to me. I know more than you think."

Leah answered in a voice scarcely louder than a whisper. "John Clapper."

I leaned closer. "I didn't hear you."

She raised her voice and gaze. "Inspector John Clapper."

"Police?"

"Criminal Investigation Department."

"CID? Esther was sleeping with a British officer?"

"Yes," Leah said. "Surprised you, didn't it? I was shocked myself when I found out."

"How *did* you find out? Did Esther tell you?"

"Of course not. Being romantically involved with a British officer was a sure way to be ostracized from Jewish society. After all, the British were the despised occupiers, keeping us from having a country of our own." She snorted. "We Jews should have been on our knees, thanking the British for importing their culture and manners and advanced knowledge to this desolate desert of a country. But instead of being grateful, most of us just wanted them gone as soon as possible. And Clapper was one of the most hated British of the lot."

"What made him special?"

"He was in charge of stopping Jewish immigration to Palestine."

I stared at her, incredulous. It seemed impossible that Esther, who was on a ship fired upon by the British and who was arrested for illegally immigrating to the Land of Israel, should become the mistress of the man who hunted other Jews like her, but it fit together with other things I'd learned.

It explained why Esther had kept her affair a secret, even from a close friend such as Natalie Davidson. It explained why Sergeant Rivlin had had to make a daily report to the CID regarding his progress, or lack thereof. Had it been Esther's lover who'd demanded those reports? The name John Clapper did not appear in the file I'd read, but that might have been intentional. In all like-lihood, Clapper had not been inclined to have his affair recorded in an official paper.

It explained other things as well. In the depths of my mind a mist began lifting and disjointed pieces started to connect like a jigsaw puzzle, painting a larger and clearer picture.

I said, "How did you learn of the affair?"

"By chance. I saw them together."

"Where?"

"At a party in an officers' club. A closed event, just British offi-

266

cers and officials and their guests. Good music and food and wine. All the men in uniform and suits and all the women in evening dresses. Everyone polite and charming and well-mannered. Just what life should be like. Like in a movie. I was there with an infantry second lieutenant I was seeing. I didn't care what other Jews thought of me. I wanted to be with civilized people, to feel that I was in Europe."

"And Esther was there?"

"With Clapper. I saw her, but she didn't see me. They didn't stay long. Clapper was eager to get her out of there, to where they could be alone. It was almost obscene. My date told me they had been seeing each other for two months or so. I was stunned."

"You never spoke to Esther about it?"

Leah shook her head, but only after a slight hesitation.

"Did you speak to her about it or not?" I demanded.

"No."

"But you told someone."

Leah didn't answer. I took a step closer, towering over her. She shrank back against the door, casting her eyes down again.

"Who did you tell?"

"Gerhard," she whispered.

"Strauss?" I asked. From the police report I knew Gerhard was his first name.

A quick nod.

"Why did you tell him?"

Again she didn't answer, and this time I grabbed her little chin in my hand and jerked her head up so she had no choice but to look right into my eyes. What she read in them started her shaking. Tiny sweat beads glistened along her hairline.

"Tell me now, damn you, or I'll—"

She blurted out her answer. "Because he wanted to know if Esther had any dirty secrets."

I tightened my grip, squeezing her jaw. "Why? To what purpose?"

She grimaced in pain, whimpering. "Because he wanted something to hold over her so she would sleep with him."

For a moment, a bubble of silence engulfed the kitchen. The only thing I could hear was the rapid humming of blood past my eardrums. Then sound returned—the ticking of the refrigerator, the chirping of a bird outside, Leah's quick, shaky breaths.

Her chin felt cold and damp. I released my grip on it, wiping my hand on my trouser leg. My fingers had left red marks on her jaw and cheeks. I took a step back from her. I wanted some distance between us. Otherwise, I knew, I might strike her. The urge to lash out was buzzing in my hands and arms. Leah hugged herself, trembling as if caught in a freezing gale without a coat. I was the opposite. I felt hot. My blood boiled with anger. The sort of anger that demands retribution.

"You knew Strauss was after Esther?" I asked, my voice thick and hoarse and strange.

"He told me. I didn't blame him. Her beauty was breathtaking. The first time I saw her, I remember thinking that *she* could really be a movie star."

"And you didn't care? Despite him being your lover?"

Leah's eyes gazed directly into mine. They were fearful, but utterly devoid of shame. "Gerhard and I weren't exclusive. I was poor. He had lots of money. Life can be hard without money and so much easier with it. Gerhard would give me money and gifts— he even paid my rent sometimes—and all I had to do was be available to him. It was fun. He's very generous. I had no claim to him. I knew he chased other women."

"But Esther wanted nothing to do with him, did she?"

"Nothing," Leah said. "Gerhard tried to get close to her a few times, but Esther always kept her distance. Even after he gave her the necklace, she didn't warm up to him. It drove him crazy."

"And he wouldn't take no for an answer."

"Gerhard is not used to being refused."

"So he decided to force her into bed," I said, acid burning in my stomach. That stinking German snake. "And you gave him the means to do it."

She said nothing. Her arms tightened around her chest.

I shut my eyes and held them closed for a count of ten, telling myself to remain calm, that this was not the time to lose my temper.

When I had my anger down to a simmer, I opened my eyes. "Tell me what happened. Leave nothing out."

She swallowed hard. This time I didn't rush her. We were past the high point of resistance. She would tell me everything.

"It was two days before Esther and Erich were killed. Gerhard asked her to stay late—he made some excuse, I don't remember what. When they were alone in his office, he started kissing her, tried to tear off her clothes. Esther resisted, pushed him away, and slapped his face. Gerhard made some remark about her owing him for the pearls, so Esther ripped them off her throat and threw them at him."

"So that's how you got the necklace. As payment for your betrayal of Esther."

"It was broken," Leah said abstractly. "Fixing the clasp cost a lot of money."

"The hell with the clasp," I snarled. "Tell me the rest of it."

Leah flinched at my tone. "Gerhard went at her again, and again she resisted. She threatened to lodge a complaint with the police and to tell his wife he attempted to rape her. So Gerhard threatened her back. If she told anyone about what had happened, he would expose her as Inspector Clapper's whore. In fact, he would do it anyway if she didn't sleep with him." Leah paused and wet her lips. "Gerhard told me Esther was frozen with shock when she heard he knew about her and Clapper."

"But Esther didn't sleep with Strauss, did she?"

"No. She ran out of the office, crying."

And later Esther told Natalie Davidson that there was a problem at work, but that she could handle it. What had she planned on doing? Had she had a plan at all?

I said, "When did Strauss tell you all this?"

"Later, when we were in—" She bit off the end of her sentence, but I would have put money on the missing word being *bed*. Strauss and Leah had used the attempted rape of Esther as fore-play, a means by which to enhance their lovemaking. My stomach flipped at the perversity of it.

"How could you do this to her? To your friend?"

Leah's eyes flashed and her face hardened into a childish mask of fury. "She wasn't my friend. I hated her. Her perfect skin, her height, her beauty, her flawless English, her grace, the way men looked at her. She could have had her pick. I'm sure she could have married some English officer if she wanted, and he would have taken her away from here, to England. I wanted her to suffer. I wanted her humiliated. I wanted her to be just like me so she wouldn't be better than me."

"But she was," I said softly. "She was infinitely better."

Leah stared at me for a breathless moment, the fury slowly evaporating from her eyes. Then it was as if an invisible hard shell around her had crumbled and a sliver of her repressed humanity peeked out. Burying her face in her hands, she broke out in tears, her small frame quaking with loud sobs.

I gave her a minute to stop crying. It took her more than twice that. Finally, she ceased and lowered her hands. Her face was a mess—eyes reddened, nose runny, cheeks slick with tears.

"I know I shouldn't have done it," she said in a choked voice. "I know it was wrong."

"It's too late for that," I said. "What I need you to tell me now is whether Strauss killed Esther and the baby."

She stared at me in shock, then violently shook her head. "No. Of course not."

"Why not? He tried to rape her and she threatened to tell his wife. It's as good a motive as you'll find."

"He couldn't have done it. He was with his wife."

"How do you know? She might have covered up for him. Wives do that, just like mistresses."

"I can't believe it. I know him. He couldn't—Gerhard couldn't."

"Yes, he could," I said. Because Strauss had a good motive and a lot to lose, and I had seen the coldness in his eyes. "It wouldn't bother him none."

"No. It's not true. I know it's not true." Leah was frantic now, desperate to believe her own words, clutching at any straw that would alleviate her guilt.

She began crying again, and a surge of searing rage came over me. I grabbed her arms, squeezed hard, and thrust her against the kitchen door. She yelped in pain.

"Stop crying!" I shouted into her face. "You're not entitled to tears. You knowingly conspired to help a ruthless man rape an innocent woman, a man who may have murdered her and her child. And you did it for the lowest reasons—greed and envy. I hope not a day goes by in which you don't see their faces before you, that they'll visit you in your sleep every night. And if your lover did kill them, I will make him pay if it's the last thing I do."

I shoved her aside, away from the door. She bumped against the counter and sagged to the floor, wailing. I slid the door open so fast it shuddered on its track, and was about to step out into the hall, when I stopped short.

There, on the floor beyond the kitchen door, huddled two children, a boy and a girl. They had their arms around each other, and both looked up at me with eyes wide with shock and terror, silent fat tears streaking down their little faces. What had scared them more, my shouting or their mother's crying?

271

The sight of them snuffed out my rage. A freezing chill of shame replaced the scorching heat of my fury. I wanted to tell them something, but I couldn't think what. For five seconds, I stood stock-still, paralyzed by their frightened faces. Then, with a conscious effort, I tore my eyes away from theirs and stepped past them and out of the apartment.

30

I walked west, stopping on the corner of Borochov and King George Streets to contemplate my options.

I could head north to the hair salon right now and tell Mira everything I'd learned. I had little doubt as to what she'd do. Eager to avenge Esther and Willie, Mira would exact her vengeance on Strauss for his attempted rape of Esther. I was certain her revenge would be deadly.

Which was fine by me. There was no other way to make Strauss pay. Leah Goldin would not break down a second time, not after she'd spoken with Strauss—a telephone call that might have been taking place that very moment. I doubted the police would ever question her. They had more pressing matters on their plate than an attempted rape that might have occurred a decade ago, for which no complaint had ever been lodged.

Strauss might also be the killer. True, his wife had provided him with an alibi, but the police had never tested it because Strauss was never considered a suspect. He'd had no motive—until I'd squeezed one out of Leah.

But I had no clear proof that he was the murderer. Strauss

might have been guilty of nothing more than attempted rape. If Mira killed him, I might never learn the truth.

And there was another reason why I did not wish to see Mira just then. I suspected that I knew what she'd kept from me, and why she had done so, as well. But I wanted to be sure, to give my mind time to process it.

So I turned left, walking south along the busy western sidewalk of King George. The air carried the mingled odors of exhaust fumes, sunbaked street dust, sweat, and the variety of perfumes and colognes of passing pedestrians. I paused for a split second at the turn to Hamaccabi Street, but decided against going home. I kept on walking, made the turn to Allenby and continued putting one foot ahead of the other till I pushed through the door to Greta's Café.

Inside it was marginally cooler. The ceiling fan rattled its steady rhythm. I mopped my wet forehead with a handkerchief and walked over to the bar. I said hello to Greta and let her pour me a cup of coffee. I carried the coffee and my chessboard to my table.

The place was busy—just one vacant table—so Greta had little time for me. This suited me fine. I wanted to pass a few quiet hours while I let my mind work. This case was nearing its end. I just didn't know whether that end included me catching a murderer or admitting defeat.

I killed a few hours playing chess, smoking a series of cigarettes, and drinking multiple cups of coffee. Patrons came and went. Greta came over to ask how I was, and I told her I was fine, and she had sense enough not to pry. At some point, I pushed the chessboard aside, got out the three pictures I'd been carrying in my pocket, and studied them one after the other. Looking at Esther and Willie, blissfully happy and oblivious to their impending doom, gave me a twinge. I did not want to fail them, but I had a sick feeling that I just might. I spent the most time on the last picture, the one Manny Orrin had taken of Esther hours before she died. I looked at it till my eyes hurt, till I could have described every millimeter of it—the hue of Esther's dress, the tone of her expression, the tilt of her beautiful face, the knobby tree to her left, the bench to her right, the crack in the pavement between her feet, and the people around her, some in focus and some blurred.

When I finally put the picture down, my sight was hazy, and my eyes felt on fire. I clamped them shut, massaging them with the heels of my hands till they no longer burned. Slipping the pictures back in my pocket, my stomach grumbled, and it came to me that I had not eaten in hours. At the bar, I asked Greta for bread and soup and vegetables, then went to the bathroom and washed my face and eyes.

When I emerged from the bathroom, there was a man seated alone at a table in the corner by the window, on the opposite side of the café from the bar. Average height, wiry build, pasty skin, mousy-brown hair that had receded to his crown. He had a beer bottle and glass in front of him.

It took me a second, but then I realized the man had been there moments ago, when I had gone to the bar to order my dinner, an anonymous presence at the edge of my field of vision. He might have been in the café for longer than that. I just hadn't fully noticed him before, focused as I'd been on the pictures.

But I noticed him now.

He sat hunched over his glass, forearms on the table, dressed in black pants and a blue shirt, its sleeves rolled back over his arms. He was staring out the window, so I only had a partial view of his face. But then, as if sensing he was being watched, he swiveled his face my way. His eyes, small and black, glided over me, not stopping till they had swept past me, giving no indication that they had registered my presence. Then he turned his head back to his glass and swallowed some beer.

Greta came out with the food, her eyes searching for me, and I hurried toward her, heart hammering, before she could call my name. With a smile and a thank you, I took the tray, the soup giving off the rich odor of cooked tomatoes. I carried the food back to my table, along the way sneaking a glance at the man.

He wore a mustache that curved downward at the corners of a mouth set in a sour expression, and his nose had a noticeable bump on its bridge. Five o'clock shadow dusted his cheeks. Along his right forearm, from wrist to elbow, a white scar curved. But what caught my eye was his lantern jaw—a slab of bone under stretched skin. It was much too long for his face and culminated in a deeply notched chin, like someone had pierced the flesh there with a fishing hook and then pulled hard on the line.

I thought I could feel his eyes on my back as I strode to my table, but when I sat and flicked my gaze in his direction, his head was turned once more toward the window.

My appetite was gone, but I forced down a few spoonfuls of soup and chewed some bread, not wanting to give a hint that anything was out of the ordinary. I slipped Esther's final picture from my pocket and slid it on the table. As I blew on a spoonful of soup, I examined the picture again. What had been a suspicion had now become a certainty.

Slightly to Esther's right and behind her was a man. Only his head and neck and one shoulder were visible—the rest was obscured partly by Esther and partly by a gray-haired woman who sat on a bench at the edge of the picture, wearing a black dress and facing away from the camera. The man himself was not facing away. In fact, the picture displayed his face in its entirety. It was a wonder he had not noticed he was being photographed, but then again, Manny Orrin must have become quite adept at snapping pictures surreptitiously.

In the picture, the man had a full head of hair, and his face was leaner than it was today. But the mustache was the same, and there was no mistaking that jaw and chin. It was the man seated at a table by the window of Greta's Café.

I considered the odds of this being a coincidence and discounted them as negligible. Then I contemplated what this meant. I came to two conclusions: I didn't know, and I was going to find out.

Feigning ignorance of the man's presence, I polished off my food, taking my time with it, trying to look as if I hadn't a care in the world. When I was done, I smoked a lazy cigarette until it was about to burn my fingers, before mashing it out. I folded up the chessboard, piled it and the empty dishes onto the tray, and brought them to the bar. Behind it, Greta was wiping glasses with a checkered cloth.

"Thanks for dinner," I told her, in a low voice. "Act natural, okay?" Then I strode to the door, put my hand on the handle, half turned and, in a voice loud enough to carry to the man at the other end of the café, said, "I'll see you tomorrow, Greta. I'm going to take a walk on the beach, do some thinking."

Greta stared at me blankly for a heartbeat, then said, "All right, Adam. See you tomorrow."

I gave her a wink, opened the door, and stepped outside.

I ambled a block up Allenby Street, pausing to light another cigarette. I did not look over my shoulder, but when I puffed out my first lungful of smoke, I tilted my head at such an angle that I could see a shadow flit across the light spilling onto the sidewalk directly outside Greta's Café as someone emerged from within.

Smiling grimly around my cigarette, I carried on up the street at a quicker pace. It was just after nine and the sidewalks were busy with people enjoying the relatively cool evening air. Laughter and music bubbled out of restaurants and cafés. Teenagers giddy with summer hustled by in packs in search of excitement. A mass of humanity swarmed the plaza outside Moghrabi Theater and the hoarse shouts of hot dog and soda vendors sawed above the din of the throng. I crossed to the other side of the street, where foot traffic was lighter, not wanting to be slowed by the crowds, and in the process caught a glimpse of the man thirty feet behind, fisted hands at his sides. With each step I took, the skin on my back prickled in increasing panic, and my survival instinct screamed at me to turn around and face my pursuer, not to leave myself exposed.

I ignored it, assuring myself that the man shadowing me would take no action on a crowded street. If he was who I feared— or rather hoped—he was, doing so wasn't his style. He liked to keep things private. And I had given him reason to believe he wouldn't have to wait long for the perfect moment to strike.

But my assurances rang hollow in my ears and a cold sweat sprang up under my jacket. My heart was doing a wild, stuttering dance inside my rib cage. A mocking voice inside my head whispered that I was being arrogant again, that this time I'd end up worse off than bruised. I took a final drag and flicked the cigarette at a nearby gutter. My hands were damp and I stuck both of them in my pockets. Earlier, at Greta's, I'd removed the Luger from my waistband and slipped it into my right jacket pocket. Now my right hand curled around the cool grip of the pistol, thumbing the safety off.

What if he also has a gun? the mocking voice in my head asked. *He can shoot you in the back.* I had no answer, so I told the voice to go away. It laughed in response, but said nothing more.

Past Moghrabi Theater, Allenby Street curled in a western trajectory, and I followed it to Ha-Knesset Square, where I verified the man was still on my tail as I pretended to check the road for vehicles before crossing it to the deserted beach.

Rows of abandoned beach chairs studded the soft sand, looking in the scant moonlight like skeletons of some extinct mammal. Waves crested and crashed on the sand with a roar, the sea choppy for summertime. The air smelled of salt and sand. There was a shed thirty feet ahead, and I made for it.

I sensed rather than heard him run toward me from behind. I whirled, whipping the Luger out of my pocket and leveling it at the man. The sight of the gun made him try to shift direction in mid-stride. His feet got tangled. He fought to remain upright, but failed and stumbled forward. He landed on hands and knees. His knife had wormed its way loose of his grip and lay there, sharp and shiny on a mound of sand.

"Get up," I told him.

He raised his head to look at me. His eyes were like two lumps of coal and his jaw was a slab of painted concrete at the bottom of his face.

He made a feeble attempt at innocence. "Hey, what's with the gun, mister? I—"

"Shut up," I told him. "Raise your hands and step away from the knife."

He twisted his lips but did as he was told. When he was ten feet away, I told him to halt. Keeping the gun aimed at his chest, I crouched down, grabbed his knife, and hurled it into the water.

"Now move. Toward that shed there."

The shed was made up of planks of wood hammered together. It listed a bit to the left. The door was unlocked, and inside, taking about a third of the space, were stacks of folded beach chairs and other stuff I couldn't identify in the gloom. Some enterprising soul had recently painted the interior, but the smell of fresh paint did not fully overwhelm that of damp, slightly rotting wood. A small window faced the sea, and moonlight filtered through it. There was no electricity, but on a peg by the door hung a kerosene lamp. I told the man to step inside and hug one wall. Then, flicking a match with one hand, I lighted the lamp, adjusting the flame low to decrease the chance of its light being spotted, and shut the door.

"Turn around," I said.

He did and once more I saw the face from the ten-year-old picture. Had he stalked Esther much as he stalked me? If I hadn't told Greta that I was heading for the beach, which he would know would be empty of witnesses, maybe he would have jumped me on the street, or perhaps broken into my apartment in the dead of night.

"What's your name?" I asked.

When he didn't answer, I raised the gun from his torso to his head. He half-smiled with his lips clamped. He had cunning eyes.

"Yossi Cohen," he said.

"Why did you kill Esther Kantor and her baby?"

"I don't know what you're talking about."

"Ten years ago, on Lunz Street. You butchered a woman and a baby and disfigured them."

"You must have me mixed up with someone else," he said, and he did not appear to be scared by the gun in my hand, though, so far, he had obeyed me.

"You don't seem too upset to be blamed for a murder you say you know nothing about," I said.

He shrugged. "I don't get upset easy."

"How did you know where to find me?"

He shrugged again. "Mister, I was out walking on the beach, minding my own business, when you drew a gun on me."

"Walking with a knife," I remarked.

"Knife?" He smiled. His teeth seemed to glint in the lamplight. "Where's my knife? I don't have a knife."

"You followed me from a café on Allenby. You were going to kill me."

He shook his head languidly. "It's no crime to sit in a café, and I never killed nobody."

I frowned. The way he was speaking reminded me of past interrogations I had conducted as a policeman. I had no doubt he had experience in such matters. He talked like a cocky criminal who knows the cops have only so much on him and that, if he were to remain alert and in control, he might not spend a good deal of his near future in a cell. But we were not in a police station. Why wasn't he afraid of being at the wrong end of a gun?

"If you don't start talking," I told him, "I'll put a bullet in you."

He snorted. "No, you won't. You're a policeman. Or you were. It don't matter. Once a policeman, always a policeman. Take me to the station if you want. You won't shoot me."

The bastard had a smug smile on his face, and I could tell by his posture that he was readying himself to spring at me when the opportunity arose. Which was probably why he'd invited me to march him to the police station, thinking I'd have to get close to him to do so. Outside, the waves smacked into the beach with a steady rhythm. I counted off five such crashes and pulled the trigger simultaneously with the sixth.

The boom of the gun ricocheted from one shed wall to the other. But I had timed it perfectly. Anyone not standing close by would likely think he'd just heard a big wave blasting into sand.

The muzzle flare caught Yossi Cohen's cocksure expression for a dazzling instant. Then he was on the ground, howling in pain, both hands latched to his thigh just above the knee, where blood was soaking through his pants.

I knelt before him, brandishing the gun in front of his gaping, panicked eyes.

"Shut up or I'll shoot you again. You hear?"

He bit his lower lip to stifle his cries. Now he whimpered instead. His face looked white and sweat had begun popping on his forehead and cheeks. Looking at his wound, I said, "From the rate it's pumping, I'd say a major blood vessel got hit. Maybe an artery. That's bad news for you."

I rose, unclasped my belt and pulled it free from its loops. I knelt again and looped the belt around his thigh, above the wound, cinching it tight like a tourniquet. The blood flow eased considerably.

"Good," I said. "You may not bleed out in the next five minutes. Now here's the score: If you don't answer my questions, you get another bullet. Understood?" I didn't wait for a nod. "How did you know where to find me?"

It was obviously an effort for him to speak, but he got the words out. "I was told to find you at the café."

"By who?" I asked, expecting to hear the name Alon Davidson.

"Strauss," he croaked. "God, this hurts."

"Strauss?" I said. I was surprised, but not for more than a second. "What's your connection to Strauss?"

"He defended me once in court."

"Strauss doesn't practice criminal law."

"He did years ago before he got married and respectable."

So that was what Strauss had meant when he talked about his current clientele being better than that of criminal lawyers. He was speaking from personal experience.

"Strauss told you to kill me?"

He didn't seem to hear me. "My leg hurts like crazy," he said, gritting his teeth. "I need to see a doctor."

"Did Strauss tell you to kill me?" I said, raising my voice a bit.

"Yes. All right? Yes. He told me you had to be taken out, that you used to be a cop and that you were sniffing around, asking questions about the murder of that woman ten years ago."

"The woman you killed."

He shook his head. "It wasn't me."

"Don't lie to me. If you lie to me, I'll blast your other leg, too. Keep in mind I only have one belt."

His face twisted in pain. The iron smell of blood wafted up from him in waves, mixed with the scent of discharged gunpowder.

"I'm not lying."

I yanked out the picture of Esther with him behind her, angled it so the light of the lamp fell on it, and held it close to his face.

"Here you are on the day she died. I know you killed her."

He squinted at the image, and I could see the recognition in his eyes. "I didn't do it. Was supposed to, but didn't. Strauss paid me to kill her, said she was a troublemaker. What sort of trouble, he never said. Told me to kill her on that specific night, because he had an alibi ready. I followed her, scouted her place, but I didn't kill her."

"You expect me to believe that? I should let you bleed out." And I loosened the belt around his thigh. Blood began oozing out of his wound again.

He got frantic. Sweat filmed his face like a sheet. "No. Don't. I'm telling the truth, I swear it. I didn't kill her. I was going to do it. I went to her apartment that night to do it. The door was open an inch. I went inside and saw them—her and the baby—dead."

"I don't believe you," I said, but I had re-tightened the belt.

"It's the truth. I swear to God it's the truth. Strauss only told me to kill the woman, not the baby. I never would have cut their faces like that. All I did was go through the apartment and take her money and jewelry."

"Strauss thinks you killed her," I said. "Otherwise, he wouldn't have sent you after me."

"If I told him I didn't do it, he wouldn't have paid me. So I told him I killed the woman and the baby too. He didn't like the baby being dead, but he didn't make a fuss about it."

"I don't see you taking the time to ransack her apartment, not with two dead bodies on the floor."

"It was the middle of the night, and I worked quietly. I thought she might have some jewelry worth nabbing, but none of it was worth a damn. Not a lot of cash, either."

I looked at him for a long moment. Outside, the waves kept on slapping the beach. He was breathing rapidly and his arms had started trembling. What he'd told me made no sense, and I had no doubt it was all lies.

I said, "You're just making this up on the fly, hoping I'll let you live to see morning. If I hadn't shown you the picture, you'd still be denying ever hearing of Esther. Not that it matters. You're a killer. You came to kill me, and you killed Esther and the baby. You must have great faith in your buddy Strauss, don't you? You figure he'll work his connections and get you off with a light sentence. He won't get the chance."

I slackened the belt and pulled it off his leg. The blood started pumping from his wound. I put the gun away.

He protested, pleaded with me, and reiterated his ludicrous claims in ever more desperate tones. When he saw I was unmoved, he cursed me and then began shouting for help. I crouched beside him, slapped one hand over his mouth, and held him down. He thrashed, but he was weak from blood loss. It took less than three minutes for him to bleed to death.

The casing of the bullet I'd fired had landed beside the kerosene lamp. I bent down, picked it up, and put it in my pocket. I inspected my clothes for blood and found none. I hung the lamp back on its peg and used my handkerchief to wipe the lamp, door, and door handle. I took a final look around, saw nothing amiss, darkened the lamp, and exited the shed.

There was no one outside. Music floated from the cafés and dance clubs facing the beach a few hundred meters away. I walked south along the water's edge where it was darkest for half a kilometer before cutting east across the beach and into the city streets. I tossed the casing into a sewer grate. Then I went home.

31

About eight the next morning I went to the hair salon. Mira wasn't there.

"She starts at ten," said the hairdresser on duty. "It's a slow morning."

I walked to the corner of Frishman and Sirkin, ascended the stairs, and knocked on her door. When she opened it, I was filled with a sense of accomplishment that I had completed the task she had given me.

Mira had on a sky-blue shirt with a high collar and a cotton white skirt that went to the middle of her shins. Her hair hung loose and tousled, as if she'd just gotten out of bed. It made her face look softer. Her lips hung slightly open and I caught sight of the tip of her tongue resting on her lower teeth.

"Can I come in?" I said, and Mira nodded, saying that of course I could. She led the way to her living room.

"Anything to drink?" she asked.

I shook my head. "Not just yet. Maybe in a little while. I have some news, but first I want some answers."

"To what questions?"

"Just one, really: Was Esther sleeping with Inspector John Clapper because she was an Irgun agent?"

Mira's mouth dropped open. She drew in and blew out a deep breath and sank onto the sofa, putting her head in her hands. I sat beside her.

"It's true, isn't it?"

Mira slid her hands off her face and nodded slowly. "How did you find out?"

I told her about Strauss and how he had threatened to expose Esther's affair with Clapper if she wouldn't sleep with him. I did not tell her where Strauss had learned about the affair—I wished to spare Leah Goldin Mira's wrath and retribution. I explained that the idea of Esther becoming the lover of a British officer, in particular one who was in charge of preventing Jewish immigration to the Land of Israel, struck me as improbable in the extreme. The only way it made sense was if Esther was working for the Irgun. I finished by relating to her the events of the previous night: how I had managed to overpower the man Strauss had sent to kill me, the same man who had murdered Esther and Willie.

"He tried to deny it by feeding me some cockamamie story, but it was clearly all lies. He killed them. Strauss had arranged for an alibi the night of the murders—not that he ever needed it."

Mira listened to me without speaking, all the while wearing an expression of such unadulterated pain that it was a struggle not to look away from her. When I was done, a single tear broke free from each of her eyes and ran in parallel lines down her cheeks.

"It's my fault," she said in a bleak voice. Her eyes were wet, shining like the flat surface of a lake on a blindingly sunny day.

"No," I said.

She wiped her cheeks with her hands. "It is. She wouldn't have died if not for me. I should have never allowed her to become Clapper's lover. I was her handler."

"Her handler?"

"I was the one she reported to, the one she gave information to."

"Information from Clapper?"

"Yes. Pillow talk, mostly. The man couldn't keep his mouth shut around Esther. He liked to paint himself as large as possible, to impress her. She encouraged him of course. She knew how to get him to run off at the mouth."

"Whose idea was it? For Esther to do what she did?"

"Hers. Esther's."

"No one pushed her into it?"

"No one. In fact, I tried to talk her out of it. I found the whole notion distasteful. I told her there were other ways she could be of service to the Irgun. But Esther was adamant. She said she could do more good by getting intimate with Clapper than by being just another run-of-the-mill Irgun member. She convinced me, and she was right. The information she got for us was priceless."

"Why did you choose Clapper?"

"For a number of reasons. One, his wife had remained in England, so he was here without a woman. Two, his position and role in the CID made him a prime target. In more ways than one, actually. The bastard's lucky to be alive."

"Why do you say that?"

"Because Clapper was marked for assassination by the heads of the Irgun. He was very effective in stopping our ships and was seen as a major threat to continued Jewish immigration to the Land of Israel. The reason why no attempt was made on his life was due to the extraordinary precautions he took. He rarely ventured out in public, kept odd hours, switched vehicles frequently, and changed his routine often. It was difficult to formulate an assassination plan that was likely to succeed. When Esther became his lover, Clapper became more valuable alive than dead and the order to have him killed was rescinded. Michael was furious."

"Why?"

"Because he had been given the task of eliminating Clapper. He did not like it when he was ordered to desist. He viewed it as a personal failure. You see, Michael did not know Clapper had been compromised."

"Compromised by Esther," I said.

Mira nodded. "Exactly. Only I knew of her actions, and only one higher-up in the Irgun knew that I had an agent close to Clapper. It had to be that way for security reasons. The more people knew, the greater chance there was of Esther being uncovered as a spy."

"Wasn't she taking an exceptional risk, being so close to a high-ranking British officer?"

"I explained the risks to her. She accepted them. Esther was very brave. Very dedicated. I remember her telling me that this wasn't a choice she was making. She felt compelled to do whatever she could to help other Jews get into our homeland."

Mira ran her hands through her hair, then clasped them tightly in her lap. She shook her head mournfully. "I knew she faced a risk of being exposed by the British. I never imagined that what she was doing might be used against her by a Jew."

"I understand that Jewish girls who went with British officers faced a severe backlash from other Jews."

"That's true. They suffered socially, but none was ever killed for it. I discussed the social risks with Esther. It didn't affect her resolve. She was willing to risk not just her freedom, not just her life, but also being hated by her own people."

"Why didn't you tell me about Esther and Clapper?"

"Two reasons. The first is I didn't want you to think badly of Esther, and of me. It's a dirty business, a woman sleeping with the enemy to get information. But you don't see it that way, do you, Adam?"

"No."

Mira had her eyes latched firmly on mine. It felt as if she was peering into the deepest recesses of my mind. "No," she said softly. "I can see that you really don't. The second reason why I kept this whole business secret from you is that I didn't think it was relevant. How could it be? No one but me knew what Esther was doing." She shook her head. "I can see now how foolish that was. Why do you think Esther didn't tell me about Strauss? I would have helped her."

I hesitated. I did not want to hurt Mira, but she would guess the reason sooner or later. "Maybe she feared you would tell her she must end her affair with Clapper, and she wasn't willing to do that."

Pain crossed Mira's face. Her eyes welled, but she shed no more tears. She nibbled on her lower lip. "So it *was* my fault. I never should have let her go through with this whole crazy, sordid scheme."

"From what you told me, Esther would have gone through with it with your permission or without it."

Mira let out a sigh. "I suppose you're right. When Esther set her mind on something, she would let nothing dissuade her. I wish you'd met her, Adam."

"I wish I did, too," I said. "She was a true hero."

Mira nodded. "The information Esther provided helped us smuggle in hundreds upon hundreds of Jews. If not for her, those Jews might have been stuck in Europe and would have been murdered by the Nazis. Do you know what pains me almost as much as her death? The fact that Esther should be celebrated throughout Israel, but she won't be. Knowing what she did to get information would make people uneasy. They would not want their daughters to have such a role model. They would not want their sons to have lewd thoughts about the beautiful Jewish girl in the bed of the British officer. Esther will not be celebrated. Her heroic sacrifice will remain unknown. She will be forgotten."

I looked at Mira and could see the guilt etched on her face. "Mira, you mustn't blame yourself. None of this is your fault."

She nodded a few times, and I knew I hadn't convinced her. Guilt was like that. It was not susceptible to reason.

Mira's face suddenly hardened. "It's good that you killed the murderer," she said. "I wish I had done it. I will take care of Strauss."

The way she said it left no room for discussion. Not that I had anything to say on the subject. Strauss had sent an assassin after me. He was responsible for the deaths of Esther and Willie. I couldn't prove his guilt in a way that would result in a murder conviction, so he had to die. Either Mira would do it, or I would have to take care of it myself.

Mira said, "Have you given Willie's mother the news?"

"No," I said, and I explained that I'd not yet told Henrietta that her son was dead, that I'd been waiting until I'd discovered who the killer was. "I'll go by her apartment later this afternoon after she returns from work."

"She will be heartbroken."

"Yes. She will. I'll tell her the killer died a violent death. Maybe it will ease her pain a little." But the words rang false, and I knew that I had held off informing Henrietta of her son's fate for no good reason.

"She will want to have the name on the headstone changed," said Mira.

"What?" I asked, distracted by thoughts of Henrietta.

"Willie's and Esther's headstones. They bear their false names to this day."

"Oh, I see. Yes, I suppose you're right. I'll talk to Henrietta about it."

"I haven't visited their graves," Mira said, looking abashed. "Not even once. I couldn't bring myself to do it. When this is all over, I think I'll go."

There didn't seem to be anything to say to that, so I kept quiet.

Mira put her hand on my forearm. Her fingers matched her physique—long and slender. Like last time, her touch was cool, but it sent heat up my arm.

We stared at each other in silence for a long, loaded moment. The air in the apartment seemed to be holding its breath.

Mira broke the silence. "Thank you, Adam, for all you've done."

She leaned a little toward me and tilted her head. After a slight hesitation, I leaned the rest of the way, closing the distance between us. Her lips parted slightly the instant before my mouth met hers, and her warm breath tickled my tongue. It had a taste, her breath, but I could not tell what it was. Something sweet and fresh.

Her lips were softer than they looked, and she invested herself fully in the kiss. When she broke the kiss, my lips felt deprived.

"I wanted to do this last time," she said, smiling softly, "but the moment seemed wrong. Now is better." She didn't wait for a response, but leaned in again.

This kiss was deeper. Her hand gripped my shoulder. My hand went around her back. She scooted closer to me on the sofa, our legs and bodies touching. A muffled moan escaped her throat. A long-dormant heat began flowing through my body.

Part of me was immersed in the moment, in Mira; another part kept its distance. Against my closed eyelids wavered the face of my dead wife, Deborah, and mingled with the pleasure of the kiss was guilt. It was an illogical guilt, but palpable, born from a feeling that I was being unfaithful to Deborah. A voice inside my head warned me that should I take this moment further, I would be cutting ties to my past, to my lost love. I had no picture of Deborah. All that she'd worn or touched or owned was gone, taken by the Germans or the Hungarians. All I had were memories, and they brought with them such agony that I kept them locked away in a vault deep down in my subconscious.

Go! Get up! Leave! the voice implored.

But another voice whispered that Deborah would not have begrudged me this moment, nor any that might follow. She would not want me to wallow in misery for the rest of my life. She would want me to seek and find happiness. And where would I find another woman like Mira? A woman who could accept and appreciate the man I now was?

The voices were still skirmishing in my head when Mira ended the kiss. She rested her forehead against mine, inhaling deeply through her nose. Then she leaned back, took her hand off my shoulder, glanced at her watch, and let out a sigh of frustration.

"I hate to do this, Adam," she said, "more than you can imagine. But Sarah is expecting me at the hair salon. I'm already running late."

She looked apologetic, and I did my best to hide my conflicting emotions. There was relief, but it was overshadowed by impatient irritation and a desire to kiss her again.

Mira said, "Can you come over tonight after you see Willie's mother? I'll cook dinner for us."

"Yes," I said, my voice slightly hoarse. I swallowed to clear it.

Mira smiled. It was a happy smile, eager and lovely, utterly exorcised of ghosts and guilt. She put her hand on my thigh and we kissed again. My hand went through her soft hair to cup the back of her head. She kneaded my thigh. It lasted a long time, that kiss, and by the time it was done we were breathless.

"God," Mira exhaled. "I wish I didn't have to go."

At the door we kissed some more—a swift series of kisses, each like a promise of more to come.

"Finish what you have to do and then come over," Mira said. "Around six should be fine. We'll eat early."

What we would do after dinner remained unsaid.

32

I was light-headed when I strolled west on Frishman. A woman walking in the opposite direction slowed her steps to study my face, then gave an amused smile and a chuckle and continued past me. It was only then that I realized I was grinning.

How was I to pass the time till evening?

I could buy something to bring with me, but what? Flowers? Or maybe something for dessert? There was a guy on Daniel Street who sold contraband chocolate. It wasn't very good chocolate, but in these deprived times, it was a luxury.

But that would not take me long, and there would still be hours to go till six. Before that I would go see Henrietta to give her my report. To destroy her world. The thought dampened my heightened spirits, and the grin faded from my lips.

There was no escaping it. I had taken upon myself the burden of giving Henrietta bad news when I took on her case. Back then, I'd assumed the bad news would be that I had not found any trace of her son and did not think I ever would. The news I would deliver to her this afternoon would be worse, but it was my obligation to do so just the same.

And then the case would be done, and I would see Mira again.

I ran the talk I'd just had with her over in my mind, pausing when I got to the bit about Esther's and Willie's graves. Mira was right: Henrietta would want her son buried under his real name.

I thought about the two graves, marked with false names, untended for ten long years, and I knew that I was not yet done with this case. There was one last place I had to go, a final goodbye I had to say.

In the next block over was a bus stop. I waited for fifteen minutes till the bus came. It wound a long, circuitous route through the city. Forty minutes later, it discharged me at the entrance to Nahalat Yitzhak Cemetery.

By the gate to the cemetery slumped a weary-faced old man on a three-legged chair next to a rickety table topped with fat candles in flimsy metal saucers. Seeing me approach, he pushed himself an inch higher from his slouched position.

"Light a candle for the soul of the deceased," he suggested in a muffled, thickly accented voice.

I shook my head and walked past him into the cemetery. The dead, I believed, could not be helped by the lighting of a flame. They were beyond such gestures. I did not believe in the power of prayer, either. I had seen it fail all too often in Auschwitz.

There was a small shack just inside the gate with a rectangular sign that read ADMINISTRATION over the open door. Inside, behind a cluttered desk, sat an overweight bearded man peering over the thick glasses straddling the tip of his nose at a copy of the *Mishna*, mouthing the words as he read.

I cleared my throat. He raised his eyes and asked me what I wanted. I asked whether he could direct me to the graves of Esther and Erich Kantor. He consulted a ledger and read off the row and plot numbers. After giving me directions, he returned his attention to his text.

I walked up the central avenue fringed by long rows of

bleached headstones. Here and there benches had been placed in the shadow of cypresses. Birds flitted from branch to branch, their chirping an incongruous merry note in this place of mourning. I saw no other visitors. I was alone in a sea of gravestones.

To my right stood a large stone marking the communal burial place of unnamed soldiers from the War of Independence. Why unnamed? Because, I suspected, these were soldiers who had survived the Nazi extermination campaign in Europe, and, like me, had arrived in Israel without family or friends. Some had gone to the battlefield straight from the ships that had brought them to the Holy Land and had not had time to acquire new friends before they died by an Arab bullet or artillery shell. Now they lay together in the earth for which they'd fought.

Pausing before the mass grave, I couldn't help but contemplate the different manner by which the dead are buried. Some have a personal resting place with a stone bearing their names; some are laid together with other anonymous dead; and there are those, like my wife and sisters and daughters and mother, for whom there is no grave at all. To those I could add the ones who are buried under false names, like Esther Grunewald and Willie Ackerland.

Two minutes later, I was standing at their graves. They had been buried side by side, as was customary with mothers and children who perished together. The headstones were simple white slabs, smudged black by time and weather, laid horizontally on a low stone base, slightly elevated off the ground. Each stone was marked by the Hebrew and Gregorian dates of their birth and death. The right one bore the name Esther Kantor; the left the name Erich Kantor. Below the names and dates was inscribed the traditional acronym entrusting their souls to the Bundle of the Living.

And there were the flowers.

The sight of them brought me up short. A scatter of desiccated petals and shrunken stalks on the headstone bearing the name

Erich Kantor. Willie Ackerland's grave. There were no flowers on Esther's grave.

How long ago had they been left here?

In this weather, no more than a week. But the bigger question was, who had left them? And why?

Suddenly, a brisk wind gusted and swept the flowers away. Had I arrived five minutes later than I did, I never would have known they had been there to begin with.

"So it's you, then."

I spun around. The scratchy voice belonged to a religious man with a bushy black beard laced with gray. He had on black pants and a vest over a white shirt beneath the hem of which peeped the tassels of his *tzitzit*. A large black yarmulke covered his bald head. He was leaning on a straw broom as he eyed me with clear blue eyes that looked too young for his fifty-something face.

"It's me, what?" I asked.

"The one who's always leaving flowers on that grave there. The little one's."

"Are you saying that there are regularly flowers here?"

He inclined his head. "So you're not him?"

"No."

He was disappointed to hear that. "It's regular, but not something to set your watch by. Sometimes a month goes by with no flowers, and then I'll find new ones one week after the next."

"And always on this grave—" I pointed at Willie Ackerland's grave "—but never on this one?" I moved my finger to indicate Esther's headstone.

"Yes. Just on the little one's."

"Any particular kind of flowers? Any special color?"

"No," he said. "They can be red one month and yellow the next."

"How long has this been going on?"

He scratched his bearded cheek. "The first time I saw the

flowers was during my first month here, six years ago. But a colleague of mine told me it's been happening for longer than that."

"And you've never seen the person who leaves them?"

He shook his head. "I start my day early in the morning—seven thirty, eight at the latest—and the flowers are already there. Whoever he is, he comes at night when the cemetery's deserted. Strange, isn't it?"

Very strange, I thought.

"I wouldn't want to be here at night," the man continued. "In the dark, with all the spirits of the dead around me."

"Is the cemetery locked at night?" I asked.

The man raised his eyebrows. "Why would it be? There's nothing worth stealing here."

So whoever it was could come and go as he pleased. He wouldn't need to scale a fence or jimmy a lock. He'd just walk right in and up the same path I had, to Willie Ackerland's grave. It could be anyone.

"I'd sure like to know who it is," the man said.

Me too, I thought. But what did it matter who had left these flowers? I had my killer. He was dead. I knew the man who had put money in his hand to kill Esther, and to kill me. Mira would soon see to him. This case was over and done with. So why was my stomach knotted tight? Why was the blood thudding in my ears? Why did I feel that this was important?

Because it was odd. Because it didn't fit. Because the flowers were left exclusively on the stone marked Erich Kantor—Willie Ackerland's grave—and not on Esther's. I could think of no one who would have reason to grieve for Willie but not for Esther. Not someone who'd been in Israel for at least the past six years.

And because someone who sneaks into a cemetery in the dead of night is trying to hide something, and whenever someone is hiding something, there is a reason for it.

"Well, anyway, I got some sweeping to do," the man said and wished me a good day. I mumbled a goodbye without turning to him, and I could hear his footfalls receding as he walked off. I had my eyes firmly set on the two graves, willing them to divulge their secrets, to tell me who this mysterious mourner was.

I might have stood there for one minute or five, my mind churning in gradually deepening desperation, knowing that it would come up with no answers. Then the wind picked up again, stronger than before, buffeting my clothes, swirling up dust and dirt against my neck and face so that I had to avert my face and shut my eyes. When I opened them, I happened to be facing diagonally to the left, looking at the row of graves behind Esther's and Willie's.

And there I saw it, at the edge of my field of vision, the upper half of an unassuming headstone engraved with the name Talia Shamir. Beneath the name was a date of death. I blinked once or twice, sure my eyes were playing tricks on me, but of course the date remained the same. Not March 1939, when the prison raid to free the passengers of the *Salonika* had taken place, but August 31, 1939, a mere five days after Esther and Willie were slain.

Could this be another Talia Shamir and not Michael's wife? Talia was an uncommon name, and the date of birth on the stone indicated that this Talia had been but twenty-one when she died, about the same age Michael had been ten years ago. The right age to be the woman in Mira's picture.

I cast my mind back, searching for the moment in which someone had specifically said that Talia Shamir had died in that raid. It didn't take long to determine that there had been no such moment. Michael had never said it, and neither did Mira. What Mira had done was mournfully say Talia's name right after pointing out the man in the picture who had died in the raid. My mind had simply jumped to the conclusion that Talia had died that night too.

Which, I now saw, was a conclusion I should have rejected the moment I'd learned that the Talia in the picture was Michael's wife. For if his wife had died in that raid, Michael would have seen to her body and not driven Esther and Willie to the Klingers.

So why had Mira said that Michael had sacrificed his family for the Irgun?

Without a conscious decision, I found myself approaching Talia's grave, my shoes crunching on the small stones that proliferated the cemetery. As I neared, the inscription on the bottom of her gravestone came into view. *Noble of heart and spirit, darling wife of Michael, loving mother of Judah.*

It was now beyond doubt. Here lay Michael's dead wife. But what snared my attention were the final three words of the inscription. *Mother of Judah.*

I had seen no trace of a son in Michael's apartment. It was obvious no child resided there with him. But the inscription told me Michael and Talia had had a son named Judah. Perhaps he was dead, too. Yes. That had to be it.

But there had been no pictures of a child in Michael's apartment. And when I'd talked about the guilt I felt over the deaths of my daughters, Michael had not mentioned that he had also lost a child. Almost as if he didn't want to be reminded that his child had ever existed.

Or didn't want me to know about him.

All of a sudden, a chill spread up my spine, making me shiver and causing the hairs on the back of my neck to stand. My heartbeat jumped to a faster, erratic rhythm. In my mind a dark suspicion began whispering that I had been wrong this whole time, that the truth I had been blind to was too awful to contemplate.

Stop it, I thought, *don't get ahead of yourself.* Perhaps it was simply too painful for Michael to talk about his son, to see his face every day. I could understand that. Or maybe I just wanted to pretend that I did.

I began walking, scanning headstones, searching for the name Judah Shamir. I wanted to see his grave. I wanted to know when he died. If I knew, maybe the whispering in my head would cease. I walked along one row of graves after another, and after a while the names of the dead began to blur, so I would not have been able to tell the name of the man or woman or child whose headstone I had just read. All I knew for sure was that none of them was Judah Shamir.

After what might have been twenty or thirty minutes of fruitless searching, I stopped, wiped the sweat off my brow, and looked around. I had covered but a small section of the cemetery. It would take me hours to go through it all. Perhaps there was a quicker way.

Back in the administration office by the entrance, I found the same clerk still peering at the *Mishna* over his glasses.

I asked him whether they kept a list of all those buried in the cemetery.

"Yes," he said, laying his book on the desk. "By year."

"I'm looking for the grave of Judah Shamir. He died somewhere between 1939 and today."

"You don't know exactly when?"

"No. But I know it was after August 1939."

"Very well," he said, though I could tell he found my request odd.

From an open cabinet, he hauled out a stack of large brown ledgers and piled them on top of other papers on his desk.

"Let's see," he said. "Here's 1939."

He flipped open the ledger and ran his finger along the list of names, finding none named Judah Shamir. 1940 through 1943 yielded nothing as well. In April 1944, he found a listing for a man named Elisha Shamir, sixty-five, and raised his eyes to mine, as if hoping I'd be willing to compromise on that person.

"Not the one I'm looking for," I said. "Mine is Judah Shamir, and he couldn't have been older than twelve."

"Hmmm," he said, and lowered his eyes to the ledger.

Fifteen minutes later, he slammed the cover of the 1949 ledger. "No Judah Shamir is buried here."

"Are those ledgers accurate?" I asked, though I anticipated what his answer would be.

"One hundred percent. I log every burial myself. Perhaps this Judah Shamir is buried in another cemetery in the area."

I asked him for a list of cemeteries and he drew one up for me. I thanked him and left.

Back in Tel Aviv, I rang the hair salon from a café. Mira picked up herself. The joy in her voice when she recognized mine was like a cold stab deep in my belly.

"I can't make it tonight," I said, coming off brusque and businesslike, though I hadn't intended to be so.

"What? Why?"

"Something came up. Something important I need to take care of."

"Oh." And in that single syllable was confusion, bewilderment, and pain. I shut my eyes. Nothing was said for a moment. In the background, a radio was playing a jaunty duet of two male singers. Then Mira said, "When will I see you? Tomorrow?"

"I don't know. I don't think so. I'm not sure how long this will take." *I'm not sure whether you'd want to see me again in a few days' time.*

"You sound strange, Adam. What's wrong? What is this thing you need to do?"

She sounded distraught now. Almost frantic. I gripped the receiver so hard it was a wonder it didn't crack. What could I tell her? I wasn't sure what was going on myself. All I had were questions, and a sense of impending...not doom, but a horrific enlightenment.

"I can't talk about it yet. I'll explain when I can. Sorry about tonight."

I said goodbye and hung up. I stood there for a while, gazing into space or into myself, not moving, until a man in work clothes asked if I was through with the phone. I ordered a beer and drank it without tasting it. Then, when the beer was done and the telephone was once again free, I got up and started making calls.

33

Four days later, a little after nine in the morning, I entered the building with the stained facade and climbed the dusty staircase to his door. I had the Luger with me, though it did little to boost my sense of confidence. We were not evenly matched, he and I, in the art of dispensing violence. If it came to a fight, I would have to be either very fast or very lucky.

I tensed upon hearing the scrape of the key turning in the lock on the other side of the door, but he greeted me with nothing but a weary smile. He had on a blue shirt and dark brown pants and black socks, but no shoes. A bottle of beer dangled from his hand. No weapons in sight.

"Adam," he said, "good morning."

"Got a few minutes, Michael? There's something I'd like to discuss with you."

Michael Shamir nodded, still smiling. As he did on my earlier visit to his apartment, he said, "Better come in, then."

I trailed him inside, shutting the door behind me.

He said, "I just started on this bottle. Want one? Oh, I remember, it's too early for you, isn't it?"

"Afraid so."

As last time, his living room/bedroom was neat, spotless, and unassuming—like a monk's cell. A fitting room for its occupant. The only sign that this warrior monk had once had a life outside of his vocation were the pictures of his wife. I stared at them for a few seconds while Michael lowered himself onto the middle of his old sofa. I remained standing.

Michael said, "Well, if you change your mind..." and took a swig from the bottle.

His tone was light, but it sounded forced. He looked tired, like he hadn't slept in days. The lines on his forehead ran deeper, and bags had gathered like storm clouds under his eyes. I waited till he had swallowed the beer in his mouth before speaking.

"I know it was you, Michael," I said.

His face showed no reaction. He didn't deny it or ask me what I meant. For a good thirty seconds, he said nothing at all. If I didn't know better, I might have believed he hadn't heard a word I said. He took a quick sip and rolled the bottle between his hands before setting it down on the floor between his feet. Again I tensed, my hand close to the Luger stuck in my waistband, but Michael stayed seated, elbows on knees, shoulders slightly hunched. His expression was difficult to read, but there was no surprise in it. Nor anger.

He said, "First time we met, after you left, I said to myself: 'A man like that, who's survived what he's survived—he's no ordinary man. If anyone can discover the truth, it is he.'" His eyes found mine. They were hard eyes, but they did not look cruel. The eyes of a man who's killed, yes, but not the eyes of a murderer. "What gave me away?"

"The flowers."

"Flowers," he said, drawing out the word like he was rolling it on his tongue, exploring the taste it evoked.

"The flowers you left on the grave," I said.

He gave an almost imperceptible nod. "What made you think I was the one who left them?"

"I happened to glance to one side and saw Talia's grave. I read the inscription. It was then that I learned she hadn't died during the prison raid like I'd originally thought, but a few days after the murders of Esther and Willie. I also learned that you had a son. Judah. A good name."

His mouth twitched into a shadow of a smile. "Judah Maccabee. The ultimate Jewish warrior."

"Like you."

Michael shrugged, the smile gone from his lips. "I did my part, as best I could." Like me, he was uncomfortable with being praised for his prowess in war.

All of a sudden, I was awash in grief. I had kept it at bay over these past few days, even as my disjointed suspicions coalesced into a harsh, incontrovertible truth. I had clung to a desperate hope that Michael would deny his guilt, that he would somehow convince me he was not a murderer.

That hope was dashed now. This man, whom I had begun to think of as a friend, as a brother of sorts, was lost to me. And his loss was like a gaping wound in the center of my body.

I inhaled deeply, taking a moment to collect myself. "My first thought was that Judah was dead. There are pictures of Talia on the walls of your apartment, but none of your son. You also didn't mention him when I spoke of my daughters. Perhaps his memory was too painful for you, I thought. Perhaps that was why you had removed all traces of him from your home."

I paused, waited for him to say something, but he remained silent. His eyes, narrowed in their permanent squint, were aimed at a point on the floor between us.

"I searched for Judah's grave. First in Nahalat Yitzhak, then in the cemeteries in Kiryat Shaul and Trumpeldor Street. When I didn't find it, I asked a policeman friend of mine to locate Judah for me. He did. Judah Shamir lives in Kibbutz Sarid in the Jezreel Valley with his aunt—your sister, Malka. I talked to her yesterday morning."

Michael lifted his gaze. His eyes settled on mine. I held my breath, but still he said nothing. He lowered his head once more. Sunlight from the window bathed his hair, and I spotted a few gray strands among the black.

I said, "Malka told me how one day, ten years ago, you suddenly showed up on her doorstep with your baby boy in your arms. You thrust him at her and asked her to care for him. You couldn't because your wife had just died and because of your work for the Irgun. Your sister also told me that before that day, she and you had not spoken for two years. You had a big fight over politics. Malka is a socialist. She did not like her brother joining the Irgun. So you broke off all contact with each other. But she still loved you, and she agreed to take care of your son. Malka said you've never visited him. Not even once in ten years. She also told me that Talia killed herself. Malka didn't know how or why. I found out later that Talia had slashed her wrists in your old apartment on Dizengoff."

I paused and wet my dry lips. I had come to the heart of the matter. This was the secret axis around which this whole sad business revolved.

"Mira Roth once told me you had sacrificed your family for the Irgun. I thought she meant that Talia had died in the line of duty, but that wasn't it. What Mira meant was that you had given your son away so you could dedicate yourself fully to the Irgun. Only she got it wrong, didn't she? I talked to some of your old neighbors. One of them was positive that your son had brown eyes. According to your sister, the boy she's been raising as her nephew these past ten years has blue eyes. Sometimes, a baby's eyes change color from blue to brown, but it's never the other way around. That boy up there in Kibbutz Sarid is not your son. He's Willie Ackerland."

Terrible truths often have weight to them. I felt that weight then, pressing on me from all sides. Michael seemed to feel it too. He hunched his shoulders further, as if he were being squeezed into a smaller space.

"And Judah is the dead baby the police found in Esther's apartment. I know you killed Esther. Did you also kill Judah?"

His head whipped up. His eyes sparked. "No. Of course not. How could you think that?"

"What else am I supposed to think?"

His voice vibrated with emotion. "I never would have killed my son. Not my son."

"So tell me what happened."

It took him less than a second to start. The confession had been there, ready in his mind. It tumbled out like an avalanche.

"I never should have taken Talia on that damn prison raid," Michael said. "She wasn't cut out for that sort of thing. Talia was a delicate woman, sensitive. But we needed the extra gun, and she pleaded with me to let her take part in the operation. I never could deny her anything." He swallowed hard and cleared his throat. The latter didn't help. When he continued, his voice was hoarse, half choked. "Talia didn't get hurt that night, not physically. Emotionally, though, she was a wreck. The sight of blood, of death, scarred her psyche. She started having nightmares, lost her appetite, became too thin. The only thing that kept her going, that gave her any happiness, was Judah. He was the joy of her life. Of our lives. I knew that as long as Talia had him, she would be all right, and that one day she would be her old self again."

Michael paused. The skin on his face was stretched tight across the underlying bone, jaw muscles flexing. He cleared his throat again.

"That evening, August 26, 1939, I'd put Judah to sleep in his crib. Talia and I had dinner and listened to the radio for a while. It was a good evening. I had a few days to myself between assignments. Later, I went to check on Judah. He was...he'd stopped breathing. He was dead."

A tear dribbled out of his left eye. He wiped it away hastily.

"When Talia saw Judah dead, she lost her mind. She began shrieking, tearing out her hair, punching herself in the thighs and stomach. I had to restrain her. I managed to give her a sedative, and she fell into a deep sleep. I knew that in a few hours, when the drugs wore off, she would awaken to a reality she could not bear. She could not live without her son, so I decided to give her another one."

"By stealing Esther's baby," I said.

"He wasn't hers." Michael's voice was sharp with anger. "She wasn't his mother. He was another woman's child, and that woman had given him away. By the time I took him, he had been in Tel Aviv for nearly six months and there was no sign of his mother. I didn't think she was ever coming after him. He was no one's child."

"So you took him."

He nodded. "I wrapped Judah in a blanket and carried him with me. He was still warm when I got to Lunz Street. It was after midnight and the street was dark and empty. I went up to the apartment where Esther and Willie lived. The lock gave me no trouble. I put Judah on the living room sofa and went into the bedroom. I must have made a noise, because Esther was up. She opened her mouth to scream, but didn't. I think that recognizing me gave her pause. She didn't see the knife. I slashed her across the throat. She died almost instantly. I don't think she felt much pain."

The anger had gone from his voice. Now he sounded clinical, as if he were reporting on an operation he had conducted.

"I found some of Willie's clothes in a closet, took them to the living room, and put them on Judah. Back in the bedroom, I lifted Willie out of his crib—he'd carried on sleeping through all this—and laid him on Esther's bed. I put Judah in the crib. Then I stabbed him through the chest."

"How could you do that?" I asked, horrified. "To your own son?"

"That was the hardest part," he said. "That, and what came next. But Judah was already dead, and I wanted to save Talia, so I did what I had to do. I stabbed Judah several times, making sure I got the heart. That was important, because a heart wound was the only way to explain the near absence of blood around his body. And it worked. The police bought it, didn't they?"

I nodded. It was easier than uttering the single syllable a "yes" would have required. Despite the heat and the jacket I had on, I was suddenly cold. I shuddered.

Michael noted my distress. "Want me to stop, Adam?"

I shook my head, finding my voice. "No. I want to know everything."

"All right," he said. "What I did next I did because I had to, not because I wanted to. It was the only way. I had to make Judah unrecognizable so the police would assume he was Esther's baby. They were the same age, the same size, they even had the same hair color. But their eyes were different. That was why I had to stab Judah through both eyes. That wasn't easy. It went against every instinct in my body. I had to force myself to do it."

"Why did you also disfigure Esther?"

"To throw the police off track. I didn't want them to focus on the baby. I wanted them to think this was the work of some madman."

And it was, I thought. *Just not the sort of madness the police had envisioned.*

"And then what did you do?"

"I had brought a change of clothes with me. After washing my hands in the kitchen, I removed my bloodied clothes and put on clean ones. Then I went back to the bedroom to take the baby. He was still asleep. I picked him up and got out of the apartment. I descended the stairs slowly, but then the baby woke and started bawling. I didn't want his crying to wake any of the neighbors, so I hurried down the stairs and out of the building. Then I was in the clear."

That explained what Haim Sassoon had heard. The baby's cries sounded louder to him because they did not come from the third floor as they usually had, but from the staircase. The crying softened gradually because Michael was putting more distance between himself and the building with each step.

Michael had stopped talking. He was rubbing his hands together, his palms making a soft scratching sound.

"You didn't take anything from the apartment? No money?"

His hands stopped moving. He shook his head resolutely. "Of course not. I'm not a thief."

No, you only stole a child, I thought with sadness. So Yossi Cohen had told me the truth. He was the one who had ransacked the apartment and stolen the money from Esther's purse, but he wasn't the murderer.

"What happened then?" I asked.

His face spasmed in painful memory. "I thought she'd be happy, but she wasn't. When Talia woke up and saw the baby, she went insane. She wanted to know where Judah's body had gone and who the new baby was. When I told her, she slapped me and threatened to go to the police. It was all I could do to get her to keep her voice down so the neighbors wouldn't know what I'd done. I finally got her to calm down. I told her we could be happy again, that we could be a family, that we could say that this baby was Judah. No one will come looking for him. No one will know. All we needed to do was move to another city, where no one knew us or how the real Judah looked.

"For the next few days, I did not let Talia out of my sight. She seemed to be getting better. She took good care of the baby. I could tell she liked him. Then I had to go out to get food. When I returned, I found her dead. She'd opened her wrists in the bathtub."

Michael closed his eyes. His breathing sounded hard and fast in the stillness of the apartment.

"Talia left a note, blaming me for her death," he said, opening his eyes. "I burned it. After Talia was buried, I didn't want anything to do with the baby. He wasn't mine. I didn't love him. So I gave him to Malka, and I did my best to forget about him, to forget about Judah. I immersed myself in my work for the Irgun. But I didn't forget Judah, so I started visiting his grave and leaving flowers there."

"Why only on his grave?" I asked. "Why not on Talia's?"

"Because she wouldn't want me to. She died hating me. And—" his voice turned ugly "—it was all because of that traitorous bitch."

"Who?" I asked, the answer popping into my mind almost instantly. "Esther?"

"Yes. The traitor. Four good men died and Talia lost her mind fighting to free her from the British, and what did she do? Become the mistress of a British officer. And not just any officer, but of—"

"John Clapper," I finished his sentence for him.

Michael looked at me in surprise. "You know?"

"It came up during my investigation," I said, goose bumps sprouting on my arms. The apartment had felt cold earlier, but now it was freezing. It would not have surprised me to see snow flurries flutter by my face—like on so many wretched days in Poland. I had guessed much of what Michael had told me, but him knowing about Esther and Clapper was unexpected. I could now see how this tragedy had come to pass. It was even worse than I'd thought. "How did you find out about it?" I asked.

"I was watching Clapper. I'd been given the task of assassi-nating him, but could never figure out a good way to do it. Eventually, my superiors called the operation off. But I kept surveilling the son of a bitch, trying to find an opening. That's when I saw Esther and him together."

"And that gave you the justification to kill her?"

"You're damn right it did." He was sitting straight now. He thought he'd found a way to convince me that what he'd done was right. "She betrayed us. She—"

I cut him off. "She was spying on Clapper for the Irgun."

His lips fell open. He shook his head. "No. There's no—"

"Mira was her handler. She told me about it herself."

His eyes bored into mine. They were begging me to admit that I was lying.

"Esther was no traitor," I told him. "She was a hero."

He sat motionless for five seconds. He didn't move a muscle, didn't even blink. Then his face came apart. "Oh, God," he said, slapping his hands over his face. He stayed that way for a while. When he finally lowered his hands, his eyes looked haunted and his face was gray.

"I didn't know, Adam. I swear I didn't know."

"Michael, it makes no difference whether you knew or didn't. You had no right to execute a woman. You had no right to steal her child. Not even if she were the mistress of an enemy officer. You murdered a woman, Michael, and you need to pay for that."

"What about all I did? In the Irgun, in the War of Independence—does that count for nothing?"

"It counts for a hell of a lot. But it doesn't change the fact that you murdered a woman."

He was silent for a long moment. "You can't prove any of this," he said at length.

"No," I admitted. "I can't. I want you to come with me to the police station and sign a confession."

He shook his head. "They'll hang me."

"They won't. You'll spend some time in jail, but they won't execute you."

"I don't want to be locked up."

"It won't be pleasant, but there are worse places," I said. "You'll survive. You'll have access to books and a radio. You'll get adequate food and a proper bed. And you'll have something even more important."

"What is that?"

"A chance for atonement. A chance to come clean and ease the guilt that's eating you. And it is eating you, isn't it, Michael? A part of you wanted to be found out. Otherwise, you wouldn't have stepped in when Alon Davidson jumped me. You weren't on your way to work that night. I talked to your supervisor. You'd taken that night off, and the one before that as well. You were following me, weren't you?"

"Yes."

"Since the first time we met?"

"Yes," he said again.

"Were you still following me last Thursday?" I asked, referencing the day I'd killed the assassin Strauss had sent after me.

"No. I stopped after Davidson attacked you. You believed my lie that I just happened to be there at the right place at the right time. If you saw me again, you'd know I was tailing you."

So Michael had not seen Yossi Cohen follow me down to the beach. He did not witness my taking Cohen at gunpoint into the shed and emerging from there alone.

"Michael," I said, "if you don't come with me to the station, I will tell the police everything I know. It won't be enough for a conviction. It may not even be enough for an arrest. But it will pique their interest. They'll have their eye on you. You won't be able to visit your son's grave ever again."

His lips curled into a bitter smile. "That's an empty threat,

Adam. After all, if I'm locked up in a cell, I won't be visiting his grave either."

"No," I said. "But I will."

He stared at me without saying a word.

"If you come with me to the station and make a full confession, I will visit Judah's grave every two months while you're incarcerated. I will lay flowers and a stone on his grave. I will recite the *kadish*. I will do those things, Michael, over a headstone that bears Judah's true name, and those of his father and mother."

I paused, scratching the number on my arm.

"I'm giving you a chance to do right by Talia, by Judah, and by Willie Ackerland and his mother. If you don't confess, it will be hard for them to be reunited. Malka may not believe that the boy she's been raising is not really your son. What would Talia want you to do, Michael? What would she tell you to do?"

He didn't answer for a long while. Outside the chirping of a songbird was drowned by the guttural bark of an angry dog. A woman in a neighboring building called out something in Yiddish. Light fell across the bed in the corner, where I was sure Michael had spent endless nightmare-filled nights. The apartment no longer felt cold. I was filled with a bleak sadness.

After what might have been five minutes, Michael reached down, picked up the beer bottle, brought it to his lips, and drained it. He wiped his lips and placed the bottle on the floor once more. Then he stood up.

"All right," he said. "Let's go."

34

I had worried Henrietta would not look kindly on my suggestion that she share her story with a reporter, but she jumped at the idea. "This way my Jacob's name will never be forgotten," she said.

The three of us met in Café Tamar the day after I walked Michael to the police station, after I went to see Henrietta and told her I'd found her son. I waited outside for Henrietta and introduced her to Birnbaum when she arrived. I had already filled him in as to the basic outline of the case—the motive, the perpetrator, the reason behind the method of killing and the disfigurement of the bodies—and his police contacts were sure to provide him with additional information. It was a sanitized, much-abbreviated outline, of course. I had held some things back—Mira Roth's desire for vengeance, Manny Orrin and his pictures, Alon Davidson and his assault on me, and Mr. Strauss and the assassin he had hired to kill me. The latter had a lengthy criminal record. Reading between the lines of various newspaper reports, it was clear that the police had no leads as to who killed him.

If Birnbaum had caught on that I was withholding information, he did not voice any protest. On the contrary, he was as happy as a boy on his birthday who had just been gifted the item he'd most longed for.

"This is a great story, Adam," he said, grinning widely as he perused the notes he'd taken of our conversation. "Perhaps the best of my career. They'll talk about this in the cafés on Dizengoff for weeks."

Birnbaum held onto Henrietta's hand for longer than he had any business to, and for a second it looked like he was about to bend over at the waist and kiss it. Instead, he gave her hand a gentle pat before releasing it, and, in a warm, compassionate voice I would not have believed he possessed, said, "I know it's not easy to talk about such hard times and experiences, Mrs. Ackerland. I appreciate you meeting with me today."

I left them so they could talk in private and took a table at the opposite end of the café, reading a western I had picked up from Goldberg's store earlier that day. They sat together for more than an hour, Henrietta doing most of the talking, Birnbaum scribbling feverishly in his notebook. Occasionally, they'd pause when Henrietta choked up or had to wipe away her tears. Finally, I saw them both rise from their chairs and shake hands again. I came over and asked Henrietta if she was all right. Her eyes were red and she looked exhausted, but she nodded and said that she was fine, happy. "Tomorrow I shall see my son. It's what I've been dreaming about for ten long, lonely years."

Outside, I hailed a passing taxi and held the backseat door open for her. She slipped inside, then leaned out and grabbed my arm. "Thank you, Adam. From the bottom of my heart, thank you."

"You're welcome," I said, uncomfortable with her gratitude, then swung the door shut and tapped twice on the roof for the driver to go.

Back inside Café Tamar, I found Birnbaum with a ruminative look in his eyes.

He said, "First impression, she looked so brittle I thought she might come apart at any second. Now I suspect that she's made of steel. An incredible woman. Utterly incredible."

"If I didn't know better, Shmuel, I might think you truly care about her."

Birnbaum draped his pudgy face in a hurt expression. "Is that what you think of me, Adam? That I am heartless?"

"On the contrary. I know you have a heart. But only for stories."

"How little you know me. It's true that I love finding and writing stories more than anything else, but I like people, too. Read my columns; you won't find one in which I was nasty to anyone. Not more than they absolutely deserved. Some of my colleagues make a sport out of eviscerating people in print. I don't. What I like most of all are stories that bring to light the indomitable human spirit, stories of triumph over adversity, stories of resilience and resurgence. Stories such as Henrietta Ackerland's. Stories such as yours, dear Adam."

I got a cigarette out, but didn't light it, just rolled it between thumb and forefinger. "Michael Shamir doesn't deserve to be eviscerated in the paper."

Birnbaum inclined his bald head. "No? He killed a woman and stole a child. I think that's more than enough reason to disembowel him, figuratively speaking of course." He narrowed his eyes at me. "Why do you care about him?"

Because I owe him for rescuing me from Alon Davidson, I thought. But if I said that, Birnbaum would demand elaboration, and I did not want to get into that. I also couldn't tell him that I feared Mira's reaction when she read Birnbaum's column filleting her hero in the newspaper she hated.

I said, "Because he did some good things. As a soldier and in the Irgun."

"The latter won't do him any good as far as my editors at *Davar* are concerned. The Irgun is our political foe, Adam, you know that. They won't allow me to squander an opportunity to tarnish the Irgun's reputation." He cast a quick look around, then leaned toward me, lowering his voice to little more than a whisper. "Listen, Adam, despite being a supporter of Mapai, I don't hate the Irgun. In fact—and if you repeat this to anyone, I'll vehemently deny it—I rather admire them. They're fanatics, but you won't find tougher, more dedicated warriors. Without them, we might still have the British lording over us." He leaned back, examining my face. "I ask again, why do you care about Shamir? Some sort of camaraderie between soldiers?"

"Something like that," I said.

"Aha," said Birnbaum. "Somehow I don't think that's quite it, Adam. I think you're hiding something, which in turn makes me very curious."

"Stop digging, Shmuel. There's nothing to find."

"If you say so, Adam." He tapped his chin with two fingers. "Normally I wouldn't let it go at that, but today I'm feeling generous. This story you brought me has made me rather fond of you. Regarding Michael Shamir, I do plan on mentioning his role in the Irgun of course, and his military service. But I can tell you right now that neither would negate his crimes in the eyes of the public."

"As a favor to me, Shmuel, tone it down as much as you can."

He nodded. "Very well, Adam. For you, I'll do what I can." He turned his eyes toward the door and the street beyond. "Do you think she'll be all right? Now that she has found her son?"

I stuck the cigarette between my lips and lit it up. "You can help her become all right, Shmuel."

He turned his eyes to me. "How?"

"Use your influence to get the kibbutz to accept her as a member. That way she can be with her son without tearing him away from his friends and familiar surroundings."

"Consider it done, Adam. Anything else I can do for you today?

If there is, don't hesitate to ask, because I doubt I will ever like you as much as I do today."

"One thing, Shmuel: Keep my name out of your column."

His jaw dropped. "Why, for Heaven's sake? Do you have any notion of how much business this story can drive your way?"

"I don't want it, Shmuel."

"Yes, I got that, thank you very much. What I want to know is why."

"I've been a hero once and didn't like it. I don't wish to repeat the experience."

"Why do I get the feeling that's not it? At least not solely that?"

"Because you enjoy fame and can't picture anyone else not feeling the same."

He wagged a finger. "Nice try, Adam. But what is really behind this request of yours?"

I smiled a lopsided smile. "There's nothing more, Shmuel. You're being overly suspicious, that's all."

"Aha," he said again, clearly unconvinced. Then he shrugged and said, "If that's what you want, then I'll do it. But you're making a mistake. A big mistake."

"Thank you, Shmuel."

He grunted, not bothering to hide how sour he was about my holding back information he desired.

After a moment in which neither of us spoke, I said, "About Esther Grunewald..."

"What about her?"

"How will you write her up?"

"In the best possible light, of course. I'll describe her selflessness in taking and saving another woman's child. I'll write about the gruesome manner of her death. Apart from a few coldhearted creatures, I doubt anyone who reads my column will finish it with dry eyes."

"You're not going to write about her involvement with a British officer?"

He pursed his lips and shook his head. "In my opinion, she's a hero, Adam, but most people won't see her that way. What they'll see is a woman who went to bed with an enemy officer, regardless of why she did it and how many Jews benefited from her actions. Do I need to tell you what words they'll use to describe her?"

"No," I said bitterly. So Mira had been right.

"I don't think she deserves that," said Birnbaum.

"What she deserves is to be celebrated as a hero."

"And one day, a few years from now, perhaps, she will be. Look, Adam, we're a young country. We need our heroes to be pure, just like a young child sees his parents. We can't process gray, only black and white. When we grow up, when we mature, then we will be able to appreciate Esther Grunewald and the hard and unseemly sacrifices she had to make."

"I understand," I said.

"I wish it were different," said Birnbaum.

35

The next night, after all the customers had gone, Greta locked the door to the café and came to sit with me at my table.

She had made a fresh pot of coffee and now proceeded to fill two cups, handing me one. I set it down on the table to let it cool. For now, the wonderful aroma it emitted was enough.

While the coffee cooled, I told Greta everything that had happened, from the night Alon Davidson attacked me to my last meeting with Michael. She listened in silence, shaking her head in disgust and anger when I told her about Leah Goldin's betrayal of Esther and of Strauss's attempted rape of her. She broke the silence when I got to the part about the assassin who had followed me from the café to the beach.

"So that was what that whole nonsense was about," Greta said. "I thought you had a screw loose—telling me to act naturally and informing me that you were going for a walk on the beach." She frowned. "Why the beach?"

"I wanted a secluded place where I could talk to him."

"Wasn't that risky?"

"It was. But I had an advantage: he didn't know that I was onto him and that I had a gun with me. Besides, there was no choice. He had information I needed."

"And you got it," Greta said.

"I did."

"And the man?"

I told her. She pursed her lips and looked away for a few seconds. Then she returned her eyes to me.

"It had to be done, didn't it?"

"Yes," I said. "It did. And he deserved it."

Greta gave a short nod to herself, sealing the matter. She sipped her coffee. She did not ask about Strauss. She didn't need to. His death had made front-page news in a couple of newspapers. He was found dead in his office with three bullets in him. The police were said to be pursuing a number of leads, but I doubted any of them would pan out. Mira would not have left any incriminating evidence. The police had also not made any connection between Strauss and the dead man who was found a few days earlier in a shed on the beach.

"What did he look like?" Greta asked, once I'd finished my story.

"The man who followed me to the beach?"

"Yes."

I described him to her. Greta shook her head.

"I don't remember him," she said, making a face. "I don't like the idea of criminals visiting my café, and I like the fact that I'm unable to tell them by their faces even less. And he's not the only one I missed."

She was talking about Michael. The story of his arrest and confession had appeared in Birnbaum's column in that morning's *Davar*.

"My first impression of Michael was rather positive as well," I said.

322

"And your second was of him saving your life. It's incredible, isn't it, the way things turned out?"

"Yes."

"And sad. So incredibly sad."

"Are you talking about Esther or Michael?"

"Both. What he did was terrible, of course. But he was driven mad by the loss of his son and his wife's condition. I can't help but feel sorry for him."

I drank some coffee. I wondered whether I had been driven mad by the loss of my wife and daughters, and if so, whether I had ever recovered.

"Are you really going to visit his son's grave?" Greta asked.

"Yes. And Talia Shamir's grave as well."

"Oh?"

"Michael asked me to, when we were walking to the police station. He thought Talia might forgive him now that he was about to confess."

"So you were right. Confessing was good for him."

"In some ways, yes."

"His future will not be easy. He will be in jail for a very long time."

"I don't think it'll be that long," I said.

"Oh?"

"He'll do a few years for sure, maybe seven or eight. Then they'll let him out."

"You really think so?"

I nodded.

"Even though he committed a murder?"

"But he's also a hero. Young countries tend to be forgiving of their heroes. Certain kinds of heroes, anyway. And as you said, Michael was driven to madness by circumstances. I believe all that would be taken into account and he will be treated with lenience."

Greta thought it over. "I'm not sure how I feel about that. Hero or not, he is a murderer. He should be punished accordingly."

"I could be wrong. They might make an example out of him. The ruling powers in Israel are no fans of the Irgun."

Greta sighed. "All this infighting amongst ourselves. So senseless."

"It's part of who we are," I said. "We Jews are argumentative. Always have been. It's our culture."

"Yes, but now that we have a country of our own again, we need to come together."

"With time, maybe we will."

"I hope so," Greta said. A frown etched deep lines in her forehead. "So the only remaining mystery is the identity of the woman Haim Sassoon saw fighting with Esther a few days before the murders."

"Oh, I forgot to tell you," I said. "I know who she is."

"You do? Who?"

"Yael Klinger."

"How do you know that?"

"The same way I discovered Michael was the killer: by accident. I was walking up King George a couple of days ago when I happened to see two men unloading produce from the back of a Tnuva truck. It reminded me of something Alon Davidson said. The night he kissed Esther by the docks, he said he saw her getting out of a truck. Moshe Klinger drives a truck for Tnuva. I paid a visit on Haim Sassoon yesterday and asked him whether the woman he saw with Esther had fiery red hair. The question triggered his memory and he said that she had. Yael Klinger has fiery red hair."

"So Esther and Moshe Klinger—"

"Were having an affair of some sort. I don't know when it began or how serious it was. They must have met pretty rarely, on nights Moshe Klinger was in Tel Aviv and Esther did not meet with Clapper. That was the reason the Klingers never had another immigrant stay with them. Yael Klinger did not want to risk her husband having another affair. It also explains why they moved so soon after Esther and Willie were killed. They needed a fresh start, at a place where there were no memories of Esther." I paused and scratched my right eyebrow. "So it turns out that Esther wasn't perfect after all. She had her faults like the rest of us."

"And she knew love before she died," Greta said. "It's good that she had that, at least."

"Yes, I suppose you're right."

Greta took another sip of coffee. She put down her cup and laid her hands on the table. Looking toward the café window, she said, "From all you told me, Esther was a woman worth knowing. I lived here, in Tel Aviv, in 1939. I might have seen her a dozen times. But somehow I think I never did. I can't help but think I would have remembered her if I had." She turned her head to face me. "Any news from Henrietta?"

"We spoke on the phone this morning. She's at the kibbutz. She met her son yesterday."

"And how was their meeting?"

"I didn't ask."

"Aren't you curious?"

"No. Not really."

"Why ever not?" Greta said. "That was what you were working to achieve, isn't it?"

I finished my coffee and examined the black residue at the bottom of the cup as I considered and rejected several replies. The truth was, I did not want to hear of Henrietta's happy reunion with her son because it would bring to mind the fact that I would never be reunited with my daughters. I wondered, not for the first time, why I found it so easy to talk to Greta about some things, and was utterly incapable of sharing others with her.

Finally, I said, "I'm just not. Henrietta did sound happy, that I can tell you. Ecstatic. The kibbutz has given her a room. They'll make her a new member soon if Birnbaum comes through, and I'm sure he will."

"That's good," Greta said. She paused, then said gingerly, "And Mira Roth?"

I forced a small smile on my lips. Greta, ever the matchmaker, had sensed a reason to be hopeful. I hated having to disappoint her. I hated the truth I was about the tell her even more. "I went by the hair salon this morning," I said, striving to keep the bitterness I felt out of my voice. "I brought with me the pictures of Esther I'd taken from Manny Orrin. I thought Mira would like to have them. She told me she never wanted to see me again. I feared as much. She adores Michael, and I brought about his arrest."

"But she can't fault you for that," Greta protested. "He's guilty."

"Mira knows that, but it doesn't change how she feels about it. In her mind, her helping me landed Michael in jail and brought shame upon the Irgun. She also resents the fact that I went to the police instead of coming to her when I learned that Michael was the killer."

Greta was silent for a long moment. "Maybe with time, she'll see things differently."

"I doubt it. Mira is the sort of woman who doesn't forget things easily. No, I think there is no future for the two of us."

"I'm sorry, Adam," Greta said.

I looked out the café window onto Allenby Street, where streetlights did battle with the darkness of night. A couple strolled past the window, arm in arm. The laughter of the woman came in faint and lovely through the glass. Loneliness settled in my stomach like a paperweight. I would sleep badly that night. My dreams would be cruel.

"Me too," I said. "Me too."

THE END

Thank you for reading Ten Years Gone.

Want more Adam Lapid?

The Dead Sister, book 2 of the Adam Lapid series, is now available.

Want a FREE short story?

Join my newsletter and get a copy of one of my short stories for FREE.

Go to JonathanDunsky.com/free to get your copy.

Please review this book!

Reviews help both readers and authors. If you enjoyed Ten Years Gone, please leave a review on whatever website you use to buy or review books. I greatly appreciate it.

A NOTE FROM THE AUTHOR

Dear Reader, (it's strange talking to you without knowing your name, but I'll give it a try).

Writing has its own rewards, but having your novel read by another person is uniquely gratifying. So I want to thank you for reading *Ten Years Gone*. I hope you had a good time with it.

The greatest pleasure I get as a writer is to hear from readers. So drop me an email at contact@jonathandunsky.com with any questions or feedback that you have, or even just to say hi.

Before you go, I'd like to ask you to do a little favor for me. If you enjoyed this book, please leave a review on whatever website you use to buy or review books. Independent authors such as myself depend on reviews to attract new readers to our books. I would greatly appreciate it if you'd share your experience of reading this book by leaving your review. It doesn't have to be long. A sentence or two would do nicely.

Still here?

Great!

I thought you might be interested in knowing about how this book came to be, and how close it came to never being written.

Ten Years Gone traveled a bumpy road on its way to publication. The initial idea came to me sometime in 2015, when I was still living in Amsterdam, The Netherlands, before I moved back to Israel. At the time, I belonged to a writers' group, and one of the other members suggested that I write a novel that takes place in Israel, because that is the country I know better than any other.

I took her advice to heart, but made it a lot more difficult for myself by setting my story not in the present, but almost seventy years in the past, shortly after Israel gained its independence. Needless to say, my knowledge of that period of time was far from complete, so I had to do quite a bit of research in order to be able to paint a vivid and accurate picture of what life was like in Israel at that time.

The reason I chose this time period was that the character of what I felt could be a great series of books had sprung in my mind one day out of the blue. That character was the yet unnamed Adam Lapid.

What I knew about Adam at that time was that he was a holocaust survivor who now worked as a private investigator in Israel. I knew that he had lost all his family in the holocaust and that he was a loner by nature. Then more details came to mind, such as his country of birth (Hungary), the fact that before the Second World War he'd been a police detective in the Hungarian police force, and that after the war had ended, he spent some time hunting Nazis before coming to Israel, where he fought in Israel's War of Independence.

After that I painted a physical picture of Adam, his fields of interest, his nature, and his views on life, death, crime, and justice. Naturally, no one could emerge from Auschwitz without being fundamentally altered by the horrors he or she experienced there and, as you read in this novel, Adam has been changed drastically by the hardship he'd faced and all that he'd lost at the hands of the Nazis.

Once I had Adam's character in mind, an idea for a plot came to me: the search for a baby who's been missing for ten years. I still didn't know what had happened to that baby, but the idea felt right for a novel. Excited with the idea, I started writing the novel back in 2015, but hit a wall about four chapters in. In despair, I set the book aside, but the character of Adam Lapid stayed with me. I decided to write another novel, this one set about one year after *Ten Years Gone,* and hoped to return to the original idea later on. That novel became *The Auschwitz Violinist,* which is chronologically the third novel in the Adam Lapid series.

Following that, I went back to writing *Ten Years Gone,* and once more couldn't get it off the ground. So I wrote another novel, *The Dead Sister,* which takes place before *The Auschwitz Violinist* and is chronologically the second novel in the series.

Now I had two Adam Lapid novels published, and I decided to let the idea for *Ten Years Gone* die a natural death. But it kept on nagging me, demanding to be written. So I did.

I was back in Israel by then, and for three months I wrote *Ten Years Gone,* and...it was a flop. I didn't like it. My wife didn't like it. The novel just wasn't good.

At that point, I was adamant. I had to let this idea go. I couldn't waste more time on it. I had tried, and failed, to write it three times. It was time to adopt baseball rules and admit that I had struck out on this particular idea.

And I did, for a while at least. But the idea kept bugging me, and eventually I figured that I would have to write this novel, if only to get it out of my system, to clear my mind for other ideas.

So I spent another three, four months on it, writing it from scratch, adding new scenes and characters and plot twists, and discarding some dull and bland scenes and characters that I had written in the earlier version.

The result is what you've just read.

As I was writing it, I could feel the story take shape, and I knew that this time it was going to turn out just fine. It wasn't all smooth sailing. There were days in which the words came slowly. There were times when I simply did not know what should happen next. But little by little, the problems were solved, the words got typed, and the story came together.

After it was done, I reread it and felt that all the hard work had paid off. The story was alive and emotional and had a good deal of action and twists. I hope you felt the same way.

I hope and plan to write more Adam Lapid novels in the future. For now, there are seven. I hope you will check out the other novels if you haven't done so already.

The next book in the series is *The Dead Sister*. Some readers believe it is better than *Ten Years Gone*. I hope you'll give it a try.

If you're a member of a book club and wish to discuss Ten Years Gone, there's a list of discussion questions directly after this author's note.

Before we part, I want to thank you again for reading my book and to invite you to join my VIP readers club at http://jonathandunsky.com/free/. You'll get a free copy of one of my short stories when you join and be notified when my next book comes out. I'll try to get it written quickly.

Jonathan Dunsky.

p.s. You are also welcome to contact me on Facebook at http://Facebook.com/JonathanDunskyBooks

BOOK CLUB DISCUSSION QUESTIONS

1. How well did the author describe the setting of Tel Aviv, 1949? Were there any historical facts that surprised you?

2. Adam agrees to take on Henrietta's case, though he believes it is hopeless. Later, he takes on another seemingly impossible case. What does this say about his character?

3. When Adam meets Henrietta for the first time, he is reminded of the way his dead mother used to hold her handbag. How predominant is the theme of motherhood in Ten Years Gone? What importance does it play in the story?

4. After Adam breaks Yuri's hand, he is surprised and dismayed by Rachel's reaction to his violence. What does this scene tell us about Adam and the manner in which his terrible history has changed and shaped him?

5. Why do you think Adam keeps the knife, the pistol,

and the picture of the dead German family in his secret box?

6. Were there any quotes or passages in the book that stood out to you?

7. In what way does Reuben Tzanani shed new light on Adam's life, psyche, and choices?

8. Adam suffers from frequent nightmares, but he sleeps soundly at the end of days in which he commits violence. What does this reveal about his character?

9. How would you describe the relationship between Adam and Greta? What role does she serve in his life?

10. After Adam shoots Yossi, the big-jawed criminal sent to kill him, he allows him to bleed out. What do you think of Adam's decision?

11. What does it say about the way in which human beings perceive heroism, that Esther's heroic sacrifice on behalf of her people must remain hidden?

12. If you could pick a character from the book and have a story written from their point of view, who would it be?

13. If you could have a conversation with one of the characters, who would it be? What would you ask them?

14. If this book were made into a movie, who would you cast as the main characters?

15. Would you recommend Ten Years Gone to a friend? How would you describe it when you recommended it?

ABOUT THE AUTHOR

Jonathan Dunsky lives in Israel with his wife and two sons. He enjoys reading, writing, and goofing around with his kids. He began writing in his teens, then took a break for close to twenty years, during which he worked an assortment of jobs. He is the author of the Adam Lapid mystery series and the standalone thriller The Payback Girl.

BOOKS BY JONATHAN DUNSKY

ADAM LAPID SERIES

Ten Years Gone

The Dead Sister

The Auschwitz Violinist

A Debt of Death

A Deadly Act

The Auschwitz Detective

A Death in Jerusalem

The Unlucky Woman (short story)

STANDALONE NOVELS

The Payback Girl

Made in the USA
Las Vegas, NV
21 April 2023

70902146R00193